WHISPERS IN THE VALLEY

THE GENTLE HILLS

———————— ✑ ————————

Far From the Dream
Whispers in the Valley

(All available in large print.)

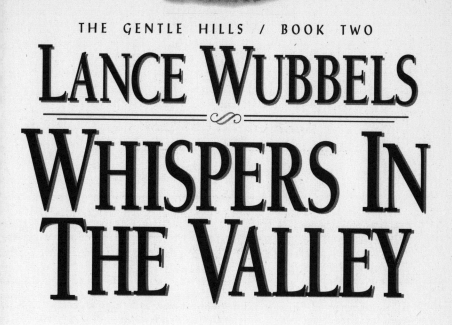

THE GENTLE HILLS / BOOK TWO

LANCE WUBBELS

WHISPERS IN THE VALLEY

BETHANY HOUSE PUBLISHERS
MINNEAPOLIS, MINNESOTA 55438

Cover by Dan Thornberg,
Bethany House Publishers staff artist.

Published by Bethany House Publishers
A Ministry of Bethany Fellowship, Inc.
11300 Hampshire Avenue South
Minneapolis, Minnesota 55438

Printed in the United States of America.

Library of Congress Cataloging-in-Publication Data

Wubbels, Lance, 1952–
    Whispers in the valley / Lance Wubbels.
      p.   cm. — (The gentle hills ; bk. 2)
    Sequel to: Far from the dream.

    I. Title. II. Series: Wubbels, Lance, 1952–   Gentle hills ; bk. 2.
PS3573.U39W45   1994
813'.54—dc20   94–49101
ISBN 1–55661–419–5 (Trade Paper)   CIP
ISBN 1–55661–630–9 (Large Print)   AC

To

Karen

———— ✎ ————

We've walked the valleys
and the hills together.
We've heard the
whispers in the wind.
Thanks for staying
by my side.

LANCE WUBBELS, the Managing Editor of Bethany House Publishers, taught biblical studies courses at Bethany College of Missions for many years. He is also the compiler and editor of the Charles Spurgeon and F.B. Meyer Christian Living Classic books with Emerald Books. He and his family make their home in Bloomington, Minnesota.

CONTENTS

1

TOGETHER AGAIN

"I'd forgotten how quiet it is," said Jerry Macmillan. He whispered the words in Marjie's ear, as if his voice might disturb the solitude of the night.

With their arms wrapped tightly around each other, Jerry and Marjie Macmillan had spent their first evening slowly strolling the bedraggled farm fields that bore the distinct marks of the fall harvesting. It was late and dark, and stars twinkled crisply through the cool air. After nearly a year on the noisy aircraft carrier, Jerry was amazed by the eerie stillness of his boyhood home. He found himself stopping over and over again to soak in the near-perfect serenity of the countryside.

"Listen!" he told his wife. "Do you hear those whispers in the breeze?"

Marjie shut her eyes and thought she could hear the hushed tones of muffled voices. "It sounds so strange," she said. "What is it?"

"I've never figured it out," replied Jerry. "I suppose it's just the way the wind swirls around in our valley. When I was a kid, I'd get spooked by it at night. Now it sounds like home to me."

"Maybe it's the wind's way of welcoming you home," Marjie suggested. "Telling you that you belong to this land, and to us."

"Sounds like it speaks the truth, then," Jerry agreed, then paused to listen again. "Another thing I forgot was how beautiful it is here. When you're at sea, the night sky is amazing, but nothing I saw compares to this . . ."

His gaze swept the sky and then dropped to take in star-frosted curls and an uptilted heart-shaped face. ". . . and nothing compares to being with you again, babe. It seemed like an eternity."

Then she was in his arms again and he was kissing her like he had just laid eyes on her after ten months at war. But it was a kiss that they had already repeated on several stops during this maiden journey around the Macmillan property. Married just a few days before Jerry reported for duty, they had a lot to catch up on.

Between kisses, Marjie murmured, "It *was* an eternity, Jerry. Those first months were terrible. I think I cried every night. It's been better here on the farm with your dad, but I still worried myself sick. Now that you're home, I can't imagine you leaving again."

"I still might have to go, babe," he told her gently. "I've still got orders to report to Norfolk in a month."

"Your discharge will come through before then," she protested. "It has to. I won't let you go again."

She hugged Jerry tightly, burying her face in his chest. He stroked her dark curls and changed the subject. "Do you still have the envelope with that hank of hair you cut off me?" he asked.

Marjie nodded yes.

"I got so lonely and scared on the ship that I finally risked someone seeing me and pulled out the envelope you gave me," Jerry said. "Funny how a few strands of hair could almost bring you to me."

"If you recall, that's why I had us do it," Marjie said. "Besides, that poor old guy who ran the bus depot needed a good laugh."

Jerry shook his head and chuckled at the memory. "You gave him that. He's probably still telling everybody that buys a ticket the one about the two crazy kids who borrowed his scissors to whack off each other's hair. You owe me for that one."

"Stick around this time, and I'll make it worth your while," Marjie suggested, her seriousness dissolving into her patented smirk.

"Sounds good to me," said Jerry, finally releasing her from his hug. "Do we need to get back to the house? Aren't you worried about how Dad's doing with the baby?"

"Martha! Our daughter's name is Martha," Marjie reminded him. "And no, there's no rush. Benjamin does wonderfully with Martha. He takes care of her all the time."

"That's a bit much to believe," Jerry stated, taking Marjie's hand and leading her along the creek again. "I can hardly imagine him holding a baby, let alone changing a diaper!"

"Well, he doesn't do that any more than he absolutely has to!" Marjie exclaimed with a laugh. "Funny to watch an old farmer who shovels manure nearly every day gagging over a dirty diaper. Your turn is coming soon, by the way."

"I was afraid you'd say that. The navy life just got to looking better in a hurry!" he joked. "Changing diapers is not a job for a—"

"Don't you dare even think that thought, sailor!" Marjie ordered, giving him a soft punch on the arm. "On this ship, all the men pitch in. Got it?"

"Aye-aye, sir!" Jerry answered, stopping to deliver another big kiss and hug. "But you're going to have to show me how. And I'm none too handy with safety pins."

"It'll be my pleasure," Marjie said. "I'm guessing that there may be a practice run waiting for you when we get back to the house."

They walked on without speaking until a loud rustling in the gooseberry bushes ahead startled them. But the unseen intruder was clearly headed in the opposite direction. They walked on, following the creek toward the still-distant farmhouse whose windows glowed a welcoming yellow.

"Dad looks like he's aged more than a year while I've been gone," Jerry mused. "Do you think his heart is really okay?"

Marjie took Jerry's hand in hers and shook her head. "I'm not a doctor," she said, "and Benjamin would never tell us a peep unless he gets so bad that he can't get up. But, no, I still think there's something wrong. The doc told me twice that everything's fine, but I'm not sure I believe him. Benjamin just hasn't been the same since he came home from the hospital. But at least he's slowed down. I've never seen any man who could work as hard as he did, especially a man who's nearly sixty."

"I know!" Jerry said. "I grew up here, remember? Dad would always push me to the limit and never give in—like he had to prove he was tougher than me or something. Strange to see him just sitting there in his big chair with the baby."

"Martha! Say it, Jerry," she scolded him. "I need to tell you, though, there's more about him that's going to surprise you. Your father may have aged while you were gone, but he has also changed in many wonderful ways."

"Like how?"

"Like sitting for hours on end holding his granddaughter when he could be fixing the shed door. Or like reading his Bible from cover to cover. When Ruthie comes over, all he wants to talk about is whether she thinks such-and-such a verse really means what he thinks it means. I can hardly steal her away from all his questions. Does that sound like the man you left to run the farm, Jerry? It's been one big change after another ever since that awful trip to the hospital."

"But not just for Dad," Jerry observed, then added, "so why didn't you write to me about what happened to you that day?"

Marjie stopped and searched her husband's starlit face. "About coming to believe in God?"

Jerry nodded silently.

She paused to collect her thoughts but continued to gaze into his eyes. "I guess I was so caught up in what to do next about your father and the farm and in all the paperwork to get your discharge, and then having the baby—"

"Martha!" he broke in.

"Touché," she conceded. "Plus . . . this may sound silly . . . but I guess I wasn't sure how to tell you. I've found that it's difficult to put words to what happened inside me that day. And I suppose I wanted to see if it was for real—if it would last."

"And did it?"

"Yes."

"You're sure?"

"Without a doubt."

"Good."

"What?"

Jerry started to laugh as he crossed over to a huge fallen oak and sat down on it. "I said good."

" 'Good' as in you're glad that I came to believe?" Marjie questioned, following him. "Or 'good' because I still believe?"

"Both," he said with a grin. "I am delighted."

Marjie shook her head in disbelief as she sat down beside him. Earlier in their walk she had told him with some trepidation what happened to her as she waited outside the hospital where she had taken Benjamin. He had listened attentively when she told him, but said nothing. "I'm delighted that you're delighted," she said. "But I thought you might think I had gotten strange or something."

"The woman who whacked a chunk of my hair off in a bus depot before dozens of people—strange?" Jerry teased. "The woman who couldn't just quit her job but had to teach her boss a lesson in how to act? You think I don't know I married someone who has a few loose marbles?"

Marjie laughed with him, but wasn't about to be deterred. "Let me try again. I was afraid that you might think that I grabbed on to faith out of desperation—like a crutch. I really was desperate, you know. I was so afraid your father was going to die. So, come clean, why are you 'delighted'?"

Jerry slipped his arm around Marjie and whispered in her ear, "Because I came to believe in God, too!"

Marjie let out a joyous scream and jumped to her feet. "What?!" was the only word that escaped her lips.

Jerry stood up and took her in his arms again. He felt her tremble, and he was suddenly overcome with awe as well. He tried to explain but found the words choked back.

"How?" Marjie whispered through her tears.

Jerry felt his own tears flowing as well, and for a while their trembling turned into shaking. Finally he regained enough composure to find his voice. "In the water . . . after they pulled Chester into the life raft. I thought I was going to die, Marjie. I was sure I'd never see you again. But there was nothing I could do. So, I prayed to God . . . and He came to me there in the water. He was so real that I could not doubt Him. And He forgave me . . ."

His words trailed off as a cold northern breeze kicked up, and the drifts of dry autumn leaves began to stir as Marjie and Jerry held each other close, feeling their strong love deepen into a reservoir of strength.

"And you were afraid that I might not understand you, either?" Marjie asked.

"Yep."

"Silly, isn't it?"

"What?"

"That we should both worry so much about this," Marjie answered. "As if God wasn't big enough to prepare our hearts for each other's change."

Jerry nodded. "You know what you said earlier—about how you found out it's hard to play God? Well, I guess that's why I was worried. And I suspicion it's a problem I'm going to have a few more times as well."

"I reckon that's true—for both of us," Marjie said, reaching up to kiss Jerry lightly on the cheek, then taking a step back to give him an appraising look. "You're a handsome man, Jerry Macmillan, but you still don't look the part of God!"

"Look or feel," Jerry said with a laugh.

"Maybe you feel like a cup of hot coffee?" Marjie asked.

"Sounds good. I had a couple other ideas, too."

Marjie grinned. "I was afraid you might have forgotten that. I'll race you to the house!"

2

First Morning

"Still sleeping, sweetheart?" Marjie whispered to the tiny blanketed bundle tucked into the old family cradle. "That's good—just stay that way a little longer. I've got a lot to do." With a glance out the bedroom window, where the sun was just making its first appearance over the hills, Marjie tiptoed back to the kitchen.

Despite the late evening, both Marjie and Jerry had been up since Martha woke for her predawn bottle. Jerry had headed to the barn to help his father with the morning chores. And Marjie had hurried to get the hen stuffed and in the oven early. She had promised the family a special dinner to celebrate Jerry's return from the war.

By the time the men came in for breakfast, the tantalizing aroma of baking chicken filled the old farmhouse.

"Smells great!" Benjamin Macmillan called out as he came into the back porch and pulled off his work boots. "Let's skip breakfast and go right to the good stuff."

"Be my guest," Marjie answered. " 'Course, the chicken's going to taste like you just cut its head off, but that's up to you."

"I guess I can wait." Benjamin came through the door, followed by Jerry.

"Where's my little babe?"

Marjie put her finger to her lips and said, "Hold the volume down. She's sleeping, thank goodness. I'd have been in a fix trying to get this food ready if she hadn't gone back to bed."

Jerry walked slowly into the kitchen and stopped to watch Marjie as she gently stirred the white flour into a batch of bread dough. Her dark brown eyes and vibrant smile were all the welcome that he needed. "You can't imagine what it's like to be here and to see you in this kitchen," he said, stepping closer and reaching his arms around her. "You're as beautiful as I remember on our wedding day."

Dropping the huge wooden spoon she was using to stir the dough, Marjie turned into his strong arms. Looking into his shining eyes, she said, "Many's the morning I looked out the kitchen window into the clear blue sky and thought of your blue eyes and what it would be like to have you here. Happy first morning home, darling. May there be many more to come." With that she took his face into her hands and pulled him down to her waiting lips.

Benjamin, caught off guard by their fireworks, ducked his head and made a beeline for the dining-room table. It seemed that he wasn't sure what might come next, so he figured the best thing was to get out of the way. But he had long since recovered by the time Jerry finished his kiss and came around the kitchen counter into the dining room. "Now that's the right way to start out the day!" Benjamin said, grinning. "But I didn't know you had it in you."

Jerry's face reddened, but he laughed. "It's all Marjie's fault. I was just an innocent farm boy until she vowed to change me into a Hollywood movie star."

"Like you need changing," said Marjie as she brought out their plates of fried eggs and steaming hash brown potatoes. "You raised a wolf, Benjamin. He always pretended to be a bashful sheep but look at him now. The man's a wolf!"

The peal of laughter that broke out around the table was cut short by the telephone's loud ringing. "Somebody's up early," Marjie said as she stepped quickly to answer it. "Must be my mother."

Benjamin and Jerry began their breakfast as Marjie answered

the call, but then hesitated, forks in midair, when they saw the strange look on her face. "Yes, he's here," she finally said. "I'll get him for you."

Covering the mouthpiece with her hand, Marjie nodded to Jerry. "It's for you. A reporter from the newspaper."

"Go on!" Jerry said with a snort. "My first morning home and you're already playing tricks on me. Say hello to Sarah for me."

Marjie threw him a convincing glare and said again, "It's Ed Bentley from the *Preston Republican*. Get over here—now!"

"What in the world could he want?" Jerry asked, swallowing a mouthful of hash browns and jumping up from the table. "You better not be fooling me."

"He says he wants to do an interview with you about the sinking of the *Wasp*," Marjie whispered, handing him the receiver.

Jerry shook his head in disbelief and took the receiver from her. "Hello. This is Jerry Macmillan," he said. "What's this about an interview?"

He listened for a while and then said, "Boy, I don't know. I ain't so good at . . . I suppose I could. . . . Today? Well, we've got family coming over about noon . . . eleven o'clock. . . . You know how to get here? . . . Okay. See you then."

Benjamin and Marjie had to wait a long minute before Jerry finally turned and said, "I can't believe it. Somebody that works at the newspaper heard I got home yesterday and thought they might get an eyewitness story. He's coming out later this morning, and they're going to press tomorrow. What am I going to do? I can't . . ."

"Just answer his questions," Marjie stated, pretending to know what would be involved with the journalist. "You'll do fine."

"Easy for you to say," Jerry chided. "You're not the one that gets all tongue-tied. And he's going to bring a camera along, too. I hate getting my picture taken."

"This is wonderful!" Marjie exclaimed. "Get your new uniform on, and maybe we'll get a nice photo out of the deal."

"For crying out loud!" Jerry barked. "I ain't gonna—"

"It's for the newspaper!" Marjie broke in. "You're representing the navy. They're going to want you looking like a big strong navy man."

"Ah, shoot," Jerry said with a grunt. "This is—"

An impatient cry from the bedroom stopped him midsentence. Marjie turned to get Martha, but Jerry beat her to the door. "Let me," he whispered. "This is my first morning."

Jerry and Marjie quietly stepped into the bedroom together. Tiptoeing to the cradle, Jerry crouched down, peeked over the edge, and was greeted with a pair of solemn, appraising eyes. Reaching down and gently picking her up, Jerry forgot all about the newspaper reporter.

"If you aren't the most precious little girl," Jerry said with wonder. He kissed the dark, downy head and then cradled the baby snugly against his arm like he'd been shown the previous day. "This is your daddy. Do you remember me? No, I ain't— Whoa! She's wet!"

Laughing and handing him a diaper, Marjie said, "Welcome to the world of fatherhood, lover boy. You make 'em, you gotta clean 'em. Come on in the bathroom and I'll show you the tricks of the trade."

After one pitiful attempt to beg his way out of the unpleasant task, Jerry got his first diaper-changing lesson and managed to skewer himself with the safety pin only once. Martha came through the experience unscathed, although Marjie had to supervise closely. Then Marjie took Martha out to the kitchen to warm up her bottle while Jerry stayed in the bathroom to clean up for the photo shoot. Benjamin headed back out to the barn to finish a couple of chores.

By the time eleven o'clock rolled around, the whole family was primped and ready for the photo shoot. Jerry had pressed his uniform and polished his shoes. Marjie had managed to squeeze into one of her pre-baby outfits. And little Martha had been fitted with a large bib to protect her dainty pink outfit from accidents. And even Benjamin had managed to get back from spreading a load of manure in time to shave and put on his best shirt and tie.

With the sound of a car in the driveway and the barking of the dogs, Marjie and Jerry jumped up from the living-room davenport and ran to the window. Benjamin, who had been dozing in his chair with Martha on his lap, came to life as well.

"Phooey!" Jerry exclaimed, looking out toward the road. "Just what I was afraid of. The reporter's late, and your mom and Teddy are early. Now I have to be interviewed in front of everybody. I told you—"

"Don't worry," Marjie reassured him. "We're your fan club—remember? We'll cheer for you."

"Just what I need."

The car doors banged, and Jerry pushed the front door open to welcome his mother- and brother-in-law. Ted stopped and gave a whistle. "We came to the wrong house, Ma," he said. "These people must be expecting President Roosevelt. Why didn't you tell us we were going dancing?"

"Just come in and we'll tell you all about it," Marjie said, but time didn't allow for explanations. Around the bend of the driveway swung another car, and the dogs repeated their barking ritual.

"You might know it," Jerry said with a sigh. "Why did I ever say I'd do it?"

"Get a cup of coffee and relax," said Marjie.

Marjie took Sarah's and Ted's coats and hung them in the closet, quickly getting everyone seated in the living room, but leaving the davenport clear for Jerry and the reporter.

"Can't I just talk with him in the dining room?" Jerry begged Marjie, bringing his steaming cup of coffee to the front door. "You're not expecting me to do this in front of everybody."

"That's why they're here early—to hear you tell your story," Marjie said with a smirk. "I called them while you were shaving!"

"You didn't!" Jerry said with a look of panic. "I'm gonna—"

The bang on the front door cut his threat short. Marjie pulled the door open and greeted a wiry, middle-aged man who introduced himself as Ed Bentley.

"Sorry to interrupt your day like this," he said, reaching to shake Jerry's hand, "but this is gonna be one heck of a story."

Jerry nodded as he returned the handshake, but he couldn't think of anything to say.

Marjie took the reporter's coat and hung it up while Ed opened his briefcase and pulled out a notebook and pen. Then they went to the living room, and Marjie introduced her mother and Ted.

Bentley went right to work, pulling out the report that had come in over the news wire about the sinking of Jerry's ship, the aircraft carrier *Wasp*, by Japanese torpedoes. He read the details released from the war department to make sure the basic information was accurate, and then he began to question Jerry about his own experience on the *Wasp*.

At first Jerry's answers were short and awkward, but as the memories flooded back he began to talk more easily, and soon the room fell silent as his story unfolded. Jerry closed his eyes and tried to put words to the experience—how the entire ship had been lifted up when the torpedoes detonated, how the exploding ammunition and ignited airplane fuel had turned the huge carrier into a death trap, how some of his fellow sailors had been engulfed in flames or sliced by shrapnel. For a time, it seemed to Marjie that he had forgotten the others in the room and was reliving the horrific drama.

Bentley wrote as fast as he could, asking Jerry to slow down at points and to repeat certain sentences. When Jerry began to describe the difficulties of abandoning the ship, the lack of life rafts, battling the waves and the burning oil slick, he paused and shuddered. The memory was too fresh to talk about easily. He opened his eyes and studied the faces of his loved ones, trying to collect his thoughts. But of those in the room, the only one with dry eyes was Bentley. Even Ted had pulled a red handkerchief from his pocket.

"Something's missing," Bentley remarked, looking back over

his notes. "This will make a great story, but what is it that you aren't telling me?"

"What do you mean?" Jerry asked. "I tried to answer what you asked."

Bentley was nodding his head. "Everything you've given me is perfect—flesh and blood, just what I hoped you'd describe. I want readers to feel this story from a local boy. But why did you go down to the hangar deck when the others were going off the flight deck? What are you hiding?"

Jerry was surprised by Ed Bentley's attention to the story's details. "I ain't hiding nothing," he answered. "I just didn't think it was as important. I went down to the hangar deck to look for a friend that worked below. Wasn't much chance of finding him, but I had to try. By the way, his name is Chester Stanfeld, from south of Chatfield."

"You're kidding!" exclaimed Bentley. "Another local boy. Why didn't you say so right off?"

"You didn't ask," Jerry said.

"So you risked your life and went down to look for this Stanfeld fellow?" said Bentley. "Weren't you afraid the ship was going to blow?"

"Sure, I was scared to death," Jerry said, recalling that he barely made it down the smoke-filled stairways. "I wasn't sure I could get there. I suppose I was risking my life, but I didn't think about it at the time."

"Take it from me—you risked your life," Bentley stated. "Did you find him?"

"I couldn't believe it," murmured Jerry, already deep into the story again. "All there was were some torn-up planes and some bodies and a few men trying to go over the edge, and so I figured I might as well go over, too—no chance of finding Chester in all that. And then I saw this pile of tarps, and there was a leg sticking out from under them, and it was him! He was alive, but his leg was cut bad, and he'd lost a lot of blood. Somehow I got him over to the railing and we went down the ropes into the water. Then there was a life raft, and I got him on board, but I lost my grip on it and it was gone. . . ."

21

Trying to describe what it was like as the life raft pulled away with his bleeding friend on board and he was left alone in the swelling waves, Jerry finally choked up. Bentley waited patiently, visibly moved by what he was hearing.

Benjamin had sat motionless as Jerry gave the account and simply let the tears run down his face, trying to not disturb his sleeping granddaughter. Although Jerry had given an abbreviated account of his experiences when he returned the day before, he had not mentioned this part. While Jerry was struggling to regain his voice, Benjamin cleared his own throat. "We love you, son! God knows how proud I am of you."

That did not help immediately, but it did seem to break the spell. Jerry waved at his father, grabbed a handkerchief from Marjie, and then was able to tell about how he and a number of other sailors had clung to ropes hanging down from the stricken carrier until a boat sent from a nearby U.S. destroyer came to rescue them.

"This is the best war story we've had from a local boy," Bentley said enthusiastically. "And your rescue of another local boy. This is headline stuff. By the way, when is your hitch supposed to be over?"

Marjie and Jerry exchanged glances and then looked over at Benjamin, who cleared his throat and spoke. "We don't know about that yet. I've had some, well, health problems, and he's applied for some sort of special discharge so he can help me run the farm. But we're still waiting for an answer."

Bentley nodded as he went back over his notes again, then he looked up and asked, "Just one more question. When you were alone, hanging on to the rope, and you had no reason to think you were going to make it, what was going through your head? Can you tell me what you experienced?"

A large grin formed at the corners of Jerry's mouth, and he looked over at Marjie, who gave him a wink and a nod. Jerry scratched his scalp and said, "I ain't sure you're gonna like my answer."

"Try me," answered Ed.

"All right," said Jerry, summoning his courage. "When I was

down there alone in the water, praying was the only thing that seemed to make any sense. If I was going to die, I suddenly realized that I wasn't ready to meet my Maker. This may be hard to believe, but in the shadow of death and in the midst of the swirling seas, God was there. He was greater than the waves, the bombs, the raging fires—even greater than my soul. If I'd have died right then, Mr. Bentley, I was ready."

Ed Bentley blinked his eyes and rubbed his cheeks with both hands. "I believe you. I do," he said reflectively. "I've heard it before. Just like that. But . . . well, my publisher doesn't go much for religion in the paper. Hope you understand." He was already putting away his notebook.

"I understand," Jerry said. "Before the ship went down, I wasn't too hot on religion myself."

"Well, that about does it, Jerry," Bentley concluded. "Just let me run to the car and get the camera. I know it's turning cold out there, but if you could come out to the front yard, I'd like to get a shot of you in the sunlight."

Jumping at her chance, Marjie said, "Ed, I was wondering . . . after you get your photo of Jerry, could you take a picture or two of us as a family. Maybe one with Benjamin and my mother and brother as well?"

Bentley, caught off guard, began to say, "I really don't—" but Jerry cut him off.

"We wouldn't want to impose on you," Jerry said. "If it's—"

"You've probably got a whole roll of film in your camera, right?" Marjie asked.

"Yes. But we don't—"

"And you'll have to develop all of it, even though you've only taken a few pictures, right?"

"True. But—"

"And you got a great story, right?"

"The best in a long time."

"So, doesn't it seem like you could do us a favor and shoot some extra photos? We don't own a camera, and we really need to get some baby pictures," Marjie said.

"All right already!" exclaimed Bentley, bursting into laughter. "You've twisted my arm as far as it goes. I'll shoot until I run out of film. But Jerry's first, and I call the shots. Understand?"

"Sort of," Marjie said. "If you stay for lunch, can I call the shots?"

3

THE FAMILY

"That was a mighty fine meal, Marjie," Benjamin declared with a contented sigh, putting his fork down on a polished pie plate. "Think I'm going to have to let out another notch or two on my belt."

Jerry nodded his agreement. "This house hasn't seen a dinner like this since Mother passed away," he said, studying his father's smile. "Why don't we do this again on Thanksgiving, if—" He didn't complete the sentence, but they all knew what he was thinking. If his discharge didn't come through, he would be reporting to Norfolk on Thanksgiving Day.

"Thanksgiving's at the Livingstones' this year!" Sarah jumped in before anyone else could speak. "It's my turn. Besides—Marjie showed me up with such good cooking. I've got to see if I can do better."

Everyone at the table broke into a laugh, and Ted said, "Nothing better than a little competition to sharpen your skills, Ma."

Sarah grinned. "Oh, I'm not so worried. The other day I was digging through my mother's trunk," she said, "and I found an old recipe she used for baking chicken in a cream sauce. Marjie's never seen it before, and I'm not about to share it. She's going to have to get up a lot earlier in the morning to beat me after I get my chance."

"I have a spy in your camp," Marjie returned, glancing at her younger brother. "Your secrets may not be as hidden as you think."

"Teddy would never betray me," said Sarah. "I've threatened to make him cook his own meals. That keeps him in line." Then a strange look flickered across her face and Marjie glanced up sharply before Sarah continued, "By the way, does anyone here care for some coffee? Marjie seems to have forgotten."

"I didn't forget," Marjie protested. "You were so busy chattering away that I couldn't ask."

Marjie and Sarah cleared the dirty dishes away and came back from the kitchen with a pot of freshly brewed coffee.

"Speaking of cooking," Ted said to Jerry, "what did they feed you on the ship? You look like you put on some weight. All muscle, of course."

"Twenty pounds of muscle!" Jerry answered with a chuckle. "I went from a scrawny one hundred fifty pounds to a solid one seventy. I guess it tells you how bad my cooking was here on the farm, because the food on the ship was terrible!"

Benjamin winked at Marjie. "Your cooking was none too good, son, but mine was worse. Marjie complained that my color was bad when she first moved out here. I think it was from the torture of eating my own cooking after you left."

"No doubt," Jerry replied, taking a sip of hot coffee. "The only thing worse than eating your cooking was eating the navy's mutton when we got in the South Pacific. And I'd thought the beans and bacon were bad. I guarantee you will never find a sheep grazing on this farm!"

"He made me promise to never cook mutton chops in this house or he'd leave me forever," Marjie stated. "I fear for the neighbors, though. I'm afraid he might take the shotgun and kill some of their sheep—out of sheer vengeance."

Ted groaned. "*Sheer* vengeance, Marjie? Very clever." Now a few others grimaced as they caught the pun. Teddy went on, "What I'd like to know, though, is if Jerry would like to take that shotgun and see if we can bag a pheasant or two this afternoon?"

"Are you serious?" Jerry asked.

"Yeah. I brought my gun along," Ted answered. "I need to work off this meal. What'dya say?"

"Sure," Jerry said. "But I'll have to change clothes. Isn't it a little late in the season?"

"Just a little," Ted replied. "But it is your land, and you've been gone. We'll call it making up for lost time."

"You seen any birds, Dad?" Jerry asked.

"There's always pheasants down around the big sinkhole," Benjamin said. "Take Blue and just wait for him to kick up the birds. Don't go shooting the hens, though. We'll need them in the spring to keep the numbers up."

"Well, if you'll excuse me," said Jerry, pushing back his chair and looking at Marjie. "You don't mind, do you?"

"Boys will be boys," Marjie answered with a shrug and another sharp glance at her brother. "You better bring something back, though, or we'll have no meat for the coming week."

"Let's hope Teddy's a better shot than I am," Jerry offered, getting up from the table. "I can't hit beans when a pheasant gets up in the air. Works better to shoot 'em from the tractor when they're sitting."

Jerry went upstairs to change, then he and Ted got their guns and shells and headed out the door. Benjamin showed no interest in tailing along, but instead headed for his easy chair and a quiet nap. Marjie and Sarah went to the kitchen to wash the dishes and put away the leftovers before Martha woke from her nap. But then Marjie followed Jerry out onto the porch and laid a hand on his arm to keep him from following Ted across the yard.

"Something wrong?" Jerry asked.

She opened her mouth to say something, then stopped herself and shook her head. "Maybe not," she said quietly. "I hope not." She gave a little shiver and hugged her arms close to her chest as she watched her brother stride toward the yard. "But see what you think."

———— ✑ ————

Seeing the guns in the two men's hands, Blue jumped up from his resting spot alongside the barn and dashed toward them, his bushy tail wagging so hard it threatened to come loose.

"Settle down, boy," Jerry said, reaching down to scratch the dog's ears. "We're going to the sinkhole to look for pheasants. Don't you run ahead. You stay when I say stay."

Blue looked up at Jerry as if he would actually obey, but Jerry knew too well that once Blue got on the trail of a pheasant there would be no holding him back.

Teddy bent down and stroked the dog's short, thick coat, then ran his fingers down the distinctive blue stripe on the dog's face and forehead. "He's one smart-looking dog," he said, looking up at Jerry. "This what they call a blue heeler?"

"Some people do," Jerry replied. "I've heard them called Australian heelers and Australian cattle dogs. At any rate, he's the smartest cow dog I've ever seen. All I gotta do is point to the pasture and tell him to get the cattle. Fifteen minutes later, he'll have the whole herd up here."

"He any good at hunting?"

Jerry squatted down to scratch Blue's ears while the dog's tongue lolled in delight. "He's pretty good at getting birds up, but he'll chase them forever if you miss." Jerry straightened. "Let's go. We'll head down the farm lane, then walk the fence-line to the sinkhole. If there are no pheasants there, I give up. Boy, it's cold for this time in October. Holding these guns, we almost need gloves."

"Gonna get colder real soon, they say," answered Ted. "I heard northern Minnesota got a half foot of snow on Sunday. You can feel it in the wind. I hate it when it comes out of the northwest."

"And I hate long winters," Jerry said. "I thought I was used to the cold, living here. But I couldn't believe how cold it got out on the North Atlantic last winter. You stand at your guns all night, and by morning you think somebody's going to have to carry you down to the showers to unthaw your blood. Say, watch Blue along here. Look at him working the pine trees.

Every once in a while we'll have a pheasant or two sneak up into the barnyard for a meal."

Ted raised his gun up and clicked the safety off for the moment. "My guess is that he might kick one up right at—"

With a sudden whoosh a rooster and hen pheasant sprang up from behind the last pine tree in the lane with Blue in hot pursuit. Ted snapped his gun to his shoulder and pulled the trigger before Jerry could even get his safety off. With a loud bang the gun thundered, and the rooster dropped instantly from the sky. A puff of feathers drifted back toward them as Blue pounced on the dead pheasant.

"Good shot!" exclaimed Jerry, clicking the safety back on his gun and patting Ted on the shoulder. "Poor guy never had a chance. Bring it here, Blue. Come on!"

Blue trotted back with his prize and dropped it at Jerry's feet, looking up with a big grin. "Good boy," Jerry said, stroking his head. "But you brought it to the wrong shooter. That pheasant would still be flying if it had been me pulling the trigger. Where'd you learn to shoot like that, Teddy?"

"My dad loved to hunt," Ted said. "Most of it I learned just by walking along with him. We never had a dog that was any good, though. He made me do most of the dog's work!"

"Well, whatever the method, it paid off," said Jerry with admiration in his voice. "I got a feeling I won't need my gun today. You can shoot 'em. Besides, my hands are already cold. Guess we can leave the bird right here on the fencepost and pick him up when we come back. Let's head down the fenceline."

The two men walked at the same speed on opposite sides of the fence while Blue worked the long grass on both sides, but they did not kick up any more pheasants. When they finally arrived at the big sinkhole, Jerry held Blue until Ted reached the other rim of the sinkhole's perimeter, then he sent Blue in to see what might be hiding in the long grass.

Blue darted down the side hill, then quickly turned at a scent that caught his nose. There was an explosion of noise as a rooster kicked up and headed right across Jerry's line of fire but out of Ted's range. Punching his safety off and pulling his gun up, Jerry led his target and pulled the trigger with a loud bang. But the pheasant did not miss a stroke as the BBs flew past.

Pumping his gun, Jerry shoved another shell into the chamber and fired again. Nothing! He pumped in another round and tried one last long shot, but the pheasant disappeared into the distance. Jerry shook his head and threw up his one free hand in disgust. "I can't believe I missed him!" he yelled over at Ted. "Once they're in the air, they're safe with me around."

Blue had dashed up the side of the sinkhole and raced a long ways after the pheasant before turning back. He stopped and gazed at Jerry with a disappointed, slightly accusing air. "Even my dog's given up on me," Jerry called out. "It's your turn, Teddy. Go on, Blue. Get back into the sinkhole."

Heading down the slope, Blue once again caught a scent that turned his attention. Following it away from Jerry, Blue was soon right below Ted's position. There was another flurry of wings, and this time two hens and a rooster went airborne. But the rooster only got about thirty feet when Ted's gun fired, ending the rooster's getaway. Once again, Blue picked up the prize and brought it up the hill to Jerry.

"You shoot 'em, I'll carry them back," Jerry called out to Ted.

Blue made several more passes before the men gave up. With every minute that went by, the raw wind seemed to pick up a bit and the temperature continued to plummet. Finally Ted walked back to where Jerry was waiting.

"How'd you like my shooting demonstration?" Jerry asked. "Sounded like Cock's Army, and I didn't hit the broad side of the barn. Three stinking shots. I had the same problem hitting targets with the twenty-millimeter guns on the ship."

"You're not leading them far enough," Ted said. "I could see your shot a couple feet behind the bird. But it's freezing. Think it's time to head back?"

"Sounds good to me," Jerry agreed, stomping his feet and shivering. "After the Pacific heat I've soaked up, this wind is murder."

"How about some liquid heat?" Ted asked, reaching inside his coat and pulling out an unopened pint of blackberry brandy.

"It's good for what ails you, and it's a great friend on a cold day." Unscrewing the top, he took a big swallow and handed it to Jerry.

Jerry stared at his brother-in-law, taken aback by the ease with which Teddy poured down the stinging drink. He didn't remember Marjie's saying anything about Teddy's being a drinking man, but it was obvious that Ted was a regular patron.

"I'll pass," Jerry said, holding up his hand, yet hoping to not offend.

Ted pulled the bottle back and took another long swallow. "Mmmm. Delicious stuff," he said, offering the brandy one more time. "You're sure?" When Jerry shook his head no, Ted screwed the top back down and slid the pint back into his coat. "I don't know what I'd do without a sip now and then. You stop drinking since you got religion?"

Jerry didn't know what to say. "No . . . well, I haven't had a drink since the ship went down," he said, trying to put his thoughts together. "I guess I haven't thought about it. I did have some drinking problems, though, before then—came close to getting picked up by the MPs. And I found out the hard way that I couldn't drink my frustrations away. But is there something wrong that I don't know about, Teddy?"

"Nothing that a good shot of brandy or vodka can't fix," Ted said, picking up the pheasant and looking it over for the damage done by the BBs. "Looks like the meat on this one's in good shape. Mostly got him in the head. You keep this one for Marjie. She always hated picking BBs out of the meat."

"Thanks," Jerry said, taking the pheasant in hand but noticing something strange in Ted's eyes. It was the same dull expression that he'd seen in the faces of many sailors the day after they returned from shore leave. He knew from experience it was usually related to pain and anger, but it always found a dark place of refuge in the barroom. "She'll appreciate the bird. But I still don't get what's up with the brandy inside your coat. You hitting the bottle?"

"Marjie didn't talk to you?" Ted snapped, starting to walk back in the direction of the farmhouse.

"About you?" Jerry returned. "She wrote me that your girl walked out on you some time ago, but she hasn't said anything since I got back."

Ted quickened his pace a bit, and Jerry had all he could do to keep up. "You ask her," Ted demanded. "I'm sure that Ma's been talking to Marjie. It's not a big deal, but I'd rather not talk about it. I take a drink now and then. I like the stuff."

"I like a beer now and then," Jerry said. "But I don't carry it in my coat."

"Hey, this isn't a problem!" Ted barked, turning around with an angry look. Then he relaxed and smiled. "Sorry. But Ma keeps bugging me about it, and I'm sick of it. I brought the bottle along thinking we'd get cold and it would warm us up. I usually only drink at the bar, and I hardly ever do it during the day. It's okay. I can walk away from it whenever I want. Just don't tell Ma, all right?"

"Fine," said Jerry as Ted turned and marched on toward the house, obviously finished with the conversation. Jerry was left to wonder what was going on, but he got the feeling that it wasn't good.

4

HEADLINES

"You two just go on now!" Benjamin insisted, holding Martha in one arm and pointing Marjie and Jerry toward the door with the other arm. "Take care of your business, and we'll be waiting for you here. And don't you worry none about this little lady. I can handle her for three or four hours without blinking an eyelash."

"Why don't you come along?" Marjie asked. "Don't you want to see the newspaper when it arrives?"

"I'll see it soon enough," answered Benjamin. "Besides, it's something special for the two of you to enjoy together. You know I like to have the baby to myself, anyway. And the sooner you get going, the sooner I can get back to some serious thinking."

"What's that supposed to mean?" Jerry inquired, stopping at the door to study his father's expression. "You're up to something, aren't you?"

Benjamin wrinkled his forehead and waved a hand. "I'll tell you later," he said with a twinkle in his eye. "I haven't quite made up my mind yet."

"You're cruel," Marjie joked. "How about a hint?"

"Forget it," Jerry commented. "He's got that stubborn Macmillan look. Let's go."

"Lovely. I've seen that same look on someone else's face,"

said Marjie, pushing the farmhouse door open and glancing back at her daughter and father-in-law. "We'll try to be back in three hours."

Jerry put his arm around Marjie to shield her from the stiff northwest wind, and they made a fast dash to the car. Slamming the car doors shut brought an instant sense of relief. With only two days left in October, the raw cold seemed to be giving a preview of the winter to come.

Heading down the driveway and waving goodbye to Benjamin, who was standing by the picture window, Marjie said, "He's a champion with that little girl."

"Unbelievable," Jerry said and shook his head. "I'll bet he's spent more time with her in one month than he did with Jack and me combined."

"I think it's a gift," Marjie said solemnly. "Like he's been given a window of time to really discover the joy of being a father. Do you think that could be true?"

"You got me," answered Jerry. "Sure looks like it. Any rate, I think it's wonderful—for him and Martha."

"And me," Marjie added. "Do you know that during the first couple of weeks, when I was dog-tired, he'd get up in the night to rock her back to sleep? It'd be the middle of the night and old Grandpa would be singing away. Then he'd get up later to do chores. I hope you're taking notes. You can learn from the man."

"I wouldn't count on it. He's got the touch."

Marjie pinched Jerry's arm and said, "You've got the same bloodline, sailor boy. By the way, are you any good at breaking arms?"

"No. Why?"

"Because before we pick up the papers we're going to pay a visit to the esteemed chairman of the county war board. We'll see whether old Jacob has made the contacts he promised, or whether you might need to do some arm twisting. Then we're going to see if Ed has any copies of the paper ready like he said. I think you deserve to get a pile of papers!"

Jerry's eyes rolled back, and he let out a loud groan. "You're going to see just how far you can embarrass me, aren't you?

Wasn't it enough to pressure him into a photo session? I'm surprised you didn't call in some more relatives to have their pictures took."

"Glad you reminded me," Marjie said with a chuckle. "I'll ask him how our family prints are coming. I wonder if he makes copies?"

"Spare me. He's not running a studio."

"But he has all the equipment. Maybe it's not a problem."

Jerry just shook his head with a little laugh and kept his eyes on the road.

The little town of Preston was quiet as usual, with only a few pedestrians shivering along the windy streets. They pulled into a spacious parking lot, then walked over to the county courthouse and through the heavy front doors.

"Remember this spot?" Marjie asked with a smirk as she stopped at the bottom of a stairway. "It's where I got my wedding kiss, right after we left the justice of the peace. I heard the secretaries upstairs called you Hot Lips after they saw you in action. The whole town heard about you."

"Maybe I should go up there and pay them a visit," suggested Jerry. "Maybe they—"

"Say no more," Marjie ordered, putting her arms around him. "You're paid for. Now pucker up—for old times' sake."

Before her last word was out, Jerry had gathered Marjie in his strong embrace and delivered a kiss that rivaled its predecessor. When he finished, Jerry quickly looked up the stairs for anyone who might be watching. Seeing no one, he gave her a second kiss even more powerful than the first.

"Whew!" Marjie said, straightening her coat as Jerry let her go. "Who put the tiger in your tank? Look. You steamed up the windows in the doors."

"I'm still catching up on the ten months I missed," answered Jerry. "All right. Let's get to our business. Where's the chairman's office?"

"Follow me. I've been here so many times in the past couple months, I know the way by heart," Marjie said. Together they negotiated the dimly lit corridors. "Are you nervous?"

"I'm only nervous about what you might say," replied Jerry. "You've got a bad track record. Let me do the talking this time."

He heard Marjie laugh and tried to catch up to her as she led the way to a small office that opened to a larger office. The secretary working at the front desk looked up and smiled. "Mr. Medlow is waiting for you," she said. "Go right in."

Jacob Medlow was rummaging through stacks of files on his desk, but he jumped up from his large oak chair and moved around the desk to greet Marjie and Jerry as they came through his office door. He was a large man in his early sixties with a generous shock of pure white hair.

"Marjie," he said, extending his hand, "good to see you again. And Jerry. Welcome home, son. I hear tell you're our first war hero from this area! Big story in the paper coming out today."

"I'm no—"

"It should be a wonderful story, Jacob," Marjie cut in. "Jerry really is a hero, but you'll never hear him say it."

Medlow patted Jerry on the back and pointed to the chairs in front of his desk. "Have a seat," he said. "I'm looking forward to seeing it in print, but Ed let me read it right after he finished typing the article. Made the hair on my arms stand up. I'm mighty proud of you, Jerry. We'd win this war in a hurry if all the boys were as brave as you."

Jerry shook his head. "I didn't see any cowards, sir. And I saw plenty of men that laid down their lives on that ship. It's a shame we couldn't save the *Wasp*. She was a fine ship. I wish I could've seen her do more damage to the enemy than she did."

Sinking down in his chair, Jacob Medlow picked up his reading glasses and settled them on his nose. Then, peering over the frames at Jerry, he said, "You did your best, son. There was nothing you could have done to make it different. Let's just hope they got the Jap sub that did it." Then he opened the thick manila folder he had been searching for before they arrived.

"See all this paperwork, Jerry? Your wife's been hounding me hard about getting you released," Jacob said. "I suppose you're familiar with her straightforward manner?"

"Very," Jerry answered and winced. "She's a little high-strung, but she means well."

Medlow laughed. "You can say that again," he said. Then he whispered, "Actually, she's a dynamo! If you're ever looking for a secretarial job, Marjie, give me a call."

"I hate secretarial work," Marjie whispered back. "Unless you're offering big bucks. But could we get down to business? I'm dying to find out what you have heard. You did call like you said you would?"

"Yes."

"So, what did you find out?"

"Not so fast," the chairman said. "I've got some questions for Jerry. Look, son, I have the sworn affidavits that Marjie has gathered from the doctor, your father, and several of your neighbors. You have also made a formal request for a Special Order Discharge based upon the assistance required on your father's farm. Since arriving home and spending time with Benjamin, do you still feel that he requires your services?"

Jerry looked at Marjie and took her hand. Taking a deep breath, he said, "There's nothing I wanted to do more than to help defend our nation, sir. But my father's health has slipped. In less than a year, he's gone from a workhorse to just barely getting by. He don't feel like he'll make it through this winter by himself, and my brother Jack can't move back to help. If I don't get the discharge, Dad's serious about selling the farm. But I'm afraid that will kill him, if his heart holds up that long. He loves that farm. He's never lived anywhere else."

"Your next assignment was to report to Norfolk on November 26?" asked Jacob.

"Yes, sir," Jerry answered. "And I'll obey that order unless the navy agrees to my discharge."

"You're made of the right stuff, Jerry," Medlow said, fishing a letter out of the folder of correspondence. He handed it to Jerry. "Read this. It came with the morning mail."

Jerry took the letter and opened it, but before he got a third of the way through the letter's formalities, Marjie had already scanned the rest. She read out loud, "The Chief of Naval Personnel hereby approves the recommendation of the Commanding Officer and grants Seaman Jerry Macmillan the Special Order Discharge from the United States Naval Reserve."

Marjie came straight up out her chair and shocked Medlow with a huge hug and then a kiss to the cheek. "Thank you! Thank you! Thank you!" she cried.

Then she turned to Jerry and hugged him as well. "You get to stay home!" she exclaimed, burying her face into his. "You get to stay with me and Martha. And the farm doesn't need to be sold!"

Jerry was stunned by the news. He hadn't told Marjie, but he really expected that he'd have to make the trip to Norfolk and try to get a hearing in the Navy Personnel Office. He hugged Marjie and then kissed her over and over, forgetting that Medlow was only a few feet away. Try as he did, Jerry could find no words to describe the relief and the regret he felt at the same moment.

Once the celebration subsided, Jerry looked up and wasn't surprised to discover Jacob Medlow grinning from ear to ear. "Thank you for all you've done, sir," Jerry said.

"Thank your wife," Jacob stated. "She did all the work. You are officially a civilian, Jerry. Thank you for serving your country so well."

"It was my privilege," said Jerry as he and Marjie rose to leave. "But I'm sorry it had to end so soon."

Jacob shook Jerry's hand again, and the couple made their exit.

"Let's get out of here fast!" Marjie said, hustling down the long hallway. "Somebody might change their mind!"

They raced as quickly as they could out of the courthouse and hopped inside the sun-warmed car. Marjie snuggled against Jerry, but they were both silent for a long while.

"I remember that terrible day you left Rochester on the bus," Marjie spoke softly. "I sat alone in this car and must have cried for a half hour straight. The thought of being separated from you again was like a dreadful dream waiting to happen. Since you got home, I haven't dared think about it for fear I'd fall to pieces."

"Thanks for all your hard work on this, babe," said Jerry as he stroked her hair and held her tight. "I didn't think it could happen so soon. It almost seems wrong that I'm home to stay, while all those other guys are still out there fighting. . . ."

Marjie lightly kissed Jerry's smooth-shaven face. "You've done your part, Jerry. And you'll be doing your part here on the farm, too. The navy people know what they're doing."

He sighed and pulled her closer. "I guess you're right."

"You *know* I'm right," she answered, her head buried in his chest.

They stayed that way a long minute, just holding each other. Then Marjie raised her head and fixed her brown eyes on his blue ones. "Several people who love you were praying a lot about this, you know, including yours truly. So maybe we should stop and say thank you to God."

"Here?"

"Sure. Go ahead," Marjie replied. "You're not stuck on praying in church only, are you?"

"In case you hadn't noticed, I ain't too stuck on praying, period," answered Jerry. "We've never done it together. Should I say something out loud?"

"Why not?"

"Does it matter?"

"I don't know," replied Marjie, "but everyone I know seems to do it out loud. I'd like to hear it."

Jerry closed his eyes. "Our Father . . . we can't thank you enough for all you've done. Thank you for saving my life, and now thank you for working everything out so well. And thank you for helping Marjie to make it through the hard times when I was gone, and thank you for our baby—for Martha—and for the special relationship you've given her with my dad. We couldn't have done any of this by ourselves. So thanks again. Uh, amen."

Opening his eyes, Jerry shook his head and said, "You didn't close your eyes, did you?"

"Was I supposed to?"

"Of course."

"You're sure?"

Jerry laughed. "You know I ain't sure of anything, especially about praying," he said. "But next time, try closing your eyes. It's going to bug me to think you're staring at me."

"You may need to get thicker skin," Marjie said. "I like watching you." She glanced down at her watch. "Look at the time. Let's get down to the newspaper building. The papers should have come in."

Jerry started the car and took a left out of the parking lot. Two blocks later, Jerry stopped the car in front of the *Preston Republican* building. Stepping inside, they spotted Ed Bentley at a desk toward the rear of the room, pounding on a heavy metal typewriter. He looked up and waved them back.

"Great to see you!" Ed called out. "You're right on time. The truck just backed up to the dock. One second and I'll finish this sentence, then we'll go get you some copies."

"Maybe a bundle?" Marjie prompted.

Ed raised his eyebrows while he finished his typing, then he rubbed his forehead. "A whole bundle? That's more—"

"I'll bet you toss copies away after every printing," Marjie asserted.

"Sure, but . . ." Ed shook his head and laughed. "I give up. A bundle it is. Did you ever think of selling cars for a living?" he asked, digging in a pile of envelopes on his desk. "Let's see here. I've got something else for you. Prints and negatives. And no, I will not make any more prints. And no, you may not open them until you leave because I can't afford for you to con me out of any more stuff. What you see is what you get. Deal?"

He stood up from his desk and held the envelope just out of her reach. "Deal?"

"Deal. You're wonderful, Ed!" Marjie said, taking the package from his hand. "Please let me open them now."

"Don't you dare!" Ed demanded. "You said it was a deal. If you open the envelope, you kiss the bundle of newspapers goodbye."

"A deal's a deal," Jerry intervened. "Let's go get the papers."

Ed turned and led the way down a long, dark hallway that opened into a noisy storage and mailing room. A couple of pallets stacked with papers sat just inside the delivery doors. Ed grabbed a bundle, cut the string that bound it, and flipped a copy open to the front page.

Marjie gasped as she saw Jerry's picture and read the bold headline: "GREENLEAFTON SAILOR SURVIVES SINKING OF AIRCRAFT CARRIER! Seaman Jerry Macmillan on USS *Wasp* When Jap Subs Got Her." She cupped her face with her hands and blinked back tears.

"It's beautiful, Ed," Marjie cried. Then she took his arm and said, "We'll never forget this. How can we thank you?"

"You already have," answered Ed. "This has been the most rewarding piece I've written in a long time. And it's going to sell a lot of papers. Actually, I may need these copies you finagled out of me."

"Oh no," Marjie protested. "A deal's a deal, remember?" She picked up the loose bundle of papers and handed it to her husband, who had gone red-faced with embarrassment. "We'd better go, Jerry," she told him. "I think we've outstayed our welcome here."

Ed broke into a laugh. "If you get another great story, you're welcome back—anytime. But warn me first. I'll hide my camera."

5

THE STANFELDS

The photos were good—not studio quality, but clear and sharp. Marjie and Jerry sat in the car outside the newspaper office studying the black and white images of the family posed outside the farmhouse. Marjie was elated, but Jerry had grown somber as he read the last part of the newspaper article.

"Something wrong?" Marjie asked. "For someone who just read a wonderful story about himself, you look like you swallowed a lemon."

"I really think we should drive up to Chester's folks before they start getting calls about Chester from Ed's article," Jerry said as Marjie carefully slid the photos back into the folder. "I should have thought to call them when I first got home. They're probably wondering if he's even alive."

"Don't you think he's written them?" Marjie asked.

"Probably," replied Jerry. "But what if he didn't? I'm sure his folks heard the radio report. They live about half an hour up Highway 52. Do we have time?"

Marjie glanced down at her watch and said, "Barely. Benjamin did say he could last four hours with Martha. We can't stay long, though."

"From what Chester said about his parents, I don't think they'll ask us in," Jerry warned.

"Meaning?"

"I ain't sure. We'll see."

"Let's stop at the bakery," Marjie suggested. "I'm starving, and I think a couple of apple fritters should tide me over."

"Pretty expensive tastes," Jerry joked as he started the car and backed up.

"Maybe you forgot I'm a big spender," Marjie said. "Anyway, we've got to do something to celebrate! Nothing like a nice, hot apple fritter, eh?"

They made a quick stop at the bakery, then headed north out of town toward Chatfield. Jerry knew where the farm was, and by the time they had downed their second fritter, they were pulling into the long driveway leading to the Stanfeld farmhouse.

A man in his early forties stepped out of the machine shed and walked toward them as Jerry pulled the car to a stop in front of the old brick farmhouse. A woman whom Jerry instantly recognized as Chester's mother came out the front door, pulling on a coat and shielding her eyes from the bright sunshine to try to get a better look at the strangers.

Jerry got out of the car and turned to greet Chester's father. "Mr. Stanfeld," Jerry called out. "I'm Jerry Macmillan. I was with Chester on the *Wasp*."

"Pleased to meet you," Chester's father greeted him with a warm handshake. "He wrote us about you. I'm Bill Stanfeld, and this is my wife, Clare."

"And this is my wife, Marjie," Jerry said as she came around the car and shook their hands. "I should have thought to call you folks when I got home on Monday, but it never crossed my mind that you'd heard about the *Wasp* and might not know how Chester was. We were in Preston this morning, and it suddenly dawned on me. Have you heard from Chester?"

"Sure did," Bill answered. "We got a letter Monday morning before that report came on the radio. Said he was in San Diego, in the hospital—that he'd been hurt. Strange he didn't say anything about the *Wasp*, but then he's a strange boy."

"I can tell you why," Jerry said. "We were forbidden to talk about the ship being sunk. I think the navy was trying to keep it a secret from the Japanese as long as possible. We're in bad shape in the Pacific for carriers, and losing the *Wasp* was a bad blow."

As he was talking, Jerry kept looking over at Chester's mother. He couldn't get over how much his friend resembled her, especially around the eyes. She pulled her coat a little tighter around her neck and cleared her throat. "Chester said you saved his life. He didn't say how, but it sounds like we got an awful lot to thank you for. Chester says he's walking and should get out of the hospital soon. I'm hoping to have him home again before he gets his next assignment."

"That's great news!" Jerry exclaimed. "I miss him already. And I'm glad to know he wrote you. Be sure and have him call me when—"

"What happened to Chester?" Bill Stanfeld interrupted. "How'd you save him?"

"It's a long story," Jerry answered, a bit taken aback by the man's abrupt question, "and we have a baby we need to get back to. But you can read the whole account in the *Preston Republican*. And it just so happens that we have some extra copies that I think have your name on them." He opened the car door, pulled several papers from the pile, and handed copies to both of the Stanfelds.

"If that don't beat all," Bill Stanfeld said, flipping the paper open. "Headlines and a photo of you to boot. Where's the part about Chester?"

"The article goes from the front page to the back page," Jerry answered. "Chester's part comes in at the top of the back page."

Turning to the back, both Stanfelds lost themselves as they found the section where Jerry discovered Chester on the hangar deck. Clare Stanfeld put her hand over her mouth as she read, and the tears began to form at the corner of her eyes. Her husband's face remained stoic, although the squint in his eyes signaled something churning inside.

Marjie put her hand on Clare's arm, thinking that the tears were about to cascade down her face. But Mrs. Stanfeld seemed to check the flow and kept on reading. She finished the article sooner than her husband, then she carefully folded the paper back together without looking up. Slowly her eyes came up to meet Jerry's, and in that moment Jerry could see the bottomless depths of a mother's love. He felt his heart begin to melt as he thought of how his own mother would be reacting.

"You saved my oldest boy's life!" she whispered. "He'd be dead today except for you."

Jerry could only nod yes through a bent smile as the tears began to stream down his face. Clare stepped forward, taking both of Jerry's hands in hers and looking him straight in the eyes. Struggling to find her voice, she said, "There's nothing we can ever do to make this up to you. But I want you to know that I would rather die myself than lose my boy. Saving him, I feel like you may have saved me."

With those words she ended her tribute and seemed to almost wilt into Jerry's arms as he reached out to hug her. Marjie put her arm around Clare as well and added her support. Whether it was the cold or the sudden surge of emotions, Chester's mother was shaking like a leaf.

Bill Stanfeld had finished reading the article as his wife had taken Jerry's hand, but his expression had not changed. Marjie thought it was as though he didn't know how to respond, so he decided to give no response rather than embarrass himself. He closed the newspaper, took it in one hand, and folded his arms across his chest. "So you went down to that lower deck in all the smoke just to see if Chester made it out?"

"Yes, sir," Jerry answered, still holding Clare.

"What made you do it?"

"He was like a brother to me," said Jerry. "I knew the chances were slim, but I had to make sure."

"And what did he say when you found him?" Chester's father asked.

Jerry shut his eyes and could hear Chester's voice as clearly as when the words were spoken. "He told me to leave him behind and save myself," Jerry said, choking back a fresh wave of tears. "Chester was always so concerned about everyone else but himself. He said I had Marjie and the baby to think about, and that he'd never make it. He said he was ready to—"

"The fool!" Bill Stanfeld spat, shaking his head, and Jerry blinked at the venom in the man's voice. "He's still on that religion kick. Said in his letter that he was spared so he could spend the rest of his life serving God. I say he was spared because of what you did. God didn't have nothing to do with it."

Jerry shook his head in return, feeling an answering anger well up in him. Remembering what Chester had told him about his father, he had hoped their discussion would not touch on religion. But now he felt he had no choice but to respond.

"I ain't a religious man, Mr. Stanfeld," Jerry declared. "And I ain't making any claim to divine knowledge. But you need to understand that I don't take it as coincidence that I happened to make it down those stairs when it was probably foolish to attempt it, or that I happened to see Chester's leg moving, or that he happened to still be conscious after losing so much blood, or that there happened to be one last life raft when I was sure they'd all left. If I were a betting man, I'd wager that Chester was right. You can call it luck or bravery, but I don't believe there was enough of either going around at the time to make it happen."

Jerry stopped to catch his breath and resolved to speak out the full story. "And I want you to know something else that the newspaper didn't put in print: God was down there in the water with us. After Chester was rescued, when I was thrashing around thinking I was going to die, God came to me. His presence was as real as you standing there holding the newspaper. And all the stuff that Chester had told me about God long before I hit the water proved to be true. I was not a believer in Jesus Christ, Mr. Stanfeld. But through the example and words of your son, and by the grace of God, I do believe today."

Marjie, watching with Clare, searched for a way to break in and end the standoff between the two men. "Jerry, we really need to be going," she said, "and Clare should get inside before she catches a cold."

Chester's father remained focused on Jerry. "Chester's got you brainwashed, too," he seethed. "So you're as big a fool—"

"That's enough, Bill," Clare broke in, stepping in front of her husband. Bill stared at his wife as if unaccustomed to being confronted by her. And Clare was clearly uneasy, though determined, as she continued, "Jerry's entitled to believe whatever he wants. And, Bill, our son's alive today because of what Jerry did. Would you rather he died?"

Slowly looking down at his wife, Bill Stanfeld pursed his lips and shook his head, his sudden blaze of anger subsiding in the face of her rebuke.

Turning to Jerry, Clare said, "I hope to see you again. If there is anything I can ever do for you people—anything—you let me know. And I thank you for what you did, Jerry." She shook their hands with quiet dignity and walked to the house without looking in her husband's direction.

Marjie and Jerry had taken a couple of steps toward the car before Chester's father moved. "Listen," he muttered, forcing the words out. "I don't like to say it, but Clare's right. I had no business talking to you like I did. And I'm grateful for what you done for Chester. There's nothing we can do to make it up to you. But I'm obliged to you."

"That's all right," Marjie returned. "Believing in God was the most difficult thing I have faced myself. It just takes some of us longer than others."

For a second the fury welled in the man's eyes again, but he tightened his mouth and simply nodded. "In any case, I'll tell Chester to call you when he gets home."

"Please do," Jerry said, shaking Bill's hand and then opening his car door. "I can't wait to introduce him to Marjie and my little girl."

Jerry and Marjie hopped into the car, then they waved goodbye and headed out the driveway for home.

"That was murder," Jerry declared as he turned from the gravel driveway onto the pavement. He gave a sigh of relief and rubbed his cold forehead as they headed south. "Chester wasn't kidding about his father. Talk about an angry man. Yikes!"

"You could have been a little clearer about that point before we got there," Marjie said. "You obviously knew more than you were telling. Clare seemed nice, though."

"Must be that Chester inherited more from her than from him," observed Jerry. "I wonder what his problem is? I thought he was ready to get out the gloves and go a couple of rounds with me just because I said I believed."

Marjie slid over in the seat close to Jerry and put her head on his shoulder. "It's like we've all got knots inside us that need to get untied so we can be free," she spoke softly. "But some of the knots are so tight that the only way to get rid of them is to cut them out. And that's painful. Something's eating that man up inside."

"You got that right," Jerry agreed. "I'll bet that Clare takes the brunt of it."

"No doubt," said Marjie. "Push the wrong button and the bombs go off. What a way to live!" She leaned back in the seat and stretched her legs out in front of her. "What a day. It's only the middle of the afternoon, and I'm shot."

They rolled straight through Preston and then on to Greenleafton without stopping. Marjie dozed most of the trip, but Jerry's adrenaline easily kept him awake. Chester's father's words—and his own response—played in his mind over and over, and Jerry felt his muscles tensing up with every mile. He wondered what it must have been like for Chester to live under the same roof with such a father.

When the car stopped by the Macmillan farmhouse, Marjie awoke and stretched. "That didn't take long," she said.

"I wonder if Rip Van Winkle said the same thing?" Jerry asked. "Let's get inside. It's been four hours since we left home."

They went into the house through the back door and found Benjamin in the kitchen heating a fresh pot of coffee. He pointed to the bedroom, and they knew that Martha was sleeping.

"How'd it go?" Marjie whispered.

"No problem," answered Benjamin. "She was as good as gold. But what else do you expect from a Macmillan baby?"

"How long's she been asleep?"

"Not long," Benjamin replied. "We should be able to have a cup of coffee, and you can tell what you found out from the war board, and I can tell you what I was thinking about when you left."

Marjie took out one of the newspapers she'd carried into the house and flipped it open for Benjamin to see.

"For crying out loud!" he exclaimed as he saw the headline. "Would you look at that!"

"Come and read the article," Marjie urged. "I'll finish the coffee. And Jerry's got a letter you'll be real interested in as well."

It was nearly an hour before Benjamin finished reading and listening to all of Jerry and Marjie's stories from the morning. He was delighted with the letter and the paper, but he asked the most questions about the encounter with Chester's parents. Benjamin was obviously troubled about what Bill Stanfeld had said.

After most of their stories were complete, Marjie turned to Benjamin. "You said you were going to tell us what you've been thinking about. I want to hear it before Martha wakes up."

Benjamin wrinkled his forehead and looked away from Marjie for a moment. "Hmmm," he sighed reflectively. "I want to warn you that you probably won't like what I have to say. But it's something I feel I need to do, and I don't want you trying to talk me out of it. Understand?"

"No. That's not fair," Marjie answered. "I hate it when you start a discussion like this."

"Just tell us what you're thinking, and we'll respect your desires," Jerry added. "But you have to let us give you our thoughts, too."

"Fine," Benjamin conceded. "I've been thinking about this long before you got home, Jerry. I didn't know when it would happen, but I hoped to live long enough to keep the farm going until you got home. Marjie and the baby needed my help, and I've needed their help. And we made it. You're home for good, and I could not be more delighted.

"But there's a wrinkle now, and I think I better be the one to iron it out. I've watched a lot of young couples trying to start a family with one or both of their parents in the same house, and it rarely works very well. I think my time on this farm is finished, so I've looked around and discovered that the little

McDuff house in Greenleafton is available to rent. I've already talked with them, and it looks like in a couple weeks it could be ready for me to occupy."

"But this is your house!" Marjie exclaimed with agony in her voice. "We don't want you to have to go. Maybe *we* should look for—"

"Please," Benjamin cut her off. "Let's not make this hard on each other. We can just sit on this for a week and then decide. But this house needs a family in it, and you and Jerry and Martha fit here. My days are numbered on this earth, if you hadn't noticed, and it's time to look ahead. Besides, even if I do move to town, it's only a mile and a half, and I'd be out every day to help with the work, anyway. But let's not discuss this anymore for now. I sprung this on you, and you need time to chew on it."

Conversation at the table fell silent, and Marjie was relieved to hear a whimper from the bedroom. She didn't know quite what to think of Benjamin's proposal, but she did know that she felt like crying.

6

POTLUCK AND PRAYERS

If the number of telephone calls and visits received by the Macmillans following the delivery of the *Preston Republican* were any indication of the weekly paper's popularity, it got a very high score. The phone did not let up, nor did the steady stream of neighbors and relatives dropping by to congratulate Jerry and welcome him home. Besides entertaining company, about all the Macmillans managed to get done was the morning and evening chores.

Ruth Buckley pulled into the driveway on Friday afternoon just as Jerry and Benjamin were getting ready to do the milking. Ruth had managed one visit since Jerry's arrival home and had listened in awe to Jerry's story. She had even asked Jerry if he'd come to the country school where she taught and tell it to the children.

"Well, I don't know. I'll have to think about it," Jerry had said.

"He'll be glad to," Marjie had amended.

Now Jerry called out, "Good to see you, Ruthie," as she pushed open the car door. "Maybe you can take some phone calls for Marjie," he added. "We're all about talked out."

"Tough being everybody's hero," Ruth replied, swinging her long legs out of the car. "But I'll be glad to take over the phones. I love to talk, and if I embellish your story a bit, you might get some more publicity."

Jerry waved her off. "I don't need any more publicity, so don't do whatever you said. Just tell them 'thank you' and 'please go away.'"

"Will do," Ruth said, heading up the sidewalk as Benjamin came out the farmhouse door. Waving her greeting, she said, "Hey, good-lookin', put your cap on. It's cold out here."

"Greetings, Ruthie," Benjamin said with his warmest smile. "There's not much left on top to worry about. But I thought you schoolteachers rap knuckles when the children say 'Hey.'"

"One of my few personal faults, Benjamin," Ruth shot back. "But I do rap knuckles."

"Marjie's got hot coffee waiting, but I guess we've kept the pot filled since that newspaper came out," Benjamin declared proudly. "Never seen the beat of this."

Benjamin plodded on in the direction of the barn, and Ruth went into the house without knocking. Marjie was already waiting with Martha tucked into one arm and a cup of coffee held out in her free hand.

"You drink the coffee, and I'll hold the little doll," Ruth said, taking Martha from Marjie and cradling the baby in her arms. "Mmmm . . . mmmm. You feel delicious to hold. And you smell as fresh as the spring."

"She just had a bath," Marjie responded. "Ruthie, it's time you get serious about finding a husband. You and babies are made for each other."

Ruth was busy making faces at Martha, but she hadn't missed what Marjie said. "Do you remember the first time we met at the church, Marjie?" she asked.

"Sure."

"Remember I told you that I hoped you might have some contacts for me?" said Ruth. "It may have sounded like I was kidding, but I was dead serious. There's no one around here that's the least bit interesting—or even the right age."

"I did think you were kidding."

Looking up into Marjie's eyes, Ruth said, "This is something I never joke about. And just between you and me, I've never talked to anyone about it. But do you know what my greatest fear is, Marjie?"

"Being an old maid."

A smile broke across Ruth's face and the flash in her dark eyes returned. "How could you possibly know that?"

"It's first-grade stuff, Ruthie," Marjie answered, "because it's so logical. You should know. You're a schoolteacher."

"It's written across my forehead, right?" Ruth said, waving her free hand up in the air. "Tell me!"

"All right," Marjie replied in a lofty, mock professorial tone. "I call it Macmillan's First Law of Human Phobias. Boiled down to its simplest terms, it states that a person's biggest fear often centers on the thing that is least likely to happen to them."

"Apply it to me."

"You are the kindest person I've ever met, Ruthie," Marjie explained. "You're intelligent, engaging, bursting with personality, and one the loveliest women I've ever seen. The most illogical thought you could have is that no one would be interested in marrying you. Yet Doctor Macmillan's research has effectively shown that people in your classification have a high probability of believing the classic fear defined as the Old Maid Syndrome. And it strikes an amazingly high percentage of single country schoolteachers."

Ruth and Marjie burst out laughing at how ridiculous the theory was, yet what made it so funny was the degree of truth it contained.

"Be serious," Ruth said when she finished laughing. "You need to add in all the factors. I'm not a spring chicken. There are no eligible men around. And I'm not a beauty. I'm just what you've said—a plain old country schoolteacher."

"Honey, you better take a look in the mirror," Marjie countered. "You're only twenty-four, you're confident and practical, and I've never seen anyone who had prettier eyes than yours. I know girls who would kill to get what you have. So trust the good doctor and take these masterful words of wisdom to heart: when Mr. Right comes along, you'll know it."

Ruth gave a sigh. "I wish it were that simple. But I'll take your medicine, doctor, and see if it helps."

"Repeat my words to yourself three times a day, and all will be well," Marjie intoned.

"I'll try it for a week," Ruth responded. "But I really didn't come over to talk about whether I'd find a man someday. I wanted to warn you about what you'll hear in church Sunday morning. I've organized a church dinner to welcome Jerry home!"

"He'll shoot you!" gasped Marjie. "You know he hates to be in the limelight."

"I know! Isn't it great!" Ruth exclaimed. "But you can't tell him. Let him discover it in church, and maybe he'll be too overwhelmed to come after me. Here's what we've planned: A week from tonight we're going to have a huge potluck dinner in Jerry's honor. It should be marvelous."

"Jerry's going to die," said Marjie.

"But that's not all," Ruth added. "Here's where you come in."

Marjie easily read Ruth's eyes and didn't like the message. "You're going to try to pull off something big, and you actually think you're going to sucker me into helping you?"

"Yes."

"This must be really good!" Marjie said, pushing her hair back. "You're right. I am a sucker. What's my part?"

Ruth nodded and said, "I'm going to ask Jerry to tell the church his story about what happened when the ship was torpedoed. You know, the part that wasn't in the paper."

"You're crazy!" exclaimed Marjie. "Jerry's never spoken before a crowd. Never. And you know it. Didn't you tell me he wouldn't even read a book report out loud in school? Why would you even think to ask him?"

"Two reasons," Ruth answered. "First, because I'm asking you to help me. Nobody's ever gotten him to do the kinds of things you can. And, second, because it's such an incredible story that everyone in the church deserves to hear it from the man who lived through it. If Jerry were to tell what happened out there, especially his experience of faith, can you imagine the impact it could have? As far as I know, no one has ever stood in front of our church and told how they came to faith, let alone with the drama that Jerry brings. It's too important not to try to get him to do it. You've got to help me, Marjie."

"My goodness," Marjie said, exhaling a big puff of air. "I thought you were talking about fun and games. This sounds serious. But, Ruth, I can't imagine him doing it—for any reason. He's scared stiff of crowds."

"The 'good doctor' said we all have our fears," Ruth reminded her. "Maybe you have some more words of wisdom tucked away in your medicine bag."

Marjie shook her head and paused as she thought it over. "What you're asking for is a miracle!" she said. "But I do have one idea that may help. If you or I ask Jerry to speak, he'll feel free to say no. But if you get Pastor Fitchen to ask him, it'll be that much harder."

"You're brutal!" exclaimed Ruth. "And brilliant. I think there's a chance that it might work."

"We'll see," Marjie said. "And I'll do what I can. But don't you dare pull my name into this. This was all your doing. I know nothing—understand?"

"Absolutely."

———— ✍ ————

Traumatic was the only appropriate word for Jerry's experience at church on Sunday morning. He had expected—and dreaded—all the attention he attracted on his first church service back since getting home. Then the announcement about the upcoming potluck in his honor took him by surprise. Waves of embarrassment almost overwhelmed him as friendly eyes turned his way. But to have the pastor pull him aside after the service and ask him to speak—that was the clincher. Jerry walked out of the church looking like he'd swallowed a wad of chewing tobacco. He hadn't said yes to the pastor, but he hadn't dared to say no either.

As it turned out, everything that Marjie said over the next few days to persuade him backfired. Despite her best attempts, Jerry only withdrew into a deeper personal agony. By Tuesday afternoon he was so miserable that she had to give up, and the last card Marjie had to play was her refusing Jerry's request to call the pastor for him and decline on the offer.

It was Benjamin who surprised Marjie by helping Jerry make his decision. As they finished chores on Wednesday morning, Benjamin said, "You look like you didn't get much sleep last night. Why don't you just tell Pastor Fitchen you can't do it? It's nothing to be ashamed about. I've never done anything like talk in front of the church, and I don't know that I could."

Jerry sat down on a bale of straw and pushed his cap back. "It's not about being ashamed," he explained. "My problem is me. Even though I'm scared, I feel something inside that wants to do it. I think about how I grew up never understanding what faith was, and then I think of other church members that might be in the same boat. If I don't tell what happened to me, and no one else tells what happened to them, and they don't hear it in clear terms from the pastor, how will they ever know?"

"What's the worst thing that could happen if you try?"

"I make a fool out of myself."

"You can face a torpedo but not being laughed at?"

Jerry scratched his scalp and stretched his neck. "Stupid, isn't it. I just wish I could do it."

"Son, the only way to beat it is to walk straight into it," Benjamin said. "I know it's not much help, but there's a lot of us folks who'd walk with you to that door."

Closing his eyes and leaning back against a wooden post, Jerry broke into a crooked smile and then a laugh. "I can't believe I'd ever even consider this," he said, looking over at his father. "But I'm going to give this a shot. It can't be any worse than trying to swim out and stop that life raft. But you may have to carry me home."

———— ✐ ————

On Friday night the church basement was packed with nearly three hundred people and the long, rickety tables were loaded with every kind of food imaginable. Most of the people who came were church members, but there were a few extras who had read Jerry's account in the paper and had heard that he was going to tell it after the dinner. The Macmillans were all seated at the front table with Pastor Fitchen and his wife. Marjie's mother and brother were there as well, sitting across from Ruth. Jerry had been surprised to see Ted walking in with Sarah, and he knew Marjie was delighted to see them both. Sarah was not much of a churchgoer, and Ted had sworn off churches altogether, but he seemed to have made an exception for this occasion. Except for a very faint hint of liquor on his breath, Ted seemed his normal, good-humored self.

For a while, Jerry was able to fool himself into thinking this was just another church gathering. But as the food on the tables dwindled and the noise level in the basement swelled and the time for his talk drew near, he began to sweat. His heart beat so hard he could hear it in his ears. A wave of nausea swept over him, and he was sure he would have to rush to the bathroom— or maybe out of the church entirely. Then Marjie put her cool hand on his and whispered in his ear, "We're praying for you, Jerry. Hang in there. You'll do fine." Though he protested, Marjie's words helped.

When it looked like most of the people were finished eating, the pastor rose and gave a short introduction to the evening, stating how glad he was to have Jerry back safely and how proud of him everyone was. Then he turned the floor over to Ruth, who had organized the dinner. Well aware of his discomfort, Ruth spoke her warm words of introduction directly to Jerry, as if he were the only one in the room, and Jerry started to believe that his fears were behind him.

But when Ruth asked Jerry to come and tell his story, the roar of the crowd's ovation ushered him back to his personal nightmare. As he stood, his heart began pounding in his throat, and his mind went as blank as a sheet of paper. Jerry wondered as he took his place behind the podium what in the world he was going to do. All he knew for certain was that sweat was pouring down his face.

Gazing out on the crowd, Jerry felt some comfort at seeing so many faces he had known since his childhood. Their clapping was long and appreciative, and many of the faces wore expectant expressions. He knew they were aware of his shyness, but they wanted to hear what he had to say. And if he could just get his story out of his mouth, Jerry felt sure they would benefit from hearing it.

He took a deep breath and waited until the crowd finally stopped clapping. Then the room went completely silent, and every eye focused on Jerry. He braced his sweaty hands on the podium and wished he had brought notes to read instead of just speaking from his heart. Seconds converted to minutes as Jerry's mind raced for something to say.

The loud click of a back door opening and the tap of a cane on the hard floor caught Jerry's attention and broke his temporary trance, though in the dim basement lighting he couldn't see who had come in. He reached down and took a drink of water, gave a nervous cough, and shot a desperate glance over at Marjie, who had settled Martha comfortably against her shoulder. She mouthed an "I love you" over the baby's silky head, and Jerry's thoughts calmed.

Opening his mouth, he was pleased to find that his vocal chords still responded to the usual signals. "I'd . . . I'd like to thank you all for coming tonight," Jerry began. "It's an honor I really don't deserve, and, if you know me, it's not something I'm very comfortable with. Maybe you noticed the pool of perspiration I'm already standing in?"

The ripple of laughter that spread through the basement caused Jerry to pause, but also served to boost his confidence. "Somebody better get a mop," he added with a laugh.

And from there, it seemed that the words began to come by themselves. Jerry started with a brief report about his friend Billy Wilson in San Diego. He told them about Billy's recovery from the burns he sustained when the USS *Arizona* was bombed at Pearl Harbor. From there it was an easy transition to telling about his own experience on the aircraft carrier *Wasp*. Jerry described the huge ship and told about his own assignment on the guns. He took them to the *Wasp*'s involvement in the South Pacific and what he knew about their role related to the Marines' landing at Guadalcanal. Except for a few lengthy pauses to take another sip of water and regather another group of thoughts, Jerry was doing fine, and the church audience was riveted to his words.

When he got to the part about the torpedoes hitting the carrier and the ensuing chaos aboard the ship, Jerry found it easiest to describe the scene with his eyes shut. Although unplanned, this action produced a very dramatic effect that mesmerized the crowd. And as he finally came to describe what it was like in the water, trying to prevent the life raft from leaving without taking Chester, many of the listeners were visibly moved, and some began to weep.

Trying to explain what it felt like to see his friend pulling away in the raft and to be suddenly left alone to face his own death, Jerry made the mistake of opening his eyes and seeing the handkerchiefs busy at work. The shock shut him down completely for a moment. But having come this far, he determined to not let a few tears stop him from getting out the whole story.

Closing his eyes again, Jerry prayed silently for the words he needed. Beads of perspiration had reformed on his forehead, and he reached up to wipe them away. Then he pressed his lips together and groped for his thoughts.

"Hanging by that rope," Jerry continued, "I was sure that I would die. But despite all my years of church, I knew I was not prepared to go. All I could see was the mountain of sins that I had committed and the fact that they condemned me to an eternal death. So I prayed the only prayer I could think of—the Lord's Prayer. Crazy to be dangling at death's door and praying a little prayer you've prayed every Sunday. But I saw those wrongdoings for what they were, and I wanted to be forgiven, and I wanted to go to heaven, so I said the only prayer that would come to mind.

"When I uttered the words 'forgive us our trespasses,' something happened—I can't describe it—almost like an explosion inside me. It was like time stood still, and right at that moment I knew that my sins were forgiven because Jesus Christ had taken them to the cross. I was ready to die, and I wasn't afraid anymore. But that's not all. I don't have the words to explain it, but in that moment God came into my soul and brought the deepest peace to my heart that you could ever imagine. The ship, the torpedoes, the burning oil, the other guys hanging there with me, even my own life seemed like nothing. God was there. And God was all that mattered."

Jerry heard the sniffles turn into actual cries from several church members, and his own emotions finally gave way, and tears now ran down his face instead of sweat. He felt an overwhelming relief that his ordeal was over, that he had given his message to the people he loved. But he didn't know how to close the meeting, and he couldn't speak anyway, so he simply stood there weeping.

As everyone in the silent basement wondered what would happen next, the person who had come in late with the cane gave a very loud cough and stood to his feet. Jerry and most of the people peered into the dim lighting as the man made his way past a few tables, then stopped and pointed his cane directly at Jerry. Murmurs circulated the room as the crowd speculated on who it was, then Jerry's jaw dropped as he suddenly recognized the man with the cane. "Chester!" he cried.

Chester Stanfeld's voice was quiet, but it rang out in the silent room. "Jerry Macmillan saved my life!" he told the crowd. "I would've plunged to a dark, watery grave somewhere in the South Pacific if the bravest man I've ever seen hadn't pulled me off that fiery casket! There's no way on earth I can ever repay him. But I want everyone here to know what kind of man he is."

Now tears were streaming down Chester's strong, square face. "Please stand up and help me give Jerry my thanks!" he called out as he dropped his cane and began to clap. One by one the dazed country folk rose to their feet and started an ovation the likes of which had never shaken their church before. Chester left his cane behind, limping toward Jerry but clapping like a madman and sobbing like a baby. People cleared a path, and the sound of clapping threatened to lift the low ceiling as Chester rounded the podium and the two friends met again with a wordless hug.

Marjie and Ruth looked at each other in tearful amazement as the entire basement seemed to melt in a crucible of emotion. People didn't know whether to laugh or cry or shout. Even Sarah Livingstone and Benjamin Macmillan found themselves hugging each other and laughing like children again. It was wonderful, it was glorious, and it was a mess.

The room finally quieted down, but there was a sense that the evening was not quite finished. Most of the people took their chairs, and Jerry and Chester stood at the podium with their arms still around each other. Jerry whispered something to Chester, then went to sit beside Marjie.

Chester surveyed the crowd, took a deep breath, and then said, "Forgive me for interrupting your church dinner, but I've traveled several thousands of miles to be able to say what I said tonight. Jerry has asked me to close the meeting, and I'd like to leave you with one thought.

"You've heard a remarkable story. I'm alive tonight because of it. But it's much more than about me and Jerry. It's the wonderful story of how God comes to us and makes himself known. It's the story of salvation. Jerry knows that many of you are no more ready to die tonight than he was when he hit the water. God is as much here now as He was with Jerry in the water. If God has moved your heart tonight, Jerry and I beg you to not wait to respond. Ask Jesus Christ to forgive your sins and come into your heart, and He will do it."

The basement crowd bowed their heads. Then Chester led them in a simple prayer that even a child could understand. And from the look on many faces around the room, it was evident that many were meeting their Creator face-to-face for the very first time.

7

THE BULL

"And then he goes and tells her I'm a preacher—"

"Well, you did your share of preaching at—"

"But you didn't have to tell her—"

"I had to say something. You were just standing there with that silly grin on your face. . . ."

It had been a late night of celebration for the Macmillans after the church potluck dinner. Chester had followed them back to the farmhouse, and soon the stories and laughter had been flying in every direction.

From the way Jerry and Chester carried on, Marjie began to think they had been separated for years rather than weeks. Jerry would start a story, then Chester would break in and tell what really happened, and then Jerry would go back and add on. When they simultaneously tried to tell the story of how Chester first met his Scottish sweetheart, Margaret Harris, the usually tranquil living room rocked with laughter.

"Enough stories for a while," Chester finally said as he held up his coffee cup for Sarah to refill. "I came over to tell you about two really big developments. Care to guess what they are?"

"You know I hate guessing games," Jerry said. "But let's see. . . . Margaret . . . the navy. . . . All right, here's my guess. You're going AWOL, then you're commandeering a cargo ship for Scotland, and we'll never hear from you again."

Chester laughed and nodded his head. "Not bad," he said, taking a sip of the hot coffee. "Closer than you think."

"You're not going AWOL?" asked Jerry, suddenly serious.

"Chester, did you meet anyone in the navy more gullible than Jerry?" Marjie inquired with a smirk.

"Actually, no," replied Chester.

"So get on with it," Jerry urged, shaking his hand and conceding that he'd been had again. "What's up?"

"It's a good thing you're sitting down," Chester began soberly. "This is pretty shocking stuff. While I was in the hospital in San Diego getting this leg healed up, one of the doctors noticed something strange about my heartbeat. So they ran some tests and said that at some point in the past my heart was damaged. They traced it back to when I had rheumatic fever as a kid, and I guess the damage is permanent."

"How serious is it?" Marjie queried anxiously.

Then Chester smiled, and his strong, handsome face lit up. "Thanks for the concern," he said. "The good news is that the problem is minor and I should live a normal life. The shocker is that my navy days are over!"

"You're kidding!" Jerry nearly shouted.

"No!" Chester exclaimed. "They won't touch me with a ten-foot pole. I'm history for them."

"Good night!" Jerry declared. "Imagine having a bad heart and not knowing it. So what are you going to do now?"

"My turn to guess," interjected Marjie before Chester could answer. "This really isn't a guess, though. I know what you're up to, Chester. You *are* going to marry Margaret."

Chester's beaming smile and red face confirmed her analysis. Everyone in the room burst out laughing, and Jerry jumped out of his chair to shake Chester's hand. "Congratulations!" Jerry exclaimed. "When's it going to happen?"

"We've still got to work all that out," sputtered Chester. "But, yes, it's going to happen as soon as I can get a job and make enough money to bring Margaret over. I want her to meet my family and have the wedding here."

"Chester, that's marvelous!" Marjie said. "We can hardly wait to meet her."

"Have you told your folks?" Jerry asked, but immediately regretted bringing it up.

Chester wrinkled his brow and shook his head no. "Not yet," he muttered.

"We understand," Marjie assured soothingly. "Just remember that we're always here, if you need us."

"Thanks," Chester replied, his lips tight. "I have a feeling we might."

Marjie could tell that Chester needed to keep talking about how things were with his parents, but he needed fewer ears in the room. Glancing over at her mother, she saw that Sarah sensed it as well.

"It's well past midnight," Sarah said as she rose from her chair, "and it just happens to be several hours past my bedtime. Benjamin, do you think I could impose on you to drive me home?"

"Certainly," Benjamin answered, pushing himself forward in his chair to get up. "I hadn't noticed the time."

"You're going to be sorry tomorrow that I came over here instead of riding home with Teddy," observed Sarah.

"Not true," Benjamin disagreed as he stood up slowly and stretched. "This has been one of the most amazing nights in my life. It would have been a shame if you had missed any of it."

Sarah nodded her head and said, "It was a delight to meet you tonight, Chester Stanfeld. This has indeed been a very special night."

———————— ⌒∕∕ ————————

"Doggone it!" Benjamin said. "Forgot again."

"Forgot what?" Marjie asked as her father-in-law wearily pushed himself back up out of his easy chair.

"Jerry asked me to feed the bull, and you might know I'd get all the way into my chair and then remember it."

"Let it be," urged Marjie. "Won't hurt that bull any to wait till you've had a nap."

"Aw, I'd rather get it over with," Benjamin said. "Can't rest with it on my mind. It'll only take a few minutes."

After the excitement of Jerry's return, the newspaper article, and the potluck dinner, life on the farm had finally settled back into a familiar routine. After the morning chores, Benjamin would usually stay in the house for a while to rest and help take care of Martha, while Marjie concentrated on cutting pieces for a quilt she hoped to sew over the winter. Meanwhile, Jerry had noticed a number of jobs around the property that had gone un-attended while he was away, so he was busy trying to get as much done as possible before the first snows came.

On this morning, the Thursday after the potluck, Jerry had loaded some fenceposts and barbed wire onto a hay wagon and headed back around the pine trees that sheltered the farm lane to work on a section of fence that was in need of repair. Benjamin had offered to come along, but Jerry had told him to stay in the house and take it easy. "I can handle it easily," he'd said. "No sense two of us fighting the wind." Benjamin had agreed with that much.

Now, however, he pulled his jacket back on and headed out the door. The cold wind grabbed at him as he stomped toward the barn, and Benjamin wished he had put on his gloves as well. *Too early to be this cold*, he thought.

Benjamin opened the barn door to find a gathering of farm dogs waiting for him with waving tails and expectant faces. "Didn't Jerry let you out?" Benjamin said. "Guess I ain't the only forgetful one around here."

The other two dogs pushed past into the yard. But Blue fol-lowed, tail wagging, as Benjamin walked through the milking parlor and grabbed a pitchfork that was propped against the wall. Then he headed to the side door that opened to an outside pen on the west side of the barn. Most of the year they kept the large Holstein bull out in the pen by himself.

Benjamin grabbed the latch to the upper half of the door and opened it, then scooped up a large pile of loose hay and tossed it through the door's upper opening. He needed to carry the feed to the hayrack alongside the barn's outer wall, but first he peered out through the upper doorway to locate the bull. The massive animal was pressed against the far fence, tail to the wind, a watchful, sullen expression on his black-and-white face. In the seven years they had owned the bull, he had never given them any trouble, but Benjamin knew better than to let down his guard.

"You stay here," Benjamin commanded Blue as he grabbed the latch to the lower half of the door and pointed with the other hand to a spot for the cow dog to sit. Pushing the door open, Benjamin stepped into the pen and closed the lower door behind him.

As he scooped up the loose hay with the fork, Benjamin glanced back toward the opposite side of the pen. The bull had not moved. Carrying the hay over to the rack, Benjamin tossed it into the holder and shoved as much as he could to the center of the rack. Then he turned quickly to go back into the barn.

It might have been Benjamin's fast movement that provoked the bull to attack, or it might have been sheer meanness. But before Benjamin knew what was happening the big Holstein was bearing down on him, moving with a speed that belied his bulk. Giving a yell and diving toward the barn door, Benjamin escaped the first attack, but before he could get to his feet the bull was on top of him. Battering Benjamin's side with his head, the big animal rolled Benjamin against the barn and pinned him to the wall. Then the bull backed off a couple of steps, nostrils flaring, pawing out clods of dirt with his front hoofs.

Benjamin lay motionless in the frozen mix of dirt and manure, not even daring to breathe. Slowly, ever so slowly, he rose to his knees, knowing he was helpless if the bull charged again. Benjamin raised his eyes to meet the bull's red-rimmed ones, hoping to win the stare-down while he carefully stood to his feet. He knew he would lose a dash for the door, but perhaps he could inch his way there in slow motion.

But the bull did not wait for Benjamin to make another move. Lowering his hornless head nearly to the ground, it lunged again, this time catching Benjamin in the stomach and slamming him against the concrete wall. Benjamin crumpled to the ground in an explosion of pain and struggled for breath. He finally managed to get a tiny, agonizing breath of air into his lungs, and after that another.

Once again Benjamin hugged the cold dirt, but this time he knew better than to try to move. The bull had taken a step back and seemed content to wait for Benjamin to try to gain his feet again. Benjamin was sure he was hurt badly, but he didn't know whether he could move or not. His only hope was to yell for help, but he knew that both Jerry and Marjie were out of reach.

Then Benjamin thought of Blue sitting just inside the barn door. Taking in several short, painful gasps, Benjamin called lightly, "Blue! Help!" He rested, struggled for air, then repeated it louder, "Blue! Help!"

There was barking and scratching at the bottom of the barn door, and the big Holstein nervously backed up another step.

"Jump through the top of the door, Blue!" Benjamin called out. "Jump, boy!"

With a sudden spring, Blue appeared, leaping through the upper half of the barn door and hitting the dirt like a stick of dynamite going off. Before the bull could get properly turned to face his new adversary, the cow dog had lunged and taken a bite from his right front leg. The bull took a swipe at the dog, but Blue danced out of his way, snarling and barking. Another nip to the right hoof, and the bull backed up and began to bellow. Blue kept dodging, barking, nipping at the bull's feet, and though the enraged creature was kicking up dust and making a terrible racket, Blue kept backing him up. Soon Blue had the bull pinned back against the far side of the pen.

Beyond the pine trees on the other side of the farm lane, Jerry heard the commotion in the barnyard. Grabbing the large hammer he was using on the fenceposts, he jumped the fence and cut through the stand of pines to the lane. From there he could see dust rising from the bull's pen, and Blue's frantic barking told him something was wrong.

Rather than go the long way around, Jerry pushed through some thorny bushes, jumped another fence, and dashed through the long dry grass that led to the pen. Shoving his way through another tangle of bushes, Jerry grabbed the top rail of the wooden fence and, still clutching his hammer, launched himself over into the pen.

He landed several feet from the spot where Blue and the bull were involved in their noisy confrontation. The bull lunged furiously at Jerry with froth dribbling from the sides of his mouth, but Jerry spun around with his hammer and landed a crushing blow in the center of the bull's skull. The massive animal staggered and stopped, frozen in place for an instant, then collapsed to the ground with an echoing thud.

Spotting his father lying beside the barn, Jerry called out, "Dad!" and raced to Benjamin's side. He knelt and gently rolled the older man toward him. "Dad! Dad! Answer me!"

With a painful cough, Benjamin opened his eyes and whispered, "I thought I was a goner, son. I'm hurt bad!"

"Where? Where does it hurt?"

"Everywhere."

"But where's it the worst?"

"My stomach. He got me in the stomach," Benjamin gasped, holding his middle. "I think he tore up my insides. Got some ribs, too, I think."

"Don't try to move!" Jerry ordered. "I'm going to get you to the hospital, but don't try to move."

"What about the bull?" Benjamin protested.

"He's out cold," Jerry reassured him. "I may have killed him. Now wait for me to come back for you."

With Blue standing guard over the vanquished bull, Jerry flashed through the barn door and then out the other door, yelling for Marjie's help. Before he made it to the house, she was out the door.

"It's Dad!" Jerry yelled. "The bull hurt him bad! I'll get the car, and you make sure all the barn doors are open."

Jerry took off for the garage, and Marjie ran to the barn. She propped open the outside door to the milk room as well as the inside door, then she dashed through the barn to the already opened door to the bull's pen. Dropping to her knees beside Benjamin, she took his face in her hands and looked into his pain-filled eyes.

"How bad is it?" Marjie pleaded.

Benjamin managed a crooked smile and whispered, "A little

worse than the last time we did this."

"You made it then," urged Marjie, "and you have to make it now."

"Promise me one thing," mumbled Benjamin. "If I don't make it, promise me you'll tell little Martha how much I loved her. . . ."

"Benjamin, you're going to make it."

"Promise me."

"I promise."

Jerry dashed through the door, and Marjie moved aside. Dropping beside his father, he said, "Dad, we can't wait for a doctor to get here. I'm going to try to carry you to the car. Marjie will help, but you've got to be as still as you can. Understand?"

Benjamin nodded weakly. Jerry got his hands underneath Benjamin and gently rolled him into his arms. Benjamin gasped slightly from the pain.

"Okay. Up we go," Jerry said, grunting as he staggered to his feet with his father in his arms. "Marjie, make sure we don't hit anything."

Marjie led the way through the barn and out to the waiting car. She opened the back door of the car, then raced around and opened the other door, crawling halfway inside to help Jerry get Benjamin all the way in. Jerry leaned over and pushed Benjamin as far as he could into the car. Marjie took Benjamin's lower legs, and she and Jerry lifted Benjamin into the center of the seat. Jerry grabbed a bulky canvas tarp that was lying outside the barn and jammed it into the back of the car to keep his father from rolling off the seat. Then Marjie propped up Benjamin's knees, and both she and Jerry slammed the car doors shut.

"You call the doctor in Preston and tell him what's happened," Jerry yelled as he flew around to the driver's door. "Tell him Dad's color is bad, and I think he's bleeding inside. Tell him to be ready to operate."

"I'm coming with you!" said Marjie.

"There's no time!" Jerry shouted, getting behind the wheel. "Call the doctor and then follow us in Dad's car!"

Jerry popped the old Ford into gear and tore down the driveway in a cloud of dust.

8

So Close

Marjie ran to the house and rifled through the phone book for the hospital's number. Little Martha had awakened from her nap, and her cries from the bedroom added to Marjie's sense of panic. Cranking through the rings, she bit her lip and hoped desperately that the doctor would be there. If he was gone, would Benjamin have any chance of making it to another hospital?

"Pick it up! Pick it up!" Marjie called out as the phone rang on the other end. The voice that finally answered was the on-duty nurse. Marjie immediately broke into her greeting and said, "This is an emergency. Is Doctor Sterling there?"

"Yes. He's right here. What—"

"Please! It's an emergency!"

"One second, please."

The second seemed to take forever. Martha's frantic wails had risen a level or two while Marjie was on the phone. "Hurry..." Marjie prayed.

A familiar graveled voice came on the line. "This is Doc Sterling."

"Doc, this is Marjie Macmillan!" she cried. "Benjamin's been hurt bad by our bull. Jerry's got him in the car and they're on the way to the hospital—should be there in ten or fifteen minutes. We think Benjamin has internal damage in his stomach area and broken ribs. He might be bleeding inside. You've got to be ready to operate."

"I'm not really set up for surgery here," the doctor responded calmly. "We'll have to take—"

"There may not be time! He looks bad! Please—"

"We'll get ready," Doc Sterling assured her. "And I'll call Rochester Methodist to see if I can get some help."

Marjie slammed the receiver down and raced to the bedroom. Scooping Martha out of the crib, she held her baby against her chest, patted her gently, tried to soothe her cries. "Please, Father," she whispered softly, "please be with Benjamin. Help the doctor know what to do."

Once Martha calmed down, Marjie wrapped her in a blanket, put her in the bassinet they used when taking her in the car, and grabbed the diaper bag. Pulling on her coat, Marjie loaded both arms and headed out the door to Benjamin's car. As she made her way across the yard, she noticed the open door to the barn and remembered they hadn't closed the door to the bull's pen.

"All we need is for the bull to get out and kill somebody!" Marjie complained to Martha as she put the bassinet on the front seat. "Come on, start!" Marjie urged as she turned the engine over. First it sputtered and spat, then it roared to life. Marjie backed up and then drove over to the barn. Leaving Martha in the car, she raced through the front door of the barn, then slowed down and cautiously approached the door to the bull's pen. She wasn't about to risk facing the angry beast alone. Slowly peeking out the door, she was relieved to see Blue standing like a sentinel over his vanquished adversary. The bull still lay motionless, but his glassy eyes were open.

"Blue! Come!" Marjie called, reaching down to scratch his chin as he left his post. "You've done your job. Good boy!"

She pulled the bottom part of the side door shut, then reached for the upper handle, firing off one final volley at the bull. "You're dead! Hear me! Dead! We're going to make hamburger out of you!"

Meanwhile, Jerry was rolling toward Preston. The road curved every mile or two, and he could only race on the straightaways, but he was making good time. Jerry had tried to keep Benjamin talking, but the last couple of minutes there had been no response.

"Dad! Are you awake?" Jerry yelled as he gunned the car down the last long straight section. "You've got to stay conscious. Can you hear me!"

"Yes" came the whisper that Jerry could barely hear above the roar of the car.

"Keeping talking! We're almost there!"

Wheeling down one last hill and across the bridge into Preston, Jerry flew past a couple of slow cars and then turned left at the block that led to the hospital. One more block, and Jerry pulled up in front of the small country hospital, braking as gently as he could.

Dr. Sterling and the nurse on duty were already waiting outside with a wooden gurney. They pulled open the back doors of the car, and Jerry jumped out to help. The doctor took hold of Benjamin's upper body while Jerry crawled into the backseat and supported Benjamin's midsection. Together they got him to the edge of the seat, then Jerry got out of the car and helped lift his father onto the cart.

As they wheeled Benjamin into the hospital, the doctor was bent over Benjamin, asking questions and listening to the whispered answers. They rushed him into the tiny examining room that had been hurriedly prepped for surgery, and the doctor took a reading on Benjamin's blood pressure while Jerry and the nurse worked at taking off Benjamin's clothing.

"Low! Way low!" Doc Sterling announced, concern on his lean, creased face. "And with the swelling and tenderness in the abdomen, guess we don't have any choice but to go in. If he's bleeding internally, he could die before we got him transferred. Let's just hope he hasn't ruptured something important. I can only do so much here."

Another nurse had been called, and she arrived just as Jerry and the other nurse finished getting Benjamin's clothes off. "Doctor Abernathy is on the way from Rochester," she reported. "He should be here in twenty minutes."

"Good!" the doctor called out, continuing to check Benjamin over. "We're going to need his surgical skills. If this gets messy, I'm in—there he goes. He's unconscious."

Dr. Sterling and the nurses slid Benjamin off the cart and onto the operating table, then the doctor turned to Jerry. "I'm going to ask you to leave now. We appreciate your help, but we'll take it from here. If you could wait outside to direct Doctor Abernathy into this room, it will speed things up."

"Yes, sir," Jerry replied. But before he turned to leave, Jerry reached out his hand to his father's face and lightly stroked the pale, stubbled cheek. He leaned over and whispered in Benjamin's ear, "Don't you go leaving us so soon, Dad. I'm just starting to get to know you." He hesitated, then added, "We'll be praying, Dad. Marjie and I'll both be praying like crazy. I love you, Dad."

Jerry left the makeshift operating room, crossed through the lobby, and pushed through the hospital's front door. He had forgotten that the car was still running and the doors were wide open, so he got in and moved the old Ford to the parking lot. Shutting the motor off, he sat there quietly, staring straight ahead with his hands still resting on the steering wheel. He felt overwhelmed by a wave of the same numbness that he had experienced when he'd finally been pulled from the warm Pacific waters by the men from the destroyer. The accident, the trip to the hospital, the examination—it had all happened so quickly that he hadn't had time to think, and for a few moments he tried to believe it really hadn't happened at all.

The sound of another car's distant approach shook Jerry back to reality, and he remembered he was supposed to direct the other doctor. Pushing the car door open, he waited to find out who it was. At the sight of Benjamin's car, he waved at Marjie, and she turned to park next to him.

Jumping out of the car, Marjie flew into his arms. "How is he?"

Jerry did not respond immediately, but held her tightly and buried his face in her hair. "He was conscious until we got him in the operating room," Jerry spoke as reassuringly as he could.

"The doc is pretty sure he's got internal bleeding, but they won't really know what's wrong till they go in and look. There's a lot of organs and bones that could have been damaged."

"Did he think he'd make it?" Marjie pleaded.

"He didn't say, and I'm sure he has no idea," Jerry replied. "But there's a surgeon on the way from Rochester—should be here in the next few minutes. Hopefully they'll have Dad opened up by then. I got a feeling that every second counts."

Martha started fussing, and Jerry said, "You take her inside where it's warm, Marjie. I'll wait for the doctor and get him inside as soon as he gets here."

Marjie left Jerry pacing up and down the sidewalk in front of the hospital door. But it wasn't long before Jerry heard another car's roaring approach, then a large green Plymouth rolled around the corner and came to a screeching halt in front of the hospital doors. A sandy-haired man jumped out, and Jerry told him, "I'll park it. Follow me." The two men raced into the hospital and down the corridor to the operating room. Jerry pulled the doors open and in went the doctor, pulling off his coat as he walked. Jerry hesitated, then reluctantly shut the door and went to park the doctor's car.

The next hours of waiting were as dreadfully long as anything Jerry had ever experienced. No one came out of the small surgery room, and no one went in. Jerry's only consolation was being able to walk the hallways with Martha in his arms and to pray with every step.

Marjie was able to call out on the hospital phone, and within an hour her mother arrived. Sarah Livingstone immediately found Jerry sitting with Martha on an oversized couch in the shabby little waiting room. Sitting down beside him, she put a strong hand on his and said softly, "I know what you're going through, Jerry. I've been here before." He had no words to answer her. He could only cling to her hand and draw strength from her quiet presence.

Three hours passed before Hilda, the nurse who had answered Marjie's first call, finally made her way into the waiting room, her weary face lightened by a look of relief. "He made it," she announced quietly. "Just barely. He lost a lot of blood, but they got him patched up and gave him blood transfusions to make up for what he lost—nearly four pints!"

Jerry gasped and buried his head in his hands. "Thank God!" was all he could get out.

"What about other damage?" asked Marjie.

Hilda shook her head and smiled. "It was remarkable," she explained. "There was a lot of bruising and shoving around, but as far as they could tell, nothing else was seriously damaged. He cracked two ribs, but they'll mend. His organs looked good, and his hips and pelvis were fine. For his age, he's one tough cookie. Even then, I'd say he was very fortunate."

"Is he conscious?" Sarah asked.

"No, and he's not going to be awake for a while," the nurse answered. "You may want to stay and talk with the surgeon, but there's not much point in you staying here the rest of the day. If he wakes up, he's going to be so groggy that he won't know what's going on. And he's going to be hurting pretty bad, so he'll have a lot of pain medication for a few days. Don't expect much from him too soon."

"I can't leave him," Jerry said quietly but firmly. "What if something happens?"

"It's up to you," Hilda responded. "There's a large chair in the room where we're putting him, and you're welcome to it. But unless something unexpected happens, Benjamin's going to be very quiet today."

"I can't leave him alone," Jerry persisted.

"Well, I'll let you work out what you want to do," replied Hilda. "I need to go get cleaned up. The doctors should be out in a short while."

Marjie got up from her chair and thanked the nurse as she left the waiting area. "Sounds like our prayers have been answered," she said, returning to her seat. "Seems like a miracle that it wasn't worse. We've got a lot to be thankful for."

Jerry and Sarah nodded. Then Sarah got out of her chair and walked to a large window overlooking the hospital's inner courtyard. "Before you stop me, Jerry, listen to me for a moment.

Sounds like not much is going to happen today with Benjamin. Why don't you go home and let me sit here for today? You've got chores to tend, and Teddy can handle things at home for me. I can stay into the evening in case Benjamin wakes up. At least one of us would be here."

"You shouldn't—"

"Think about it, Jerry," Marjie broke in. "You can't be here every minute, and it's probably more important that you're here tomorrow rather than today."

It didn't take long to convince him, but it was still a couple hours before he and Marjie left for home. They spent a long time talking with the doctors, gathering as many details as possible until Jerry felt reassured that the worst was behind them. He was particularly amazed when the surgeon explained how little time they had left to stop the bleeding. If they had not been prepared ahead of time, Benjamin would have died shortly after they got him on the operating table.

The family also went to Benjamin's room before they left and found him lying perfectly still in the hospital bed, looking very pale and fragile. Already his body had a yellow tint from the blood that had not been contained. His breathing, fortunately, was deep and regular.

Marjie took out her brush and lightly stroked her father-in-law's sparse hair back into place. Jerry held his father's hand and searched in vain for a way to express all the thankfulness he felt inside. Then he and Marjie reluctantly left, while Sarah sat down in the chair by the window and took up her silent vigil.

It was nearly afternoon chore time when the Macmillans pulled up beside the farmhouse, but Jerry had another immediate agenda.

"I'm gonna shoot that bull right now," he muttered through tight lips.

"But how are you going to handle the meat?" protested Marjie.

"I don't care! That beast deserves to die! Now!"

"Tomorrow!" Marjie pleaded. "Wait until tomorrow. I'll call the meat locker at Lime Springs, and I'm sure they can come first thing in the morning. If you kill that bull now, we could lose everything."

"I don't care," retorted Jerry, grabbing the handle to the farmhouse door. "I'm killing him now."

"Tomorrow!" repeated Marjie. "I won't let you waste the meat. We can't afford it. It's going to cost a lot to replace the bull."

"Okay. Tomorrow," he finally grumped. "But I kill the bull!"

"If you don't, I will," Marjie agreed. "But tomorrow."

9

BEN

At first, all Benjamin could manage was to get one eye open. He tried to speak, but his throat and mouth were so dry that his lips moved without making a sound. Jerry jumped up from the big green chair, grabbed a washcloth and a small container of water, and gently dabbed Benjamin's dry, cracked lips. Then he picked up a glass of water and put the straw in Benjamin's mouth.

"Take a tiny suck, but be very careful," Jerry urged. "Whatever you do, don't let it get you coughing."

Closing his lips around the straw, Benjamin closed his opened eye and managed to take in a small amount of water. Then he took another. Finally, he took a sizable swallow and then gave the faintest of smiles. Jerry relaxed his tense shoulders, relieved his father hadn't gotten the water down his windpipe.

Just then the door to the room opened. "Are you in charge here?" snapped Hilda, the nurse.

Jerry jumped and nearly spilled the water, pulling the straw and glass back from Benjamin.

"Were you instructed to give him water when he woke?" she scolded. "What would you have done if he had started coughing?"

"I'm sorry," Jerry apologized. "He just came to, and he

looked so dry. I guess I thought—"

"I don't want to be an ogre, but before you do something on your own again, come and get me." Then she softened. "Was he able to get any down?"

"Yes."

"Good," she added. "Benjamin. Are you still awake?"

The one eye struggled to open, then finally emerged.

"Great!" Hilda exclaimed, bending down closer to Benjamin's face. "Glad to finally have you back in the land of the living. You've been to death's door and back, you know. Now, try to take another sip of water." She put the straw to his lips again, and he took a few short sips. "Good."

After scribbling something illegible down on a chart, the nurse took Benjamin's temperature and blood pressure. Then she turned to leave and said to Jerry, "I'm going to call the doctor and let him know that Benjamin finally woke up. He's so weak, he won't be awake long, so don't worry if he doesn't respond now. And don't go messing around with stuff I should be doing, okay!"

Jerry nodded and thanked her as she left. Then he bent over his father again, figuring that Benjamin was probably already out. "Dad," he whispered in his ear, "are you still awake?"

To Jerry's delight, one eye popped open and then the other one. Both eyes were incredibly bloodshot, but there was a hint of a twinkle left. Then Benjamin slowly tried to clear his throat.

"You don't have to talk, Dad," Jerry urged, putting his hand on Benjamin's shoulder. "Save your energy. But I want to tell you what's going on. We almost lost you, Dad. You were bleeding inside, and we almost ran out of time. Doc Sterling and a surgeon from Rochester saved your life. So I suggest you stop calling the doc a drunk old sauce anymore. You're lucky they had enough blood here to replace what drained out of you."

Benjamin's eyes were sagging as Jerry talked, but Jerry went ahead and finished the report. "They said your liver and kidneys and such are bruised but in one piece. And your bones are going to hurt for a while, but nothing was broken except for a couple of cracked ribs. Somebody was watching out for you, and we've been thanking Him every chance we get."

Now Jerry was sure Benjamin was asleep, but then his lips moved. Jerry bent down close to his father's mouth, and he caught the faint whisper, "I hope the bull is dead."

Jerry's laughter reverberated in the sterile room. "This morning," he assured his father as the tired eyes finally shut. "Right after breakfast, I dropped him with a twelve-gauge slug. He's hamburger by now, Dad. Sleep tight."

The first three days, Benjamin slept most of the time, lulled by a heavy dose of pain medication. After that he was alert, but so weak that the doctor ordered him to stay until he could walk the length of the hallway. He failed to see the humor in Marjie's teasing that she had been walking the hallway's length three days after having Martha.

During the next week, a constant stream of visitors flowed through the room, and he seemed to thrive on the company. "You know, it's strange," he remarked to Marjie one afternoon after his neighbor Bud Wilson and a couple of church ladies had left the room. "I've been living around here for most of my life, but I feel like I'm just getting to know a lot of them. Maybe that's the curse of being too busy all my life."

"Could be," Marjie answered, looking up from the quilt square she was piecing. "Isn't it wonderful you're getting a second chance."

"Wonderful," he said, sinking back against the flat hospital pillow with a smile, "don't begin to describe it. But when did the doc say I could go home?"

"You know what the doctor said," she shot back, pretending to be cross. "If you would just concentrate on resting instead of doing too much and driving the nurses crazy, you'd be home in no time." Then she returned his smile. "But the doc told me this morning you'll be out before Thanksgiving."

Two days later, Benjamin was lying on top of his hospital bed, dressed in his regular clothes for the first time since his injury and impatiently waiting for his ride home. When Marjie's mother knocked on the door and stepped into his room, he wasn't sure what to think.

"Sarah," he sputtered, "now this is a surprise. Didn't Marjie tell you that I'm getting out this morning? Jerry'll be here any minute. I'm afraid you've made a trip—"

"Of course, they called me," Sarah interjected. "But I'm your ride home, Benjamin. I had to sign some documents down at the courthouse this morning, so I told Marjie you might as well ride with me. Sound all right to you? I owe you a ride at any rate."

"Sounds good to me," Benjamin replied, carefully swinging his legs over the edge of the bed and dropping his feet to the floor. "Uhhh! The worst part is getting up and down."

"Mighty stiff, I'd guess."

"I swear they sewed a two-by-four in my stomach." Benjamin straightened slowly and reached for his coat. "Feels good to get my clothes back on again. If I never have to put on one of those hospital gowns again, I'll die a happy man."

"Where's your suitcase?"

"Right in the closet there—behind you."

Sarah opened the door and pulled out the small old leather suitcase.

"Here, let me take it," Benjamin demanded, reaching out his hand.

"Sorry. Doctor's orders," Sarah reminded him. "You're not supposed to be lifting anything until he checks you in a couple of weeks."

"What he don't know won't—"

"Let's go before he hears you talking like that," she teased. "If I can feed the pigs, I can handle this little suitcase."

Benjamin mumbled something and sluggishly plodded out of his room as Sarah held the door. He stopped at the desk to say goodbye and was forced into signing one last batch of paperwork before leaving. The nurse on duty gave him a kiss on the cheek and her best wishes, then Benjamin and Sarah walked out.

"Whew!" gasped Benjamin as he finally got his feet into her car and she slammed the door shut. "That really tuckered me out. Hard to believe that something so easy can be so difficult."

Sarah started the car and backed away from the curb. "You've come a long way since that first night," she said. "It scared me."

"You were there?"

"Jerry was all worked up about someone staying with you that first night, but it was chore time for him. So I figured I was the best candidate to be with you."

"No one told me that, or else I forgot." Benjamin shook his head. "I've been forgetting a lot lately. I looked pretty rugged, eh?"

"You were as white as a ghost—or a corpse."

"And now I look like a giant bruised apple. My entire body is black and blue."

"Where else was all that blood supposed to go?" asked Sarah. "Oh, by the way, you put on a pretty good show that first night."

"I ain't so sure I want to hear about it," Benjamin said. "I was told I didn't wake up until the next afternoon."

Sarah burst out laughing and headed the car up the hill out of Preston. "You didn't wake up," she explained. "But you did mumble and ramble on about this and that. The best part was when you said that your nose itched. But you were so doped up that when you'd reach your hand up to your face, you couldn't hit your nose! That arm was flopping around like a chicken with its head cut off."

Benjamin laughed, too, then winced and held his stomach. "Don't make me laugh," he pleaded. "It feels like somebody's knifing me."

"Sorry!" she responded, but kept chuckling. "It was comical, though. Reminded me of when your arm falls asleep at night, and you wake up and try to move it. Whop! It hits you right in the face, and you can hardly revive it."

Laughing and wincing again, Benjamin shook his head. "I do appreciate you staying there so Jerry could go home. He was wound up like a top for the first several days. I know he needed his rest that night."

"I'm not sure how much he slept, but at least he was home in his bed rather than pacing the floor at the hospital," Sarah reasoned. "That boy thinks the world of you, you know."

Benjamin nodded but did not say anything, so Sarah continued.

"I been meaning to say thanks to you. Seems like this is a good time to bring it up."

"Whatever do you have to thank me for?"

"For raising such a fine son as Jerry," Sarah said softly, looking over at Benjamin who was staring blankly at her. Her smile warmed her expression and highlighted some of the beauty that time and a difficult life had diminished. "I couldn't be happier that Marjie got such a good husband. It means a great deal to me. Thank you for what you gave him as a father."

"Hmmm. Thanks for saying that," replied Benjamin, shaking his head. "But you're far too generous. Jerry's a fine man, all right, but it's no thanks to me. I was awful hard on the boy, especially after his mother died. Whatever's good about him must've come from his mother."

He stared out the windshield, suddenly reflective. "You know, many's the time that I wish I could start over being a father."

Sarah nodded. "Wouldn't we all. You can imagine how many spankings I gave Marjie, thinking I needed to take the sassiness out of her. She deserved some of them, of course, but I'm afraid that many times it was just Marjie being Marjie."

"She's a beautiful girl, Sarah," Benjamin said, "and not just on the outside. Whatever you did, a lot of it must have been right. Do you know what a change she brought to our empty farmhouse after she quit the restaurant and moved out here? I was so lonely I was climbing the walls, but Marjie livened that place up in a hurry!"

"That girl is full of it," Sarah agreed and laughed. "Just about teased her brothers to death when they were little!"

"I can imagine," Benjamin said knowingly. "So, how's Teddy doing? Marjie told me he was having some problems with the bottle. Things getting any better?"

"Worse. At first he kept it to the tavern, but now it seems like wherever I turn I find stashed bottles. He's in a bad way, Benjamin."

"Cotton picker," he mused, scratching his head. "Anything you can do?"

"I can't talk with him. That I've tried. Seems like his girl walking out on him exposed every raw nerve in that boy. He's a walking powder keg. Either of your boys ever get like that?"

"Guess I was lucky," Benjamin answered. "My oldest boy Jack—the one that's out West—seemed to buck me on everything I decided, but it never got explosive."

"I've thought of threatening to kick him off the farm if he doesn't stop," Sarah stated. "But with his pa gone and his brother in North Africa, he's got me over the barrel. I can't work the farm alone, and I can't afford to pay a hired hand, so what do I do? I've faced a lot of hard things, but I can't remember anything being more discouraging than watching Teddy hit the bottle."

"Maybe you'd rather not have me keep prying into your business?" asked Benjamin.

"No, please," Sarah assured him. "Since Robert died, I haven't had anyone to talk with, really . . . except Marjie. I really appreciate the listening ear. Let me ask you this: What would you have done if Jerry had turned into a drunk?"

Benjamin wrinkled his brow and stared out at the harvested cornfields along the road. "That's a rough one, Sarah. It's easy to talk about what I'd do when I don't have to do it. But I don't think you can let Teddy get away with acting this way, and you can't let the farm keep you trapped. Somehow there's got to be some consequences if he won't stop drinking."

"How?"

Benjamin shook his head again and held up a cautioning hand. "Look, it's a lot easier to give advice than to live with it, so you've got to take my thoughts with a grain of salt. But here's what I think. If it were Jerry that was drinking, I think I'd tell him he had two choices. One, no booze at the farm, ever, and no boozing in the taverns during the workweek. In other words, treat him like a hired worker. The other choice would be for him to make an offer to buy the farm, to get his money together, and I'd move somewhere else. He could live however he wanted, but at least I wouldn't have to be there to watch. If he didn't want to make an offer to buy, then I'd put the farm up for sale."

Sarah was silent for a while, staring straight ahead over the steering wheel. Finally she shot a glance over at Benjamin, "You're a tough old bird, aren't you?"

"I've been accused of it."

"Actually, I need to thank you," Sarah continued. "You're right. I can't just let it go on. I guess I'm so scared I'm going to end up losing the farm that I've been willing to let Teddy kill himself without getting in his way."

"I understand how you feel, though," Benjamin said gently. "We'd have lost the farm this fall if Jerry hadn't come home. And I'm too old to start over."

"That makes two of us. I can't do it alone. But I can't stand to watch my boy destroy himself, either." Her face was bleak as she glanced over at Benjamin. "I don't know if you ever felt like this, but it's gotten to the point where sometimes I wish I could die rather than see him so bad off."

Benjamin looked at Sarah over the lump in his throat, groping for words that might bring her comfort. "It's not something I've ever told anyone, and it's different than what you're going through with Teddy," he replied, "but after my Martha died— my wife Martha—I really didn't care to be alive anymore. I wasn't going to commit suicide. But looking back, I can see that I was pushing myself extra hard and maybe thinking I could die early. At any rate, I was miserable, and I made life on the farm a misery."

He stared blankly into the distance as though reliving those difficult days again, then turned back to Sarah. "It's only been in the last year that I've wanted to live again," he confessed. "What made the difference was finally recognizing that my happiness couldn't be dependent on having Martha with me. I let her absence in my life be filled with emptiness and bitterness rather than opening my heart to God and letting Him fill the hole with something new. I wasted a lot of time, but He's been very patient with me."

Sarah was listening intently. "And how does that relate to me and Teddy?"

"As hard as it is," replied Benjamin, "you can't let Teddy be your life. You love him, and you've shown your love faithfully. If he chooses not to love himself and not to show you love and respect your wishes, then you've got to let him go."

"And if I lose the farm?"

"Then you lose the farm," Benjamin reasoned. "But you're selling, not losing. And then you have to believe that God has another place for you. If one door shuts, you have to believe that God's going to open another one."

"No one has ever said anything like that to me," Sarah said. "I'm going to have to chew it over awhile."

"No one ever told me, either," Benjamin added. "It's too bad we have to learn the hard way."

"That I can agree with, Benjamin," Sarah said quietly, nodding her head. Then, suddenly, "Do you mind if I call you Ben rather than Benjamin?"

"I'd like that," he answered. "It's been a long time."

10

HOME AGAIN

Marjie and Jerry stood at the dining room picture window relishing the sight of Benjamin walking slowly up the steps followed by Sarah carrying the suitcase. Jerry burst out laughing when Benjamin glanced up at him and gave him a "don't say a word" look.

"Welcome home," Marjie called out, giving her father-in-law a big hug at the door. "You almost look normal in your everyday clothes. Where's the hospital gown?"

"Very funny," grumped Benjamin. "You probably thought the wide-open behind was nice. I caught you sightseeing a couple times."

"Very interesting moon!" Marjie teased and broke out laughing. "Full, wasn't it?"

Everyone joined in the laughter, but Benjamin bent over and held his hand over the incision area of his stomach. "Can't be laughing," he sputtered. "Hurts like the dickens when I do."

"You look tuckered out," observed Jerry, taking the suitcase from Sarah. "Maybe you should lie down and rest."

"Sounds good to me," Benjamin responded. "I hate to be a party pooper, but the doc said it's going to take a long time to get my strength back. I'm afraid he might be right for once in his life."

Benjamin turned and opened the door to the upstairs, but

Jerry said, "Wrong way. Were you figuring you could fly up the stairs? We traded rooms with you. You're back in this lower bedroom now."

"Thought maybe you'd carry me up," Benjamin cracked. "Listen, that was kind of you, but you shouldn't have. With the railings, I figured I could pull myself up. What about Martha? Now Marjie's going to have to keep running up and down the steps."

"We set up her own bedroom while you were gone," Marjie reassured him. "It was time to get her separate from us, anyway, so she won't wake us up every time she makes a funny noise. We got her crib in place, and it's working well. Besides, we left her cradle down here in your room. She can take her naps in there with you. Figured you might like that."

Benjamin broke into a bright smile and a slight, careful chuckle. "Yes, indeed. That is an excellent idea. Does she mind snoring?"

"Test it out," Jerry suggested, pointing toward the bedroom. "She's sleeping in there now, and you better get to your bed before you fall over."

"Mmmm. Sounds delicious," Benjamin agreed, shutting the stairway door. "That hospital bed was like sleeping on a lumpy rock. Oh, and thank you again for the ride, Sarah. You should give your daughter driving lessons. When I get my strength back, I'll tell you the story about the time she tried to kill me."

"I thought you were having a heart attack, for Pete's sake!" Marjie protested.

"She tried to kill me," Benjamin repeated. "But that's for another day when my head's not so light. Will you be staying for the afternoon, or is this goodbye?"

"Got to get home," Sarah answered. "But Marjie tells me that I should bring the chicken here on Thanksgiving Day. So, I'll see you Thursday. Rest well, Ben."

Benjamin gave a crooked smile and said, "Thanksgiving dinner here. Wonderful. See you then." Benjamin gave a small wave and followed Jerry and the suitcase into the bedroom.

"Got time for a cup of coffee?" Marjie asked her mother.

"No, but I'll take one anyway," Sarah replied, taking off her coat and hanging it on the back of one of the dining room chairs.

Marjie grabbed a couple of coffee cups and filled them, then joined her mother at the table. "How was he on the way home?" Marjie asked.

"Good. Seemed tired, but that's to be expected," Sarah said. "He's a tough old bird. Ten days ago I didn't figure we'd see him walking out of the hospital on his own."

"That's for sure," Marjie agreed, passing her mother a plate of sugar cookies. "When I saw him lying in the dirt behind the barn, I never thought he'd survive."

"Hope you rewarded that little cow dog with a piece of the fresh beefsteak you cut up," Sarah said. "He deserves a medal."

"It would take a lot more steaks than that tough old bull produced to give Blue what he deserves," Marjie replied. "Benjamin would have bled to death, for sure, or else that bull would have pounded him to pieces."

"You should call the paper and give them the story."

"I don't think they'd be interested," Marjie stated with a smirk. "Jerry says that Ed Bentley's going to need some time to heal after the last story."

"Lots of time," Jerry said, coming around the corner to the dining room. "Listen, I don't mean to be rude, but I have a load of corn to take to the mill in Greenleafton. Thanks for getting my dad, Sarah. He's resting. See you Thursday."

"You're welcome, Jerry," Sarah answered. "It was a pleasure. And I certainly understand about the corn. Go right ahead."

Kissing Marjie on the forehead, Jerry said goodbye and disappeared out the front door.

"He's a good man, Marjie," Sarah said as Jerry walked past the big dining room window. "You were wise to wait for him. But are you ever sorry you didn't grab a couple of those Rochester fellows you brought home before Jerry?"

Marjie laughed and shook her head no. "They were rich and smooth as silk. But they had no heart. Jerry is poor and just starting to get over being shy. But he has a heart as big as the ocean."

"Like his father," Sarah added quietly.

"Yes, like Benjamin. You've noticed it, too. But what's with you calling him 'Ben'?"

Sarah rubbed her left thumb with her right index finger and paused. "I'm not sure," she said. "We had such a good talk in the car that it seemed like we didn't need to be quite so formal. He said it was all right. Do you think I shouldn't?"

"No, not at all," Marjie assured her mother. "It just caught me by surprise. I haven't heard anyone call him anything but Benjamin."

"Somebody must have," replied Sarah. "But he said it had been a long time."

"Probably Martha," Marjie reasoned.

"Oh. Then I shouldn't."

"Hold on," Marjie urged Sarah, putting her hand on her mother's hands. "He said it was all right and if he didn't like it, let me assure you, Benjamin would have said so. I think it's good that he feels so comfortable with you. And I'm glad you had a good time with him. What did you talk about?"

"I asked him for advice on what I should do with Teddy," Sarah replied. "You know, he's the first man that I've talked to like that since your father died. It felt good."

Marjie smiled and squeezed Sarah's hands. "Like having a friend," she whispered. "Since Pa died, you've really been on your own."

Sarah sighed and nodded. "It was strange how everything changed after Robert died. I thought I was a pretty good friend to some of the neighbors, but it was like they didn't know what to do with me once I was alone. I just didn't seem to fit anymore. Guess I finally gave up trying and stayed to myself."

"That's a shame."

"It beats getting invited over to the Mosleys' for dinner and discovering they've also invited that strange old bachelor, Martin Sheldon!" Sarah piped in, rolling her eyes. "Now, that was a delightful evening. At least he washed before coming."

Marjie broke out laughing. "You never told me about that!"

"Guess I was too embarrassed," Sarah said. "Do you know that the hermit never said a word all night?"

"They say he's loaded, though," Marjie teased. "Lives back in the woods with that big mean dog and his team of horses. I heard he buries his money in the barn. Maybe you should stop by and give him another try."

"No chance of that," Sarah said. "If I ever got interested in another man, it sure wouldn't be because he had a stash of money. I've lived long enough to know that money doesn't go very far."

"Well, you've made a good friend in Benjamin," Marjie reasoned, taking her mother's hand, "and that's good. I know there are some things it's better to talk about with someone your own age, someone who's been through what you've been through. And Benjamin needs that as well. So keep calling him Ben."

"That I will." Sarah smiled and squeezed Marjie's hand back. "Hmmm. Thanks for the coffee, but I've got to get going. I have a special batch of lefse I hoped to make yet today. I found that Norwegian recipe of my grandmother's that uses cream, and the stuff just melts in your mouth. I'm going to show you how to do a real Thanksgiving spread."

"We'll see," Marjie answered.

———— ✍ ————

Benjamin slept most of the afternoon and never wiggled when Martha woke with a cry. He was snoring so loudly that Marjie wondered briefly if her great idea of having the cradle in his room was really so great. But she changed her mind after supper when she saw him seated contentedly in his chair with Martha in his lap.

They were gathered in the living room as they did every night to listen to news of the war on the radio. Tonight the report was grim, an account of the Russians' brave attempt to hold the Germans out of Stalingrad.

"Hitler must really hate the Russians," Benjamin commented. "This is the second winter he's gone in there. Do you know, I heard that at one point the battle line stretched five hundred sixty miles. Can you imagine?"

"Hard to," Jerry responded, looking up from the stack of get-well cards he was reading through and sorting. "It was cold enough out on the North Atlantic. I can't imagine what it must be like on the Russian front during the winter."

"Worse for the Russians," said Benjamin. "I read that two million people fled Moscow last winter. You wonder how many thousands have starved. Hitler better hope that the tables are not turned on him this winter. After what the Germans have done over there, I wouldn't want the Russians knocking on my door."

"I think the Germans have met more resistance than they anticipated," Jerry suggested. "The Russians may be short on guns and tanks, but they're fierce fighters. Proud. I ain't got much use for Stalin, but I have to admit that speech he gave and the stand he took in Moscow last winter was magnificent. I think it saved the nation—at least for a while. They had a bad summer, though."

"One defeat after another," Benjamin reported. "But the Germans are a long way from home. Maybe they've strung themselves. . . . What's wrong, little sweetheart? You getting hungry again?"

Marjie stood to take the fussy baby from Benjamin and carried her into the kitchen to heat up some milk.

"I forgot to tell you we got a letter from Billy Wilson," Jerry announced. "He's coming home for good around Christmas time."

"He's really doing better, then," Benjamin commented, "after being burned so bad? What's he planning to do?"

"Farming, if his legs can take it," answered Jerry. "But I don't think that scar tissue is going to like our winter cold. Don't know what else he'd do, though."

Benjamin rubbed his forehead, then the whiskers on his cheeks. "Bud Wilson's not as old as me, and he's in a lot better shape. They really don't need two men to run their eighty acres."

"Hadn't thought of that," Jerry mused. "You know, Billy never was all that fond of farming, anyway. I wonder if it's going to work."

"Farming's not a good occupation unless you love it," Benjamin said. "Too much work and too much risk for too little money if it's not planted in your soul first."

"Well, it'll just be good to have him home," Jerry stated. "I saw him in the hospital out in San Diego, but we still have a lot of catching up to do. Something real happened to him out there, Dad. He only told me a little bit about what happened after Pearl Harbor, but what he told me was incredible. He's a different man from the one we used to know."

"He's going to want to hear your story as well," said Benjamin as Marjie came back into the room with Martha and a bottle of warm milk. "Maybe he can light up the old church building like you did!"

"It wasn't me that did the lighting," Jerry said. "I may have put down the kindling, but it was Chester who torched it!"

Marjie handed the bottle and the baby to Benjamin, who was more than happy to assist with the feeding. "Benjamin," she said softly, "there's one other thing that Jerry forgot to tell you about."

"You were eavesdropping from the kitchen?" Jerry scolded. "I was getting to it."

"Of course, you were," Marjie replied. "Then tell it."

"Tell what?" Benjamin asked.

"We got some news you're not going to like," Jerry said. Taking a deep breath, he continued, "Mr. McDuff called this morning, and it turns out that things didn't work out for their daughter who was working in Minneapolis. She's moving back, and they need to use the house in Greenleafton."

Benjamin looked down at Martha who was busy sucking on the bottle. "That is disappointing news," he said. "But I'm glad I didn't get in there and then she needed the house. That would have put them in a predicament. You know of any other houses that are open?"

"That was the only one in town," Jerry answered. "I've heard of a farmhouse here and there, but nothing close."

The conversation in the room went silent, and the radio started to garble with static. Jerry jumped up and turned it off.

"Benjamin," Marjie said.

"Yes?" he answered, looking up from the baby.

"I've been a guest in your house for around nine months, and you've treated me like a daughter. This house feels like my home, and I treasure what I've been able to share here. When you told us about the McDuff place, I didn't say anything at the time. I deeply appreciate your willingness to let us take over the farm and the house, and I respect your desire to let us be a family, but I wonder if you'd listen to what I really think?"

"Go on," Benjamin said.

"I was reading in Ecclesiastes the other day," she continued. "There's a lot I don't understand there, but one phrase made a lot of sense to me. It says that 'to every thing there is a season, and a time to every purpose under the heaven.' When I read it, I thought of you moving to Greenleafton, and it just didn't seem right to me. It seems to me that for a time we've been brought together in a special way. Maybe it's 'a time to heal' or 'a time to build up' or 'a time to embrace,' I don't know, but it's been a special time—for me at least."

She paused and fixed her eyes on his. "Could I ask you to consider not rushing your decision? Of course, you need to get your strength back before you go anywhere, and the doc said that would be a couple months at least. But even after that, would you go into it slowly? I don't want to miss whatever it is that we've enjoyed so much. And I know that Jerry is looking forward to spending time with you and learning about what you've been learning. Everything's changed so much in the past year that I think we all need more time together. Would you please think about that?"

Benjamin picked up Martha and gently placed her against his shoulder, patting her lightly as her dark head lolled. "I'll do that," he said quietly. "Actually, I lay awake a couple nights in the hospital wondering about it. But I don't want to be in the way here. Are you with Marjie on this, Jerry?"

"Absolutely."

"Well, let's wait awhile and see what happens. Sometimes we don't know the future until we get there."

11

THANKSGIVING

"If there's one thing I hate," groused Benjamin as he shuffled into the kitchen for his early morning cup of coffee, "it's going out to chore when it's pitch black outside. Seems like it stays dark forever this time of year."

"Happy Thanksgiving to you, too," Marjie teased. "Were you up early?"

"I was awake before Jerry went to the barn," answered Benjamin. "I guess I've gotten up early for too many years—can't get it out of my system."

"You have much pain in the night?"

"Just when I try to move. Feels like every bone in my body is frozen in place by morning."

"Did you take your medicine?"

"No."

"And you're complaining about not sleeping? Haven't you noticed how tired that medicine makes you?"

"I'm trying to stay off the stuff. The sooner you cut—"

The phone rang, catching Benjamin off guard and making him jump. Marjie chuckled as she moved to pick up the receiver. She listened for a long time, her frown deepening into lines of concern. Benjamin sat down at the dining room table and waited to hear what was wrong.

Finally, Marjie took a deep breath. "It's all right, Ma. We understand. Just come as soon as you're ready. You can't control what he says or does, so just let him do what he wants. Do you want one of us to come and get you?"

Marjie paused and listened again, then she said, "You're sure? . . . All right. See you around noon. Don't be in a rush."

Hanging the receiver back on the hook, Marjie stood silently staring at the telephone. Benjamin noticed that her knuckles were white.

"Trouble at home?" he asked.

Marjie walked over to the picture window and still did not look Benjamin's way. "All I can say is that Theodore Livingstone was lucky I wasn't there this morning. If I didn't slap his face, I'd have given him a good piece of my mind."

"What's wrong?"

"He came in from the barn this morning already smelling like the bottom of a bottle of whiskey, and he told Ma that he wasn't about to bring her over here today and listen to more of our stinking church stories. Said that she better stop complaining about his drinking, and just to show her who was boss, he let her know that he was headed somewhere to booze all day. Told her she better be home in time to do the evening milking without him."

"Whew!" Benjamin gasped, shaking his head in disgust. "That's dirty pool. Nothing like a bottle of booze to make a man mean. How's your mother doing?"

"Not good. She was crying at first," Marjie sputtered. "He's going to pay for it, if I have anything to say about it. He really hurt her this time. Seemed like talking on the phone calmed her down, though. She said she was going to be late getting here with the food. And she has to drive herself. He already stomped out of the house and headed somewhere."

"I could drive over and help," offered Benjamin.

"That's kind of you to offer, but she said she could handle it," Marjie replied. "It's probably good that she has some time to get her composure before she comes. Plus, you're in no shape to drive yet."

Benjamin looked out the window toward the barn and saw

Jerry coming up the sidewalk from morning chores.

"Jerry's not going to take this well," Benjamin suggested as the back door opened. "He thinks the world of your mother."

"My dander's up this time," Marjie said, her red face confirming the statement. "She should dump all of Teddy's junk out at the end of the driveway and lock the gate. If he wants to suck on the end of bottle, let him. But he—"

"So what did Teddy do now?" Jerry said from the back door. He quickly put his coat away and joined them in the dining room where Marjie was pacing in front of the window.

"I believe I'll go check on the baby," said Benjamin. "You probably want to talk about this without me."

Benjamin tiptoed into the living room, where Marjie had laid Martha to nap on a soft blanket. The baby was wide awake but not fussing yet, so he picked her up and they had a little conversation. Then he took her into the bathroom and changed her diaper before coming back into the dining room. He was relieved that Marjie and Jerry had pretty much wrapped up their discussion about Ted.

"Look who's up," Benjamin announced as he came around the corner from the bathroom with the baby in the crook of his arm. "She says Happy Thanksgiving to everyone."

"Glad she's happy," Jerry groused. "Somebody needs to be cheerful around here."

"Here," Benjamin urged, handing her to Jerry. "Let a little sunshine in."

Jerry smiled as she rewarded him with a big gummy smile. "You've got the cutest face," he said softly to Martha, "and an uncle whose neck I'd like to wring. I think your Uncle Teddy's going to have a little chat with his older brother-in-law one of these days. And it's not going to be pretty."

"I'm going to pull every hair out of his head," Marjie assured them. "He'll be as bald as a bowling ball."

Benjamin sat down and scratched the back of his neck. "I know what you're feeling," he said. "Teddy deserves a poke in the nose or something worse. But I have to tell you, we have to be careful what we say to Sarah. There may be a time that one of you needs to confront Teddy, but it has to start with Sarah. And it has to be something that she does when she's ready to do it, not because we tell her she's got to do it or one of us jumps in and tries to do it for her. I guarantee you that the whole thing will only get worse if we don't let her handle it her own way."

"But he's walking all over her!" Marjie protested.

"That's between your mother and Teddy," Benjamin cautioned. "She needs to say when enough is enough, and perhaps her expression of pain will be what turns him around. Who knows?"

"When I was growing up, nothing made me feel worse than knowing that what I was doing or saying was hurting Mother," Jerry confirmed.

"Well, Teddy better stay clear of me today," Marjie warned. "I'll shove the whole bottle down his throat if he dares show his face."

The sound of dogs barking outside ended their conversation as a car rolled down the driveway and stopped by the sidewalk. Jerry was the first to figure out that it was Chester. Handing Martha to Marjie and stepping out the front door, he called out, "Happy Thanksgiving! What brings you over on a holiday?"

"Big news!" Chester yelled, waving his hands in the air and striding up the sidewalk. "Big news! Had to come right over and tell you."

"What's up?" Jerry asked as Chester threw an arm around his shoulder and tugged him toward the door.

"Not here," Chester protested. "This is something for all of you to hear."

Entering the house with a brilliant smile, Chester ordered Jerry to sit at the dining room table with Benjamin and Marjie, then he began. "I got the letter last night when I checked my mail, but it was too late to drive out. I'm so happy that I'm busting up to tell you this. You remember I told you that as soon as I could get the money together, I was going to pay for Margaret to come here?"

"Yes . . ." Marjie prompted as Chester delayed.

"Well, I got a job in Preston at the Iron Works," he declared.

" 'Course, I hadn't saved a nickel yet, and I hadn't even figured out how long it would take to get enough for her passage here. But last night, I got to my apartment late and found this letter in my box from Margaret. She said I shouldn't worry about the money, that it's already come in—and she's gonna be here around Christmastime!"

A collective gasp exited from the three shocked adults around the table. Their mouths were open but nothing was coming out; they could only stare at Chester in disbelief.

"Try saying congratulations!" Chester urged Jerry. "I didn't drive all this way for you to sit there gaping at me!"

Jerry got out of his chair and slowly moved toward Chester shaking his head. "I'm sorry, but I just can't believe it could be happening so fast," Jerry said, stooping to give his friend a big bear hug. "Congratulations! I couldn't be happier for you."

"Thanks!" Chester exclaimed. "I knew at least you would be excited for us."

Benjamin rose from his chair and shook Chester's hand. "Congratulations! She must have fallen head over heels to be in such a hurry!"

Everyone broke into laughter, and Chester's face went beet red. "I guess so," he said sheepishly.

"Wait till you meet her, Dad," Jerry urged. "You're going to swear that she's an angel. When I saw her for the first time, I—"

"You better be careful what you say, farm boy," warned Marjie.

"I . . . said that next to Marjie, she was the most beautiful girl I'd ever seen!" Jerry announced, bowing from the waist toward Marjie.

"That's my man!" Marjie declared, jiggling the baby on her shoulder. "But what do you mean, Chester . . . at least we would be excited for you. What did your folks say?"

The glow on Chester's face sputtered out. "I didn't dare tell them yet. They already kicked me out of the house."

"What?"

"Kicked me out. Or Dad did. Caught me reading the Bible one night and he laid down his old law. Said if I wanted to practice my religion, I'd have to pack my bags and find another roof to sleep under as soon as I got a job. Mom said she wasn't going to buck him on this one. So this past week I took a room in one of the apartments above the bank across from the courthouse. It's not pretty, but it'll do for a while."

"I'm so sorry," Marjie said. "I didn't mean to spoil your good news."

Chester shrugged. "No, that's all right. Gotta take the good with the bad. I guess I've known for a long time that it would come to this, but I kept hoping it would change."

"So what are you doing today?" asked Benjamin.

"Nothing much. Dad told me to not bother them."

"Doggone, that makes me mad!" Jerry snorted. "You're going to stay here and celebrate Thanksgiving with us."

"I couldn't—"

"Don't you dare say another word," Marjie broke in. "My mother's coming over with a huge chicken dinner and a heavy heart. You're going to stay and help us cheer her up. Any questions?"

"To tell the truth," Chester admitted, "I dreaded going back to that empty room. But I don't want to get in the way of your family day."

"You are family, Chester," Benjamin declared. "And we're delighted you can join us. Besides, we need to put you to work on caring for the baby. Sounds like it might not be too long and you'll need to know the ropes."

Once again Chester got flustered and his face went crimson red. Marjie put Martha into his arms and said, "Like this. Your buddy Jerry didn't even know how to hold her!"

"Say, before I forget, Chester," Benjamin interjected, "you said something about Margaret's money 'coming in.' What did she mean by that? Is that something the Scottish people say?"

"No ... no," replied Chester and laughed. "I'll be honest with you and tell you right off that I've never heard of this happening. But Margaret says she simply asked God to supply her with the money when the timing was right. She had determined to save what she could, but that would have taken forever. Less than a week later she received an envelope in the mail with the amount she needed to travel, plus a bit more. There was no letter of explanation and no return address on the envelope."

"Wow! That is amazing," Benjamin whispered. "I've never heard of that happening to anyone. She must be a special lady."

"She's special all right," Chester agreed. "I've never met anyone like her."

"You have to promise to share her with us," Marjie said. "I could use some help when it comes to praying."

"Couldn't we all?" Jerry agreed. "Now, just in case it has slipped someone's mind, this farm boy has come in from choring and is starving. Where is breakfast?"

"Shoot!" exclaimed Marjie. "I got so distracted with everything that I forgot. You take Martha, and I'll have food ready in ten minutes. Have you eaten, Chester?" One look at him and she said, "I should have known. Ham and eggs, coming up."

———————— ❧ ————————

It turned out to be a wonderful Thanksgiving Day for everyone. Marjie's mother arrived shortly after noon with a carload of special foods she'd been working on for a couple days—right down to the delectable chicken in a cream sauce. Despite the war rationing, the farm provided everything they needed for a big meal. Marjie had pulled out the Macmillans' good table service for the first time since she had been there, and the carefully polished silver picked up the gleam of the delicate blue-sprigged china and sparkled on the snowy embroidered tablecloth.

As they finally sat down to eat, Benjamin asked everyone to join hands and surprised them all by suggesting that they take turns thanking God for something special from the past year. With all that they had been through, Marjie was afraid that the lunch would be ice cold by the time they were through. But it was an extraordinary experience, and it turned out that no one had just one thing to be thankful for.

After the food was finally put away and the dishes were washed, Benjamin lay down for a rest while Marjie and Sarah whipped Jerry and Chester in a couple of games of Rook. Marjie rattled the men with her constant chatter and teasing, and Sarah's nearly perfect poker face kept them guessing and laughing. The afternoon was excellent medicine for Sarah's dampened spirit, although the specter of Teddy's absence still cast a shadow in the room.

Benjamin got up about the time the second game was finishing and Marjie decided she and Martha needed a nap. While mother and baby climbed to their upstairs bedrooms, Jerry offered Chester a tour of the farm. It wasn't long before Benjamin and Sarah were left to themselves in the living room.

"Rough morning, eh?" Benjamin asked.

Sarah nodded. "I guess I remember a couple worse. But it ranks right up there in the top ten. You were right, you know."

"About what?"

"About my making Teddy face up to what he's doing. When he walked out on me this morning, I realized he can't even see what he's doing. That booze has such a tight grip on him that he doesn't care what happens—to him or me. It's like he's not Teddy anymore."

"What are you going to do?"

"I'm not sure yet," Sarah deliberated. "But I'm not going to put up with it. Even if I have to sell the farm and go to the poorhouse, that'll beat getting put through the wringer watching him kill himself."

"You're right," said Benjamin. "But what about your other son, Paul? Doesn't he. . . ?"

When Marjie came downstairs an hour later, she was delighted to find Benjamin and Sarah talking like old acquaintances who had come together after years apart. It was clear they had been swapping stories the whole time—and clear that they were quickly becoming the best of friends.

12

WINTER RUN

"Oh, Marjie, that apple pie hit the spot," Bud Wilson remarked as he wiped his mouth with a napkin and surveyed the Macmillan dining room. "And the coffee's starting to warm me up inside. How about a refill?"

"Did you ever think of wearing a hat?" Marjie asked their neighbor. "How could you sit on that tractor pushing your way through the snow and not at least cover your ears?"

"Ain't that cold yet," Bud explained, warming his hands on the coffee cup. "Wait a couple months, then I'll have it on."

"I sure wish somebody would come out with a tractor scoop to clean out the driveway," Jerry commented. "But we appreciate you coming over with your homemade blade to push some of it out of the way. How much snow you think we got last night?"

Bud rubbed his shiny red cheeks and stretched his neck as he deliberated. "I'd say at least eight inches, maybe more. It's dry as a bone, though, so it's not so bad. Great snow for sliding. My kids are already trying the hill behind our place."

"So, do the Macmillan boys pay you for pushing the snow to the side?" inquired Marjie, giving Benjamin a wink. "Or is it such a delight that you do it for fun?"

"It's not for fun, that's for sure!" Bud shot back. "We work a trade. I use my contraption to push the snow in the winter, and

Benjamin plants my corn in the spring. As early as this snow is, looks like Benjamin might get the better deal this year."

"Hope he plants your corn rows straighter than I planted my raspberries last spring," teased Marjie.

"I'm going to dig that row under just as soon as the first dandelion pops its head out of the ground," announced Benjamin, taking his last bite of pie. "She tormented me all summer with her infamous crooked row."

"You heading into town next?" Jerry asked Bud.

"Just as soon as I can feel my fingertips," he replied, rubbing his hands together. "Want to come along and collect for me?"

"No thanks," answered Jerry, then explained to Marjie. "He pushes the snow out of the driveways of the townsfolk, and the most he's ever gotten from a few of them is a thank you. Why do you keep doing it, Bud?"

Taking another sip of coffee, Wilson shook his head. "I guess I just like to do something for my neighbors when I can. There's no money in it, that I know. And that blade don't do a very good job."

"Still, it ain't right that they don't pay you something," Benjamin protested. "It must take you most of the day to clean 'em out."

"Did you ever think of plugging their driveways rather than opening them up?" Marjie asked. "Then when they hollered, you could suggest that the sight of a greenback or two might help."

"The thought has crossed my mind," Bud admitted. "Say, how you been feeling, Benjamin? You're looking a lot better."

"Pretty good, thanks," replied Benjamin. "Some of the bruising has finally cleared, and I've been feeling better every day, except for last night. That snow got my joints to aching something fierce. And I still feel like the doc left a plank in my stomach."

"Bud, have you heard anything more from Billy?" Jerry asked.

"Just that he'll be home for Christmas," he responded with a pleased smile. "Home for good, he says. Best Christmas present he could ever give Ella and me."

"Jerry and I were talking about that the other night," Benjamin said. "You think he'll stay on the farm?"

Bud Wilson shook his head and stroked his chapped fingers. "Figured we'd cross that bridge when we get there. For now, all we care is that he's alive. We take it as a gift from God that we even get the chance to see him again. Can't believe it's been a year since the *Arizona* went down. You remember how you came over, Jerry?"

Jerry nodded. "Wish I could forget it," he said. "I thought Ella was having a nervous breakdown—holding Billy's picture and just rocking and rocking in her chair."

"You just don't know the difference it made when you came racing into our living room that day," Bud stated. "We thought Billy was dead for sure. Somehow your being there brought in a little ray of hope. But now he's coming home, and we're just planning to enjoy having him with us again.

"But to answer your question, Benjamin," continued Bud, "no, I don't think he'll stay at the farm. Unless the navy has changed him, it'll only take an hour or so in the milking parlor before he's looking out the barn door for something else to do. I won't say that he hates farming, but it's close."

"What else would he do?" Benjamin asked.

"Hard to say," Bud answered. "With his burned-up legs, it gets complicated. Seems like he's been doing all right at the hospital—helping out and all. Maybe that's what he'll want to do. But we'll see when he gets home."

"He'll find something," Jerry said reassuringly. "With so many men away in the service, there's plenty of jobs, and he's one of the few around here who went to high school."

"I'm glad we sent him," Bud commented. "I could have used him for the field work. But as much as he disliked farming, I thought I better get him into town and make sure he got an education."

"If he needs work," Marjie said. "I know of a dozen jobs in Rochester that he could do."

"It'll work out," Bud agreed. "But I need to get these old

bones moving. Thanks for the lunch, Marjie. The food's improved considerably since you moved in. You should ask Jerry to fix you some of his famous pancakes sometime. Remember?"

"The ones with the double dose of chunky baking soda?" Benjamin interjected and laughed.

"Enough already!" Jerry pleaded, throwing up his hands. "Why else do you think I asked Marjie to marry me?"

"Don't let him in the kitchen, Marjie," Bud advised as he pushed his chair back and reached for his coat and gloves. "His first three wives lasted one meal, and that was the end of them."

"Time for you to mosey on," Jerry responded. "You're telling my secrets."

"See you all again," Bud called as he pushed through the doorway.

They watched as Bud Wilson got back on his tractor, and they waved at him as he headed down the driveway. The brilliant sunshine on the fluffy white snow hurt their eyes, and Marjie tried to shade her face.

"What a lovely day," she observed. "It's a shame to just sit around the house, especially with Martha asleep."

"You're suggesting we go to Greenleafton and help Bud with the snow?" Jerry teased.

"No, but didn't you hear him say his kids were out sliding? I spotted a toboggan in the shed that looked like it hadn't been used for several years. How about we dust it off and take it for a spin?"

"Now?" Jerry muttered.

"Why not?" Marjie continued. "What else did you have planned?"

"Nothing, but—"

"Go ahead," Benjamin broke in. "I'll watch the baby when she wakes up."

"I don't know if—"

"Come on, you big chicken!" Marjie egged Jerry on. "You probably don't even know how to steer it."

Jerry scratched behind his ear. "You're going to be sorry you said that. I'll give you the ride of your life and see just how brave you are. Let's go."

In no time they had on their warmest clothing and boots and were pulling the old toboggan through the large pine trees that sheltered the south side of the farmyard. Jerry pulled open the farm gate that spanned the picturesque opening between the snow-laden trees, and they both stood gazing for a minute. Below them spread a long hill that led to the creek, and finally, to the wide field in the valley that was easily the most valuable piece of land on their property.

"What a sight!" Marjie exclaimed. "Think what a lovely photograph this would make. We have to get a camera, Jerry."

"The cameras we can afford wouldn't capture what you see," Jerry said. "It really is something, though. The wind usually blows the snow off this hill and makes it impossible to slide down. But this time there's no wind, and the snow's like a heavy blanket. Perfect!"

Marjie reached over and pulled Jerry close to her. "I really lured you out here to tell you again how much I love you and how good it is to have you home. It's been so crazy around the house since you arrived that we've hardly had a chance to kiss."

"You are a very clever woman," returned Jerry, throwing his sturdy arms around her. "And with very good timing. I was starting to wonder if the magic was wearing off."

"No chance of that, mister," Marjie said sweetly, then she gave him a big shove that pushed him straight over backward. Jerry landed in a large puff of snow with a shocked look on his face, but before he could jump up Marjie was on him like a cat. She pinned his arms down and sat in mocked triumph over him. "I love you, Jerry Macmillan, and don't you ever talk about the magic wearing off again!" she demanded. "Promise?"

"I promise," he declared but then quickly flipped off her arms and tossed her sideways into a snowbank. "My turn," he said as he pounced on top of her and gently pinned her arms down. "I can't tell you how good it is to be home, but I don't ever want to leave again." Bending down, he kissed her long and firmly as the snow filled in around their faces.

"We keep on like this, we're going to melt the snow off the hill," Marjie sputtered as Jerry pulled away from her face and wiped the melting snow off his cheeks.

"Let's give it a try!" Jerry shouted and pulled her toward him. Wrapping her tightly in his arms, he kissed her warmly and held her for the longest time. Then he suddenly spun both of them around, and together they rolled down the hill. By the time they stopped, they both looked like skinny, laughing snowmen.

"I haven't had so much fun in years!" Marjie declared between gasps, struggling to clear some of the snow from her face and hair. "I didn't know an old man like you could be so lively."

"Or an old married lady like yourself," Jerry teased. Pushing her over again, he kissed her a third time and refused to quit until a loud wolf whistle pierced the air. Looking up the hill and to the east, they spied the mailman waving from the opened window of his car.

Jerry hopped up and gave an embarrassed wave back as the window slowly closed and the car pulled away. "I can't believe he caught us," Jerry complained, then he and Marjie burst into convulsive laughter.

"I think he's got one on us," Marjie said when she finally caught her breath. "Should we try the toboggan? Or do you want to try melting snow again?"

"I think we better save the heat for the house," Jerry replied with a crooked grin. "Let's give the hill a couple of runs."

"Will you carry me to the top?" Marjie asked. "You wore me out already."

Jerry helped her to her feet, then dusted some of the dry snow off her coat. Then he gathered her in his arms and began to slowly climb the hill.

"I was kidding!" she called out. "Put me down."

"Save your energy," he ordered. "I told you I was going to see how brave you are."

About halfway up the hill, Jerry could go no farther and put her down. "You're not as light as I remember," he said.

"That was a year and one baby ago," Marjie protested lightly. "You should try it some time."

Reaching the top of the hill, Jerry took the toboggan and pointed it down the steepest section that led toward the creek and the valley. Marjie looked down the slope and shook her head. "Too steep for me," she announced. "I can barely see the creek from this angle."

"Trust me," Jerry said with a smile. "I've shot this hill a thousand times, and it's great. Besides, the deep snow is going to slow us down."

"I bet!" she snapped. "So what happens when we get to the creek?"

"We cruise right across it and into the field beyond," Jerry assured her. "Hop on the front, and I'll take care of steering in the back."

"Oh my," Marjie said regretfully as she plopped down on the toboggan and got her legs situated. "I think I'm going to be sorry for suggesting this."

"All right now, hang on," Jerry ordered as he sat down and shoved off.

Despite the sharp incline, the old wooden toboggan cut slowly through the deep snow at first, then it finally picked up some speed. Marjie began to scream and Jerry hollered as the wind whistled past their faces. Hanging on for dear life, they sped down the hill with the snow flying out from the front and the sides of the toboggan. Then, as they reached the bottom, the deeper snow overcame their speed and brought them to a gradual stop.

"That was incredible!" yelled Jerry as he jumped up. "Wow! What a ride! How'd you like it, Marjie?"

Marjie was laughing and brushing the tears and snow from her face. "Wonderful!" she gasped. "Let's try it again."

Jerry took her hand and helped her to her feet, then they trudged back up the hill. Stopping several times to rest, they finally got to the top and sat down on the toboggan to catch their breath.

"You sure you want to try it again?" Jerry asked between gulps of air.

"One more time," Marjie answered. "I think I can only climb this hill once more."

"If we go down the path we just cut," Jerry explained, "we're going to pick up a lot more speed."

"Speed!" Marjie exclaimed. "I love the wind roaring in my ears. But I still don't trust the creek."

"We'll get there this time, that's for certain," Jerry assured her. "We'll cruise right over it. There's so much snow on it that I can hardly tell where it is."

"Let's ride, then," urged Marjie.

"Hang on!" Jerry called as he gave the toboggan a big running push and hopped aboard.

Sitting tightly in the path they had made on their first trip, the toboggan picked up speed quickly, and it wasn't long before their cries filled the countryside. Both Marjie's and Jerry's eyes teared as the wind whistled past their faces and they hurtled down the steep descent toward the creek. They rocketed past their previous stopping point, and once again the snow sprayed in every direction. But even with their great speed, the unpacked snow slowed them to where they could see again, and Jerry called out, "We're almost to the creek! Just over this ridge."

The heavy toboggan skipped over a bump, then they hit much deeper snow and came to a hurried stop. The riders sat motionless and breathless for a moment, then Marjie turned to Jerry, "Are we on the creek?"

"Yeah! Don't move."

"Why?"

"I forgot. It's not been cold enough—"

There was a sudden crack, and the toboggan instantly tipped sideways. Before they could utter another word, Marjie and Jerry were plunged into the freezing water. Fortunately, it was only up to their waists and neither rider went in head first.

Finding her footing and hanging on to the now floating toboggan, Marjie turned slowly toward Jerry, who was slipping on the rocks under his feet. "We'll just cruise right over, right?"

"A slight miscalculation," Jerry feebly explained.

"After you get me out of the creek and back to the house,"

Marjie demanded, "you will sit patiently and wait until I have spent as much time as I want in a hot tub of water. Is that clear?"

"Crystal clear." Then his face brightened. "But maybe we could share?"

13

NIGHT VISITORS

"Who could that be at this time of night?" Marjie asked Jerry as they peered out the kitchen window at a car that had just pulled into the farmyard. "No one called today about coming over."

Jerry pressed his face against the frosty window and squinted hard. "Looks like Chester's car," he answered. "But there's somebody with him. A woman!"

"Could it be her—so soon?"

"It has to be," Jerry concluded. "Look at him opening the door for her like the perfect gentleman. If that don't beat all!"

Jerry turned and rushed toward the front door. "Better wake Dad up!" he called back as he headed out into the cold.

Marjie poked her head into the living room, but Benjamin was already yawning and stretching in his chair. "So what's going on now?" he sputtered. "All this noise—hard to get a decent nap in around here."

"You were sawing logs pretty good, so stop complaining," Marjie said. "Chester's here, and we think that Margaret's with him. Better check out your hair quick. Looks like a sparrow's nest in the back."

Benjamin pushed himself up out of his chair and tried to press his hair back into place with his fingers. Then he followed Marjie as she went to the front door and held it open for Jerry

117

and Chester and a petite, dark-haired woman with enormous blue eyes.

"You must be Margaret," said Marjie, taking the woman's hands and then giving her a hug. "Welcome to America, and welcome to the Macmillan house. I've heard so much about you that I feel like I know you. I'm Marjie."

"It's such a pleasure to meet you, Marjie," replied Margaret in a gentle, lilting burr. "Chester's told me a great deal about you as well. I believe I'm to ask you if you're still givin' Jerry haircuts."

Everyone burst out laughing, and Marjie piped in, "I thought about cutting off his ear. That would have kept the other women away, I'll bet."

"The scary part is that she's serious," Jerry added. "Margaret Harris, I'd like you to also meet my father, Benjamin Macmillan. He's been looking forward to this since Chester first spoke about you."

Benjamin stepped forward with a wide grin and took Margaret's hand. "The pleasure is mine, Miss Margaret Harris," he said in a courtly tone. "These two boys have raved about your beauty, but I see now that their description was nothing in comparison to such a rare elegance. I can see why Chester said he felt like his feet were nailed to the floor the first time he saw you. You really *are* an angel."

Margaret's clear pale cheeks were bright pink by the time Benjamin finished, and she reached up to chase back some stray curls. "I'm certainly no angel, Mr. Macmillan, but I thank you indeed for your kind words," she whispered. "You remind me of my good father back in Scotland."

"Let me take your coats," Jerry offered. "Let's head for the living room."

"I need to put some coffee on first," Marjie said. "Maybe you'd like to see our kitchen, Margaret."

"Oh yes," Margaret replied as she followed Marjie. "And where's your wee bairn?"

Marjie turned and gave her visitor a quizzical look. "I'm sorry," she said, "but I'm not sure I understood you. You can see the barn from the kitchen window, but it's a very large one."

Margaret burst out laughing and shook her head. "You're going to have to forgive me. I meant to ask you where your baby is, but I said *bairn*. It's a word we use for a little child. I'm afraid I'll be mixing my words up quite a bit."

"This is going to be fun," replied Marjie. "And I love the way you talk. Our—what did you say?—bairn is upstairs sleeping, but I suspect she'll be up before too long. She's finally started sleeping through the night, but she conked out early tonight."

This time Margaret looked blank. "I'm sorry . . ."

"Conked out—oops!" Marjie exclaimed and laughed. "This is going to work both ways. It means that she fell asleep early."

Laughing as well, Margaret said, "That's good. We have a game called conker that I couldn't imagine her playing so soon. But perhaps she's a wonder child."

"She's wonderful," Marjie replied, crossing over to fill the coffeepot with water. "But she's not playing games yet."

"Such a large kitchen." Margaret's blue eyes widened as she surveyed the cupboards and counters. "And so new. It must be wonderful."

Marjie gave Margaret a slightly bewildered look as she followed Margaret's gaze over the worn cabinets and the battered stove. "But this house is almost seventy-five years old. I love it here, but I'd hardly call it wonderful or new. My aunt's kitchen in Rochester has all the newest things."

"I'd like to see it, then," Margaret continued, running her hand over the wooden counter top. "All the houses in our part of Glasgow are hundreds of years old, and you can hardly turn around in my mother's kitchen. She'd think you were the Queen of England! Or the Queen of Minnesota, perhaps!"

Both women laughed, and Marjie mentally congratulated Chester on finding a woman with a sense of humor.

"Can I be of any help?" asked Margaret. "I already feel so at home."

"No. Just let me get this coffee on the burner and we should go into the living room. I'm glad you feel comfortable here,"

Marjie said. "I think this is a friendly house. I felt at home the first time I walked in here."

"You're very fortunate—" Margaret said tentatively, cutting off her sentence abruptly.

Marjie looked at her new Scottish friend and said, "Didn't things go well with Chester's parents? You're supposed to stay there, aren't you?"

"I dinna think they like me," Margaret spoke in a hushed tone, and her elegant lips began to quiver.

"How could anyone not like you, Margaret?" whispered Marjie as she reached out to give her a hug. "What happened?"

"Nothing, I suppose," answered Margaret, holding her head against Marjie's shoulder. "But I feel as if I must be a traitor or a harlot or something worse. Chester's father won't talk to me at all. His brothers seem to be afraid of me. And I get the distinct feeling that Mrs. Stanfeld just wishes I'd go away."

As much as she hoped that Margaret was overreacting, Marjie didn't think so. She held Margaret a bit longer and then said, "After Jerry left for the navy and I found out I was pregnant, my mother reminded me that even in the worst of times, things had always worked out for her and my pa. I knew those words were true, and I hung on to them as my strength. And though I've had my share of doubts, things really have worked out. Somehow God has been here helping us make it. But it's been one little step after another."

Margaret lifted her head off Marjie's shoulder and a faint smile crossed her thin lips. "I thank you for the words of cheer," she said. "My own mother told me those very words as we waited at the docks for my ship, but I'm afraid my memory is poor. Forgive me for troubling you, especially on my first visit with you."

"I think I understand something of what you're feeling," Marjie assured her. "Mr. Stanfeld seems to have a big problem with anyone or anything that's connected with religion, and Chester says your father's a minister. I felt sorry for Chester's mother. I got the impression that she really didn't agree with her husband, but that she didn't dare disagree, either."

"I think that must be true," Margaret said, a tender comprehension dawning in her round blue eyes. "Oh, but, Marjie, it's still so very difficult. The plan is for me to stay with them until we can be married, and Chester's father frightens me. I don't know if I—"

"Are you two going to talk all night?" Chester called out as he came around the corner into the dining room. "We have business to take—oops, sorry! Looks like I'm interrupting something important."

"It's all right," Marjie assured him. "Margaret was just filling me in on how she's adjusting to life on the farm."

"I wish it were better," Chester said soberly, putting a protective arm around Margaret's shoulders. "My father can't stop his crusade against God, even for his soon-to-be daughter-in-law. We were hoping Margaret could stay with them for a couple of months before we got married, but I don't know how long she can put up with him. You never know what's going to set him off."

"Well, we can't solve it tonight," Margaret said, her blue eyes warm on Chester's rugged face. "I'm glad I could speak with Marjie about it, and we'd appreciate it if you could pray about it, Marjie. Chester's father won't even consider coming to the wedding."

"For crying out loud, I'd like to give him a piece of my mind," Marjie spat. "He should be thankful his son's alive to—"

"No sense in you getting worked up, too," Chester broke in. "If anyone gives him a piece of their mind, it will be me. But let's drop this part for now. But Margaret's right, Marjie. Please channel some of your energy into prayer. If God doesn't soften my father's heart, all the fighting in the world isn't going to change him. Let's go into the living room and talk. We have some things we'd like to settle tonight."

"Wedding plans!" Margaret whispered.

"That's more like it!" Marjie said. "Just let me check the coffee, and I'll be right behind you."

Once they were all settled in the living room, an awkward

silence fell, and everyone seemed to be waiting for someone to begin.

"So what's going on?" Jerry finally said to break the ice. "The smiles on your faces tell me you came over for more than a cup of coffee."

Chester looked over at Margaret, who simply nodded back at him in return.

"Cat got your tongue?" Jerry asked Chester. "Or are you going to do your guessing game with us again?"

"If you'd be quiet for a second, I could put my thoughts together," protested Chester. "It's about our wedding plans. Shoot! I've been thinking about it all day, and now I can't get it out."

"You'd like our help?" prompted Marjie.

"Yes, exactly," Chester responded. "Everything's happened so quickly that we don't know when or where the wedding will be. But we do know that when it happens, I'd like you to be my best man, Jerry. Margaret would not be here tonight if you hadn't spoken to her for me. I am forever in your debt."

Jerry grinned from ear to ear and nodded. "It would be an honor. You just needed a little grease to take the rust off your lips—and I should know!"

"And I've not yet had the chance to thank you for bringing us together," Margaret said softly, "and also for saving my Chester's life." Leaning over, she took Jerry's face in her hands and planted a delicate but resounding kiss on his cheek. "You are a wonderful friend, and I can never repay my debt to you!"

Jerry's face flamed an instantaneous red, and the hug that followed intensified the glow. Everyone burst out laughing, and Jerry finally relaxed enough to return the hug and to kiss her cheek as well.

"Don't get too frisky," Marjie teased. "That's a beautiful woman you're kissing and hugging."

Margaret laughed and looked a bit embarrassed, too. Turning to Marjie, she said, "And I was hoping that you'd be my matron of honor. I know we've just met, but I already feel we've been friends for a long time. And with Jerry and Chester being so close, it just seems right. Would you do it?"

"I'd love to," Marjie said, although for a rare moment she was nearly speechless. "Are you really sure—"

"Oh yes," Margaret broke in. "I'd be so disappointed if you said no."

Clearing his throat, Chester looked at Benjamin. "And we were wondering if you would be willing to take the place of Margaret's dad? He's an ocean away, and my dad refuses even to come to the wedding. Besides, you remind me more of my future father-in-law than any man I know."

Benjamin shook his head and tears began to pool in his eyes. Reaching a hand up to brush aside the moisture, he shook his head. "I would be pleased to help you in any way I can. But it's not right to compare me with this young lady's father. Jerry's told us he's a fine man of God."

Margaret looked intently into Benjamin's eyes as if she was searching their depths. "Chester has told me about you, but I hope to learn more for myself. He says that you have a great heart for God in the same way that my father seeks God. I believe that is true."

"I have never met a man with a bigger heart than Benjamin," Marjie agreed. "He turned my heart toward God as well."

"Please, stop!" pleaded Benjamin, waving his hands. "You're gonna get me crying, and this is supposed to be a celebration. I ain't a saint in nobody's book, but I am proud to be one of God's little children who's still working on the ABCs."

"But that's what a saint is, Mr. Macmillan," Margaret declared. "And I'd be honored to have you stand in the place of my father. Please say you will."

"It will be a pleasure," conceded Benjamin.

"Marjie, how's the coffee coming?" Jerry asked. "It's not wine. But Marjie's coffee's fit for a fine celebration."

Marjie headed for the kitchen with Margaret following to help. Putting some cookies and the cups of coffee on individual plates, they came back into the living room and passed them around.

"Excuse me," Marjie said as she handed Benjamin a plate. "I need to check on the baby. I'll be right back."

When she came back down the stairs, Marjie was holding Martha in a soft pink blanket.

"Oh, she's a bonny one!" Margaret exclaimed, putting her plate aside and rising to take Martha from Marjie. "May I hold her?"

"Be my guest," Marjie responded, carefully arranging Martha in Margaret's waiting arms. "But I've got to warn you about celebrating. If you celebrate too hard or too often, there's a high probability that you'll get yourself one of these little bundles—it's amazing how quickly it can happen! So a word of wisdom from one who learned the hard way: Be careful!"

14

JAIL

"Boy, it feels good to sit down," Jerry said with a gust of relief as he collapsed in a heap onto the davenport. "I didn't think we'd ever get that calf born. Good thing you called old Charlie when you did."

"Don't pay to wait, that's for sure," Benjamin agreed. "If the vet saves you one calf a season, that covers all the trips when you could have gotten along without him. Why don't you head for bed? You look bushed."

"I thought I'd wait until Marjie got Martha to sleep," Jerry responded. "What time is it, anyway?"

"Quarter past nine," answered Benjamin, checking his watch. "And you had a late night last night—late calf delivery, late chores, late dinner. You're running on empty, son."

"Aw, this is nothing compared to standing all-night watches on the *Wasp*," Jerry said. "I'd get so tired I'd start seeing things, and I had to keep telling myself it couldn't be what I thought it was. Made me wonder what I'd do if I ever actually saw something real."

"Well, you look like you've done your shift for today," Benjamin continued as Jerry rubbed his face and eyes with his hands. "The wind didn't make it any easier today."

"Felt like the North Atlan—"

Jerry's reminiscing was cut short by the telephone's ring.

125

With Marjie upstairs putting Martha to sleep, Jerry rose wearily from his peaceful repose and went into the dining room to answer the call.

"Yes, this is Jerry," he addressed the caller. Hearing Marjie's steps on the creaking wooden stairway, Jerry wished he had stayed on the couch. "I'm aware of the problem, yes. . . . Oh no. . . . Is he hurt? . . . How about the other guy? . . . I can be there within the hour. Do I need to bring cash? . . . I'll be right down."

Slowly and deliberately, Jerry set the receiver back on the hook and exhaled a deep breath of frustration.

"Teddy's in jail, isn't he?" Marjie said coldly as Benjamin walked in to hear what was wrong.

"Drunk and fighting," Jerry replied. "The Spring Valley police asked me to come take him home. I guess he was riding with one of his buddies, but they'll keep him overnight unless one of the family comes and gets him."

"Let him sit and rot," snapped Marjie. "Maybe he'll get the message. I'm not paying a cent to spring him loose."

"There's no bail," Jerry explained. "The other guy was just as much at fault, and nobody's pressing charges. They're just holding him for a sober ride home. I already told the police I was coming. Let me handle it."

"I'm coming along," demanded Marjie, stepping toward the closet to grab her coat. "It's time I give him both barrels. If he thinks—"

"This one's mine, Marjie!" Jerry cut in. "Your brother's not in any shape to hear what you have to say. He deserves it, but it's not going to help."

"So what is going to help?" Marjie asked sharply.

"I ain't sure," Jerry answered softly. "But your anger ain't gonna overcome his anger or whatever's going on inside him. Maybe I can say something to him that'll sink in, though."

"Does Sarah know?" Benjamin asked.

"No. Teddy had the police specifically ask for me," replied Jerry. "I think it's better that Sarah doesn't know."

"Why?" Marjie protested.

"What good will it do?" Jerry said. "It's just going to trouble

126

her more, and it seems to me she's got plenty on her mind already. She knows he's drinking like a fish. Is it going to help her to know that he's been fighting?"

Marjie sighed and shook her head. "No, but somebody's got to make him pay."

"He's paying for it the hard way," Benjamin said. "Whatever's driving him to the bottle must be worse than all the misery the booze brings with it. If he asked for Jerry to come, maybe he's wanting to open the door."

"Don't bet on it," Marjie warned, although she was calming down. "He's probably just hoping we won't tell Ma on him."

"Maybe he is," conceded Jerry. "But I'd like to show him I care before we get tough."

———————— ✑ ————————

The moonlit sky was hard and clear, and the snow crunched under the black Ford's wheels as Jerry rolled down the road bleary-eyed and teeth-chattering. Spring Valley was about the same distance from the farm as Preston, but to the northwest rather than the northeast. The miserable cold inside the car warred against Jerry's bone-weariness, but with every mile he wondered if he should have taken Marjie's advice and let Teddy sit in a warm jail cell for the night.

The bright lights of the town were a welcome sight, and Jerry turned off the main highway and headed for the downtown streets. As he pulled up in front of a building with a white sign that read "Spring Valley Jail," Jerry instinctively glanced around the dimly lit street, hoping to sneak inside without anyone spotting who he was. To his relief, there was no one moving anywhere.

Jerry pulled open the large wooden door and peeked in to make sure it was all right to enter.

"Come on in and shut the door!" yelled a heavyset policeman from behind the only desk in the office. "Can't be letting all the heat out of here."

"Sorry." Jerry jerked the door closed behind him and looked around the area. "I wasn't sure if I needed to wait to check in or something." He spotted Ted seated with his head in his hands in an oversized leather settee that looked like a donation from an old widow's house. Ted did not bother to even look up.

"You Jerry Macmillan?" the officer asked, pushing himself back away from the desk and moving toward Ted.

"Yes, sir."

"This fine young brother-in-law of yours can't hold his liquor," the officer announced, "and he seems to think he's pretty tough." He reached down and grabbed Ted by the chin and roughly jerked his head up. "Don't you, sunshine!"

Teddy shoved the officer's hand away and glared into his face. "Keep your greasy hands off me, you fat—"

"That's enough!" Jerry shouted and stepped close to both men. "You're in enough trouble for one night, Ted. Get your coat and come with me, or you can stay and see how you fare here in the Spring Valley jail."

"Let me tell you something, sunshine boy," the officer warned. "You and your buddies stay out of my town if you're looking to get plastered. If I catch you here again, you and me are going to spend some time together—and you're going to be very sorry if that happens. You're nothing but trouble, and I can't stand the sight of a punk like you."

"That makes two—"

"Take your coat!" Jerry broke in, stuffing Ted's coat in his face. "You say one more word, and I leave. Are we free to go, officer?"

"Unless sunshine here wants to see if he's a man yet," sneered the policeman.

"Let's go," Jerry demanded, pulling Ted up. "Out the door."

Ted's short time in jail seemed to have sobered him up. He still hadn't taken his bloodshot eyes off the officer, but he did not protest again. As he pulled on his coat, Jerry noticed Ted's swollen hand and bloody nose.

"What happened to your hand?" asked Jerry. "Looks like it's broken."

Ted did not answer, but headed for the door without looking back.

"This ain't his first fight," the officer said to Jerry. "He's got a problem with the booze, and when he's drunk, he loves to fight. Sooner or later, he's going to hurt himself or somebody else. Every cop in this part of the county is watching for him. I'd suggest you get him to sign up and do his fighting for a better cause."

"Thanks for the advice," said Jerry. "I'll see what I can do."

"You do that," agreed the officer with a superior smile that made Jerry clench his fists involuntarily. For a brief moment Jerry wondered how Ted had held back from trying his good hand on the officer's jaw.

Jerry stomped out of the jail and hurried to the car. Ted was sitting motionless on the passenger's side, looking straight ahead. Jerry turned the ignition, and the old Ford sputtered to life.

"It's freezing out here," Jerry said, holding his hand by the heater blower to see if there might be some warm air left from the trip in to town. "Are there any cafes open around here? Maybe you want a cup of coffee?"

"Just the tavern," Teddy mumbled. "I don't think we better try that place tonight." He had tucked his swollen hand in his jacket to keep it warm.

"Or tomorrow night, or the night after that," Jerry commented, pulling out and heading down the street. "That cop wants to put you out of commission for a long time, and like it or not, he's in charge. He reminded me of some of the MPs we'd see in port. They ruled the world, and woe to the man that bucked them."

Teddy just turned his head and seemed to study the houses as they passed. Soon they had left the city lights behind and were rolling down the highway toward the Livingstone farm. Finally Jerry ended the silence.

"Is your hand broken?"

"No. I think it's just sprained. I laid the other guy out doing it."

"Looks like he managed to find your nose before that."

"That may be broken. Made me so mad that I unloaded everything I had."

"What was the fight about?"

Teddy sighed and shook his head in disgust. "The jerk made a joke about my girl Linda dumping me for another guy. I had to make him pay."

"Was she really worth fighting over?" Jerry asked. "I heard she's already running around on whoever she married. That what you wanted?"

"No!" snapped Teddy, then he relaxed again. "But I loved her anyway. She was everything I ever wanted in a woman."

"You wanted her even when you knew she'd run around on you?"

"I didn't believe she had," Teddy said quietly, rubbing his forehead with his good hand. "She always said I was the only one for her. I even had an engagement ring."

Jerry rounded a curve and wondered what to say next. "So why are you killing yourself with the booze?" he asked. "Don't you know how your mother feels when you come stumbling into the house in the middle of the night?"

Teddy sat shaking his head. "Yeah. I think I know how she feels," he muttered. "If she didn't need me to keep the farm going, I'd leave so she didn't need to watch. But I don't have any choice."

"You have some other choices. Like telling yourself the truth instead of listening to the lies you're feeding on."

"You going to start preaching now? I suppose Marjie wants you to try a sermon on me."

"You better stay clear of Marjie," warned Jerry, laughing and relaxing a bit. "The mood she's in, a whip would be the only sermon she cares about. No. I ain't here to deliver a sermon, but I am here to try to tell you the truth."

"Which is?"

"That you can get along just fine without Linda whatever-her-name-is," Jerry stated. "She hurt you bad, and that's the truth, but you don't have no reason to keep pouring whiskey on the wound. I saw dozens of women just like her in the port taverns, and they go from one guy to the next. The truth is that you're going to get over her, and you'll find somebody else who really loves you. Unless you insist on killing yourself first."

Teddy stared intently out the window, seeming to search the moonlit fields for signs of life. Jerry slowed the car and turned onto the gravel road that led to the Livingstones'. The farm was about a mile and a half from the turnoff.

"What you said, I wish I could believe it," muttered Teddy. "But I don't, you know. My life's over. Did you notice that big oak tree back there? Many nights as I'm driving by it, I've thought about piling my truck into it."

"That's crazy," Jerry said gently. "She didn't deserve your love, Teddy. Let her go."

"I can't. And the booze helps. I don't want to stop."

"God can help," added Jerry. "He helped me when I needed it."

"He doesn't care about me. Never has."

"Give Him a chance," Jerry urged. "Don't waste your life away on someone who didn't even love you."

Teddy blew out a cloud of frosty steam. "Let's drop it, okay. I'll try to quit drinking for a while and see how I feel. But I don't believe in God—period. You and Marjie can say whatever you want, but it's not for me."

Jerry pulled into the Livingstone driveway and stopped in the farmyard to let Teddy out. Fortunately, the house lights were off and stayed off as they had approached.

"Thanks for the ride," Ted said as he reached for the door handle. "I won't forget it."

"Teddy, one more thing," Jerry said as Ted turned toward him. "This is going to sound funny, but I've gotta say it. We want you to know that we love you, and that we want to see you get better."

Teddy's red eyes brimmed with tears, and he shoved down on the handle. "I appreciate that," he whispered, then stepped into the cold night.

15

DOCTOR'S APPOINTMENT

"You're looking sharp this morning," Marjie observed as Benjamin sat down next to Jerry at the dining room table. "What time's your doctor's appointment?"

"One o'clock," answered Benjamin. "Apart from getting the stitches snipped, it seems like a waste of time. What're they going to tell me that I don't already know? Except for the stiffness, I feel better than I have in a long time."

"Taking it easy for a change has done you a world of good," Jerry said, looking at his father. "I've never seen you so relaxed. I think you look ten years younger than before the accident."

"Right," Benjamin said with a chuckle. "I suppose if I sit in my chair long enough, someone will mistake me for a twenty-year-old and sign me up for the army."

"You never know," Marjie teased. "Jerry's right, though. You look healthier now than you did when I first came to visit you a year ago. I think you were just worn out."

Benjamin put down his fork and looked out the window at a cardinal that had just stopped at the bird feeder for a snack. "Funny, isn't it," he said. "You work like a madman all your life, thinking you have to get everything done and keep making things better. Then you get one step from the grave and you realize it wasn't worth it. What you thought was living turns out to be merely existing. That I regret."

"You're not dead yet," Jerry said, trying to lighten the mood. "Weren't you the one talking the other night about that scripture verse—something about the locusts?"

"The book of Joel," Benjamin said, then quoted, " 'And I will restore to you the years that the locust hath eaten.' But if He's going to do that, I hope He hurries up. Once you start having physical problems, you may as well start counting the days until the old ticker gives out."

"What side of the bed did you get out of this morning?" Marjie asked. "Don't tell me you've been getting your calendar out and checking off the days one at a time. All you can do is live one day at a time. But you know, I've thought about that verse since you mentioned it, especially regarding my pa. Once he came to terms with God, he didn't live long afterward. But when I look back, I'm amazed at what happened in so short a time. If nothing else, think of the difference his Bible and his favorite verse meant when Jerry needed it."

"We're definitely not wise enough to figure out what it all means," Benjamin concluded. "Say, do you think Sarah would like to ride into town with me? Maybe we could stop at the cafe for lunch."

"The Coffee Cup?" Jerry teased. "Living high on the hog, aren't you?"

"I got all this hard-earned money," retorted Benjamin, "and it's time I spend some of it. But seriously, Marjie, do you think she'd want to go along?"

"Probably," Marjie replied. "Why not give her a call and ask?"

Benjamin smiled sheepishly. "Would you call her for me? You know how I hate the phone. And then she doesn't need to feel any pressure from me. Just tell her I hate to go alone."

"You're sure you're all right with driving?" Jerry asked. "I could drive you in."

"There's no problem with me driving now," answered Benjamin. "If I can walk down into the woods and cut down our Christmas tree, I can drive a car. Besides, you've got plenty to take care of here with the calves coming in. I can handle this. How about it, Marjie?"

"I don't know what your problem is with the phone," Marjie said. "If you just did it occasionally, it wouldn't be so difficult. You're a grown—"

"Please."

"All right, already!" Marjie gasped, pretending to be put out. "But not until I get the kitchen straightened up. And if Ma does want to ride along, you've got to promise to stop here on the way back so I can see her for a while."

"Fine with me," Benjamin agreed. And when he left the house a few hours later to pick up Sarah, Marjie was almost sure he was wearing aftershave. She couldn't remember him doing that even once in the year she'd been with him.

———— ⌒∕ひ ————

About three that afternoon, the sound of tires and the usual chorus of barking dogs announced that Benjamin and Sarah had turned into the Macmillan driveway. Marjie and Jerry were sitting in the dining room enjoying a talk and an afternoon snack before he went back to the barn to begin the evening chores. Martha was nearly asleep on Jerry's shoulder.

Marjie jumped out of her chair and ran to the window. "Something good must have happened," she remarked as Sarah and Benjamin got out of the car and walked up the sidewalk together. "They're both smiling from ear to ear, and they're talking up a storm. I wonder what's going on?"

"We'll soon find out," Jerry said as the front door opened.

"Good news?" Marjie asked, taking her mother's coat and giving her a hug. "You two look excited about something."

"Very good news!" exclaimed Sarah. "But I'll let Ben tell it. Let me have the baby. Look, Ben, we got here just in time. Those eyes are still open—barely."

Benjamin was beaming with smiles. Taking off his coat and boots, he sat down and took one of Martha's little hands, gently rubbing it with his cold thumb. The baby offered her grandfather a tired smile before burying her face in Sarah's shoulder.

"Well?" demanded Marjie in frustration. "Do I have to get a crowbar, or are you going to be nice and tell us what's going on?"

"You don't need a crowbar today," he answered. "I just wanted to greet my granddaughter before she goes night-night. Yes, there's good news. The doc said I'm healing real good, and in about another month he figures I can go back to my usual activities. He also said the stiffness is normal, and it's probably just a matter of time before that feels better again."

"That's wonderful!" exclaimed Jerry. "Just what you expected."

"But there's more," Sarah added.

Benjamin's laugh had a joyful ring to it that Jerry couldn't remember ever hearing, and both Jerry and Marjie leaned forward to hear what was coming next. "You're not going to believe this," said Benjamin. "I couldn't believe it until the doctor wrote it down on my chart."

"Spit it out, will you!" Marjie scolded.

"My blood pressure's down to nearly normal!" Benjamin announced with a chortle. "And they said my heart's in good shape. They say I'm as healthy as a horse!"

Marjie and Jerry sat staring at the jubilant Benjamin. The exuberant look on his face made it plain that he was telling the truth, but that did not change the intensity of the shock they felt.

"So I guess I ain't dead yet, just like you said this morning!" Benjamin declared, patting Jerry on the back. "Looks like I've got back some of those locust years, eh, son? That little girl of yours might get to know me better than I figured."

Marjie reached over and gave Benjamin a big hug, groping to find the words she felt welling up from within. "This is the most wonderful news you could have ever brought us," she said softly. "Next to Jerry not going down with the ship, it may be the best news I've ever heard."

"God is so good," Jerry affirmed as he joined Marjie in hugging his father. "It's nearly too good to believe. Did they say how things could improve so drastically?"

"They said what we already knew," Sarah replied. "Ben was

pushing so hard that his body couldn't take it. Maybe if that bull hadn't slowed him down, we wouldn't be celebrating today. The doc said that if Ben's blood pressure would've kept going up, something would've had to give. But he stated again that Ben's heart has not been the problem. His heart's fine!"

"What a wonderful day!" Marjie gushed, still hugging Benjamin. "I suppose you're going to want your farm back?"

"Not on your life," Benjamin replied. "The doc said I could resume a normal schedule, but he gave me orders not to try running this farm again by myself. We've got time to work out what I'm going to do. I'm just glad it looks like I've got some more years under my belt."

"We all are," Sarah said softly, reaching out and touching his hand. "Are you going to tell them the rest of the story?"

"More?" Jerry and Marjie chorused as they sat back up in their chairs to listen.

"It's not about me," Benjamin said.

"So who is it about?" asked Marjie.

"Margaret and Chester," answered Benjamin. "We saw Chester at lunchtime in the cafe, and he came over and ate with us. Problems with Chester's dad have gotten worse, and it looks like Margaret's going to have to find another place to live."

"But where?" Marjie asked. "She doesn't have a job or anything. Can Chester afford two places?"

"No," explained Benjamin. "But they've decided to go ahead and get married as soon as they can find a bigger apartment, even if that's not what they planned."

"But what are they going to do in the meantime?" asked Jerry.

"They don't have any ideas," Benjamin said. "But I do."

"What?" Marjie asked.

"They're coming here for Christmas dinner in a couple of days, right?" he asked.

"Yes," said Marjie. "I can't believe all the things I still need to get done before then."

"I want you to call and ask Margaret if she'd like to bring her bags and stay with us until the wedding," declared Benjamin with a look of pleasure spreading across his face again. "We've got an extra room upstairs. No sense in her staying where she's not wanted. Maybe we can make her wedding something special, even though she's been disappointed by Chester's family. What do you think? I wanted to check with you before inviting her. We don't know how long she might stay."

"I think it's a wonderful idea," said Jerry, still shaking his head over how much had changed in a year's time. "I'm sure she'll be easy to have stay with us. But do you think Chester's folks will be offended?"

"I doubt it," Benjamin replied, shaking his head. "And if they are, it's their own fault. Chester told us that Mr. Stanfeld asked her to leave."

"What a beastly thing to do!" snapped Marjie. "How could anyone who's so kind and gentle be treated so horribly? He may be Chester's father, but he needs—"

"Chester already had a long talk with his pa," Sarah broke in. "Actually, it was that talk that brought the issue to a head. I think Chester's hurting pretty bad over it. But at least his father knows where Chester and Margaret stand now. Seems like it was important for Chester to say what he did before they got married. He's his own man now, but they're really on their own."

"That really burns me up," Jerry seethed. "Looks like we'll just have to be Margaret and Chester's family. She must feel terrible."

"I'm sure she does," Benjamin said. "But Chester said she's been strong despite all the rotten treatment. So, what do you say, Marjie?"

"I'll call her right away," Marjie said. "It'll be our chance to get to know her better. But I've got one question. Was this whole thing your idea, Benjamin? Or did you get a little help from Granny?"

Sarah smiled and looked down at Martha, who was sleeping soundly despite the noisy conversation around the table. Benjamin looked slightly sheepish.

"You should have been a detective," Benjamin said. "Actually, the whole thing was your mother's idea. When we were driving back from Preston, she asked me what I thought of her offering Margaret a temporary room at their house. With all of Teddy's problems, that didn't seem like such a good idea. Then I thought of the extra room upstairs and felt like this was the place."

"That was very kind of you," Jerry said to Sarah. "You haven't even met Margaret yet, have you?"

"No. But one good favor deserves another," Sarah replied, looking at Jerry.

"What's that supposed to mean?" asked Jerry.

Sarah smiled wryly. "My grandmother used to say kindness begets kindness, and I believe she was right. You were kind to me, and I guess I figured I should offer some kindness to Margaret."

"I still don't get it," Jerry said.

"You think I didn't recognize your car when you dropped Teddy off the other night?" asked Sarah. "I knew right off that he must have been in trouble and was doing his best to keep it from me. The sprained wrist and the puffy nose told me the rest of the story in the morning light."

"But the lights were off when we got in," Jerry protested.

"That doesn't mean I was sleeping," Sarah explained. "It's a rare night that I sleep until that boy is home in bed. I keep thinking that one of these nights he may not come home. Makes it mighty hard to doze off, I tell you."

"You'll understand when your little Martha gets to be eighteen and is out for the evening with some boy you don't know very well," Benjamin added. "You can't sleep a wink until you see the lights in the driveway."

"So I want to thank you for getting Teddy out of whatever trouble he was in," Sarah declared. "And you must have said something that got under his skin. He stayed home the last couple of nights. That's a change."

"You never told me what you talked about," Marjie said to Jerry. "Did you chew him out or what?"

"No. I'll leave the chewing out for you," Jerry teased. "I simply let Teddy know I care about him, and I tried to show him some of the lies that he's believing about the woman he was going to marry. But we've got to keep praying for that boy. He can't keep racing down the road he's on for long. To be honest, I'm scared for him."

"Is he coming here with you for Christmas day?" Marjie asked her mother.

"I can only hope," Sarah replied softly. "He won't talk with me about much of anything except the daily work. But he gets worse when he's alone, so let's hope he comes."

16

CHRISTMAS

"What do you think of the pine wreath in the window?" Marjie asked her mother as she finished putting the silverware around the Christmas dinner table. "Benjamin made it special for today."

"It's . . . big," Sarah said with a smile. "I don't remember ever seeing one that huge."

Marjie laughed and walked over to straighten it. "He's so excited about everyone coming over for Christmas. I guess I am, too," she added as she returned to her place settings. "So you couldn't talk Teddy into coming?"

Sarah was busy carving the turkey, carefully separating the light meat from the dark. She looked up and answered, "Nope. He said he had some things to do, although I don't think he was going anywhere with his drinking friends. He told me I didn't need to worry about making it home in time to chore."

"That's a switch. At least he's giving you one Christmas present this year," Marjie replied, looking out the picture window and down the driveway. "I wonder how late Margaret and Chester are going to be? Guess we'll need to cover the hot food and keep it in the oven."

"I covered the potatoes and beans and put them in to warm while you were changing Martha," Sarah said, sneaking a small piece of turkey and popping it in her mouth. "Mmmm. This tastes scrumptious!"

"Well," Marjie announced, "that's everything except for finishing the turkey. Guess I better wash my hands and see how I look. Do you think this dress is all right? You really dressed up."

"You look fine," her mother assured her. "I never get a chance to wear this dress, so I thought I'd drag it out today. You like it?"

"I love it," answered Marjie, studying her mother's attire. "You always look good in flower patterns. Makes me feel like summertime. I like the necklace, too. I can't remember the last time I've seen that on you."

"That's because I haven't worn it for a few years," Sarah said. "Sort of like the dress."

"I've thought about pilfering a few of those items from your jewelry box that never get used," Marjie teased. "They'd look nice on me, I'll bet."

"You keep your sticky fingers to home, darling," joked Sarah. "There's precious little there to pilfer. By the way, that was kind of Benjamin to come pick me up. I could have driven myself."

"He said he didn't like the thought of you driving alone with the possibility of the car breaking down on such a cold day. But if you ask me, I think he just likes an excuse to get out of the house. And I think he enjoys being with you."

Sarah looked up at Marjie, who was waiting to see how her mother would respond. But Sarah just smiled and went back to work with her knife. "Some reason he shouldn't?" she asked, pausing for a few moments. "Old people should just sit around and twiddle their thumbs all day? Maybe do a little crocheting and talk about the old days?"

"That's not what I meant, and you know it," Marjie protested. "And you're not that old."

"What did you mean?" her mother asked, turning the tables.

"Oh, nothing," Marjie sputtered, walking back to the window and looking down the driveway again. "I shouldn't tease about it, I guess. Actually, I think it's great that you and Benjamin have become friends. It's good for both of you."

"Why's that?"

"You do enjoy tormenting me, don't you?" asked Marjie,

laughing with her mother. "I'm being serious, and you keep making light of it. Do you really want me to say what I think?"

"Certainly. I think."

Marjie looked around to make sure that Jerry and Benjamin were still in the living room, then walked over close to her mother. "Because it's good for Benjamin to have a woman his own age in his life, someone he can talk with. And the same's true for you. It's good for you to have a mature man for a friend."

Sarah had finished getting the meat off the bones and put down the knife. "Well, I think—"

"Here they are now!" Jerry called out from the living room. Sarah and Marjie looked out the window as Chester's car rolled past.

"You were saved by the bell," Marjie whispered to her mother. "Whatever you were going to say, save it. You're not leaving this house until you tell me."

"Don't bet on it," Sarah said, washing her hands in the sink. "Go on, now. You've got guests to attend to."

Jerry had already grabbed his coat and was heading out the door to help Chester carry in Margaret's bags. Marjie had taken time out of her Christmas preparations to make new curtains for the empty bedroom upstairs and to find a couple of pictures to hang. Despite Jerry's assurances that Margaret would like the room, Marjie was worried that Margaret would be disappointed with it.

Margaret was the first one up the sidewalk, struggling to balance a large box and several brightly wrapped packages. Jerry and Chester followed her, slowly lugging massive leather suitcases that nearly touched the ground.

"Merry Christmas!" welcomed Marjie, hugging Margaret as best she could with the box in the way. "We're so delighted that you'll be staying with us."

"Merry Christmas to all!" Margaret announced in return, putting her box on the floor and taking off her coat. "I'm so happy to be here. I can't thank you enough for asking. And this must be your mother?"

"Yes," replied Marjie. "Margaret Harris, I'd like you to meet my mother, Sarah Livingstone."

"Pleased to meet you, Margaret," Sarah declared, taking Margaret's hands. "If things get boring here, you're invited to stay at my house as well."

"I'm happy to meet you, Sarah Livingstone," Margaret answered. "I won't forget your kind offer, though I hope not to have to hold you to it."

"Jerry, why don't you and Chester take those bags straight up to Margaret's room," Marjie said. "She may need to get something out."

"Merry Christmas to you, Father Macmillan," Margaret said to Benjamin, who had come into the room with Martha tucked in his arm. "Do you mind my calling you Father?"

"Not at all," Benjamin said with a handsome smile. "And Merry Christmas to you. You can call me whatever you like."

Everyone laughed, and Sarah went over and took Martha.

"My turn, Ben," Sarah said. "You'll have to get used to sharing the baby with him, Margaret."

"Let's go upstairs, and I'll show you your room," Marjie said to Margaret as the heavy tramp of the men's feet descending the stairs signaled that the bedroom was clear. "I'll bring your box."

Marjie picked up the box and headed up the stairs and down the hallway, with Margaret following closely. Jerry and Chester had set the suitcases in the hallway, so they had to wind their way around them to step into the sunny bedroom.

"Oh, Marjie, it's grand!" Margaret cried, covering her mouth with her hands. "You shouldn't have gone to so much work."

"I just made new curtains, that's all," explained Marjie. "I wanted a little something to say that we're so glad you're here."

Margaret paused and looked intently at Marjie, then she pushed the door shut quickly and leaned against it with her eyes closed. She shook her head as if she was in pain, then her shoulders began to shake up and down and the tears came, but only a muffled groan was uttered.

Marjie dropped the box on the bed, took the young woman into her arms, and held her for the longest time. Try as she might, Margaret could not stop the avalanche of buried emotions that had been waiting for a crack to escape through. Marjie finally nudged Margaret to sit on the bed and whispered that she was going to the other bedroom to find a handkerchief.

When Marjie returned, Margaret had nearly regained her composure and welcomed the handkerchief. Drying her eyes and cheeks and hands, Margaret took a deep breath and shut her eyes again. "I suppose I'm all bloodshot now," she whispered hoarsely, then popped open her eyes. "They'll all know I've been cryin'."

"So what if they do?" Marjie said. "We're your family now. And we all know what you've been through. You'd have to be a rock not to cry."

Margaret broke out laughing, and a few straggler tears surfaced but were quickly dried before they could find her cheeks. "I'm no rock," she confessed, "and I'm not as strong as Chester thinks I am. Another day in that house, and I'm afraid I'd have been on the next boat back to my country!"

"I'm so very sorry for the pain you've gone through," Marjie said. "I don't understand how anyone could treat you so badly."

Shaking her head and taking another deep draft of air, Margaret gently pressed the corners of her eyes with the sodden handkerchief. "I don't want to spoil Christmas for everyone. I'm a terrible guest."

"Would you stop it already!" Marjie demanded. "You'll be fine, and we'll all be fine. Besides, it's good to make the men wait awhile for the meal. That way they appreciate it. They're the ones who cause us so much grief, anyway. Chester probably didn't even warn you about his father, did he?"

"Not really," answered Margaret. "I knew Mr. Stanfeld was an unbeliever, but I didn't know he would despise me."

"And Jerry somehow managed to join the navy and didn't tell me that he'd gotten me pregnant!" joked Marjie. "Talk about poor communication."

Margaret laughed, and the deep frown gave way to a relaxed smile. "I think I'm going to like it—"

"You girls going to stay up there all day?" Jerry yelled up the stairs. "We're hungry. What's going on?"

Marjie jumped up and opened the door. "We'll be down in a few minutes, babe," she called back. "We're looking at Margaret's—"

"Wedding dress," whispered Margaret.

"Wedding dress," Marjie called out. "Give us five more minutes."

"Times two equals ten minutes," Jerry concluded and shut the stairway door.

Margaret pulled the box toward her and carefully undid the ties surrounding it. "I do want you to see my dress, Marjie," she said. "It's the only really precious thing I brought over. Most of my best things are still in a trunk in Scotland."

Taking off the lid and unfolding two layers of fine paper, Margaret stood up and pulled an armful of white out of the box, then turned it for Marjie to see. "It was my mother's," she said with pride. "She made it herself."

"My goodness!" gasped Marjie as the sunlight beaming in through the window shimmered on the snowy silk. It was a full-length gown adorned with delicate ruffles and immaculate stitching. "I've never seen anything so perfect. May I hold it?"

"Surely," Margaret said, delighted that Marjie liked it. Holding it up to Marjie, she said, "You would look lovely in it. Would you like to try it on?"

"No-no-no," replied Marjie, waving her hands. "Having the baby worked wonders on my figure. I'd pop every seam in your dress!"

Margaret laughed and handed it to Marjie. Then she reached into the box and pulled out the veil. "Mother made this special for me," she said.

"Beautiful!" exclaimed Marjie, holding the dress next to the veil. "It's perfect. I can hardly wait to see you in it. And I can hardly wait to see Chester's eyes pop out of his skull when he sees you. You haven't shown the dress to him, have you?"

"Never!" Margaret announced. "Not till the wedding."

"Good," said Marjie. "This is going to be so much fun!"

Margaret put a hand on Marjie's shoulder and looked into

her friend's dark eyes. "I can't tell you what it means to hear you say that," she said. "Everything was going so poorly, I thought I might not bother to wear it at all."

"Oh, you're going to wear it, all right," declared Marjie. "And Chester's never going to forget the sight. I guarantee it! Matter of fact, I'm glad I beat you to Jerry. I might have lost my man if he'd have got a load of you in this dress."

"A load?"

"Oops," explained Marjie. "I mean if he would have gotten a look at you. You better be careful, though. Old Benjamin might step in and try to ace Chester out!"

"Ace! I do know that one. I learned it from the Yanks back in Glasgow." Margaret and Marjie laughed out loud as the two of them carefully folded up the gown and veil and tucked it back into the box.

"We better get downstairs before they start thinking we've been talking about more than a wedding dress," Marjie suggested. "Are you ready?"

"I feel much better—thanks to you. Do I look like I've been crying?"

"Buckets," Marjie replied, catching Margaret off guard for a second. "No, you look fine. Nobody's going to notice a thing."

They went downstairs and into the dining room, where a smiling Sarah was standing patiently beside the table with all the food ready to serve. Steam was rising from several of the dishes, and the delicious scent of the roasted turkey permeated the house.

"I thought I was going to have to come up and get you," declared Sarah. "Figured you must be talking serious, so I got the food into bowls."

Marjie looked at Margaret. "There are no secrets when this woman is around. When I was a little girl, she knew what trouble I was going to get into before I did it."

"You have a mother's heart," Margaret said to Sarah. "That's the way my mother is too. With my mother so far away, I hope you stay close. I may need your help."

"Time to eat," Jerry called back to Benjamin and Chester as

he entered the dining room. "Wow! Look at the feast, will you? Chester, remember last Christmas? Slight improvement, eh?"

"Boot camp. Great Lakes Naval Base. Business as usual, sir!" joked Chester, saluting Jerry as he and Benjamin came into the room. "In some ways it seems like yesterday, and in other ways it seems like a lifetime ago. But I'll take this any day!" he added, putting his arm around Margaret.

"I can't imagine why," Benjamin piped in. "Now let's get to the meal. Then we've got presents under the tree to open. Where do you want us to sit, Marjie?"

Marjie pointed out each person's chair, and they all found their spot and stood waiting for Benjamin to pray.

"Is Martha sleeping?" Marjie whispered to Jerry. He nodded.

Benjamin looked thoughtfully around the table into the faces of his family and guests. "This is a wonderful day," he said slowly, brimming with a smile. "It's been years since we've truly celebrated the birth of our Savior in this old house, but today is an easy day to give Him thanks for coming to earth as a baby and giving His life for us. Less than two months ago, when the bull had me pinned to the ground, I never thought I'd get the chance to spend another Christmas around this table with the people I love. And you are the people that I love."

He paused for a moment and looked down, placing his hands upon the back of his chair and gathering his thoughts. Then he looked up again and met the eyes of each person around the table in turn. "Jerry, a year ago I sat at this table alone and prayed for your safety. God knows the sorrow He spared me in getting you off that carrier alive. Marjie, you helped bring joy and meaning back into my life. God knows how much I had come to dread the emptiness of this house until you moved in.

"Chester, your life and words made the difference in my son's coming to faith. God knows your heart's desire to reach other lives like you did Jerry's, and He will honor it. Margaret, you've come to us from far away because of love. God knows that love, and He will honor it. He also knows the valley you have walked through, and He promises His rod and staff to comfort you.

"And Sarah, you have become a true friend, and it's a rare privilege to have such a friend. God sees the grief of your heart for your one son and the anguish for the other who's at war, and He will be with you.

"Let's join hands and give Him our praise."

17

A NEW YEAR

"Happy New Year to you, too!" Marjie called out as Chester and Margaret started down the Macmillans' front sidewalk toward Chester's car. "I won't wait up, Margaret."

Marjie shut the door and turned to her friend Ruth. "So what did you think of her? Is she a doll or what?"

"I'm so jealous I thought I was going to turn green," Ruth replied, sitting down at the dining room table. "It'd be one thing if she was just beautiful, but she's got a sweet personality and an accent to boot. Why couldn't Jerry save the life of a great-looking guy who's not already taken? I'm sure I'm jinxed. And with women like Margaret Harris around, I don't stand a chance."

Marjie laughed and sat down at the table as well. "I guess you failed to follow the good doctor's advice. Remember?" she asked, but Ruth shook her head no. "You were to repeat three times daily: When Mr. Right comes along, I'll know it."

"I tried it for a week, but nothing happened," Ruth joked. "What if there's no Mr. Right?"

"Would you stop spinning that old record!" Marjie exclaimed. "You keep saying it, and you're going to believe it."

"Okay! I was just kidding," said Ruth. "Actually, I did go out with a new guy the other night."

"What? Who?"

"Just an older guy who teaches at a country school outside Canton," Ruth said and smirked. "No one around here knows him. We met at some teachers' meetings."

"And you didn't call me!" exclaimed Marjie. "How could you?"

"It's nothing serious," replied Ruth. "Besides, I hardly know him."

"Is he good-looking? Do you like him?"

"Yes, very . . . and I'm not sure," said Ruth. "We went to see *Heaven Can Wait* at the Strand Theater in Preston. We didn't talk much."

"So you must have—"

"No!" Ruth broke in and laughed. "We enjoyed the movie, then he drove me home. He was a perfect gentleman."

"That's all?"

"So far. You were expecting a diamond ring?"

"Why not? What's his name?"

"Peter Boyd. And that's all I'm telling for now," Ruth stated. "He's just a friend, anyway."

"I want to know before you go out with him again," Marjie demanded. "I've got to keep track of all you young couples. What did you think of Margaret and Chester together?"

"They really do make a wonderful couple," Ruth replied. "And with his strength and her sweetness, I'll bet they'll make a fine pastoral team someday."

"They're something special, all right," agreed Marjie. "Margaret's been with us for a week, and she already seems indispensable. She and Benjamin have been talking Bible stuff since she got here. And she helps around the house so much that I'm going to be spoiled by the time she leaves. I've already managed to forget how to change a diaper!"

"If she and Chester are getting married at the end of the month, you better enjoy it while you can. A month goes by so fast," Ruth said. "They didn't say where they were getting married. I suppose it'll be at his parents' church?"

"I wish," replied Marjie. "His parents are anti-God, anti-church, and anti-believing. Or his father is, anyway. He kicked

Chester out of the house for his faith, and after Margaret was with them for a short time he asked her to leave as well."

"Goodness!" sputtered Ruth. "I had no idea. Margaret acted like everything was fine. And they were going over to his folks' for the evening?"

"I can't believe it, either," Marjie answered. "But Chester said they were invited for a New Year's Eve dinner, and Margaret said it was a chance to keep the door open to the family. I'm not so sure I would have been so gracious."

"Me either," Ruth agreed. "So when's the wedding going to be? And where? I'd really like to go, now that I've gotten to know Margaret and Chester."

"They've set the date for January 30," Marjie replied, "but they're not sure about the 'where' yet. I think they've about decided just to go over to the pastor's house and let him marry them there. They'll only have enough money saved to afford renting the upper half of a house in Preston, so they..."

"Yes. So they what?"

"I just had a brilliant idea."

"From the look on your face, I suspect it involves me," Ruth deducted. "Will you stop that smirk! This better be above the table."

"It is. Trust me."

"You pull too many tricks to think that I'd ever trust you," Ruth protested mildly. "But let's hear your brilliant idea before you forget it."

"Margaret carried the most lovely wedding dress that I've ever seen all the way from Scotland," Marjie said as she got out of her chair and began to pace around the dining room table, "and now she's not even going to get a chance to wear it. We can't let that happen, can we?"

"Meaning?"

"Ruthie, in one month's time, you and I are going to organize a church wedding—at our church!" exclaimed Marjie, beaming a smile at her puzzled friend.

"How will we get anyone to come? No one even knows them but us."

"Exactly," suggested Marjie. "Because we know them, we're going to tell others about this wonderful couple who are going into the ministry and need a good church to be a part of. You know how quickly most of the church people welcomed me into the church, and everybody loves a wedding. What do you think? You're the expert at this."

"You're stretching it, Marjie," Ruth commented. "Jerry was a hometown boy, so everybody came to your shower. But they hardly know Chester. I don't know."

"You can do better than that, Ruthie," urged Marjie. "I know you too well."

Ruth rubbed her forehead, and her dark eyes began flashing signals toward Marjie. "All right, you know her better than I do. Other than being really nice, what is most unusual about her?"

"She's a wonderful singer," Marjie replied. "She sings when she's working around the house, and I've never heard a voice so captivating in my life. I can hardly keep working when she's doing it."

"That's where we start, then," Ruth declared confidently. "In fact, this is going to be easy."

"How?"

"We need to take advantage of what Chester and Margaret do best," explained Ruth. "If I can talk the pastor into it, next Sunday we'll be hearing the Scottish nightingale sing a solo in the morning worship service, and she'll be followed in the Sunday school hour by a fine young Bible teacher who already made a big impression on the church at Jerry's potluck dinner. Give them a couple of weeks' publicity, and I'll bet we fill the church for their wedding!"

Marjie stopped her pacing and clapped and laughed. "You're amazing, Ruthie!" she exclaimed. "But will Pastor Fitchen go for it?"

"You leave him to me," Ruth assured her. "Give me five minutes on Monday, and he'll be on the phone asking both of them to help out. Now, you'd better get a sheet of paper out. We've got a wedding to plan before your Martha wakes up."

———— ✑ ————

"What you two been up to?" Jerry asked as he and Benjamin came in from the barn. Ruth was feeding Martha a bottle, and Marjie was adding scribbles to a sheet of paper already covered with writing. "Looks like trouble. Not another potluck?"

"Better," Marjie said.

"What?"

"A full-blown church wedding for Margaret and Chester!" Ruth declared. "And you're the best man, and the fine-looking gentleman behind you will be giving away the bride."

"Where? Not at our church."

"Yes, at our church," Marjie said. "And it's a secret for now, so keep a lid on this. We'll tell you about it after you get cleaned up. You smell like the barn."

"That surprises you?"

"How'd choring go for you, Benjamin?" Ruth asked.

"Pretty fair," he answered. "I'm only doing the easy stuff. But what I'm doing feels great."

"When're you leaving for my mother's?" asked Marjie. "She should have come here tonight, seeing as Billy Wilson's finally coming over. You're going to miss him."

"Sarah thought you youngsters might enjoy an evening without us old folks," Benjamin explained. "Besides, she doesn't know Billy, and he'll still be here when I get home. I'm leaving just as soon as I wash up and change my clothes."

"Don't you want to eat?"

"Sarah said she found a pint of oysters in Lime Springs and is making stew," Benjamin said with a smile. "Now that's a meal for New Year's Eve, eh?"

"Beats our leftovers," Marjie agreed. "What are you two going to do? Bang pots and pans at midnight, or what?"

"I don't know that it's any of your business," Benjamin joked. "But we'll probably sit and talk. Pretty exciting, right? Like your card game."

"Right. We could have dealt you into the game if you wanted to play. I know how much you like cards, so you must be really hungry for oysters," Marjie said. "Say, you better hustle and beat Jerry into the bathroom. He takes forever, you know."

Benjamin excused himself and cut straight across to the bathroom. In a short time he was heading out the door, leaving behind an aromatic trail of aftershave. He only paused to say good-night.

———— ✑ ————

Jerry's oldest friend, Billy Wilson, arrived about an hour later, carrying an apple pie with a thick sugar crust that his mother had sent along. Rather than making it home for Christmas, he had stopped in Kansas City to visit a friend who had also been injured on the *Arizona*. He'd just arrived home the day before, and this was the Macmillans' first time to see him.

Marjie greeted Billy and took the pie from him before Jerry could grab his hand and then give his best friend a backslapping hug. After they were done, it was Marjie's turn.

"Welcome home, Billy!" Marjie exclaimed and hugged him tightly. "You're a sight for sore eyes."

"It's great to be home—and alive," Billy said softly, his eyes brimming with unshed tears. "Congratulations on your marriage to that goofy-looking friend of mine. You finally snared him."

"Took a war, but I bagged him," replied Marjie. "How many double dates did you arrange to try to keep us together?"

"I did my share," answered Billy. "You owe me."

Billy let go of Marjie and smiled a bit awkwardly at Ruth, who was standing behind Marjie. Although he and Jerry and Ruth had gone to school together, Marjie knew that it had been a long time since they'd seen each other.

"Welcome home, sailor," Ruth said warmly, stepping forward to give him a hug as well. "I was afraid I wouldn't have anyone to fight with anymore."

"No such luck," Billy assured her with a laugh. "You may have toughened me up for what I had to face. I wonder if two kids ever battled as many times as you and I did at school."

"You got me into so much trouble," Ruth said, stepping back

from Billy. "Maybe we should go a round, and you can let me get even."

Billy threw up his hands in mock surrender. "No need to bother. The Japs got even for you. If you give me the old trip move, I may never walk again."

They all laughed, and Marjie took Billy's coat and hung it up. "Ruth and I will bring in the coffee. Why don't you and the goofy-looking friend of yours go into the living room and meet your little niece. We've declared you an official uncle."

"I'm thrilled!" exclaimed Billy. "This is a first."

Jerry led the way while Ruth and Marjie ducked back into the kitchen.

"Boy, I can't believe he looks so good," said Marjie, pulling down some cups from the cupboard. "Jerry said we'd never know he'd been hurt, except for the limp. But I guess I didn't believe him."

"It is amazing," Ruth said. "He even seems different somehow. Not so cocky and brassy. He used to make me so mad. Did you ever have someone who you loved to hate?"

"No. You'll have to explain that later," replied Marjie. "I'd forgotten how good-looking he is. Those big green eyes and strong arms . . ."

"You can also forget whatever ideas are wandering through your overactive imagination," Ruth warned. "He broke the heart of every pretty girl in the county. Just about the time that they were falling all over him, he'd drop them and take out their best friend. So I'm happy to have him as a friend, but that's it. He's dangerous. Do you understand?"

"That I understand," Marjie replied as they finished getting the coffee and sandwiches ready. "I remember he dated some of my friends. Talk about a lady-killer. But Jerry says he's changed."

"Looks like the leopard's still got spots to me," Ruth whispered and winked. "And I stay clear of leopards."

"You didn't go out with him, too?" asked Marjie, staring into Ruth's dark eyes.

Ruth gave her a twisted smile and an imitation of Groucho

Marx's eyebrow tricks, then picked up two trays and headed for the living room.

"You did, didn't you!" gasped Marjie, grabbing her trays and trying to catch up. But Ruth was already in the living room before Marjie could dredge up any more nuggets from the past.

The four friends sat in the living room and ended up getting distracted from their game of Hearts. Marjie and Ruth wanted to hear the complete story of what happened to Billy, then Billy wanted to hear about the sinking of the *Wasp* and about how Marjie came to live with Benjamin on the farm. Ruth added in all the details that were skipped over. They laughed together; they listened to each other and were filled with wonder; at moments they were moved by one another. When Marjie told how she had come to God in the hospital courtyard while waiting to hear about Benjamin's heart, Billy had to reach for the napkin on his tray to use as a handkerchief. None of them had seen Billy cry since he was a little boy, and his tears got them all going.

After they had told and retold their stories, Jerry asked Billy, "I realize you just got home, but have you thought any more about what you're going to do now?"

Smiling, Billy shrugged his shoulders. "Yes and no," he said. "I wanted to just get home and farm for a while, maybe rest for a time and then make some decisions. But I've been home for twenty-four hours and I know that I won't be farming for long."

"Your dad didn't say something, did he?" Ruth asked.

"No. Nothing like that," Billy answered. "He'd love to have me on the farm. But let's face it. The farm's too small for two grown men, and I just don't fit on a farm. Even if I did, these legs just can't take the cold. That I quickly discovered. Five minutes outside in these temperatures, and they hurt so bad I can hardly take it."

"So what's next?" questioned Marjie.

"I've had a lot of time to think about it," Billy responded. "When that old battle-axe of a nurse was scrubbing off scar tissue, I'd try to concentrate everything I had on the future and what I was going to do. But I still don't know. All I've ever done is farm during the day and run around at night. Now I don't feel much like doing either."

"We were just talking about that," Marjie said impishly.

"About what?" asked Billy.

"Never mind," Ruth broke in before Marjie could say more. "You have your high school diploma, which is more than most men in the area. Did you ever think about going into business?"

"I hate selling," Billy said. "I could never make a business profitable."

"But not every business job is selling," Ruth said. "You were very good at math. Maybe accounting or something?"

"I do like math, Ruthie, but I can't imagine sitting at a desk pushing paper all day. I want to do something where I'm helping people. That's what I liked about helping at the hospital. I don't want to go into medicine, but I want to be involved in people's lives and make a difference."

"Whew! That's a tall order," Jerry remarked. "Sure doesn't sound like the old Billy I used to know."

"A lot has changed," Billy added, but he was looking at Ruth instead. "You may be in for some big surprises."

18

STUNNING

With the exception of Margaret Harris, everyone in the farmhouse was moving at a dead run to get ready in time for church. During the morning chores, Jerry had noticed that one of the milking cows was starting to develop a case of mastitis, and treating her had kept him and Benjamin in the barn way past schedule. That delay had slowed Marjie in getting their breakfast together, which in turn delayed getting the noon meal ready, which delayed her getting ready.

Margaret was fortunate that Chester had picked her up earlier to practice her song one more time with the church organist. Margaret was nervous enough about singing for the first time before an American audience, and the pandemonium that was now in full swing around the house would have heightened her anxiety.

"I'll never get my hair ready in time!" Marjie called down the stairway to Jerry, who was in the bathroom shaving as fast as he could. "You and Benjamin just go when you're ready. I'll come later in the other car."

"That car's been sitting all week," answered Jerry. "I don't even know if it'll start. We can make it if we keep moving. None of us are going to miss her singing."

Marjie went back into their bedroom and ran the brush feverishly through her long, wavy brown hair, then she slowed down and decided to concentrate and make sure every stroke counted. Martha lay on the bed, kicking and wiggling with pillows propped on both sides to keep her from rolling.

"There we go!" Marjie rejoiced when the last strands fell into place. Then she paused for just a moment in front of the big dresser mirror. "Well, Martha, what do you think of your mama? Do I get a passing grade?" She sighed. "Could be better. But it'll have to do for now."

Scooping up her baby, Marjie dashed into Martha's bedroom to deck her out in the cute yellow dress Sarah had made as a Christmas present. Jerry's pounding footsteps on the stairway told her he was only moments away from being ready as well.

Fifteen minutes later, the Macmillans were entering the church with ten minutes to spare. Taking off her coat in the basement, Marjie checked herself one more time for fear that she might have forgotten her belt or that perhaps her slip was showing, but all was well. Then, to the delight of the silver-haired grandmother in charge, Marjie reluctantly dropped Martha off in the nursery. This was only the second time she'd left Martha there, and Marjie would have preferred to stay with her herself.

Benjamin and Jerry were waiting for her in the foyer, and Marjie noticed that the church was nearly full.

"Ready?" Jerry whispered.

"I guess," responded Marjie softly. "We'd better move, or we'll end up in the front row."

"I'll just be a minute," Benjamin said, motioning with his hand for them to go. "Hurry or those pews may fill up, but save me a place."

Marjie wanted to find out what he was up to, but there was no time for questions. So she and Jerry walked down the side aisle and found an empty section of a pew.

"What's he doing now?" she whispered to Jerry.

"Who knows?" Jerry replied. "Look—there's Margaret up there with the choir. Glad they let Chester sit with her. But she doesn't look nervous to me."

Marjie looked beyond the pulpit into the choir loft and discovered that Margaret's eyes were fixed on her. She gave Margaret a little wave, and Margaret nodded back and smiled.

Then Jerry leaned over and whispered, "What's Billy doing in the first row with those two young boys?"

Marjie turned her focus to follow Jerry's eyes. Two young farm boys were sitting next to Billy, who had the aisle spot. "I have no idea," she said with a shrug of her shoulders. Opening her bulletin, Marjie showed Jerry a line after the announcements stating that those who had applied for church membership would make a public declaration of faith.

Jerry shook his head no. "Billy did that years ago. Must be something else."

A hand lightly tapped Marjie on the shoulder, and she instinctively nudged Jerry to slide over. When she turned to see who it was, Marjie gave a start to find her smiling mother and Benjamin waiting for them to make room.

"For crying out loud," Marjie muttered softly as Sarah sat down next to her. "Somebody could at least warn me you were coming."

"Surprises are fun," her mother said. "Besides, I'm too old to miss hearing an angel sing. It only happens once in a lifetime, my grandmother used to say."

Marjie looked at Jerry and gave him a did-you-know-about-this look, but he simply whispered, "I had no idea." She wanted to ask her mother another question, but the pastor and choir made their entrance, and the organist began to play. Marjie spotted Ruth in the midst of the choir robes, and she gave Ruth her traditional wink.

The bulletin listed Margaret's solo after the announcements and before the time when new members would be welcomed into the church. As Pastor Fitchen began the service and went into his long congregational prayer—really a mini-sermon complete with scriptures—Marjie felt her head begin to droop. Too many hours up in the night with the baby rolled together with a fifteen-minute prayer that the pastor read were more than she could endure. She hoped that Margaret's singing could pump some life into the preaching that would follow.

The elderly pastor finished his prayer and then made a few

routine announcements about upcoming events. Then his somber expression changed and actually warmed to a smile. Turning to Margaret, he declared, "We have a very special soloist this morning who's come all the way from Scotland to sing for us. I'd like you to welcome Miss Margaret Harris into our congregation, and I hope you take a few minutes after church to get to know her. I'd also like to announce that on Saturday, January thirtieth, at two P.M. sharp, Margaret Harris and Chester Stanfeld will be married in this church, and Ruth Buckley and Marjie Macmillan say you are all invited!"

A small ripple of surprise passed through the congregation, but the weight of the shock fell upon Margaret and Chester. A "What!" slipped out before Margaret could silence it, and she quickly glanced at Chester to see if he knew what was going on. Then she flushed as the realization dawned that Ruth and Marjie were the culprits and that the two connivers had kept both her and Chester in the dark.

Margaret took a few seconds to compose herself, then stood, turning a smile toward Ruth in the row behind her. Then she stepped to the podium and beamed a smile out at Marjie as well. " 'Tis an honor to be with you this morning," she said simply. "I was so nervous about singing before so many of you Yanks at one time, but the unexpected announcement about our wedding in this lovely church has shaken my nerves clean away."

The congregation broke into laughter, and Margaret had to wait for the din to die down before continuing.

"Thank you, Marjie and Ruth, for making these arrangements," Margaret continued. "I thought I'd carried my wedding dress all the way from Scotland for nothing, but it looks like I'll have my chance to wear it after all. My mother will be so proud!

"Now, I'd like to sing my favorite hymn for you this morning, *Fairest Lord Jesus*, but I need to explain that it's become even more lovely to me since riding the train across your grand United States. If you've ever been to Scotland, you know how beautiful our countryside is, but as I studied the many landscapes and was overwhelmed by the breadth of your nation, I found myself humming this melody over and over again. And now that I've been at the Macmillan farm and enjoyed the solitude of your charming hills, I think I can better express the wonder of the songwriter as he compared the elegance of nature with our indescribable Savior."

Margaret took a step back from the podium and signaled for the organist to begin. Then, shutting her eyes and taking in a deep breath, she began singing in a sweet clear tone. There was an intrinsic power and purity to Margaret's voice that washed over the listeners and left them awed and breathless.

The organist played the first three stanzas quietly to give Margaret's singing the focus, but on the final stanza both she and Margaret opened up the volume all the way. Something like the sound of thunder rumbled within the church as the resonating words were indelibly etched on every listener's heart:

Beautiful Savior! Lord of the nations!
Son of God and Son of Man!
Glory and honor, praise, adoration,
Now and forevermore be Thine!

Before Margaret was even halfway through the last stanza, many of the church members rose to their feet almost involuntarily and joined in finishing the glorious words of praise. Several looked around in embarrassment as the song ended, but so many people were standing that sheer numbers made their participation acceptable. Many of the members were shaking their heads in wonder and mumbling to themselves, but their wonder soon turned to an awkward silence and everyone sat back down quickly.

Marjie had been holding Jerry's hand when Margaret began singing, and by the finish of the song she had nearly squeezed all the blood out of his fingers. Jerry was so caught up in the song that he didn't notice the numbness setting in until the prickles started, and then he had all he could do to get his hand away from her.

"It was more beautiful than I could have imagined," Sarah whispered to Marjie as they sat down with everyone else. "I wonder if it's something like what your pa hears up there?"

Marjie nodded in agreement and felt a quick wave of loneliness for her father, but the sound of the pastor's voice diverted her attention back to the podium.

"I've been a pastor for a little over thirty-five years," Pastor Fitchen began, looking back toward Margaret, who had taken her seat next to Chester. "But I have never heard anything so extraordinary, and I've never seen such a response. Margaret Harris, I'm hoping you'll sing for us again next Sunday?"

Margaret smiled and nodded a yes.

"Thank you," he said, turning to face the congregation. "I'm sure that none of us will want to miss your encore."

Pausing to study the faces of the three young men in the front pew, the pastor continued, "This has been a highly unusual week for me. First thing Monday morning, Ruth Buckley called and asked me if I would allow an angel to sing in our church if she could guarantee the delivery. How can you resist an offer like that?

"Then I got a call yesterday that has changed the rest of our morning's service. It happened too late to change the bulletin, but as a result, I will not be preaching a sermon as indicated. I realize the irregularity of it, but I believe there's something more important for you to hear than my sermon.

"Yesterday morning, Billy Wilson called me and then stopped by in the afternoon. As you may know, Billy grew up in this church. He was a crew member on the USS *Arizona* and was injured at Pearl Harbor, and I know he and his family appreciate all your prayers for his recovery. But that's not really what Billy came to talk to me about. I believe that what he told me deserves to be heard by everyone here, so I'm going to ask him to come now and share his story with you. Afterward, although he made a confession of faith as a young teen, he will join David Vandermere and Gus Jenson in publicly confessing their faith in Jesus Christ. If that confuses you, I think what Billy has to say will make it clear."

Billy had stepped out of the pew and was waiting for the pastor to finish the introduction. Pastor Fitchen stepped down, shook Billy's hand and whispered something in his ear, then took a seat.

Billy moved to the podium and paused momentarily to survey the congregation, his striking green eyes and handsome smile covering the nervousness that Jerry knew was inside. Although he had always been more outgoing than Jerry, Billy was a stranger to speaking in public, especially in church. When he spotted Jerry, Billy nodded and seemed to catch a fresh breeze of confidence. His first words were, "I can't tell you how good it is to be home . . . and alive!"

Billy ran his fingers back up through his short brown hair and took a deep breath. "This is going to surprise many of you this morning, but ten years ago I stood in the exact spot in the front pew and lied about my faith—before you and before God. I'm glad I can be here this morning to tell you I'm sorry for not having told the truth. At the time, I had no more faith in God than the man on the moon. But having gone through the confirmation process, I felt the pressure to follow the others in my class and join the church, regardless of what I truly believed. And the truth was that I didn't particularly believe anything. Today I do believe, and I'm here to take a public stand upon that fact.

"A little over a year ago, on a beautiful tropical Sunday morning, I had just finished a breakfast of hotcakes and eggs on the *Arizona* and gone topside for a smoke. As I came out on the deck, I could hear the church bells ringing across the harbor, and I remember thinking how glad I was that I didn't have to go. Funny how a few seconds later a church is the one place I wished I could be.

"I hadn't even gotten my cigarettes out of my pocket when all hell broke loose around me. Before I heard the first explosion, I felt the tremendous shock of the Japanese torpedo that hit the battleship *Oklahoma* and keeled her over, trapping four hundred sailors below the decks. I thought for a moment that a tornado must have touched down, but then I heard someone screaming that we were under attack.

"I looked up and saw a gray plane with a large red dot on

the fuselage flying past, and I tried to make a dash to man one of the guns. But before I could get close to a gun, a tremendous explosion tore our battleship open and knocked me to the deck. I looked up and saw a blast of flames come out of the No. 2 gun turret, followed by an explosion of the forward magazine. The foremast leaned forward, and it seemed like the whole forward part of the ship was immediately enveloped in flames and smoke.

"It was a sight so terrifying I can't describe it. If you have a vivid imagination and can conjure up an image of what hell is like, this might have been close to it. I was sure I would die.

"I can't tell you how I survived, because I haven't been able to recall parts of what happened. Perhaps I need not tell you that more than a thousand fellow crewmen lost their lives—a lot of 'em are still trapped down there in the wreckage of the *Arizona*. I do remember running for the railing with my legs on fire and leaping through the air into the blue waves in the winter sunshine. And I remember swimming for the docks and crawling for what I thought was a safe place. I remember waking up hours later on a cot in the naval hospital, feeling like my legs were still on fire. I remember screaming with pain and the nurses tying my hands to keep me from doing more damage to my legs.

"But more important than all of that, I also recall the terror of stepping so close to death's door and not knowing what would happen if I died. It was sheer terror. But in the middle of the terror, I saw something greater—both wonderful and terrible at the same time."

Billy paused to run a hand across his close-cropped skull, then leaned forward against the podium. "While I can't describe it," he said, "and you may think I'm crazy, for an instant I believe God gave me a glimpse of himself. It was not a physical seeing, but an amazing opening of the eyes of my soul. Without a shadow of a doubt, I knew that He was the great God over all, and that He held my life in the center of His hand.

"And somehow," Billy added in a near-whisper that still managed to ring through the building, "somehow I knew that all He was asking me to do was to believe."

19

FEARS

"I'll be back before dark," Benjamin announced as he opened the front door of the farmhouse. "You can finish those wedding plans without me, I reckon. No sense me sitting around here in the way."

"I thought you were eavesdropping on our conversation about Ruthie's second date with her schoolteacher friend," Marjie replied. "Who you going to see, anyway? You could at least let us know in case someone calls looking for you."

Benjamin wrinkled his forehead and shrugged his shoulders. "Who Ruthie dates is none of my business," he answered, "and if anyone's looking for me, tell them to try again after dinner. I've got someone who's been on my heart for some time to go see, and I got a feeling today's the right day. I'll tell you later what I discover. Fair enough?"

"No. You never play fair." Marjie rolled her eyes. "You better have a good story to tell, or there's no dinner for you tonight!"

"I guess I'll stop in town then," Benjamin joked back. "Maybe Chester would like some company."

"Not tonight, he won't. Chester's coming here for dinner," Margaret corrected with a gentle smile. "We want him to feel like he's helping with the wedding plans."

"Very crafty," declared Benjamin, pointing a finger at Margaret. "Seems like you women always get this way right before a wedding. Ruthie, be careful what goes on this afternoon. You're with two devious ladies who have the power to corrupt your good name."

"It's too late," Ruth conceded with a hearty nod. "I'm already damaged goods."

"That's a cold breeze you're letting in," Marjie complained to Benjamin. "You born in the barn?"

"Maybe I was," Benjamin suggested, stepping out into the bright winter sunlight. "See you later."

A chorus of goodbyes followed him out the door, and Benjamin waved as he strode by the big picture window.

"When I first came here to stay," Marjie spoke slowly, "that man was as predictable as his old pocket watch. Now I don't know when he's coming or going, who he's seeing, or what he's doing. He even calls on the phone when he thinks I can't hear because I'm upstairs with Martha."

"And we thought he'd be dead by now," Ruth said and laughed. "Looks like he's got a lot of miles left in him."

"Let's hope so," Margaret added, looking out the window as Benjamin's car rumbled down the driveway. "He's as dear a man as God ever made, and his tender heart has helped me so in feeling at home here, especially when I'm missing my mum and dad. I'm delighted that he's willing to walk me down the aisle."

Marjie laughed out loud and said, "He's so proud to be involved that he'll be popping his buttons. I hope he doesn't start crying and mess up the service."

"I'd love it if he did," Margaret said with a sigh. Then she looked down blankly at the various sheets of wedding plans they had been working on. "Maybe it would drive the fear away."

Ruth and Marjie looked at each other in disbelief. Margaret had shown nothing but elegant poise since she moved in with the Macmillans, and the sudden crack in her armor caught them off guard.

Marjie took the pencil out of Margaret's hand and gently laid it on the table. Then she placed her hand over Margaret's and said, "If you're afraid of something, Margaret, I'd be glad to talk with you about it. When Jerry was gone, Benjamin once called me the Queen of Fear, and he was right. In the middle of the night I'd get so overwhelmed with being afraid that I thought I was going crazy."

Margaret took a deep breath and shook her head in disgust. "I hate to be such a ninny," she moaned, closing her tender eyes. "It should be so simple, and I've tried repeating the verses a hundred times: 'Rejoice evermore . . . pray without ceasing . . . in every thing give thanks: for this is the will of God in Christ Jesus concerning you.' But it doesn't get any better."

"My mother once told me that the greatest distance in the world was between her head and her heart," Ruth said soothingly. "I wish it weren't true, but I've certainly found it true for me. I can know something in my head and can quote it verbatim, but that doesn't mean it's gotten down into my heart."

"But I had no idea that you were worried about something," Marjie said. "Did it just come up?"

"No, no," Margaret sputtered. "It started before I left Scotland, but it gets more difficult with each day that the wedding gets closer. I'm ashamed to tell you that I've been covering over it. I was afraid that you'd think I was foolish. Maybe we should forget I said anything and just finish our work here."

Marjie spoke very carefully. "We don't want you to feel like you have to tell us anything. But I think you'd feel better about it if you did."

"And I think you're right," Margaret said softly, relaxing her shoulders and slowly stretching her neck muscles. "Only I'm not sure where to begin. It's such a mess. It seems as if everything's wrong."

"Like Chester's family, for instance?" asked Ruth.

"Exactly!" gasped Margaret, letting loose some of her pent-up anguish. "I prayed for them and tried so hard to be kind and gentle and not offend them. But it all has gone so badly, and now they barely tolerate Chester coming into their house. It's all my fault."

"You don't really believe that, do you?" said Marjie. "I suspect that the problems you had with Chester's parents go back before Chester was born. It doesn't have anything to do with you or Chester. Both of you just happen to be lightning rods for whatever their problem is. Anyone with faith who gets too close to Chester's father is going to get a blast. Jerry and I did, and we barely know them!"

"Maybe we're looking at this from the wrong angle," Ruth interjected. "If you could go stay with Chester's parents again, what would you do different?"

Margaret shook her head and sighed. "I've thought it over a hundred times, and I can't think of anything. I've wondered if I made a mistake by trying so hard to be what they wanted me to be. I was in a place where I felt I couldn't express any of my real thoughts or beliefs. But when I did say what I thought, that made everything worse."

"I think you need to face it, Margaret: you couldn't win," reasoned Marjie. "Whichever way you turned, you would have been up against the same situation. They simply don't want what you or Chester represent."

"Which doesn't mean they always won't," Ruth suggested. "Maybe your time with them was more profitable than you think. We can never tell when something we say or do makes an impression on another person."

"Like the time back in country school when you talked about the poor girl who could only afford lettuce sandwiches?" Marjie laughed. "I may have forgotten who you were, Ruthie, but I never forgot what you said."

Ruth laughed as well and said, "You promised to stop dragging up my ancient history, Marjie. How was I supposed to know you brought lettuce sandwiches because you liked plain lettuce sandwiches? Have you ever met anyone who eats lettuce sandwiches, Margaret?"

Shaking her head no, Margaret laughed out loud. It seemed that the friendly bantering was doing more for Margaret's worries than Ruth and Marjie's most convincing arguments.

"What else is troubling you, Margaret?" asked Ruth. "If we can't take the fear away, at least we can be concerned."

"What you said about not being able to win makes sense to

me," mused Margaret. "The whole time I was with them, I felt I was losing. I just wish I could have done something to change the situation. They even refuse to come to the wedding!"

"That's their problem," Marjie protested. "You can't change them. Not even their son's gentle way over all these years has swayed them. You have to let it go."

Margaret smiled a crooked smile and said, "All right. I'll let it go. I hope."

"Good," Marjie declared. "One fear down and . . . how many to go?"

"Just a couple more Goliaths," answered Margaret. "But they're very big!"

"Bring 'em on," Marjie challenged. "The bigger they are the harder they fall. Besides, Ruthie has an answer for everything!"

"You must promise never to tell Chester or anyone else," Margaret requested. "I'd die if he found out. Will you promise?"

Marjie and Ruth nodded.

"All right. I'm afraid we will be married a few months and Chester will discover how dull I really am," confessed Margaret. "And then he'll be so disappointed he'll wish he would have never met me." She leaned forward, her blue eyes full of worry. "He's so excited now, but when he sees me every day, how can it possibly last? And we really haven't had much time to be together. What if he's in love with someone who's really not there at all?"

Marjie sank back in her chair, amazed that she could have spent so much time with Margaret without knowing these thoughts were swirling around in the other woman's head. Then she leaned forward and asked, "Has Chester given you any hint that his love is not genuine? Do you have any reason to doubt his love?"

"No. His love is so strong it frightens me."

"Does he seem like the type of man who walks away from commitments easily?" continued Marjie.

"Oh no."

"And you love him?"

"More than I ever imagined I could love anyone."

"Well, then," Marjie reasoned, "it sounds like you've got what every girl dreams about." She picked up her pencil and used it to tick off an imaginary checklist in the air. "Here's a mature man who's crazy about you, and you love him. You've known him long enough to see how faithful he is to what he commits himself to. Yes, his emotions are probably going to rise and fall, but that doesn't mean he'll stop loving you. Besides, if that were true, you're as vulnerable to it as he is."

"There's really no way to guarantee we can hold on to anyone's love," Ruth added gently. "Love is a choice you keep making over and over again. And there are going to be times when Chester is disappointed with you, and you with him. We all disappoint each other sooner or later, and we're never all that others hope we are, but that's life.

"I have failed my schoolchildren at times," Ruth continued, "and they've disappointed me. But that hasn't kept me from going back the next day or kept them from forgiving me and moving on. Your love for each other is going to be stronger than your disappointments, and the strength of both your commitments to God will serve you well."

"Was your father always madly in love with your mother?" Marjie asked.

Margaret laughed and said, "No. My father was never very emotional. And, yes, I know what you're going to ask next, Marjie. My father did disappoint my mother, and she sometimes failed as well, but they have kept on loving each other for more than twenty-five years."

"Case closed," declared Marjie, bringing down the pencil like a little gavel on the tabletop. "All right?"

"I suppose," Margaret replied. "It still frightens me, though."

"But isn't love always scary?" Ruth asked. "If God's love is our model, and He was willing to have His heart broken and allow His Son to die for mankind's sin, knowing that people would reject His love every day . . . well, our love is going to be a risk as well."

"I know it's true," acknowledged Margaret. "But it's still difficult to accept. Maybe this Goliath doesn't breathe his last until

174

you're married and work through some of the problems?"

"I think that's probably right," Marjie said. "Much of life is that way."

"Most of it," acknowledged Ruth. "Now, what's the other Goliath, Margaret?"

Margaret's face got red, and she placed both hands over her eyes. "I'll embarrass all of us if I say it."

"You're not going to embarrass me," Marjie responded. "I've been around the block a few times."

"What?" Margaret peeked out from behind one hand.

"Sorry. I thought we'd worked through most of these funny sayings," Marjie said. "I just mean that I lived on my own for four years, and I've seen others do a lot of shocking things. You won't embarrass me."

Margaret mumbled something out from behind the shield of her hands, but neither Ruth nor Marjie could understand, so they asked her to repeat it.

Through a whisper, Margaret said, "I'm afraid of what our first night will be like. I've never been with a man before."

Ruth's dark eyes darted over at Marjie, and Marjie knew Ruth was leaving this problem to her care. Marjie sat silently, wondering where to begin.

"See. I did embarrass you," Margaret murmured softly with her hands still covering her face. "I shouldn't have said anything. You mustn't tell Chester!"

"I'm not embarrassed," Marjie responded quickly. "But you have to give me a few seconds to think about it. It's not something Ruth and I talk about all the time. Let me ask you this. Did you and your mother ever talk about it?"

Dropping her hands, Margaret nodded her head. "A couple of times," she said. "I understand the physical part, I think. But still . . ."

"Most of my friends who got married never talked to anyone about it," Marjie said. "Not even about the physical part. It was pretty scary for them. But if you understand that part, you're a lot further down the road than they were."

"But the rest of it?" Margaret hesitated, then asked. "Do you mind me asking what your first night was like?"

"Only if you promise not to tell anyone," Marjie responded tentatively. "Both of you."

Ruth and Margaret both nodded their promise and waited.

"Hmmm," Marjie sighed. "This is a little more embarrassing than I thought. . . ."

"You don't—"

"Hold your horses," Marjie interrupted. "I want to say this right, so just let me gather my thoughts. First of all, you need to know that it wasn't perfect by any means, and I got very nervous, but it turned out to be very special and wonderful. And you need to know that I'd never been with a man before either, so it doesn't require an expert."

"What did it require?" Margaret questioned.

"I'm not saying that what worked for Jerry and me will work for everyone, but there were a couple things that helped me, and they may help you. First, we talked for a long time about it, and I told Jerry that I was scared. I told him I wanted it to be special for both of us, but that we'd have to take our time, and he'd have to help me relax. So let it be romantic, let it be a time of discovery, and don't rush the physical part. Take your time, and ask Chester to take his time. Tell him what you like and what you don't like. You may be surprised at how he responds. And listen to him as well. There's no hurry.

"The other thing to remember is that if it doesn't go well the first night, it's not really that important. Think about it. Why does the first night have to be so perfect? The two of you are going to have a lifetime together, so one night becomes insignificant. You have years to make your life together what you want it to be, so don't expect all the bells and whistles the first night!"

The three of them laughed, and Margaret looked somewhat relieved.

"You know, I do feel much better," she said. "We should have talked sooner. Now, I just have one more question."

Ruth and Marjie met each other's glance, then nodded, ready for another bombshell.

"Whyever would you tell me to hold my horses," asked Margaret with a trace of a smile, "when I haven't even a wee dog to my name?"

———————— ✍ ————————

Benjamin was not home when he'd said he would be. Chester arrived after a full day at the Iron Works, and they were already eating dinner by the time Benjamin drove in.

Coming in through the front door, Benjamin smiled and greeted everyone. "Sorry I'm late," he called out, tugging off his coat and hanging it in the closet. "Glad you didn't hold dinner for me."

"With the crazy hours you've been keeping," Marjie joked, "we don't hold anything anymore. Where have you been?"

"I did some visiting, just like I said," replied Benjamin.

"And?" Jerry asked. "Marjie told us you were going to clue us in to whatever discovery you made. What's up?"

"Well, I've been more than one place today," said Benjamin. "But the one visit I made that really counted worked out better than I'd hoped. Chester, I called on your parents today."

A wave of shock rolled around the dining room table, but Chester and Margaret were clearly the most shaken.

"Why?" Chester responded slowly. "You knew they—"

"Precisely why I went to talk with them," interjected Benjamin. "Particularly your father. I thought it might help if an old man like me had a chat with him."

"About what?" Chester continued, perplexed beyond words.

"About the wedding, of course," Benjamin answered. "And, father to father, I talked to him about how he's been treating you and Margaret."

"I can't believe you did that," gasped Chester. "Did he get mad?"

Benjamin nodded. "Very—well, at first. But I don't give up easy. Just ask my son."

"You can say that again," Jerry said.

"So what happened?" asked Margaret. "Can you tell us?"

"Sure." Benjamin's smile widened and he broke into a laugh.

"It took some persuading, but I'm happy to announce that Bill and Clare Stanfeld and family will all be in attendance Saturday at the wedding of their son Chester Stanfeld and the lovely Margaret Harris of Scotland!"

20

MARGARET'S SPECIAL DAY

Marjie sat quietly in front of the bedroom dresser, staring contentedly into the mirror. She was certain it was a miracle that she had managed to squeeze into the tweed suit she had worn on her wedding day. It was the only outfit she owned that seemed nice enough to complement Margaret's beautiful wedding gown. It seemed a miracle, as well, that Ruth had come up with two precious pairs of nylon stockings for her and Margaret—she'd been hoarding them in a Mason jar for just such a special occasion. Marjie's last remaining pair, bought before rationing began, were in sad shape.

Benjamin and Jerry and the baby were downstairs in the living room waiting for her and Margaret. Chester was going to meet them at the church. Margaret had insisted that he not see her before the ceremony, and though he had protested, his words had fallen on deaf ears. If Chester wanted to marry her, she had stated, then he could wait one more hour to see her.

For the first time in about a year, Marjie was truly pleased with how she looked. With Jerry safely home and helping with the baby, and Margaret and Benjamin pitching in, she had finally caught up on her sleep and been able to give her hair and skin the attention they needed. And without a lot of effort, she'd been able to get her figure nearly back into shape. *I think Jerry's going to like what he sees today*, she thought with satisfaction, running the brush through her hair one last time and repositioning the tortoiseshell combs.

Then it dawned on Marjie that Margaret's room had been silent for far too long. Both of them had gone to get dressed at the same time, and even though Marjie had taken her time, she hadn't heard a single creak of the floor or the sound of Margaret's customary humming.

Tiptoeing out of her bedroom and into the hallway, Marjie sneaked toward Margaret's closed door to listen for any movement inside. But she forgot about the creaking floorboard right in front of Margaret's door, and in the hallway's eerie quietness the noise seemed to echo. Marjie grimaced and hoped against hope that Margaret hadn't heard it.

"You're welcome to come in, Marjie, if you like," a muffled voice spoke from behind the painted wooden door.

Marjie shook her head, regretting that she'd been caught, and took the large doorknob in hand, slowly pushing the bedroom door open. Margaret, already in her wedding dress, was sitting motionless on the edge of her bed, her hands folded neatly on her lap.

"I'm sorry," apologized Marjie, looking a bit sheepish. "It was so quiet, I got a little worried you might have escaped out the window or something. Is everything all right?"

"I think so," Margaret responded with a half-smile. "I was just thinking about all the people I love that are here, and all the people I love who're so far away. But it can't be time to go already, can it?"

"Just about," answered Marjie with a look of sympathy. "We need to be there in at least forty-five minutes if you don't want to get Ruth upset with you. She can be a bear when it comes to making sure everyone's on time. I'll bet she's got the ladies on the food committee on a dead run."

"No. We mustn't be late," Margaret agreed, breaking into a sunny smile. "You look just splendid, Marjie. The suit is perfect, and your hair—it's just right. Everyone'll think it's you who's getting married when you walk down the aisle."

"Don't I wish," Marjie said. "They won't even notice me

when they see you. But I am delighted that this suit fits again. I was afraid I'd have to sew up some of those old gunnysacks from the feed mill for a new dress."

"You could make a gunnysack dress look nice today," Margaret spoke softly. "Your face is glowing with life."

"It's called rouge, silly!" Marjie said. "Are you sure you don't want me to add a little color to your cheeks and just a touch of lipstick? Just enough to make Chester's jaw drop when he lifts your veil. How about it?"

Margaret laughed out loud, and her deep blue eyes sparkled with delight. "I've never worn cosmetics before," she confessed, "but there couldn't be a more perfect day to see how well it works! What do I need to do?"

"Just follow me," Marjie urged, turning to go back to her bedroom. "I'll have you fixed up in no time. Say, I forgot that you don't have a long mirror in here. How did you know how your dress looked?"

"I didn't."

"What? Why didn't you come to my room? You know I don't mind."

"I was too nervous to look," Margaret said with a short laugh. "I was frozen to the bed."

"Why?"

"I just don't think I'm ready for this," Margaret murmured. "Chester deserves someone better."

Marjie looked at Margaret and gently shook her head. "If you don't beat all, Margaret Harris. You're serious again, aren't you?"

"Oh yes."

"Take my hand and let's finish getting you ready," Marjie said, reaching out to Margaret and gently pulling her up from the bed. "Marriage isn't about deserving anything. It's about being a gift to each other. And today Chester Stanfeld is requesting that you become a gift to him. That's what you want, right?"

"More than anything in the world."

"Then accept his love for you just the way you are," Marjie

counseled. "You don't have to become anything different than you are. But you've got to relax and enjoy this. This is your special day, Margaret. Once in a lifetime. Let's celebrate it!"

Marjie gave Margaret a big hug, and they both broke into laughter.

"You're just the sister I always needed!" exclaimed Margaret. "This is going to be grand, in spite of me. So take your paintbrush and see what you can do. I've a hankerin' to see Chester's jaw drop!"

––––––– ∽ –––––––

Half an hour later the Macmillans and Margaret were climbing out of Benjamin's car in the church parking lot, and Ruth immediately whisked the bride and the matron of honor to the back office of the church, which doubled as a bridal room for weddings. Jerry hurried to the basement to join Chester and the pastor before going up the back stairway to take their places at the front of the church. Benjamin, wearing a burp cloth over the shoulder of his carefully brushed old suit, took little Martha and went to find Sarah, who had already found a seat near the front of the church. After handing the baby over to her grandmother, he took a seat in the back and waited for his time to walk Margaret down the aisle.

"Everything's ready, Margaret!" Ruth announced as she and Marjie helped pin the veil into place in Margaret's hair. "There must be at least two hundred people out there already."

The wedding co-conspirators pinned the last loose strands of Margaret's hair back into position, then stepped back to take one last look.

The afternoon sunshine streaming into the office dazzled her dress to an intense whiteness. The narrow waistline and gently flaring skirt highlighted her graceful figure, and the delicate veil floated gently over her shimmering brunette curls. Narrow, upturned lips broke into a smile, and Margaret asked, "You approve, then?"

"I've never seen anyone more beautiful in all my life!" whispered Marjie, shaking her head in wonder.

"Magnificent," Ruth spoke in a hushed tone, nodding her agreement. "Truly magnificent. I doubted before, but now I believe."

"What?" asked Margaret.

"That you were in fact an angel," confessed Ruth. "Forgive me."

All three broke into laughter, and both Marjie and Ruth took turns giving Margaret a hug and wishing her the best. Then, as if on cue, Ruth snapped back into her coordinator role and grabbed her "to do" list.

"Let's see," she mumbled to herself, pointing her index finger two-thirds of the way down the page. "Marjie, you've got Chester's ring, right?"

Marjie gave Ruth a blank stare and replied, "No. I thought you had it."

"For crying out loud, I don't have it!" Ruth scolded. "Didn't you have it, Margaret?"

A deep frown creased Margaret's serene expression as she shook her head no. "I gave it to you yesterday."

"No, you didn't, Margaret!" Ruth protested. "I would have remembered. Think! Think hard! What did you do with it? We've only got a couple of minutes to go!"

Margaret put her hand up under the veil and covered her eyes, then her shoulders began to shake up and down.

"Don't cry!" Ruth gasped. "Don't cry! We'll think of something. Just pretend. That's it. Just act like you're putting the ring on Chester. We can find it later. Oh, please don't cry!"

With that, neither Margaret nor Marjie could hold it in any longer, and they both burst into laughter. Ruth's expression instantly changed from intense anxiety to suspicious bewilderment.

"Gotcha!" Marjie sputtered as she laughed. "You've misjudged Margaret, Ruthie. She's no angel, but she's a wonderful actress. I have the ring right here!" She opened her hand to reveal a shiny gold wedding band.

Margaret was still laughing so hard that she couldn't talk. The combination of Ruth's comical panic and her own wedding nerves reduced her to helpless hilarity. "Hook, line, and sinker," Margaret gasped as she struggled to contain herself. "That's how Marjie said you'd swallow this. I'm sorry. It was Marjie that thought of it."

Ruth curled her lips, then slowly broke into a mild chuckle. "Very funny, ladies. And I thought we were friends. With Marjie involved, I should have expected a trick—but I wouldn't have dreamed you two could set me up like that. There's no time now, but I guarantee that I'm not through with the two of you. Before the sun falls this fine day, you shall indeed feel the intense burning of my eternal wrath!"

This time they all laughed together, and Ruth moved toward the door. "You're on, ladies," she said as she pushed it open with a courtly sweep. "No more jokes, and give it your best. Save some of that lovely smile for Chester, Margaret."

Marjie stepped out the door first and was immediately greeted by Benjamin who stood beaming in the foyer. He looked every bit the proud father waiting to give away his only daughter in holy matrimony.

"The organist is down to the last arrangement before the processional," he whispered to Marjie as she gave him a kiss on the cheek. "We better get into position."

"Do you really dare walk such a grand lady down the aisle?" Marjie asked, pointing back at Margaret.

Benjamin turned and smiled from ear to ear. "You bet I dare," he answered without hesitation, formally offering her his arm. "Miss Margaret Harris, you look exquisite! Are you ready, bonny lass?"

"As ready as I'll ever be, Father Macmillan," she answered shyly, crooking a delicate arm through his.

"Then let's go," Benjamin declared, patting her hand with his free one and stepping with her behind Marjie.

They followed Marjie until she stopped at the back of the long sanctuary aisle. Marjie turned around and whispered to Benjamin, "Are Chester's folks here?"

"Front row on the right," he nodded, turning toward Margaret. "Suit and tie, fancy dress. They look as happy as peas in a pod."

"Did my ma make it?"

"Front row on the left, just where Margaret asked that she'd sit. Next to me."

Margaret gave Marjie a smirk and opened her mouth to say something, but then held it back and simply shrugged her shoulders. Just then the organist paused for a moment, catching everyone's attention, and moved into the processional. Marjie got the distinct impression that Margaret knew something she wasn't telling, but with the congregation standing and turning to look at them, now was not the time to discover the secret.

To the rhythm of Wagner's bridal march, Marjie smiled and stepped slowly and elegantly down the aisle. Her dark brown eyes were focused solely upon Jerry, who stood waiting for her at the front of the sanctuary in the center of the aisle, beaming a smile of loving anticipation. For just a few steps Marjie forgot that it wasn't her wedding. *I love you, Jerry Macmillan,* she thought, *and I take you to be my husband this day.* And when she remembered where she was, she decided to go ahead and treat the ceremony as if it were their own.

As she reached for Jerry's arm, Marjie glanced over at her mother quickly and was surprised at how young and pretty she looked at first glance, with a freshly pressed navy blue dress and her hair newly permed and even some rouge on her cheeks. Little Martha, held upright in her grandmother's lap, kicked and waved her arms at the sight of her mother. But there was no time to stop and greet any of them. Marjie took Jerry's arm and they stepped up the stairs in the front, then separated at the landing to find their positions on either side.

Turning toward the congregation, Marjie nearly burst into tears at the sight of Margaret and Benjamin slowly moving down the aisle. The congregation was transfixed by Margaret's elegant beauty. Benjamin was smiling so hard that Marjie was afraid his face would crack. And poor Chester looked like he was about to faint in disbelief, overwhelmed with wonder that this radiant creature was choosing to marry him.

Then Marjie's attention was caught by Bill and Clare Stanfeld, who stood in the front row with Chester's two teenaged brothers. Of all the people to be crying already, Marjie couldn't believe that Chester's father would be red-faced, with what looked like tears of joy pouring down the hard lines of his face. Through his tears, which he made no attempt to hide, he was beaming at his daughter-in-law-to-be with a wide smile of approval. His wife, smiling a bit more nervously, cast an occasional glance sideways toward her husband, as if she was waiting for him to change his mind.

Margaret stopped as she reached the front and whispered something to Benjamin. Then she let go of his arm and moved over to Chester, whose jaw was still in the upper position but looked suspiciously close to dropping to his knees. She took his arm, and they stepped up the stairs together while Benjamin remained standing in the aisle.

Jerry and Marjie locked eyes as Chester and Margaret came to the landing and took their positions in front of Pastor Fitchen. Then they turned to face the pastor as well, and the processional was ended.

A spirit of joy seemed to have fallen upon the aging minister, and Marjie thought for a second that he had forgotten his opening lines. He just stood there grinning and studying the faces of the two young people whose hearts he was about to join together as one. Whatever was going through his head, he finally recovered and took a deep breath.

"This is the day that the Lord hath made, let us rejoice and be glad in it," he called out in a tone of authority that the members hadn't heard for years. "Yes," he continued, "let us rejoice in this happy occasion."

And then began the familiar ceremony, "Dearly beloved, we are gathered together here in the sight of God and in the presence of these witnesses to join this man and this woman in holy matrimony, which is an honorable estate, instituted by God, and signifying unto us the mystical union which exists between Christ and His church. It is not to be entered into unadvisedly, but reverently, discreetly, and in the fear of God. Into this holy estate these two persons now come to be joined.

"Who giveth this woman to be married to this man?"

Benjamin had stood his ground patiently and let a pause shift the congregation's attention to his words. Looking directly at the pastor, he called out, "The Reverend Thomas Harris of Glasgow, Scotland, and his wife Barbara do."

And with his duty done, Benjamin took his seat next to Sarah Livingstone, who looked as proud of him as he did of Margaret.

21

ONLY ONE, AND THAT'S YOU

"I'm so tired I could curl up and die," Jerry moaned. He and Marjie were snuggled together on the davenport. "This choring-alone business in the morning after a late night is for the birds."

"Benjamin would have come out," replied Marjie, running her fingers through his lank blond hair. "I think he felt bad about leaving."

Jerry pinched his lips together and shook his head. "Not too bad. With the cold snap, he seemed pretty set on driving out to take your mother to church this morning. Besides, it gave us a good reason to skip. The wedding yesterday filled my quota for church-time this week."

"Do you realize this is the first time in a month that we've had this place to ourselves?" Marjie asked.

Jerry nodded. "I've noticed," he said quietly, his kisses growing a bit more intense. "That was another reason I thought it might not hurt to miss a church service once. How long's Martha going to be napping?"

"Plenty of time," Marjie answered, kissing him lightly on the cheek. "And plenty of time for you to take a bath. You smell like a cow."

"I took a bath yesterday," Jerry protested mildly.

"Good for you," teased Marjie. "Two baths in two days. Is that a record, or what? I want you to smell good and to shave those whiskers."

"It's a deal, if I can take a nap this afternoon," he bargained.

"You got a deal, sailor boy," Marjie laughed. "By the way, Teddy's coming over after lunch sometime, but you don't need to get up. Said he had something important to talk with *me* about."

"I wonder what's wrong now?" Jerry grumped. "It's probably a good thing I'll be sleeping."

"He wouldn't say what's on his mind," Marjie added. "Hopefully it's nothing big. But I wouldn't bet the farm on it."

"You can say that again," Jerry replied. "Whatever it is, don't even think about giving him any money."

"And I have money to spare?" Marjie raised her eyebrows and shook her head. "That's one worry that shouldn't affect your nap, Mr. Scrooge."

Jerry did not respond, and for the moment the living room fell silent. An occasional gust of icy wind rattling the front door and the creaking of the house were the only noises to disturb them.

"I love the quiet here on the farm," Marjie said after a while. "But it's going to be strange around here without Margaret, don't you think? I'm going to miss her."

"I think I will, too," Jerry said. "Funny how easy she fit in, like she'd lived here all her life. Chester really got himself a sweetheart."

"I never met anyone like her," Marjie agreed. "Are you jealous of Chester?"

"Now, what kind of question is that?" he asked, pulling away from her a little.

"I'm serious," she said. "Do you wish you would have found someone as wonderful as Margaret instead of me?"

"This is stupid."

"No, it's not," Marjie insisted. "She's always kind and gentle. She's beautiful, even without makeup. She sings like an angel and knows the Bible forward and backward. She's perfect."

"No one's perfect," Jerry stated. "She's everything you say, and probably more, but she's not perfect. And I have one very big problem with Margaret that I haven't dared talk about."

Marjie stopped rubbing Jerry's head. "What? Did she do something?"

"Of course not!" exclaimed Jerry. "Nothing bad. But I ain't sure I want to talk about it. You're getting upset already."

"You better keep talking or you will see me upset," she demanded. "Are you joking with me?"

Jerry laughed and realized he had better stop teasing before he spoiled the morning for both of them. "Okay. No more jokes. My big problem with Margaret don't have nothing to do with whether she's pretty or sings good or knows the Bible. It's more basic."

"So what is it?"

"Just that I happen to be in love with you," Jerry declared, then kissed her long and warmly. "And I ain't in love with Margaret Harris Stanfeld or any other woman on this earth. Only one, and that's you. Besides, I got married to you again yesterday."

"What?"

"I said my vows all over again when we were standing there with Chester and Margaret. When you were walking down the aisle, I wished we were getting married all over again, so I decided to just pretend it was our wedding, too."

"So did I," Marjie whispered with a pinch of wonder in her voice. "When Margaret repeated her vows, I did it too. I almost felt like I meant those words more yesterday than I did when we were married."

Jerry laughed to himself quietly. "That's what I thought, too. I suppose it's because we understand what they mean a lot better now."

Marjie just smiled and nodded.

"Are you ever sorry you said the words a year ago?" Jerry asked.

"You can't mean it."

"I can mean it," he answered. "I thought about it as I was saying those vows to myself. You could've found somebody like Chester that's going to be a preacher, or you could have married a businessman or one of them doctors in Rochester. So maybe you've had some second thoughts about being stuck with a dumb farmer who stinks like a cow?"

"You make me so mad," Marjie blurted and pinched him hard on the arm. "I love you because you're you. And I happen to be crazy about farmers! I even like the smell of cows!"

"Enough to—"

"No. There's a limit, and you're over. Head for the bathtub, and don't forget to use the soap!"

———— ✎ ————

Marjie heard the old truck's rattling fenders before she actually saw it pull into the driveway. Carrying Martha over to the window, Marjie watched as Ted Livingstone jumped out of his truck and pulled his coat up to try keeping his ears warm.

"Just like always—no hat," she commented to Martha, shaking her head. Then she remembered all the times they'd played together in the snow when they were kids, and how he hated to wear any type of headgear. Marjie chuckled and suddenly felt a wave of sisterly love well up, refreshing the part of her heart that had grown parched by anger and resentment.

As Ted dashed up the sidewalk, Marjie stepped to the door and pulled it open. The bright sunshine off the fresh coat of snow blinded Martha's eyes, and she gave such a jerk that Ted thought she was going to fly out of Marjie's arms.

"Whoa! little dolly!" he called out as he hustled through the doorway, causing Martha to jerk again in surprise. "I'm sorry! Didn't mean to scare her. You must have been feeding her some Mexican jumping beans!"

"I guess," Marjie said, backing into the dining room. "Put your coat in the closet. Where's your hat, Teddy?"

"You know better than to think I'm going to answer that question," Ted replied as he shoved his coat in the closet and turned around with a smile. "How's my favorite niece?"

"Favorite as in only niece," Marjie corrected. "She's been missing you lately. And so have I. Why don't we ever see you anymore?"

"It's a long story," answered Ted. "You don't want to know."

"Try me," Marjie suggested. "You hungry?"

"No. I'm fine. I ate before I came. Ma had a roast ready for Benjamin after they got back from church, and I had a nibble."

"Meaning you left enough for them—maybe," said Marjie, looking at her brother suspiciously. "The last time I heard you say you had a nibble, you'd devoured a whole chocolate cake."

"You don't forgot a thing, do you?" Ted responded with a tight little laugh, taking Martha from Marjie's arms and finding a seat at the dining room table. "I left them plenty, I promise. But I will take a cup of hot coffee. The heater in my truck gave up the ghost, and I'm stiff as a bone from the cold."

Marjie went into the kitchen to get Ted his coffee, but first she put a bottle of milk on to warm.

"Where's Jerry?" Ted called out.

"He's trying to take a nap, so hold it down a notch," Marjie urged, coming around the kitchen counter into the dining room. "As soon as her bottle is ready, you can feed Martha. I thought you might like that."

"Thanks," Ted said, taking a sip of the coffee. "Being the youngest didn't give me many chances to hold a baby. Other than your dumb dolls."

"You liked those 'dumb' dolls when you were little," Marjie said. "But I'll never tell."

"Right," he mumbled. "Like you wouldn't play the ace of spades if you had a chance."

"I never said that," Marjie replied innocently, turning to go check on the bottle. "There's no mercy when we're playing cards."

"Don't I remember?" Ted said. "Paul used to call you Matilda the Hun. You were mean."

"He's older than us," Marjie said, returning to the dining room and handing Ted the warm bottle of milk. "He's just not very good at counting cards."

Marjie sat down across the table from her brother and stared at him affectionately. He was busy getting the nipple into Martha's mouth and watching her take the first few sucks. *I wish we could go back and be kids again*, Marjie thought. *Everything was a lot simpler back then.*

"So what's up, Teddy?" Marjie asked when he finally looked at her. "Are you going to tell me the long story, or is there something else on your mind?"

Ted took a deep breath and leaned back in his chair as far as he could. He fixed his eyes on Marjie, and she could clearly see the pain that he had stuffed deep down inside. He hesitated, seeming to consider whether he really wanted to talk.

"I'm sorry Linda hurt you so bad, Teddy," Marjie began, hoping to get him to open up. "You really did love her, didn't you?"

Ted nodded and kept staring into Marjie's dark brown eyes. Drawing in another deep breath, he finally said, "I had my whole life planned around her. Had the wedding day all set. Then she spots another good-looking guy and tosses me away like an old bone. I should've seen the writing on the wall, I suppose. She'd done the same thing to a dozen guys in front of me. But I thought she loved me, for some stupid reason."

"She was one of the prettiest girls in the county," Marjie responded. "Suppose that had something to do with it."

A curling smile broke out on her brother's face, and he nodded again. "You hit the nail on the head with that one. I couldn't believe anyone so beautiful would think I was handsome enough to go out with me. She'd bat those baby blues at me and I'd fall off my chair. And I ended up face down in the gutter."

"Nobody said you had to stay there," Marjie challenged.

"I been trying to get out," he responded. "Especially since Jerry drove me home that night. What he said helped more than anything else—even more than getting thrown in jail. Trouble is, the only time I feel good is when I'm drunk."

"And I reckon you feel even better in the morning?"

"You reckon wrong," he said through a rueful grin. "But it doesn't seem to make much difference. Feeling good for a few hours always seems worth it."

"Do you realize how much you're hurting Ma?" asked Marjie. "Ask her what it was like to watch her uncle die when the booze wrecked his liver. I love you with all my heart, Teddy, but I'm going to be honest with you. You may as well drive a spike in her heart as keep this up."

For a moment Marjie saw a spark of anger in his eyes, but it was quickly tamped down. "That's why I'm here." He spoke determinedly. "If only for Ma's sake, I've got to get away."

Martha had pushed away the nipple, and Ted handed her across the table to Marjie. "Better show me what you do next," he said. "I've never burped a kid before."

Putting a towel across her shoulder, Marjie placed the baby there and lightly patted her on the back. "You keep talking," she said. "What do you mean by 'get away'? Leave the farm?"

"That's right."

"But where?" she queried. "Are you moving in with one of those guys you've been running around with?"

"Nope," he answered. "I have to 'leave' leave—get clean away from this area—or I'm gonna go crazy."

Marjie kept patting Martha's back, but she was too stunned to be aware of what she was doing. "You're going to leave Ma alone to care for the farm? You can't be serious."

Ted shook his head that he was in fact serious, but his smile was long since erased. He rubbed his temples and cheeks with his hands. "If I stay, I'll keep on drinking, and that'll kill her to watch. If I leave, maybe I can make a new start. And if not, at least Ma won't have to see me in the gutter anymore."

"She'd have to sell the farm. You thought about that?"

"Is that worse than watching me kill myself?" he retorted. "Sure, I've thought about it. Do you think I'm that stupid? I don't want to see her off the farm, but I just can't live there any longer."

Marjie looked down at Martha, who was nearly asleep already. "Have you talked to Ma yet?"

"No," he said. "I thought I'd talk with you first."

"So where're you thinking about going?"

"The army," he said promptly. "I've already talked with the county war board. As soon as I say I'm ready, I'll be gone."

"Paul's already out fighting in North Africa under Eisenhower, and now you're going to join as well?" Marjie asked, still hoping he didn't mean it. "Ma's going to have to sell the farm, move somewhere, and then worry herself sick about two boys surviving the war."

"The farm is the only reason I'm not in the war with Paul now," Ted countered. "If I'm not working on the farm, I have no choice but to go. Besides, I'm sick of feeling like a coward who's hiding behind his mother's skirts. I've waited long enough. I want to be there when they drive Hitler back to Germany. Maybe I'd be the lucky one to put a bullet in him."

Marjie could see that there was no talking her brother out of his decision. But she still searched for words to protest it.

"Give it up, Marjie," Ted said. "I can see the gears grinding in your head. I'm going. I have to get out of there. Sooner or later I would go anyway, so Ma would have to face it sometime. I don't want to farm for the rest of my life, and I don't think it's fair to expect me to stay home forever just so Ma can stay there. It's gotten so bad that I hate the place."

Marjie didn't like the way he said the last sentence, but she could see his point. If Ted truly didn't want to farm, she agreed with him that something should be done. "Could you at least wait until the farm is sold and Ma has somewhere to go?" she asked by way of a compromise. "The war's not going to end tomorrow, much as I wish it would. Could you wait until everything here is settled?"

"I'll give it until spring planting," replied Ted. "If I don't set a date, you know full well that Ma won't get serious about the move."

Marjie nodded grimly. "When are you going to break the news to her?"

"Tonight. After chores. I thought you might want to come over."

"Not tonight, Teddy," she said. "I'm the one who'll have to help her cope once you leave. It's your decision, and you've got to learn to start taking responsibility for your decisions. If it breaks her heart, you better not run away from her and grab your bottle. Bravery in war starts with courage at home," she added, getting to her feet, "and you can start being a man tonight."

22

THUNDER AND LIGHTNING

"Ruthie, aren't you hanging around for Sunday school?" Marjie asked after the morning worship service. "If we have to stay and listen to Edna, you've got to be there to protect us poor ignorant folks who swallow everything she says."

"Sorry," Ruth answered, stopping to talk, "but you're on your own today. Dad asked the Weavers over for lunch, and I'm not finished cooking the meal. Don't tell Edna I said that, though. She'll launch her infamous story about not sewing up a hem on Sunday. Why don't you skip, too? Chester's going to be back teaching next week."

"Normally I'd love to skip, but I have a hunch there's going to be a thunder and lightning show," Marjie suggested with her wry smirk. "I'll bet you're going to regret missing today."

"You're the worst pest," Ruth scolded, rolling her dark eyes and pinching Marjie's arm lightly. "What's going on? I *can't* stay, so tell me!"

Marjie shrugged and smiled blankly. "I can't say for sure, because I really don't know. But Benjamin's been studying the Sunday school lesson all week, and I think he's got his gun loaded for bear. By the time this class is over, I'm willing to bet some cold cash that Edna Harper will wish that Benjamin Macmillan had stayed to home."

"What did he say about it?" asked Ruth, pulling Marjie off to the side of the foyer.

"Nothing."

"So how do you know what he's thinking?"

"I don't," answered Marjie. "But he's got the look in his eyes that's only there when he's got something brewing inside, and the quieter he gets, the more important it is. Are you absolutely sure you can't stay, Ruthie?"

"Shoot, you should have called me yesterday," Ruth answered, shaking her head. "I told the Weavers to come right after church, and if I stay for Sunday school I just can't be ready in time. But they'll be in the class, so maybe they'll give me the scoop on what happens. By the way, I see your mother is here this morning. Did Teddy actually talk to her like he said he would?"

"Who knows?" said Marjie. "If he did, she's not said a peep. I think he chickened out. But I don't dare ask Ma, because I'm not about to tell her for him. He used to sucker me into doing his talking for him. It would be just like him to do it again."

"Don't let him do it," Ruth counseled. "But let me know if you find out anything. And I'll call you this afternoon to find out what happened in Sunday school, so take notes! See you."

Marjie had wanted to ask Ruth about her date with Peter Boyd the evening before, but she only barely managed to say goodbye before her friend was out of earshot. She laughed at how fast Ruth could move when she had a job she wanted to get done, then she headed downstairs to the Sunday school classroom.

Sitting on a hard wooden folding chair between her mother and Jerry, Marjie looked around. She was surprised by how many church members had stayed. Since Chester had taken over the class, the attendance had doubled, and it appeared that many of them didn't realize that Chester was taking off one more Sunday after his wedding. When Edna made her starchy appearance, a few daring souls made a quick dash for the doors.

But the rest were trapped before they could gather their wits.

"Look at her," Marjie whispered to her mother, directing Sarah's gaze to the front of the class. Edna Harper's jet black hair was tied in a severe bun, and Marjie thought Edna's frown had deepened since the last time she'd seen her. "I hope you're ready for this."

Sarah raised her eyebrows and nodded. "Benjamin warned me," she murmured. "He told me I might want to cover my ears."

Marjie chuckled and noticed that Benjamin had his Bible open and was studying a section intently. "What's he got up his sleeve?" she asked her mother.

"I don't have a clue," Sarah answered. "Why?"

Marjie whispered, "Never mind. We'll see what happens. But hang on to your chair."

The class began with Edna's usual deadly monotone, and Marjie was amazed at how quickly some of the veterans of the class could doze off. It was almost as if they had a switch inside that could be thrown at a moment's notice, ushering them into dreamland. As Edna droned on, Marjie's own eyelids began to feel heavy but she forced them to stay open. She wanted to know what the topic was in case Benjamin got into a discussion. Marjie wished she had picked up a copy of the printed lesson, but it appeared that only Benjamin had one, and his copy had several pencil notations scratched on it.

When she finally figured out that the lesson was about the Holy Ghost, Marjie looked over at Jerry, whose eyes were already dropping into a deep swoon. Poking him in the side, she whispered, "What is a Holy Ghost? Something like a graveyard ghost?"

The poke in Jerry's ribs had temporarily resuscitated him, and he shrugged his shoulders. "I really don't know," he answered softly. "We say it every Sunday in the creed, 'I believe in the Holy Ghost,' but your guess is as good as mine."

Marjie gave him a "thanks a lot" look and wondered what it was about this lesson that could have caused Benjamin to study so hard. Edna droned on without seeming to say anything meaningful, and after another five minutes, Marjie threw in the towel, giving up hope of making any sense of the mysterious ghost business. Jerry struggled to keep his head erect, and Marjie's attention switched to counting his nods between attempts to open his eyes.

When Edna finally paused and asked if anyone had questions about what she had covered so far, the only one who raised a hand was Benjamin. Edna gave a smug smile and said, "Yes, Benjamin."

"You're covering a lot of information that I don't understand much about," Benjamin piped up. "But I've done a lot of reading about it this week. Do you mind me asking a few questions that have me stumped?"

"Not at all," Edna replied. "But I'd like to stick to the lesson."

"I'll try," Benjamin assured her. "You said earlier that the Holy Ghost is a person, right?"

"That's right," Edna commented. "The third person of the Trinity. There is God the Father, Jesus Christ the Son, and the Holy Ghost. You're familiar with the Apostles' Creed?"

"Yes, of course," Benjamin stated, "but I've said it for over fifty years and I still don't understand much about the Holy Ghost. If the Holy Ghost is a person, can I know Him like I know you?"

A puzzled expression spread across Edna's face, but she didn't attempt an answer. The question, though unanswered, did serve to perk up the ears of most of the people in the class, however.

"Did you read the beginning chapters of the Book of Acts?" Benjamin continued.

"Parts of them," Edna responded, trying to recover, "but I'm well acquainted with those chapters. What about them?"

"If the Holy Ghost is a person," Benjamin queried as everyone in the class turned to listen, "and if He came in a powerful rushing wind on the Day of Pentecost and filled the house where the disciples were praying and then filled the lives of the disciples and caused them to speak with other tongues . . . well, then, should we expect that He'll do the same thing today if we asked Him?"

"No!" sputtered Edna, totally caught off guard. "That was only for the Book of Acts."

"Where does it say that?" persisted Benjamin.

"Well, I'm not sure, but—"

"This week I've read the accounts in the Book of Acts and several references in Paul's Epistles," Benjamin explained, "and I didn't find anything that suggested the Holy Ghost was supposed to be limited to Acts. And I discovered many references that tell of other people who were filled with the Holy Ghost *after* the Day of Pentecost. Obviously, He didn't change His method after the first day.

"And there's something else," Benjamin went on. "We're commanded in several places to be filled with the Holy Ghost. But what does that mean, exactly? I've gone to church all my life, and I've never once heard someone say they were filled with the Holy Ghost. How could something that was so clearly understood in the early church become such a mystery in ours? Do you know?"

Edna's expression was now a complete blank. Marjie could see that Benjamin may as well have asked her to explain how big God is. But that did not mean that Edna had given up. It took her just a few minutes to regroup.

"The Holy Ghost has given us the Word of God to live our lives by," she defended, lifting up her large black Bible. "It is our only standard for life and godliness. Once the Word of God was complete, the outward demonstrations of the Holy Ghost ceased. To abandon the scripture standard is to come under the sway of emotionalism. Are you proposing that we call the Holy Rollers back and all start jumping up and down this morning?"

Several of the class members broke out into laughter, and Edna surprised everyone by smiling herself. No one there, including Marjie, wanted to see a return of the traveling "revival" shows that set up camp periodically in the area and left emotional chaos in their wake. But Benjamin was not about to give in so easily.

"Edna, you mistake my purpose," he persisted, raising his voice above the whispers the discussion had aroused. "I ain't suggesting we jump up and down, and I ain't suggesting we should speak in other tongues. But it troubles me that we don't see God at work in our lives like He was at work in the early church. Doesn't that trouble you?"

"I suppose," Edna conceded uncertainly. "But God is sovereign, Benjamin. He does what He wants, when He wants."

Benjamin rubbed his forehead. "God's sovereignty is another issue for another lesson. Could I tell you about the Bible verses I've been studying for this week's lesson?"

Edna nodded for him to continue.

"Well, I've become convinced that the difference between us and the New Testament Church is that they knew what it meant to be filled with the Holy Ghost and power. I've never understood it myself, so I came hoping that you or someone else here this morning could help me out."

At this point Benjamin paused and looked around. But nobody spoke, not even Edna, so he went on, "I've been reading the Bible all my life, but it's only been in the past year that I felt I understood it in a way that helped me live my life. And then I read what the apostle Paul prayed for the church in Ephesus"—here he flipped the pages and then read aloud—" 'that the Father of glory may give unto you the spirit of wisdom and revelation in the knowledge of him: the eyes of your understanding being enlightened; that ye may know what is the hope of his calling.' And that's what I think's been happening to me— the eyes of my understanding are being opened. Now, who could do that to my blind eyes but the Holy Ghost?

"And then there's what Jesus said in John's gospel." He flipped again. " 'Howbeit when he, the Spirit of truth, is come, he will guide you into all truth.' Now, that verse seems pretty clear that even the Word of God remains a darkened book unless the Holy Ghost shines His light upon it. Yet we don't claim to know the Holy Ghost. How can we be guided by someone we don't even know?"

He closed the Bible and tucked it under his arm. "You know

what I think happens when the Holy Ghost isn't involved in our lives today? The truth that Jesus said would set us free ends up being cold and sterile, and we use it sort of like the Pharisees we're always poking fun at. We build our own lists of what it means to be a Christian, yet Christianity's never come alive inside our own hearts.

"I personally have felt like one of those poor disciples of John the Baptist that Paul discovered living in Ephesus. He asked them, 'Have you received the Holy Ghost?' And they answered him that they hadn't even heard of the Holy Ghost. And I wonder, are we any better off than they were?"

Edna had no response this time, except to look down at her notes as if she were going back to where she was before Benjamin took over. But before she could restart the class, Billy Wilson spoke up.

"I believe that what you're saying is the absolute truth, Benjamin, even if it pinches our toes. Back some weeks ago I made my confession of faith, and I heard later that some people thought it was wrong for me to say that God revealed himself to me, that God no longer does that. But if God can reveal himself to Paul on the Damascus Road, who am I to tell Him He can't give me a glimpse of the same? Now I ain't even close to being the apostle Paul, but I know that He opened my heart. And I know that I can say, 'Once I was blind, but now I see.' If that's not the Bible, what is? And if that isn't what the Holy Ghost does, who else brought me to believe? The devil?"

Marjie noticed that the longer Billy went, the more agitated Jerry became. He sat up straighter and straighter and began to quietly clear his throat. Then finally the need to speak overcame his fear of speaking and he addressed the group as well.

"Who met me in the water and filled my heart with the peace of God? And who was it that reminded me of all my sin, all the bad things I had done? When I bowed my head, I saw my sin as plain as the waves and the oil and the flames. Chester told me that was the work of the Holy Ghost, although I don't claim to know much about it."

One of the older women in the class had been searching

through her Bible, then turned around to listen to Jerry. "I never thought I'd dare tell anyone what happened to me when Bud was lying in the hospital bed after the stroke," she said when Jerry had finished. "I guess I thought no one would believe me. Late one night after all the visitors had left the room, I knelt alongside his bed and tried to pray, but I couldn't. All I could do was cry out to God for help."

She hesitated, almost as if she were gathering her courage, then continued, "All of a sudden I found myself praying for Bud with words that I knew I wasn't thinking up. When Hannah was praying for a son, the prophet Samuel thought she was drunk because all he saw was her lips moving. And as I prayed and the words rose and fell from my heart, I was overwhelmed with a sense that Bud was truly in the hands of God, and that if he died, I would be okay. There was someone bigger than just me in that hospital room that night.

"Later I came across a verse in Romans that I think makes sense of what happened." She picked up her Bible to the place she had found and began to read, " 'Likewise the Spirit also helpeth our infirmities: for we know not what we should pray as we ought: but the Spirit itself maketh intercession for us with groanings which cannot be uttered.' "

She let her Bible drop and spoke intently to the people around her, "If that wasn't the Holy Ghost, I have no explanation for what happened to me in the hospital. It certainly wasn't me. But it helped me."

Several more members who were never known to say much in the class added their personal stories of how they felt the Holy Ghost had intervened in their lives. Marjie was wishing Ruth had stayed, for a time like this was rare in their church; people simply did not talk about anything so personal. Then Marjie noticed that her mother was sitting forward in her chair, waiting for her chance to break in. *Now I believe in miracles!* she thought.

"I'm not a member of this church," Sarah said respectfully, looking at Edna. "May I speak?"

Edna simply nodded.

"I don't understand much of what's been said here," Sarah acknowledged. "And I've never been big on church. To tell you the truth, I didn't see or hear much that ever impressed me. But I faced a problem with my son recently and asked my daughter, Marjie, to pray for him with me. When we bowed our heads, I can only describe what happened by saying that the presence of God filled the room. I was afraid to open my eyes for fear that I'd lose sight of what my soul could see. Call me crazy if you like, but I'll never trade that reality for anything else in this world. God was with me, and He was as real as anyone in this room.

"I think it would be good," Sarah continued, "if we stopped and asked the Holy Ghost to do in our lives just what the Scriptures say He will do. I'd like to spend the rest of my life, however long or short it is, walking in God's presence. And I want Him to live inside me so that I become more like what He is like. I know that won't happen unless He does something special in me."

A hush fell, and Sarah's suggestion did not require an answer from anyone in the room. One by one, all around the room, members bowed their heads and hearts to God and sought Him in a way that they had never sought Him before. And many that day found healing as they touched the hem of His passing garment.

23

GORILLA

Jerry pumped his brakes lightly to keep the black Ford from swerving, but his most seasoned ice-driving skills could not prevent the car from slowly gliding through the stop sign and toward the deep ditch.

"Hang on!" Jerry called out, pumping the brake pedal in one last desperate attempt to keep control. "We're going over!"

Marjie hung on to the leather handrest and braced herself for a crash. But the Ford's front wheels simply dropped over the edge of the ditch into the deep snow and brought the car to a sudden halt.

"Whew!" gasped Jerry. "That was close!"

Marjie loosened her grip and let her head fall back against the top of the car seat. "Close to what?" she whispered. "The whole front end is in the ditch."

"Close to dropping the whole car in," answered Jerry, taking a deep breath of cold air. "A couple more feet and this old buggy would be sitting here till spring."

"Sounds like a good idea," Marjie sputtered, shaking her head. "I've never been so scared to be on the road before. The road is like an ice rink. Let's leave the car here and walk the rest of the way. Maybe the sun will cut through the glaze before we need to head back."

"We can't leave the car sitting here with half of it hanging out for the next guy to smack into."

"What guy?" protested Marjie, looking both ways down the road. "We're the only one's crazy enough to be out on the road today."

"This wasn't my idea, if you recall," Jerry said. "It's *your* brother that's got problems with that breech calf. And *you* were the one who promised we'd come over and help deliver it."

"And *you* were . . ." Marjie's voice trailed off as she realized the truth in what he was saying. "You were crazy enough to listen to me. Don't you know better than that by now."

She gave a little chuckle and smiled at Jerry. "This is a stupid thing to fight about," she said. "We're just lucky that we didn't bring Martha along. Good thing she's safe and sound with her grandpa."

Jerry nodded and took Marjie's hand. "I'm sorry for getting so worked up," he confessed. "Guess I'm a little edgy from the roads. But we need to get the car out of the ditch."

"How?"

"I've got the shovel in the back to dig us loose," Jerry answered, pulling his cap down over his ears and looking down the road again. "You stay in here and get behind the wheel. When I wave, I want you to try backing the car up. Maybe we can manage to get ourselves out. Otherwise, I'll walk down to that farm we just passed."

"Matsons' place."

"You know them?"

"I know everyone around here," Marjie reminded him. "I went to school with their son, Clarence. We called him Gorilla. If you saw him, you'd understand why."

"Sounds like he might be useful," Jerry said as he pushed the car door open and stepped into the frigid February breeze. "Watch for my signal."

Jerry pulled the shovel from the trunk and stooped to assess the predicament. Shrugging his shoulders, he jumped into the ditch and began to clear the snow away from the bottom of the car.

It didn't take long for Marjie to grow impatient, so she

opened the door and carefully stepped around to the front of the car. "How's it look?" she called out.

"Not too bad," Jerry answered, pausing for a moment and studying the mess he was in. "The front's not as packed as I thought it would be. Give it a try. Maybe she'll go."

"I'd prefer you to try it," Marjie suggested. "I'm still shaking from going in the ditch."

"Just give it a try," Jerry pleaded, wiping the snow from his coat. "I'll need to stay down here and push. You're not going to have any traction with those back wheels."

"What if it does come out?" asked Marjie. "How do I stop?"

"Don't worry about it," Jerry answered. "If she starts to move, don't let up until the front wheels are back on the road. Then just shove in the clutch and gently pump the brakes."

Marjie reluctantly hopped back in the Ford and hoped that backing it out was as simple as Jerry made it out to be. Popping the gears into reverse, she slowly let out the clutch and felt one of the tires begin to spin helplessly. Jerry pushed until his face was red, but the car did not budge. Finally he raised his hand for her to stop.

"We gotta get some more weight in the back of the car," Jerry yelled as he tossed the shovel back onto the road and pulled himself up out of the ditch. Stepping onto the slick road, he slipped and nearly went down before he was able to catch himself by grabbing the front of the car and hanging on.

Laughing at how comical he looked, Marjie rolled down her window. "You look like you must have learned some new steps in the navy. You need skates."

"You aren't kidding!" agreed Jerry. "We'll never get this car out of here at this—say, who's that?"

Marjie looked down the road toward the Matsons' turnoff and saw a small red Farmall tractor heading their way. "That's old man Matson driving and Clarence hanging on the back. See why we called him Gorilla?"

"He looks as wide as the tractor," Jerry declared with amazement. "Wonder why they bothered to buy a tractor at all—he could pull a plow easy enough. Must be a job feeding that boy."

"Don't call him a boy," Marjie warned. "No one's dared to call him that since he was ten."

Pushing down the door handle, Marjie stepped out of the car with Jerry's support and waved at the Matsons as they pulled up to the rear of the Ford. "Howdy," she called out. "We got ourselves a little problem."

Clarence was holding a section of heavy chain and smiling broadly. "Not for long, Marjie," he replied in a friendly voice as he stepped down from the back of the tractor. "We seen you go by and thought you was going a mite fast. We pull a lot of speedy drivers out of the ditch on this corner when it ices up."

Jerry rubbed his chin sheepishly but refused to look at Marjie's taunting smile. "We'd appreciate you giving us a pull," he said. "I dug the front end out already, so she should come out easy."

"Don't bet on it," Ned Matson barked over the noise of the tractor engine. "Once them wheels drop down, it's tough to get the frame off the edge. Got it, Clarence?"

"Got it!" yelled Clarence, who had slid under the back of the Ford to hook the chain around the rear axle. Crawling back out, he jumped onto the rear of the tractor to add his bulk for traction. Marjie and Jerry got back into the car and waited for a signal.

"Okay, give it a try!" Ned hollered to Jerry, nudging the tractor ahead to take the slack out of the chain.

Jerry put the Ford into reverse and slowly let out the clutch. The tractor gave an initial tug that Marjie thought moved the car ever so slightly, but then both car and tractor wheels began to spin in futility. Clarence shifted his weight as far back as he could, but it didn't help. Finally, the elder Matson let off on the gas and gave up pulling.

Both Matsons stepped down carefully from the tractor and made their way to study the front of the car. Marjie noticed Clarence break into another beaming smile as his father pointed to a spot in the middle of the car's front bumper.

Ned Matson climbed back out of the ditch and leaned into the open car window. "Can't get no traction on this ice," he announced, "but I think the boy can get you out of there. When you see me signal, give her the gas again."

Jerry wasn't sure what the plan was, but he looked at Marjie and whispered, "Boy?"

"Only his daddy calls him that," she explained. "Don't you dare try it. And watch him now. Clarence is going to try to lift us out!"

"There's no way he can budge it!" Jerry protested. Then he turned toward Mr. Matson, who was back on the tractor and pulling the chain up tight again. When Ned waved, Jerry again let out the clutch and pressed down on the pedal. But this time Clarence gave a mighty heave, and the entire front end rose. Slowly the Ford inched backward out of the ditch with the smiling Clarence providing most of the power.

Once the front wheels were back on the pavement, a stunned Jerry let off the gas, and the tractor came to a halt. "He's not human!" Jerry mumbled to Marjie. "He's—"

"Mostly gorilla!" Marjie interjected and laughed. "But he's a nice gorilla."

Clarence ascended triumphantly out of the ditch, and Jerry got out of the car to shake his hand.

"Thanks a lot, Clarence," Jerry congratulated him. "That was amazing."

"Ain't nothing to it," suggested Clarence as he crushed Jerry's right hand in a massive paw. "I've always been big. Fact, most people call me Gorilla."

"That's my boy!" Ned Matson yelled with pride from the tractor. "If you think that was something, you'd get a kick out of seeing him pull out tree stumps. Say, we read about you in the paper. We're mighty pleased to meet a war hero. Clarence here wanted to join up, but we can't run the farm without him."

"I'm no hero," Jerry said, shaking his head. "I just did what I could. Kinda like what you just done for us. What do I owe you?"

"Go on with you," Ned assured them with a wave. "Me and Clarence, we're just glad to be of service. Y'know, I always kinda hoped that little Marjie might take a shine to my boy, here, but

I guess it weren't in the cards. You take care of her, y'hear. She's a keeper."

"You're right there," Jerry agreed, walking over and shaking Ned's hand as well.

"And slow it down a notch," advised Ned, winking at Marjie. "Ain't no point in trying to rush it today."

"I'll be more careful, that's for sure," Jerry conceded. "Thanks a million."

Clarence got down and yanked out the chain, then hopped on the back of the tractor as it pulled back down the road toward home. Jerry took one last look at the hulk that dwarfed the tractor, then slowly turned the old Ford south and carefully maneuvered it toward the Livingstone farm.

"Just think," Jerry joked, "you and Clarence—that would have been an interesting match."

"He's an interesting catch for any girl," suggested Marjie. "Not much to look at, but he's got a heart of gold. And you'd never have to worry about getting stuck in the ditch."

"Good point," Jerry conceded as he pulled the car into the Livingstone farmyard. "We should have brought the guy along with us. If we had problems getting that calf delivered, he could probably lift the cow into the best position."

"I don't think *probably's* the right word," Marjie corrected him. "More like *no problem*."

Ted Livingstone stepped out of the barn and waved for Jerry to come straight in. Marjie could read Jerry's thoughts and said, "Don't worry, I'll save you a nice hot cup of coffee. And the barn's warmer than the ditch you just crawled out of."

Marjie jumped out of the car and headed toward the house. "Come on in," her mother said, pushing open the outside door. "Be careful on the porch steps. They're slick as glass."

"Don't I know," Marjie said as she gingerly negotiated the three wooden steps. "We dipped into the ditch up by the Matsons'. Gorilla lifted us out, if you can believe it."

"I'm a believer," Sarah answered, giving Marjie a warm hug. "Ethel already gave me a call and told me the whole story. That boy is as strong as a bull."

Taking off her coat and hanging it up, Marjie noticed a white tablecloth draped across the large wooden rocking chair and her mother's sewing basket beside it on the floor. "This is a gorgeous pattern," Marjie said, walking over to pick up the tablecloth. "I thought you'd given up on needlework. When did you take up embroidery again?"

"Since I got a granddaughter," Sarah said with a twinkle in her eyes. "Think she'll like it?"

"She'll love it!" exclaimed Marjie, studying the intricacy of the design. "Whatever made you think of it?"

"Benjamin."

"What?"

"Benjamin," her mother repeated. "He mentioned how much you love the one I made for you. Thought I better get busy on Martha's before all the spring work hits. Won't have much time after that, I reckon."

Marjie watched her mother's expression closely for any sign that Ted might have told her about his plans to enlist in the army, but she saw no hints.

"What's on your mind?" Sarah asked.

"Is it that obvious?" questioned Marjie.

"You're an open book," answered Sarah. "Besides, when I called about the cow having trouble, I got the impression that you were glad for the chance to get over here, even if the weather was bad. Thought you must have something that was bothering you."

"And nothing's bothering *you*?" Marjie queried.

"You look like you need a cup of coffee and a chair," Sarah suggested, moving toward the kitchen. "There's some fresh brewed on the stove—and I used all new grounds. Just for you, of course."

"Of course," Marjie joked. "Better let me inspect for sure."

Sarah and Marjie filled their familiar chipped coffee cups and sat down together at the kitchen table. "Now," Sarah said, "what's troubling you?"

Marjie took a couple of sips before answering. She had

hoped that her mother would volunteer the information without her having to tease it out.

"Has Teddy talked with you recently?" Marjie began tentatively.

"About what? He lives here, you know, so we talk several times a day," replied Sarah.

"About his future?" Marjie tried again. "Has he said anything about what he hopes to do?"

"Can you be more specific?" her mother asked.

"Oh," groaned Marjie, shaking her head. "I was always a sucker for Teddy to get me to talk for him. I hate to be the bearer of bad news, but I take it that he's not said anything about joining the army by the time spring planting rolls around?"

Marjie was confused when Sarah showed no surprise. She just took another sip, then looked straight into Marjie's dark eyes. "Yes," she said. "He told me a few weeks ago. I didn't know he'd talked with you, though, and I didn't want you to worry about it."

"You didn't want it to worry *me*?" Marjie blurted out. "What about you? You're the one I'm worried about. You could lose the farm."

"Could?" Sarah questioned. "More like will. Seems clear enough to me."

"Why didn't you call me, Ma?" asked Marjie. "Aren't you worried? What are you going to do?"

"Long term?" Sarah reflected quietly, swirling the last bit of coffee in her cup. "I don't know. Short term, I'm not going to do anything."

"What?" Marjie was incredulous. "He said *by* spring planting. If you're going to sell, doesn't every day count?"

"Absolutely," Sarah agreed. "But he'll be here through the spring planting. Count on it."

"That's not what he told me," Marjie countered. "Did something change?"

Sarah gave a crooked smile and nodded. "Sometimes evil works for good," she said. "Do you believe that?"

"I'm not sure. Try me."

"Along with the booze," Sarah stated, "it seems that your brother and his buddies have taken to gambling at their card games. And apparently Teddy's none too good at it. He's racked up enough losses that even if he sold his truck, he couldn't pay off his debts. It's going to take him longer to leave than he hoped."

Marjie was caught somewhere between immense relief and overwhelming sadness. She knew that the gambling made the drinking all that much more dangerous. And she knew that the inevitable move would still come.

"But what happens when time runs out?" Marjie asked. "He's going to go—sooner or later."

"I plan on doing what I'm doing right now," her mother answered.

"Which is?"

"Trusting that somehow God will work all of this out," Sarah replied. "Isn't that what you'd recommend? I don't have many other options."

Marjie nodded her head, wishing she had something helpful to say but discovering nothing that seemed appropriate. She was amazed by the strength of conviction that she read in her mother's eyes.

"And I've talked with a couple of neighbors about buying the property," Sarah added, finally allowing the dull ache of pain to show in her eyes. "It seems I'm going to be looking for a room in town before long."

24

NOT JUST ANOTHER DAY

"Oh, my," Marjie groaned and plopped down on the living room davenport. "Why'd you have to go and spoil a perfectly good day?"

"I'm only asking a question," Benjamin protested mildly from his favorite chair. "And I ain't saying it's gonna happen tomorrow. All I asked was what you thought. It's been over three months since I got banged up. Seems like I ought to be moving on."

"You really don't understand, do you?" Marjie replied, sitting up and turning her full gaze upon Benjamin. Taking a deep breath, she continued, "Let me try to make it clear one more time. We love having you here. It's given all of us the time we wanted to spend together. I see no reason why you should go. Think of how close you and Martha have gotten."

Benjamin smiled and looked down at the warm little bundle who was snoozing in his lap. "I sure ain't complaining," he said softly. "I've never felt so close to a baby before—not even my own. And I couldn't have made it without you and Jerry. Actually, I've loved everything about this time except for those first few weeks after the bull got me—those I could do without. But I can't stay here forever."

"Why not?"

"Shoot!" Benjamin snorted. "You know full well. As long as

I'm here, you can't really be your own family. Besides, you're still practically newlyweds. If I were in your shoes, I wouldn't want an old man hanging around the house all the time. Tell me that's not a problem."

Marjie opened her mouth to protest but immediately realized that he was right. "It's not a problem we haven't been able to handle," she answered. "If we're missing out on something now, we've got a whole lifetime ahead of us to make it up. But we know this time with you is special."

Benjamin rubbed his whiskers and then looked down at Martha again. "I recall you saying that you thought it was one of those times 'for every purpose under heaven' that Solomon talked about," he remarked. "You remember that?"

"Sure."

"Do you have any idea what that meant to me?" asked Benjamin.

"I guess I never thought of it," answered Marjie. "At the time I thought the words were mostly for me."

"Maybe they were—partly," Benjamin reasoned. "I just remember coming home from the hospital with an incredible sense of dreading how terrible it would be to sit around all day doing nothing. A couple of years ago I would have preferred to die, and the quicker the better. Hearing you say that you thought there was a purpose behind it all gave me hope—though I'd have still preferred to be working."

"You did a good job of fooling me," Marjie commented. "I had figured you'd go crazy around here, but there were times when I actually thought you liked it."

Benjamin burst out laughing, and the baby stirred. He took both her hands and held them in one of his hands, and she settled back into her sleep. Then he looked back at Marjie and continued, "There have been many wonderful moments around here the past few months, but I can't tell you how many times I sat in this chair and told myself to remember that there must be a purpose for the resting I was doing. I pretty much chewed that message down to the bone."

"So why talk about moving out again?"

"I told you why, and you know I'm right," Benjamin persisted. "Besides, this is the healthiest I've been in years. *My* reason for staying has been accomplished—thanks to all your help and good cooking."

"I appreciate your gratitude, Benjamin, but you're not at one hundred percent yet."

"A hundred percent of what?" countered Benjamin. "When I was lying around here, one of the things I had to tell myself was that I was fifty-nine years old and not getting any younger. I look back, and it seems stupid to have pushed myself so hard to pretend I was still a young man like Jerry. I'm strong enough now to put in a good day's work, but I'll never be twenty-five again. I figure I better start acting my age."

"You got me there," Marjie acknowledged. "Just bringing your blood pressure down has made such a difference. But what about the limp?"

"What about it?" Benjamin questioned with a smile. "Just because my hip didn't break don't mean it'll ever be the same again. I feel fortunate to be able to walk—period. Besides, the limp seems to be generating a fair amount of sympathy."

"That's just like you, isn't it!" Marjie teased. "Always looking for attention."

"You got that right."

"Mr. Attention-Getter. Right," Marjie responded, but then she got serious again. "So what are you thinking?"

"I need to start looking for a place nearby," Benjamin deliberated. "Then I'm thinking about where I might get a job."

"What?" Marjie gasped, sitting up and changing her expression to bewilderment. "Why in the world would you even think such a thought? This farm is your life."

Benjamin shook his head no and puckered his lips as if he were weighing her words. "*Was* my life," he stated. "Too much of my life, to tell the truth. But I want it to be yours and Jerry's now, and Jerry can do most of it on his own. I promise that I'll be here when he needs me."

Marjie took a deep breath and shook her head back. "Jerry's not going to want to hear this," she warned, running her fingers nervously through her hair. "Maybe you're right about finding a place of your own, but I hate for you to talk about getting a job. I'm telling you, Jerry's going to hit the roof."

"You just agreed that my health is good," Benjamin explained. "I could live for a long time, and I need a steady job."

"Hold on!" demanded Marjie. "Let me collect my thoughts before you close the book on this. First of all, you and Jerry need to strike a deal in writing on what this farm is worth. Once that's done and we start making payments, you're going to have steady income and we can pay you to work here. You can tell us the hours you want to work. How about that?"

"Sounds simple enough," Benjamin agreed. "But you've got to remember that most farmers with this amount of acreage don't have much left at the end of any month to live, let alone pay for help that you can get along without. You've seen how tight money is here. And I'm still going to have bills to pay as well."

"Where would you work?"

"There's plenty of jobs around with so many men gone," Benjamin answered. "I've heard that Bernard's looking for a man to run the feed mill part time. If I got that job, I could probably work my hours around what's needed here. That wouldn't be so bad, would it?"

Marjie stood up and walked over to the south-facing window. Placing her hand on the windowsill, she watched the pine trees and elms sway with the strong westerly wind. "I don't like it at all," she said sorrowfully. "This old house won't ever be the same."

———— ✑ ————

Neither Jerry nor Marjie had said much to each other on the way to Ruth's that evening. Benjamin's talk with Marjie had given her a bad case of melancholy, and the last thing she wanted to do was bring it up for discussion with Jerry. And Jerry seemed to be absorbed in his thoughts as well.

"Who'd she say was coming over?" Marjie asked. "Hope I know everyone."

"Sounded like a bunch of people," Jerry answered. "Billy and Margaret and Chester for sure. Probably a dozen, I'd guess."

"Ruthie really frustrates me sometimes," grumbled Marjie. "She wouldn't tell me why she wasn't inviting her teacher friend from Canton. And she wouldn't let me bring something for tonight. Thinks she has to fix everything. The more I tried to get her to budge, the more stubborn she got. Guess I got a little mad at her on the phone. Don't you think she should be able to let somebody help her once in a while?"

Jerry slowed the car down as they approached the long driveway to the Buckley farm. "Ruthie's usually got a good reason for whatever she does," he commented. "Maybe you should ask her about it."

"I tried," she said. "I don't know. Maybe I was having a bad day, but she sounded strange. I got the impression that she was hiding something."

"Come on," Jerry said sarcastically, pulling the Ford into the oval-shaped farmyard that was filled with cars. "It's just a card party. What would she be hiding?"

"I have no idea," Marjie answered. "But look at all the cars. We must be the last ones here."

"Not quite," Jerry corrected. "Looks like we just beat Billy."

Billy Wilson had followed them into the yard and come to a quick halt right behind them. Jumping out, he joined them as they climbed out of their car.

"How's it going!" Billy called out. "Beautiful night, eh? Not bad for the first week of March."

"It's great," Jerry said, taking Marjie by the arm. "Getting the itch for spring. If we can keep the wind from the west, the snow'll be melting soon."

"Heard you got a birthday coming up, Marjie," Billy said as he led the way up the sidewalk toward the front door. "Twenty-four big ones, eh? Tuesday, I believe."

"Where'd you hear that?" Marjie scolded. "Jerry, did you tell?"

"I didn't tell him anything," Jerry muttered. "Tell her, Billy."

"He didn't say a peep, Marjie," Billy defended as he knocked on Ruth's front door, then he turned and gave her a taunting smile. "You must have told someone else!"

"What are you talking—"

Before she could finish, the door flew open to reveal a whole entryway filled with people yelling out, "Surprise! Happy birthday, Marjie!"

Marjie screamed and tried to cover her face, but just as she did, someone inside popped the flash on their camera and caught her with her mouth wide open. She gave another scream, and everyone burst into laughter.

Billy Wilson and Jerry were nearly in hysterics, and Marjie punched both of them in the arms to try to get them to stop, but her protests were futile. The trap had been set, and Marjie had fallen in all the way.

"Where's Ruthie?" Marjie demanded, shaking hands with the first well-wishers at the door. "She's behind this, isn't she?"

She spotted Ruth and Margaret standing at the back of the crowd laughing so hard that they were hanging on to each other. "You rats!" Marjie called out. "You are terrible! How could you do this to me?"

That threw them into a fresh round of convulsions. Tears were pouring down Margaret's face. "That was the funniest face I've ever seen!" she cried.

Hearing Margaret's peals of laughter, Marjie broke down and joined in as well. She only wished that she had been the one who was pulling the trick.

Chester stepped beside Marjie, put his arm around her, and announced, "I got it all on film, Marjie. What's it worth to you?"

"How about your life!" blurted Marjie. "If you show anyone that picture, so help me, Margaret's a widow. Where did you get a camera?"

"Wedding present," Chester explained. "Takes good pictures, too. But this should be worth some cash."

"All right, Ruthie, it's your turn," Marjie warned, turning to the obvious instigator. "How could you?"

"How could I not?" Ruth countered, still wiping tears away.

"I told you the day of Margaret's wedding that you'd pay for the gag about me having the rings. I figure you shaved a good year off my life that day. So why wouldn't I have a little surprise party up my sleeve? You don't think you're the only one who can pull off a trick or two, do you?"

"I don't now, obviously," Marjie acknowledged. "I'm impressed."

"You should be," Ruth agreed, reaching out and giving Marjie a hug. "Your mouth was open so far I could have popped an orange into it."

"Forget it," Marjie bantered. "This doesn't compare to the rings. I owe you."

"We'll see," Ruth replied. "Let me take your coat. You look a little warm!"

"It's called embarrassed, if you're searching for the right word," suggested Marjie as she pulled off her heavy coat and handed it to Ruth. "I'd like to hide."

"You may not!" exclaimed Margaret, taking Chester's arm. "We're here to celebrate your birthday. And to give you thanks for being such a wonderful friend!"

"That's right," Ruth added as she turned from the hallway closet.

"This is your way of saying thanks?" teased Marjie. "I hope to never be on your enemy list."

"Don't worry about that," replied Ruth, taking Marjie by the arm and leading her into the living room, where most of the other guests had already moved. Then she stopped and whispered into Marjie's ear, "You're a friend forever. Watch me now."

Raising her hand, Ruth got everyone's attention, and the room fell silent. "Less than a year ago," Ruth announced, "Marjie Macmillan stepped into our community and became a part of our lives. Some of you are just getting to know her, and some of us feel like we've been friends with her forever. Until I met Marjie, I didn't realize how wonderful it is to have a best friend. Now I know what I've been missing all my life.

"From all of us, Marjie, but especially from me," Ruth said, "tonight we want to wish you the happiest of birthdays and a wonderful year to come!"

Then the door to the kitchen was pushed open and out marched Jerry and Billy in tandem, carrying the biggest birthday cake that Marjie had ever seen. Twenty-four candles flickered brightly as the two men made their way across the room to a very delighted Marjie.

They stopped to present her the cake, and Jerry said in a hushed tone, "To my best friend and only love, Happy Birthday, babe."

25

NOT JUST ANOTHER NIGHT

"Who dealt this mess anyway?" Jerry moaned as Ruth slapped down the last trump card and pushed her and Marjie's score over five hundred.

"I did, and Billy cut them," Marjie replied and blew him a kiss. "You country boys are just sore losers. Thought the navy would have honed your skills."

"You just got lucky again," said Billy, winking at Jerry and tossing his cards down on the table.

"That's four games straight, if I'm remembering right," Ruth reminded him with a tilt of her head. "I can't recall ever having so much luck before, can you, Marjie?"

"If this is luck, we'll be something special when we figure this game out," Marjie threw back. "Wouldn't it feel good to finally have some competition?"

"You keep it up, and we'll throw another birthday party like last weekend," Jerry countered. "Took her two days to recover from the shock. I wonder if Chester got that roll of film developed yet."

"You may have to sell some acres to pay him off," Billy added with a hearty laugh. "Didn't somebody tell me how Marjie conned the newspaper reporter into all those pictures when you got written up in the paper? I'll bet he'd love to run one of Marjie in the paper."

Marjie gave Billy a playful shove and warned, "I'm only going to say this once, and it's for every breathing soul at this table. If anyone so much as dares hint that Chester talk to Ed Bentley, I guarantee that what he or she will face from me will make the Gordon Stilwell incident look like a walk in the park. Understood?"

Jerry threw up his hands in mock surrender.

"I know nothing about a photo," Ruth responded with a chuckle. "I'm already at the top of your most-wanted list!"

"Won't breathe a word," conceded Billy, pushing his chair back from the Macmillans' dining room table. "I was hoping to live to the ripe old age of thirty."

"Good," declared Marjie. "I'm glad that's settled. Anybody care for some warm apple crisp?"

Jerry's and Billy's hands shot up quickly, and Marjie and Ruth headed for the kitchen.

"This losing business is getting ridiculous," Billy suggested quietly to Jerry. "I think we're going to have to try cheating."

"I heard that!" called Marjie from the kitchen. Then she added as she came around the kitchen corner with four china cups on a tray. "I actually believe you'd try it."

"Without a twinge of guilt," joked Billy, taking the coffee cup that Marjie handed him. "You've beat on us long enough."

"We take no prisoners," Ruth declared. Setting her tray of dessert plates down on the dining room table, she continued, "Marjie's just getting even with you and Jerry for all those times we beat her team in softball. And I'm getting even for what hard times you used to give me when we didn't win."

They all laughed, and the memories of more innocent times flooded over them.

"I don't remember ever playing with anyone who loved to win more than you did, Billy," Ruth said, passing out the plates and sitting down. "Except for Jerry, perhaps."

Billy laughed again, then rubbed his forehead. "We both loved to win, but at least Jerry was a good sport when we lost.

I'm not sure why I was so mean to you about it."

"You certainly were mean," Ruth responded with a gentle smile. "But I think I gave you back some of your own medicine."

Something in the air had altered during that last exchange. Marjie looked across the table at Jerry, who met her glance with a bewildered expression of "what's going on here?"

"You did, and then some," Billy was assuring Ruth. "When I was in the hospital, sometimes I used to think about how rotten I was to you. It's been bothering me again the last couple of days. So it seems like a good time to say I'm sorry. I was wrong for taking my frustrations out on you. Will you forgive me?"

It took Ruth a couple of moments for what Billy was saying to sink in, and her face got a little red. "Of course," she responded softly, then sat quietly for a minute, pushing a piece of apple crisp around her plate. Finally she looked up at Billy. "I have some things to say to you, too. A couple of years ago, when we broke up, I said some things to you that were as cruel as I've ever spoken to anyone. I should have apologized a long time ago."

Billy focused on Ruth's dark eyes for a few seconds, but before he could respond, Marjie broke in.

"Perhaps you two would like some time alone?" she asked. "We can go into the living room if you'd like."

Billy shook his head no. "It's all right," he sighed. "You know us like family."

"It really is all right," Ruth assured Marjie. "Jerry knows the whole story backward and forward, I'm sure. I acted pretty terrible."

"I deserved it," Billy stated. "Didn't I, Jerry?"

Jerry still couldn't believe they'd suddenly jumped from a bantering card game to a remorseful confession. "You really want me in the middle of this?"

"Not in the middle," Billy replied. "But you were there. Ruth deserved to be mad, didn't she?"

Jerry wrinkled his forehead and squinted his eyes. "I don't much care for taking sides, but ... seeing how you asked, I'll tell you what I thought. How you broke up with Ruthie would hurt anyone, but it seemed like you ended up treating all the girls you dated pretty bad."

Jerry looked at Marjie for reassurance, then back at Billy. He'd never told Billy what he thought about such matters. Billy was staring at him somberly, but then he smiled.

"I was a selfish jerk," Billy said, looking back at Ruth. "I thought I could have any girl I wanted, so I treated dating like something I could buy and sell, and I hurt a lot of nice girls in the process. But I'm especially sorry that I treated you that way, Ruthie. You were my friend a long time before we ever dated."

Tears glistened at the corners of Ruth's eyes, but she held her gaze steady. "What you did hurt me . . . a lot . . . for a while. But I told myself a hundred times that I should have known better. There were six girls before me and six girls after me. I was just another number."

Billy pursed his lips and shook his head slowly. "You weren't just another number, believe me," Billy pleaded with her. "You could never be a number. But I was a fool. Please forgive me."

"I told you, you're forgiven," whispered Ruth, blinking back the tears. "But however wrong you were, that didn't make what I said right, Billy. Please forgive me, too."

The muscles in Billy's jaw were tight and his eyes were pinched nearly shut. Marjie held her breath, waiting for his response and wondering if everyone at the table was about to burst into tears.

"I forgive you," he said slowly and deliberately to Ruth. "I wish I could make it up to you, but I can't."

"We could start by being the friends we once were," Ruth suggested. "How about it?"

The intense solemnity of Billy's face relaxed, and his green eyes began to dance again, but he did not take them off the softness of Ruth's expression. "I'd like that," he responded. "It's time to start over."

Marjie looked at Ruth and was amazed at how beautiful she looked; putting away those old hurts seemed to have visibly changed her. But Marjie thought she saw the familiar flash return to Ruth's dark eyes as she said, "Let's do that."

An awkward silence fell around the table, and the four friends quietly sipped their coffee and picked away at their apple crisp. Jerry kept looking over at Marjie in hopes that she'd start a new conversation, but she was no more sure what to say than he was.

"I'm sorry if we've made you uncomfortable," Billy finally said to Jerry and Marjie. "This conversation went much further than I thought it would. But I appreciate your bearing with us. It feels so good to get all this off my chest. Since I got hurt and had so much time on my hands, some of this stuff has been eating me alive. I've been going to several people to talk since I got back. So if it's any comfort, you're not the first ones to have to put up with me dragging up the past."

"If you're not uncomfortable, we're not uncomfortable," Marjie responded. "You just surprised us a little."

"More like a lot!" Jerry added, getting everyone to laugh and lightening the mood.

"This apple crisp really is superb, Marjie," Ruth said, taking in her last forkful.

"Thanks," replied Marjie. "I used a handwritten recipe from Jerry's mother that I unearthed in the back of one of the cupboards. Seems like the Macmillan baker boys tossed most of her recipes."

Jerry gave a sheepish grin and shrugged his shoulders.

"She was some kind of cook," Billy said as if he was reminding himself. "Didn't matter what time of day it was, she always had something warm and delicious in here. I spent so much time in this house when we were young that she was like a second mom to me. It's always been strange coming in here since she died. She was a live wire."

"She really was," Jerry agreed, smiling in remembrance. "We just about drove her crazy playing cowboys and Indians in here. She whacked our bottoms with her broom more than once."

Everyone laughed again, and Ruth got up to refill coffee cups.

"So what's the scoop on you?" Jerry asked Billy. "We know that your legs have been too sensitive to work outside in the cold, and you said that the farm's not big enough for you and your dad to work together. Any thoughts of what you're going to do?"

Billy pushed himself back up straighter in his chair and wiped his lips. The solemn look pushed back over his countenance, and he mumbled, "Maybe we've had enough serious talk for one night?"

"What's up, Billy?" asked Marjie. "If something's changing, we want to know."

"Nothing's really changed," he replied.

"Like mud," Marjie scolded. "Talk!"

"She must drive you nuts," Billy said to Jerry, who shook his head yes. "Okay, I'll tell you what I'm thinking, but I haven't finalized it yet. I've got two big problems with these legs. The burn area can't take the cold, and I'm not sure how it'll do in the heat of summer. And my bum knee can't take the heavy lifting. As you might guess, neither of those situations is gonna mix well with life on the farm."

"So what are you saying?" Jerry questioned.

"I'm thinking that I may need to try to find work where it's drier and warmer. The climate in San Diego was perfect, and there were plenty of jobs. Maybe that's what I should do."

Billy's three friends tried to take in the thought of him leaving after only being home such a short time, and it left them dumbfounded. Marjie glanced at Jerry who looked as if he were going to be sick.

"Don't everybody talk at once," Billy offered. "It's not like I want to leave you folks. It's these legs of mine. What else can I do?"

"Have you looked around here for indoor work?" asked Ruth, who obviously had her thinking hat on. "Office work?"

"Not much," sputtered Billy, shaking his head reluctantly. "There's still the cold."

"If you moved to town and lived close to an office job, seems like it might work," she suggested.

"Ah . . . I don't know," replied Billy. "I ain't much on living in town."

"You'd live outside San Diego and drive in to work?" Ruth challenged.

"Well, no . . . maybe," stammered Billy. "I'm not sure what I'd do. I suppose I'd probably live in town if I went there."

"So let's find you an office job here in the area and see if you can live close-by," Ruth continued. "If it doesn't work, what have you lost? Just a little time."

"Sounds good to me," Jerry seconded with a sigh of relief.

"Hold on," Billy demanded, breaking out in a bright smile. "This is my life, and I appreciate your concern and help. I do want to stay, but what kind of a job can I get here? In a city like San Diego, jobs are a dime a dozen."

Marjie looked at Ruth and could see a determined fix in her eyes. She knew that Ruth must have an ace or two left in her hand.

"If I were able to help you get started at a really good job in Preston," Ruth stated, "would you try it?"

"What job?" Billy asked.

"First, you tell me whether you're willing to try," she countered. "If you don't think it's a job you'd like, you can say so. But I need to know that you're willing to try this."

Billy took a deep breath and threw up his hands. "Okay, I cry uncle," he said. "I'm willing to try. What's the job?"

"Well, it's at a bank," Ruth explained. "It's a beginning position, but I know that if the president finds the right man, he'll advance quickly. We know you're good with numbers, and you'd even have a chance to help people like you said you wanted to do. What do you think?"

"Whew!" Billy puffed. "Slow down. Guess I'll have to think about it. You're sure the job is available?"

"Absolutely."

"In the bank?"

"That's what I said."

"And what would I do?" Billy asked. "Just walk in and apply? I don't have any experience."

"There's no experience required," Ruth added. "And you can tell Mr. Stockdale that I sent you. He'll sit up and listen."

All three friends looked at Ruth with different thoughts running through their heads on how she knew about the job and what her relationship was to Stockdale.

"No tricks?" Billy questioned her.

"None."

"Honest?"

"Honest."

"Hmmm," Billy sighed, eyeballing Ruth hard again but still smiling. "I'm going to check this out. But if you're pulling my aching leg on this, Ruthie, I take back all the apologies I made tonight."

Ruth gave Billy a wrinkled smile. "Don't you worry. You won't be taking anything back."

By this point, Marjie was about to burst with curiosity. "Ruthie," she asked, "could you help me take the dishes to the kitchen?"

"Sure," Ruth said with a smile. "I need to get on home anyway. It's late."

Once in the kitchen, Marjie placed her dishes on the counter and cornered Ruth. "What in the world are you up to?" she whispered. "How do you know the banker will even consider Billy?"

Ruth broke out laughing and clapped a hand over her mouth to keep the sound from carrying. Leaning close back to Marjie, she whispered, "I knew Billy would never stay on the farm, so I did a little checking around. I heard about the bank job, so I went down and had a chat with Stockdale. A couple years ago I caught a fairly major mistake he made on my father's farm loan, and it saved him a pile of money and a bigger pile of embarrassment. He owes me a favor, and it's collection time."

Marjie looked at Ruth with a sense of wonderment. "You really are something," Marjie said softly. "You'd do that for him after what he did to you?"

Ruth simply nodded.

26

SPRING BREEZES

Marjie pulled on her boots, then jumped up and headed for the living room to say goodbye to her daughter and father-in-law. Jerry was already outside waiting for her. Stepping around the corner of the stairway, she was startled to find both grandfather Benjamin and baby Martha on hands and knees.

"Like this," Benjamin was pleading. Slowly moving his hands and legs forward, Benjamin demonstrated his crawling technique as the seven-month-old swayed back and forth in excitement. "See!" he was saying. "Like this. Now you try."

Benjamin stopped and swung around to coax her toward him, but then he saw Marjie standing in the doorway holding her hand over her mouth to keep back the laughter.

"She's almost crawling!" exclaimed Benjamin, straightening up on his knees. "Any minute now and she'll take off!"

"You said that a month ago," Marjie laughed. "If I only had a camera. You're going to get lame if you keep this up."

"Beats getting old," Benjamin assured her. "Which way are you two going?"

"I'm not sure," answered Marjie. "Jerry's leading the way. But I suppose we'll follow the creek at least to our property line. Maybe farther."

"You be careful," Benjamin warned. "That creek can be dangerous in the spring. Billy fell in once when he and Jerry were exploring. Nearly sucked him under."

"Don't worry yourself," Marjie replied. "I don't want to get that close. You take good care of my girl, and get off the floor while those old bones are still moving."

"Just you go," Benjamin suggested with a wave. "Fella can't have any fun with you around."

"See you two later," Marjie returned cheerfully, then she turned and pushed the front door open.

Stepping into the brilliant spring sunshine, Marjie was greeted by southerly breezes that were busy licking up the snowbanks and turning the ground into a swampy mush. Pools of water stood everywhere, while on the hillsides the melt-off snow was turning rivulets into torrents. Spring had made its sudden arrival and was making short work of the long winter's stay.

"Sixty-two degrees! Can you believe it?" Jerry called out from in front of the barn, where he stood shaping a wet handful of snow into a ball. Blue stood by him, wagging his tail furiously and waiting for something to happen.

"If you throw that thing, it's war!" Marjie yelled a warning.

Jerry laughed, then wound up and fired the snowball right at her feet, hitting a mud puddle and splattering dirty water up her dark blue slacks. Blue came dashing up, grabbed the remnant of snowball, and gobbled it down.

"You've had it!" Marjie screamed, picking up her own handful of snow and packing it hard, then running straight at Jerry with Blue jumping up and down at her side. But Jerry was laughing too hard to take her seriously. The closer she got, the bigger the show he put on for her.

Marjie got within fifteen feet, reared back, and fired her snowball. Jerry went to duck, but he miscalculated and ducked directly into the projectile's path. The snowball popped Jerry's ear and knocked his old choring cap off his head.

"Ow!" Jerry yelped, clutching his ear and bending over in agony. "My ear!"

Now it was Marjie's chance to laugh at the sight of Jerry dancing around in pain and Blue dancing around him, but her merriment was tempered with a measure of sympathy. Walking over to Jerry, she bent down and picked up his cap. "You asked for it," she said with a chuckle.

Jerry looked up at her through one opened, one squinting eye, still holding his ear. "You didn't have to put so much mustard on it. I didn't throw at your head."

"Let me kiss it," Marjie offered, handing him his cap and giving him a hug. "I'll make it all better."

Jerry lifted his hand and slowly revealed a flaming red ear that still dripped with icy water. "You nailed that sucker," he moaned.

Marjie reached out her hand and touched it gently. "I'm sorry," she said, then leaned forward and kissed his ear. "But you did start it."

"And I'll finish it," he replied, managing to smile. "Try that again, but right here." He pointed to his lips and puckered up.

"Mmmm," Marjie responded. "This'll cure what ails you." Then she planted a sizzling kiss on his lips that soon had him forgetting about his ear.

Pausing for a breather, Marjie asked, "Better?"

"Just a little more will do it," Jerry replied.

But before they could get in a second kiss, Blue ran up and splattered the lovers with his muddy paws.

"Blue! Get down!" Marjie cried as she pulled away from Jerry's embrace. "Look what you've done."

Several brown paw tracks were neatly imprinted on her coat. Blue had turned tail and headed for the safety of the barn. "You better hide!" she called out after him, then looked at Jerry. "Good thing this is my old coat."

Jerry brushed off the mud from his jacket as best he could. "Calamity just seems to follow wherever you go," he joked. "Let's get moving before something else happens and we don't get our walk in. This is the perfect day to see our sleepy creek turn into a mighty river."

Marjie took his arm and asked, "Which way are we going?"

"Straight over to where we went sliding, then we'll just follow the creek a ways," Jerry replied, leading south from the barn toward the large pine trees. "You never got to see a big spring runoff?"

"Never," Marjie answered. "Our land at home was too flat. And this time last year Benjamin wouldn't let me walk down by the creek. Too worried about the baby. Do you know what I just caught him doing?"

"No."

"He was down on the floor showing Martha how to crawl."

"You're kidding."

"I'm not kidding," laughed Marjie. "Sometimes I think he likes to get us out of the house—just so he can have her to himself."

"It's worth it, you know."

Marjie nodded her head as they passed the opening in the pines that overlooked the valley below. Much of the snow had already disappeared, leaving behind greenish brown tufts of grass from the year before. Marjie's eye followed the path down the long, gentle hill to the creek. But its usually placid surface had been transformed into a foaming torrent of icy runoff that raged and rolled at its banks.

"That is incredible" exclaimed Marjie. "Is it like this every spring?"

"No," Jerry replied, obviously pleased with Marjie's reaction. "Only when we get a big thaw. This is the best I can ever remember seeing it."

"Let's go down as close as we can," suggested Marjie as Jerry opened the barbed-wire gate. "What's the story about Billy falling in?"

"Dad warned you, eh?" Jerry asked, closing the gate and heading down the hill. "See that spot down by that big elm tree?" He pointed to an area a fair distance downstream. "Billy and I were staying just as close as we could to the water, and Billy suddenly dropped through a snowbank and went in up to his shoulders. Luckily the current wasn't cutting through that spot; otherwise, he'd have been a goner. I pulled him out, but our folks wouldn't let us come down here again in the spring for a couple of years."

"I can understand why," Marjie said, following Jerry toward the creek. "I shudder to think of all the trouble you two must have gotten into."

Jerry laughed and nodded in agreement. "Huck Finn and Tom Sawyer," he said. "Every trip into the woods and every walk to school was an adventure. If my mother'd known half of what we did, she would have skinned me alive."

Leading her toward a limestone outcropping that leaned out over the angry creek, Jerry said, "In the middle of the summer when it was really hot, Billy and I used to jump off there into about two feet of muddy water."

"How could your mother not notice?"

"We'd jump in the cow tank when we got home and wash up, then let the air dry us out."

"What about your clothes?"

"You've heard of skinny dipping?"

"I can't believe you," Marjie protested as they crawled up onto the rocks. She had to raise her voice a bit to be heard over the roar of the water. "Did you ever tell your dad?"

"Didn't need to. He caught us."

"And he didn't tell your mother?"

"He snuck up behind us and scared us so bad that I reckon he figured we'd never dare do it again," explained Jerry, breaking into a hearty laugh. "He roared so loud that we took off running for home buck naked. Then he made it real fun by hiding our clothes."

It was an intriguing mental picture, but Marjie quickly forgot it as the sight of the swirling waters captivated her. From the outcropping, they could peer straight down into the center of the stream. The rust-colored water had swollen the creek to three times its normal width and in many places it threatened to escape the upper banks. Chunks of unmelted snow and ice, wooden fenceposts, and even small logs rolled beneath them. Wherever they looked, the turbulent water seemed to be tearing and carving out new territory for itself.

After she had gazed on the powerful sight for a while, the warmth of the large limestone slabs seemed to offer Marjie their invitation. She sat down on the rock and leaned back on her hands, taking in a deep draft of refreshing spring air, closing her eyes, letting the sunshine warm her face.

"Perfect day," Jerry proclaimed as he sat down beside her. "Absolutely perfect. Wish it was like this all summer."

Marjie did not open her eyes, but nodded in partial agreement. "It's not quite perfect," she said quietly, then looked over at Jerry.

"Why not?" asked Jerry.

"Good question," responded Marjie slowly. "Your story about your dad reminded me that he's still planning to move out as soon as he finds a house to rent. Seeing him play with Martha on the floor, I sort of got a sick feeling in the pit of my stomach. I can't imagine him leaving."

Jerry's eyes saddened; he looked away and appeared to be preoccupied with the creek again. Pushing his cap back and rubbing his forehead, he said, "I hate to see him leave, but there's no talking him out of it. He's convinced it's time for us to become our own family, and he's probably right."

"I understand what he's saying well enough," Marjie reasoned. "I just can't stand the thought of him working in a place like the feed mill all day, then going home to an empty house, fixing himself supper, and then sitting alone all night."

"He managed it before," offered Jerry.

"And just about crawled the walls," Marjie finished. "You know as well as I do that he isn't made for living alone. He needs somebody around to share his life with. Besides, the way he cooks, he'll starve to death."

Jerry gave a short laugh and patted his stomach. "Twenty pounds added in the navy either indicates pure fat or previous malnutrition."

Marjie pinched his waist, but didn't feel like following it with a joke. Instead, she said, "What can we do for him, Jerry? I feel like we're letting him down."

Taking her hand and rubbing her palm with his thickly callused fingers, Jerry mumbled, "I wish I knew what to do. His health used to be so bad that I didn't figure we'd have to worry about where he went or what he did. Maybe we can invite him over for supper every night?"

Marjie shook her head and twisted her lips. "He won't come. And even if he did, it won't be the same. I'm afraid life will never be the same for him again."

"I'm sure it won't be—for him or us," Jerry conceded. "I may be the one who's benefitted the most from having him around the house. After all these years, I feel like I'm finally finding out who my father is, and he probably says the same about me. But life goes on, and it changes. We'll just have to adjust."

"Adjust, yes, but why does Benjamin have to go back to what he hates?" Marjie asked. "Can you see him being alone again?"

Jerry sighed deeply and scrunched up his mouth. "No," he muttered. Then his face brightened a bit. "But maybe we're looking at this backward."

"Meaning?"

"Well," Jerry reasoned, "when I left for the navy and he was on his own, that was hard on him. But as a result, his life changed for the better. You came to stay with him, and then Martha came, and since then he's had the time of his life."

"I still don't get your point."

"Maybe we're not seeing the big picture," explained Jerry. "We only see the difficulties—which are real. But perhaps there's something better for him ahead that's just as real. Just 'cause we don't see it, that don't mean it can't happen."

Marjie finally broke into her patented smirk and nodded. "What you mean is that God did something good before, and He can do it again."

"That's what I mean," Jerry agreed. "But it might not look anything like what we want it to look like."

"That's the part that troubles me."

"I know. But isn't that what faith is for?"

Marjie closed one eye and gave Jerry a long Popeye expression. "I still don't like it," she whispered.

27

SPRINGTIME SPARKS

"How far away is this place?" Marjie asked Jerry as their car rolled down a steep, rocky road in the shade of a stand of towering pines. "We've never been down this road before."

"*You* haven't," Jerry replied, gripping the wheel hard and braking because of the sizable rocks that lay strewn across the way. "We used to come down here fishing when I was kid, but the road's in terrible shape. Must be the frost coming out tore the rocks loose. Where we're going is a couple of miles from here."

Marjie looked down at Martha and smiled. "All this bouncing knocked her out like a light," she said. "We should drive around every night and see if it works."

The car finally reached the bottom of the hill, and Jerry sped up as they crossed the flat stretch of bottomland bordered by barren fields on both sides.

"Looks pretty wet down here yet," Jerry remarked, slowing the car again as they approached an old wooden bridge and a cluster of buildings on the other side. "We'll have our crops in before they touch this property."

"What's the name of this place?" Marjie asked.

"Forestville," replied Jerry. "And this here's the south branch of the Root River." Rattling across the bridge, he made a quick left and pulled the car to a stop just off the edge of the road. To the right was a large brick and wood structure that appeared to be long since abandoned.

"That's the old Forestville general store," continued Jerry, pointing up at the fine woodwork that graced the front of the building. "This is one of the oldest settlements in the county, and that was one of the earliest stores. Pretty spooky-looking place, eh?"

"What happened to it?" Marjie questioned. "Looks like there's stuff still in there."

"The place was abandoned years ago," Jerry explained. "I don't know why they did it, but one day the people who owned the store locked the doors and moved to California. Left all the merchandise right where it was. It's been that way ever since. We should ask my dad for the story. My grandpa used to come here with the wagon for supplies."

"All this way?" Marjie asked.

"Yep," answered Jerry, pulling the car back onto the road and heading south. "It was the only store around, and the county seat was there too."

"There? There's only a few other buildings and that huge barn on the other side of the road."

"Times change, and I guess that ol' place didn't keep up," Jerry reasoned. "Seems like there's a lesson there."

"I guess," Marjie agreed. "But I'd like to get inside and pick out some of that merchandise. It's not doing anyone much good in there."

Jerry nodded. "Maybe they'll make a museum out of it some-day. Oops! Here's the turn already."

He braked hard and pulled the car into a narrow farm drive-way that led through dense woods. There was no gravel, and the muddy potholes and tree roots tossed the car from side to side.

"You weren't kidding when you said this place is in the boondocks!" exclaimed Marjie, bouncing up and down in the front seat. "And we have to drive across the river yet?"

"We don't *have* to drive across it, but you're not going to want to wade," Jerry assured her. "The water's ice cold, especially this time of the year. This is a great place for a picnic, though. Trust me."

Suddenly the shady lane opened into a rolling meadow that was only beginning to break out into the green of spring. Jerry followed the bumpy trail as it led up a slight incline.

"Do you think we'll have enough food?" Marjie asked.

"This was Ruthie's idea, remember?" Jerry replied. "And you know Ruthie! I'm sure she's got everybody bringing something. But if all we have is your fried chicken, I'll be fine."

Rising over the knoll, the thin road curved right, and they were immediately in someone's farmyard. Jerry drove past a barn on the left, pulled up to a large gate, and honked his horn.

"Now what?" Marjie asked, looking toward the neatly kept white farmhouse. A tall man in bib overalls stepped from the house and gave a friendly wave.

"We have to get permission to go through the gate," Jerry answered as the lanky farmer sauntered around the front of the car. "And he charges to get through."

"Fred, how's it going?" Jerry called out.

"Just fine," the man acknowledged. "Been a busy day, though. This is the fourth car. Little early in the season, ain't it?"

"We know trout season's not open yet, but we're not fishing. Just a picnic today," Jerry said. "What do I owe you?"

"Not a nickel," Fred replied. "I read your story in the paper, Jerry. This one's on me."

"Thanks!" Jerry said, tucking his billfold back into his pocket.

The farmer unhooked the large wooden gate and pushed it wide open. Jerry rumbled past him and headed the car cautiously down a treacherous incline, braking all the way down the slippery, rocky descent. Marjie clutched Martha tightly as they approached a river that looked to be about twenty yards across.

"You're sure we can make it through!" exclaimed Marjie nervously. "Looks deep to me, and the water's fast."

"We'll make it," Jerry assured her. "See the cars up on the bank across the stream?"

Pulling the car to a stop right at the river's edge, Jerry looked at Marjie and asked, "Ready?"

Marjie refused to look anywhere but straight ahead at the cars that had already made it through. She saw Ruth and Margaret walking toward them, followed by Billy and Chester, then Benjamin and her mother.

"Are you sure they came this way?" Marjie demanded.

"They either came this way or they sprouted wings and flew in," teased Jerry, waving at the friendly spectators who had gathered on the other side.

"Let's get this over with," growled Marjie, clasping Martha tightly and bracing her feet. "Give her the gas!"

Jerry nudged the Ford forward, and the front tires dropped into the shallow rapids. The force and the roar of the water gave an eerie sense of impending doom inside the car. The slick back tires then entered the stream and began to spin and slip on the limestone rocks beneath.

"Give her the gas!" Marjie barked.

The car began to shift sideways; Jerry adjusted the steering wheel and pushed down on the accelerator. The others on the bank began to whoop and cheer them on, then suddenly the front end dropped another degree lower, and water began splashing up into the engine. Halfway through, the motor gave a prolonged sputter and nearly died.

"Uh-oh!" Jerry called out. Pushing in the clutch, he revved the engine, and the motor came back to life. Jerry popped it back into gear and sped through the rest of the way. Rising up out of the water, the Ford slid past their friends and pulled to a stop alongside Benjamin's car.

"Whew!" muttered Jerry, turning the car engine off. "That was exciting!"

"I'm walking back!" Marjie spat, still sheet white from fright. "Did you do that on purpose?"

"Me?" Jerry protested. "How could I stage that?"

"I have no idea," Marjie gulped, then she gave a long sigh. "But I thought you were smiling until the motor popped."

Jerry laughed and said, "I was. Guess I didn't think about

the water being higher this early in the year."

"Let's get out of this boat," Marjie said, pulling down on her door handle and feeling very relieved as she stepped safely onto the dry land with Martha still sleeping contentedly in her arms.

Billy was the first one to the car and greeted Jerry with a generous pat on the back. "That was a fine piece of driving," he declared to the others, then he turned to Marjie. "And on behalf of all of us, I declare Marjie Macmillan as the undisputed champion of the most-frightened-looking-face contest. Let's all give Marjie a big hand!"

Seven sets of hands began clapping, and a few wolf whistles broke the air. Marjie shook her head and acknowledged her victory. Then she retorted, "There'll be no fried chicken for you today, Mr. Wilson!"

The laughter continued while Sarah sidled up alongside Marjie and whisked Martha away. Jerry and Marjie opened the back doors of the car and rattled around pulling out their basket of food, a couple of chairs, and their card table. Then they followed to where the others were already seated.

The picnic area was on a lovely grassy bank that overlooked the joining of the main stream of the river with an adjacent smaller stream of spring-fed water. Stately elm trees leaned out over the bank, their tiny spring leaves rippling in the light breeze. The farmer's cattle grazed on the land, but the herd was across the valley on a slope where the sunshine had already greened the hillside.

Marjie plopped her basket down on the card table that had been designated for the food, studied the variety of foods there, then poured a cup of coffee and joined the others who were seated around the other card tables.

"Margaret, did you bring the glazed doughnuts?" asked Marjie, settling back into her chair. "I love doughnuts."

"That I did," Margaret replied.

"She made them herself," Chester stated proudly.

"You're kidding!" exclaimed Marjie. "They're beautiful. I thought you got them at the bakery. How could you possibly have made them at home?"

"I didn't," answered Margaret with a coy smile. "They were made in the bakery."

Giving Margaret a confused look, Marjie reasoned, "If you made them, but they came from the bakery, what am I to think?"

"Simple," Margaret assured her, then she broke into a laugh. "I have a job at the bakery!"

"Congratulations!" exclaimed Marjie. "See. I told you you'd have no problem getting a job. Why didn't you call and tell us? How's it going?"

"First, we have no phone, so I couldn't call. And, second, I like it," Margaret replied. "Mr. Olson is a very nice man, and his wife keeps slipping me sacks of yesterday's pastries. Chester is going to turn into a blimp!"

Everyone laughed, and Chester puffed his cheeks out and began to rise up out of his chair until Jerry pushed him back down.

Benjamin cleared his throat and said, "We got some bad news for you, Jerry. Before you got here, Billy told us he won't be around for spring planting."

"What?" Jerry gasped. "You're leaving?"

Billy's expression sobered, and he simply nodded that it was so. "We did talk about it," he reminded Jerry.

"I know, but still," sputtered Jerry, covering his frustration. "What's the rush?"

"I got a job offer, and it was too good to pass up," Billy grinned, then looked at Ruth, who obviously knew something Jerry didn't. Marjie immediately picked it up.

"In San Diego?" asked Jerry.

"In Preston," Marjie said matter-of-factly. "The Farmers and Merchants Bank. Am I right, or am I right?"

"The lady wins another prize!" Billy stood up and mimicked a huckster from the carnival. "Give her the biggest glazed doughnut in the house."

Jerry burst into laughter and reached over and shook his best friend's hand. "That's wonderful news," he declared. "When do you start?"

"Monday," answered Billy. "And I'm moving into Chester's

WHISPERS IN THE VALLEY

old apartment. I hope to leech a few meals a week from our two friends here."

"Anytime," Chester piped in.

Marjie laughed along, but she wasn't finished with her detective work. "Ruthie, where's your car?"

Ruth gave Marjie a blank stare, then answered, "I didn't drive—afraid of crossing the stream. So Billy called and suggested I ride with him."

"You could have ridden with us," Marjie said.

"I owed her," Billy interjected quickly. "I got the job at the bank because Ruthie twisted Stockdale's arm."

"I see," Marjie concluded, studying Ruth's eyes, then looking across at Billy. "It's obvious. I don't know how I could have missed it."

After the picnic had been devoured and the conversation slowed down, Sarah and Benjamin volunteered to take care of Martha while Marjie and Jerry went for a walk up toward the spring that fed the smaller stream.

Stopping to gaze into one of the deeper holes of the narrow stream and watch the small brown trout that were schooled toward the bottom, Jerry asked, "Why did I get the impression that your mother was in a hurry to get rid of us for a while?"

"Maybe she was," Marjie replied. "I think she and Benjamin like to talk without us getting in the way."

Jerry nodded and said, "Sarah has a way of getting him to talk like my mother used to do."

"They've got a lot to talk about," Marjie added. "They've both been through a lot in their lifetimes."

"Say," Jerry asked, "speaking of best friends. What were you and Ruth talking about when you snuck off there for a couple minutes?"

"You noticed that," Marjie said, "but you didn't notice the other?"

"What other?" queried Jerry.

"Take a gander back down the stream at your old buddy

247

Billy," Marjie suggested. "What do you see?"

Jerry turned and shaded his eyes against the bright sunshine. "Billy's walking with Ruth down toward the big pool. So what?"

"So what?" Marjie railed. "So you're blind as a bat! Think about it."

"They're—" Jerry cut himself off, then scratched his forehead. "Are you sure?"

"Absolutely," Marjie replied quietly.

"What about this guy Ruthie's been dating?"

"He's too slow. What you see is where the action is."

"They're just friends—"

"Want to put some money on it?" Marjie teased, taking Jerry's arm and pushing him on down the trail. "I give them six months maximum. We're either going to hear wedding bells, or they're going to crash and burn."

"How do you know that?" Jerry wondered. "Did Ruth tell you?"

"She wouldn't say a peep, but she doesn't need to," Marjie replied. "It's written in the eyes, Jerry. Look for the sparks the next time you see them together."

28

BADGER STEW

Warm breezes were gently puffing Jerry's light blond hair to one side as he turned the small Ford tractor at the end of the newly harrowed field and came to a halt. The black earth was rich and clean, and with the early rains the field had worked up as smooth as a ball field. It was as though the tender soil was waiting to embrace the precious seed he was placing in its care.

A dog's sudden barking in the ravine just beyond the fence-line brought Jerry out of his daydream, and he reached down to shut off the engine.

"Blue!" he yelled, but the dog's barking only got louder. "Blue, come here!"

Just then Marjie came up over a knoll in the pasture carrying a picnic basket with Jerry's lunch. Waving at Jerry but hearing the barking, she called, "What's wrong?"

"Blue must have—"

But a shrill yelp from the dog cut through Jerry's words. Grabbing a long steel wrench out of the tractor's tool box, Jerry jumped from the Ford and raced toward the deep ravine. Leaping over the pasture fence, he made his way down the ravine's steep incline. Blue had cornered a big badger against the rocks.

"Blue!" Jerry screamed, racing toward the scene. "Back up!"

Blood was already dripping down the side of the dog's face where the badger's long claws had raked him, but the little cow dog wasn't about to let his savage enemy go. The badger's muscular black-and-white body was hunched up and ready to attack.

As Jerry approached, the badger turned toward him as the larger enemy. The dark eyes flashed beneath the streamlined white stripe that ran from nose to shoulders. The white teeth were bared in silent menace. Jerry knew from many years in the country that a cornered badger could be bad news for either dog or man.

"Get away from him!" Marjie called as she reached the rim of the ravine and looked down. "He'll tear you up!"

Jerry raised his empty hand for Marjie to be quiet, then he reached down and lightly touched Blue on the back. The dog did not take his eyes off the enemy. "Back off, Blue!" Jerry commanded, but he did not dare take his focus off the badger either. He held the wrench poised, ready for the badger to make a move.

A second touch on the back, and Blue slowly stepped back. "Call him!" Jerry yelled to Marjie.

Marjie called with as much authority as she could muster, "Here, Blue. Come on, boy!"

Blue turned toward her for a moment, and Jerry commanded, "Go!" With that, the wounded dog made his retreat.

"Come on, Jerry!" Marjie called as Blue approached her at the top of the ravine. "Leave him before he hurts you, too."

But with Blue out of the way, the badger hissed and began to inch his way toward Jerry. Standing his ground, Jerry raised the large wrench with his right hand and stretched out his left hand and waved it in a teasing motion toward the badger.

"Don't!" cried Marjie, but it was too late.

The large badger sprang forward toward Jerry's left hand and opened its mouth to bite, but in a lightning motion Jerry delivered a blow that struck the badger squarely between the eyes. The short, broad body dropped lifeless against the rocks, and the badger's dull-yellow underside showed as it lay in a heap on its side.

Marjie grabbed Blue before he could make his dash back to

Jerry's side. "Is he dead?" she called.

"As a mackerel," Jerry replied, tapping at the vanquished foe as if he wasn't quite sure. "That's the last dog this old boy tears up. Blue was lucky. How is he?"

Marjie held Blue's face and shook her head in relief. "Just a long scratch. Maybe he learned his lesson."

"Did he look like he learned his lesson?" Jerry muttered as he picked up the badger by its short, bushy tail. "Blue was going to fight to the death. And he'd have lost. This badger's big—twenty-five pounds, I bet. Want him?"

"For what?" Marjie asked, wrinkling her nose.

Jerry shrugged and picked his way up the side of the ravine toward them. "Soup?"

"Yuck!" sputtered Marjie. "Why do you even talk like that?"

"They say badger meat's not that bad," Jerry persisted with a grin. Reaching them at the ravine's edge, he dropped the heavy badger on the ground, and Blue bent down to sniff at it.

"Tell you what," Marjie suggested. "I'll cook him on one condition."

"Which is?"

"You eat him."

Jerry and Marjie burst out laughing, then Jerry knelt down beside Blue and proudly congratulated the cow dog for his bravery.

"You should skin him and make yourself a badger cap," teased Marjie, lightly touching the badger's thick fur. "You looked like Daniel Boone fighting a 'bar' down there. But that wasn't the smartest thing you've ever done, you know. If he'd have gotten your hand, there'd be nothing left but a stump."

Jerry chuckled and nodded in agreement. "I reckon you're right. I thought he had me there for a second. But I still got my quick right! He never saw it coming, let alone felt a thing."

"Oh, brother!" Marjie gasped, shoving Jerry and sending him tumbling over backward. "You're so tough!"

Marjie took off running back to where she'd dropped the picnic basket, but before she got there, Jerry had caught her and picked her up off the ground.

"Tough enough to take care of you," he suggested with a wide grin, holding her in his arms. "Marjorie Belle Macmillan. I still love the sound of that name. Time for a kiss."

Marjie put her arm around Jerry's neck and kissed him gently at first, then followed up with several more that were not so gentle.

"Mmmm!" he murmured as he let her back down to the ground. "Delicious. How about. . . ."

"Sorry," she told him. "Not now. Your father's bringing Martha out here to join us pretty soon."

"So. . . ."

"So, not today," Marjie countered, walking back to the picnic basket. "Now, let's get you some lunch before you and Blue tackle another critter. Where shall we eat?"

"Under that tree," answered Jerry, pointing to a gnarly old oak. "We used to eat there when my mother would bring lunch out to us. Been a long time since I ate there. Shall I bring the badger?"

"Leave it right there," Marjie warned, "or you'll be eating last year's acorns instead of chicken sandwiches."

Jerry and Marjie walked over to the oak and spread a tattered white tablecloth over the long grass. Then they sat down, and Marjie pulled out the sandwiches and potato salad and a jug of milk.

"Can't beat a picnic!" Jerry exclaimed as he leaned his back against the knobby tree trunk. "What a beautiful day, eh?"

"Here, wash your hands," Marjie said, handing him a Mason jar of water and a bar of soap. "Who knows what that badger was carrying."

A gust of wind blew some of Marjie's wavy brown hair into her face; she reached up and pushed it back with a smile. Looking around at the lovely valley below them and the tiny buds on the oak tree, she took in a deep breath of air and said, "Wonderful! A little better than the North Atlantic, I'll bet."

Jerry chuckled and nodded, swishing water through his hands and getting them as clean as possible. "Doesn't compare," he stated. "It's hard to believe that a year ago I was shuttling

Spitfires to Malta. Sometimes it's almost like a dream—it's hard to believe it really happened. I can still see that one Spitfire circling overhead again and again and then putting down on our deck. He came so close to crashing."

"Scary," Marjie said as she handed Jerry a sandwich. "But let me assure you that it wasn't a dream. Last year your father was seeding this field by himself. This year he's playing with his granddaughter."

"And . . ."

"And what?"

"Did you look at your garden before coming out here?" Jerry asked with a broad grin.

"No."

"Check out your raspberry row," Jerry continued, taking a large swig of milk and wiping the corners of his mouth. "He straightened it."

"No!" Marjie protested. "Are you kidding?"

"Nope. He was busy at it when I left the yard," Jerry replied. "He said he just couldn't take that crooked row anymore."

Marjie laughed and shook her head. "Here's your fork," she said, passing him the utensil. "I thought he looked a little guilty when he came in this morning. I'll chew him out good when he gets here."

"I can't believe you held him off last year," Jerry stated. "If it was anybody but you that'd planted those berries, he'd have fixed it the next day."

"Guess I did pretty good, eh?" asked Marjie with a smirk.

"Pretty good at what?"

"Tormenting him."

Jerry nodded and laughed. "You are an expert at torment."

Pulling a big bone out of the picnic basket, Marjie looked over at Blue, who had lain down beside them. "I almost forgot your reward, old boy. Compliments of your friend the bull. Enjoy," she said, tossing it over. "It's all you get."

"So when are you going to get my garden ready?" Marjie asked Jerry. "I've got the seeds, and the potato eyes are cut and ready to plant."

"You better get Dad to help you," Jerry said, stretching his arms and yawning. "I'm allergic."

"To what?"

"Gardens," answered Jerry. "I hate gardening with a passion. Makes me ill just thinking about it."

"You seem to have been enjoying what we canned last summer," replied Marjie.

"I didn't say I hated eating out of it, especially when it's fresh," he explained. "It's working in the garden I hate. We used to have a garden the size of a football field when I was a kid. Mother had enough tomatoes to feed an army."

Marjie laughed, but she wasn't about to give in. "You're still going to help me, buster," she persisted. "Let me quote you one of Edna's favorite Sunday school verses. 'If—' "

"Hold it!" interjected Jerry, holding up the last bite of his sandwich. "Let me try: 'If any would not work, neither should he eat'!"

"You got it!" exclaimed Marjie. "You're very good."

Jerry and Marjie laughed, and Jerry added, "It's about all I do remember. She must have drilled that one into us."

"Say," Marjie said, "we never decided on what we wanted to do about church. Remember?"

"Sure," replied Jerry. "I've been thinking about it for a couple of days now. I think you and Martha and I should join the church together."

"But you're already a member," Marjie commented. "You planning on doing what Billy did?"

"Why not?"

Marjie shrugged, then took Jerry's empty plate and set it back into the picnic basket with hers. "I thought it was amazing," she stated. "Won't it seem strange, though, the three of us joining together? Has anyone ever done that before at your church?"

"Not that I remember," Jerry replied with a smile. "But I was reading in the Book of Acts the other day that whole households were baptized together. Sounded like that's what we should do."

"I like that," Marjie said. "I hope the church people think it's okay. Do you think we should ask them to dunk us like they do over at the Baptist church?"

"That would go over big," Jerry suggested with a chuckle. "Like your crooked raspberry row did with my dad. Do you think sprinkling or dunking makes any difference?"

"Why should it?" asked Marjie. "Benjamin keeps saying that it's what's in your heart that matters."

Jerry nodded. "That much I'm sure about. I guess I just wonder what the big deal is. I've never thought about it much—until now."

"Well," Marjie added, "I suppose it wouldn't hurt to ask the pastor . . . or Benjamin. I'll bet he knows. My guess is that someone read the verses one way and someone else read them another way, and never the twain shall meet."

"Seems sort of dumb to me," Jerry concluded.

"Like a lot of other stuff," Marjie replied.

Blue had been busy crunching away on his bone, but now he jumped up suddenly and gazed out across the field. A few seconds later Jerry and Marjie heard a car engine and the rattle of a loose fender. With a small cloud of dust following, Benjamin's car appeared over the ridge, coming toward them on the tractor lane that ran along the fenceline.

"That's strange," Marjie said, getting to her feet. "He said he was going to walk out."

Jerry got up as well and followed Marjie to the fence. Holding down the top strands, he helped Marjie get through the barbed wire and then walked back to get the basket and cloth.

"What's up?" Marjie called as Benjamin pushed the car door open.

Benjamin did not answer, but turned to pull out the little bassinet that held Martha in place when he drove the car. The baby was kicking vigorously and giving gurgled opinions to the world, obviously in a good mood after a late morning nap. Picking her up, he passed her over to Marjie as Jerry crossed the fence behind them.

"What's wrong?" Marjie demanded, seeing Benjamin's sober look. "Is it my ma?"

Benjamin shook his head no. "She's fine," he said. "But she called just before Martha woke up. Seems that Teddy got all worked up this morning after chores—walked out and said he wasn't coming back. He and your mother had some sort of argument. She said he stuffed some things in a bag, threw it in his truck, and pulled off. He was supposed to finish seeding the oats today, and your ma's afraid he might be serious about staying away this time."

"Oh, phooey," Marjie spat. "That knucklehead's stubborn enough to do it. What's she going to do?"

"She sounded pretty nervous, Marjie. And she's got good reason to be nervous. On top of worrying about Teddy, she could have real problems if a rain were to blow in with only half the field planted."

Marjie turned toward Jerry and asked, "Can you help her?"

"Now?" he questioned, looking out at his own dark fields. "I'm only halfway done myself. If we—"

"Hold on!" Benjamin broke in. "I've taken care of it already. Marjie, I told Sarah that you and Martha and I would be over as soon as we could get there. You can talk with your mother, see how she's taking all this, and I'll get those oats in the field. If Teddy doesn't come home tonight, I'll help her with the milking as well."

"You're wonderful!" exclaimed Marjie, giving Benjamin a hug. "Let's go!"

29

No Time to Give Up

Benjamin slowed the car for the sharp turn into the Livingstone driveway, and a large cloud of road dust threatened to catch them from behind and engulf the car. Turning quickly off the dry country road and speeding up the farm driveway, he managed to escape the mushrooming cloud and its choking bite.

"Looks like Teddy didn't come back," Marjie said as she surveyed the quiet farmyard. "There's the tractor—all set to go, looks like. You sure you can handle a John Deere?"

"I told you twice already that a tractor's a tractor," Benjamin assured her, pulling the car up close-by the farmhouse and stopping by the front steps. "Simmer down now or you'll get your mother more upset than she already is. I'll have the oats in before dark."

"Wonder where Ma is?" Marjie wondered, looking at the empty screen door where her mother usually met them. "Strange that she didn't hear us coming."

"You go on in the house and look for her, Marjie," urged Benjamin. "I'll bring Martha in and her bag. Maybe your mother's on the phone or out in the barn."

"I don't like the looks of this," Marjie murmured and pushed the car door open. "She knew we were coming. This isn't like her."

Marjie jumped out of the car and turned toward the barn.

"Ma! You down there?" she called, but the only noise to be heard was the rattle of the metal feeders where the pigs were busy eating.

Turning back toward the house, Marjie bounded up the front steps and entered without knocking. "Ma!" she yelled as she stepped into the living room, then stopped. "You here?"

An eerie silence gripped the dreary farmhouse, and for a moment panic seized Marjie's heart. Then she heard the sound of Benjamin slamming the car door shut and his footsteps on the wooden steps behind her.

"Ma! Are you here?" Marjie called. Again she stood silently and received no response. The screen door opened, and she turned to Benjamin and Martha with a bewildered look.

"Is she gone?" Benjamin asked.

"No one's here," Marjie replied. "Where would she have gone?"

"Did you check the rooms?" questioned Benjamin, setting the diaper bag down and resettling Martha against his shoulder.

"No, I—"

"Better check her bedroom," Benjamin said.

Marjie hurried to the stairway and quickly climbed the steps. Knocking on her mother's door, she opened it and stepped into the empty room. The only sign of life was the breeze gently pushing the curtains from side to side.

"Marjie!" she heard Benjamin call. "Down here."

Panic fled and true fear took over as Marjie made her way back down the stairs. *She couldn't have. . . . She's too tough to let him push her over the edge. . . . She's probably just. . . .*

Stepping off the bottom step and into the living room, she looked over at the opening to the kitchen. Benjamin was standing by the door, pointing inside and nodding for her to come.

Marjie walked to the doorway and scanned the kitchen. Her mother was seated alone at the round oak table, her elbows resting on the wood, her gaze fixed out the window toward the clothesline and lilac bushes. In her hand was a white handkerchief that she was turning ever so slowly.

"Ma," Marjie spoke softly, then walked to the table and sat

258

down beside her mother. Taking Sarah's hand, she whispered, "It's going to work out, Ma. Something always does."

Sarah smiled ever so slightly, but continued to stare out the window. "Hmmm," she sighed and nodded to herself. Then she took a deep breath and turned toward Marjie and smiled. Noticing Benjamin and Martha still standing in the doorway, she waved for them to come in.

"You'll have to excuse me," she said wearily. "This hasn't been one of my better days."

"Maybe this little bundle of sunshine can help," Benjamin suggested, handing Martha to Sarah. "She cheered me up on some pretty gray days."

Sarah gratefully took her granddaughter from Benjamin. Martha pushed her legs against her grandmother's lap and waved her arms excitedly, flashing an infant copy of Marjie's familiar smirk. Sarah chuckled, then Martha laughed, then they all laughed together.

"Aren't you my little dolly," Sarah said as she untied Martha's white bonnet and handed it to Marjie. Then she bent down and gave the baby a kiss on the cheek and another smile. "I wish Grandma was in as good a mood as you."

Marjie got out of her chair and headed for the stove to make a pot of coffee, but was surprised to discover that her mother had already brewed it. She placed the blackened pot back on the burner to reheat.

"So what happened, Ma?" asked Marjie.

Sarah made a face at the baby and did not look at Marjie. "Not much to tell," she replied. "Nothing new, that's for sure. Before I went out to the barn this morning, I found another bottle of whiskey in Teddy's room. I've warned him before that if he dragged any more of that stuff in here, he'd have to move out. So I went to the barn and told him how disappointed I was.

"He blew the roof off the barn," she continued, finally looking up at Marjie. "Told me he was clearing out for good and I could have this stinking farm. Looks like he meant it."

"Maybe he'll come back tonight," Marjie hoped aloud, "when he cools down."

"I wish it were true," her mother replied. "But if I know anything about that boy, he's gone for good. He's had time to cool down, and he didn't forget about planting the oats. Matter of fact, he suggested that if I wanted to keep the farm, I better get out there and get it done myself."

"The jerk!" spat Marjie, shaking her head in disgust. "He better not come around here today—"

"Won't do no good, Marjie," Benjamin cut in, raising his hand for her to stop. "It would probably only make it worse. No sense making an enemy out of your brother, especially if he goes into the army like he said."

Sarah silently nodded her head in agreement, then turned her focus out the window again. "I should have gone ahead and sold this place when he first talked about going," she said flatly. "I guess I've just been hoping all this trouble would go away. I knew it was coming, but it's still hard. I've been here so long— I hate to give it up."

Marjie was so angry with Teddy that she wanted to cry, but she fought back the tears for her mother's sake. Sarah seemed to have worked through her anguish to a place of calm, but Marjie sensed that an outburst could easily set her off.

"Maybe you shouldn't give it up yet," Benjamin offered and put his strong, farm-worn hand on Sarah's arm.

Sarah turned her attention back to Benjamin and gazed solemnly at him. Finally she spoke. "I hate to sound rude, Ben, but under the circumstances I don't understand why you'd even say that."

"I'm sorry," he replied, but he didn't look sorry. "Sarah, I've been thinking about this since I first heard what Teddy was planning to do. I should have talked with you before, but I guess I didn't know how to bring it up till now. Sarah, what if I were to come work for you?"

"Wha—what are you talking about?" Sarah placed her hand with the handkerchief in it over her mouth. "Work for me?"

Marjie noticed how quickly her mother was getting upset, so she quickly turned off the stove and took Martha from Sarah.

Benjamin burst out laughing, but Marjie thought it was primarily from nerves. "I mean that . . . well . . . at least for a while, until you get this sorted out, I could be your hired hand. I can get here early in the morning and stay until the evening chores are done."

Sarah continued to hold her hand over her mouth and stared into Benjamin's eyes. "I know you too well to think you might be kidding, but why would you do that?"

Glancing up quickly at Marjie, Benjamin gave a funny smirk and then looked back at Sarah. "That's not so easy to answer right now," he replied, reaching back up and rubbing his ear. "But you need help, don't you?"

"Desperately."

"And I'm available, right?"

"That's what you've said."

"So why shouldn't I come work for you?"

Sarah shrugged her shoulders, but not having an answer didn't lessen the surprise.

"The way I see it," reasoned Benjamin, "it's a shame that a woman as young as you should have to move to town and try to find work. I'm not needed on our farm anymore, and I swear I'll curl up and die if I get put out to pasture. I was already going to find a house to rent and get a job in Greenleafton. Ain't that the truth, Marjie?"

"It's the truth," murmured Marjie, still struggling to catch up with what was happening.

"So why don't we help each other out and see if you can keep this place," Benjamin urged Sarah. "If we can't do it . . . well, at least we tried. How about it?"

Rubbing a hand across her lined forehead, Sarah took a deep sigh. "Ben, if you don't beat all. One minute I'm finally ready to sell the farm, and the next minute you got me thinking I don't have to. Has he lost his marbles, Marjie?"

Marjie shook her head in disbelief. "That bull might have knocked a few loose," she responded, "but we better check again. The rest might have rolled out by now."

They all laughed, but Marjie recognized the persistent look in Benjamin's eyes.

"I know I'm an old man," he said with a nod toward Marjie. "And that bull helped me realize it. But the marbles are all there yet, I promise you. I really would like a chance to help here. So what do you think, Sarah?"

Sarah pushed her chair back, stood up, and stepped to the window. "I've been looking out this window for so many years," she whispered as she studied the shrubs that were growing greener every day. "There ain't much to look at, but it's been mine. And I don't like the thought of living in town. But as much as I appreciate your offer, Ben, I just don't see that it can work."

"Why?" Benjamin protested.

"For one thing," she continued, turning toward him, "this farm has never generated enough extra money to pay for a hired hand."

"That's not a problem," Benjamin countered. "I've given Jerry and Marjie a price for them to buy the farm, and their monthly payments will cover my needs."

"But," Marjie broke in, "you told us you'd need to be earning more money than that to cover your expenses. Remember?"

"So I was stretching it a bit," Benjamin confessed. "Figured it was the only way to get you off my back about moving out and working. If I have the monthly payments and I get all my meals provided here, I'll be all right. And if we could make this farm more profitable, perhaps we could split the profit down the middle?"

"Just ain't right," Sarah mumbled. "I can't ask you to do that."

"You didn't ask me to do anything," Benjamin urged. "I am asking you to let me help. What have you got to lose?"

"Nothing . . ." she confessed. "But it don't seem right, Ben. Besides, you were supposed to be slowing down, weren't you? I've got milking cows, and I can't make it without the milk money. But you shouldn't be milking."

"Who said that?" Benjamin jested. "Suppose Marjie told you that? I'm supposed to slow down, but this is only eighty acres and . . . how many milkers?"

"Eight."

"Huh!" Benjamin snorted. "We've had up to eighteen. I can handle it."

There was a long pause, and Sarah again began to fidget with the handkerchief in her hand.

"Ma," said Marjie soothingly. "Maybe you better let the old man give it a try."

Turning toward Benjamin, Sarah wrinkled her brow. "You're sure, Ben?"

"No doubts," Benjamin assured her. "I'd be pleased if you'd give me the chance to try. I like farm work a heap better'n shoveling grain at the mill."

Sarah gave a half-smile, then closed her eyes and quietly laughed to herself. "No one's been so good . . ." she whispered. Then finally the tears broke loose and rolled down her tired face. Her body shook like a leaf from the sudden explosion of joy and relief.

Marjie stepped toward her mother, but Benjamin was out of his chair faster. He wrapped his arms around Sarah and held her tightly, letting her weep and laugh within his caring strength.

"We'll give it our best shot," mumbled Benjamin, who was nearly in tears himself. "Maybe we'll even have some fun doing it!"

Marjie looked on and felt strangely out of place. It seemed like this was a moment reserved for Benjamin and her mother to share alone. But by the time Sarah had regained control of herself and Benjamin had let her go, Marjie was grinning. "It's a good thing you gave in, Ma. He's the devil to live with when he doesn't get his way!"

The laughter gave each of them a chance to relax again.

"Well," Benjamin stated, "enough talking for me. Time to get them oats in the field. You want to show me where everything's at, Sarah?"

Sarah nodded, but said, "How about coffee first?"

"No thanks," replied Benjamin. "You and Marjie can sit and talk after I get in the field. I always get worried about the equipment breaking down or a rain blowing in. The faster I get it done, the happier I am."

"Let's go, then," Sarah responded with a large smile and took his arm. "I always like to keep the hired man happy!"

30

NO STRINGS

"So when did he say he'd be there?" Jerry asked, pushing his plate aside and stretching back in his chair. "You're going to be there, too, aren't you?"

Marjie fed Martha another spoonful of mushed peas, then looked over at Jerry and raised her eyebrows. "All of us will be there," she responded. "And that includes you, mister. If Teddy thinks he's going to get away without facing us, he's got another thing coming."

"What time are we supposed to go?" Jerry repeated. "I've still got a lot of field work to finish."

"Around noon, Ma said," replied Marjie. "You've just got to make the time for this, Jerry. Family's more important than the crops."

Jerry nodded, staring out the dining room window and focusing on nothing in particular. "Family's always most important," he agreed. "But I gotta tell you that I really don't want to be there."

Marjie put down her spoon for a moment and let a wave of frustration pass before she responded. "You think I do?" she asked. "No one wants to be there. Just because it's unpleasant, that doesn't let us off the hook. We have to do this for Teddy's sake."

"Maybe," suggested Jerry, continuing to gaze out the window.

"Would you please talk to me?" Marjie insisted. "Are you saying we should just let Teddy walk away and leave Ma holding the bag?"

Jerry turned his attention back to Marjie and sat forward in his chair. "No," he said, shaking his head. "But it sounds to me like you're going to give it to Teddy with both barrels. And I guarantee you that the whole thing will turn into a shouting match, and everybody's gonna lose. You've got your cannon loaded, don't you?"

"Packed," Marjie commented with a frown.

"Well, you'll unload, then Teddy will unload," Jerry reasoned. "And then Teddy'll go and enlist, and he'll be so mad he'll never want to come home again. We'll feel like we had to confront him, but it'll bother us as long as he's gone. So I'd just rather do something fun tomorrow—like get a tooth pulled or clean the pigpens."

Marjie laughed, then wiped the mess from Martha's face with an extra dish towel. "Here you go," Marjie said, passing her over to Jerry. "Just don't shake her too hard, unless you want those peas and some other goodies on your shirt."

Sliding his chair back from the table, Jerry sat Martha in his lap and kissed her lightly on the top of her wispy dark head.

"All right. So you think it's going to turn into a feud. And it probably will," Marjie conceded. "If we confront Teddy, it blows up and everyone's upset. But if we don't, he walks away like everything's fine. That really makes me mad."

Jerry wrinkled his forehead and stared out the window again. "Makes me mad, too," he admitted, turning toward Marjie. "But maybe there's a way to beat this thing."

"How?"

"What do you think Teddy's going to be expecting tomorrow?" Jerry queried.

"He probably won't expect you or Benjamin to be there," replied Marjie. "But he'll figure on Ma and me. And he knows that he hurt Ma and that I'm angry with him. He'll expect a fight."

"What if he walked into a going-away dinner instead?"

"What?"

"A big dinner—like you did for me when I came home," Jerry explained.

"Why?"

"Nothing you say or do is going to stop him from going, right?"

"Right."

"Do you want him to leave thinking that you hate him?"

"No, but—"

"Wouldn't you want him to go knowing that you love him no matter how upset you may be with him?"

"Yes, but he's not—"

"So treat Teddy in a way that he doesn't deserve," Jerry continued, "and give him the love that he can never forget. Perhaps you can disarm him and still let him know how you feel without it tearing everyone even further apart."

Marjie's dark brown eyes glistened in the bright sunshine streaming into the dining room as she stared intently at Jerry, then she stood and began gathering the plates and cups. Carrying a load to the kitchen, she placed them in the sink and gazed out the window past the barn. "The Prodigal Son," she whispered.

Stepping back into the dining room, Marjie asked, "So you've been reading about the Prodigal Son, eh?"

"No," Jerry shook his head. "Never thought of it. Matter of fact, I don't remember it all that well."

"Ruth and I were reading it last month. It's the story Jesus told about a young man who demanded his inheritance, and then he spent it all—"

"Now I remember," interjected Jerry. "He ended up feeding pigs. Like me."

Marjie laughed and teased, "Almost. Except he was in such bad shape he had to eat the stuff he *fed* the pigs—sort of like you did eating your own cooking. But then he remembered his father and returned home, hoping his father might allow him to work as a servant."

"Right. But instead the father put on a dinner and threw a big party in his son's honor," commented Jerry.

"Exactly," Marjie replied. "When you mentioned making Teddy a dinner, I thought you were thinking about that story. Teddy's a prodigal, if there ever was one. But maybe we could do the dinner first—before he leaves."

"Sounds like a great idea," Jerry added with a smile. "Glad you thought of it."

———— ✍ ————

With the long cloud of gray dust trailing behind, Ted Livingstone's truck could be seen a long way off as he rolled down the gravel road from south of the Livingstone farm. Crossing the little wooden bridge spanning the creek where he and Marjie had played as children, he slowed down and cut sharply into the driveway.

Sarah Livingstone and Marjie had been watching and waiting at the living room window, but now they stepped back from the light so as not to attract Ted's attention. Benjamin was holding Martha on the davenport, and Jerry was nervously moving back and forth in the rocker.

"Shall we surprise him?" Marjie wondered out loud, looking toward her mother.

"This ain't no birthday party, Marjie," Sarah replied. "Why don't you go out and meet him halfway. He knows that Benjamin's here helping, and he knew you would be here."

"That's a good idea," Jerry added before Marjie could protest. "Hurry! Don't let him get his dander up."

"His dander's been up for a long time," Marjie said with a sigh, then headed for the door. "Why do I always get stuck with the hard stuff?"

Marjie could hear the truck door creaking open as she stepped down from the farmhouse porch. She could see that Ted had one foot on the ground, but he looked like he was waiting to see what she had in mind. Marjie smiled and waved as she approached, hoping she could alleviate some of his concerns.

"Howdy, stranger," she said softly as she stopped and leaned on the truck door. "Why don't you come on in?"

"You got your boxing gloves on?" Ted asked, but did not return her smile. "I'm in no mood for this."

"No gloves, today," Marjie assured him, lifting her hands where he could see them. "I might go for the hair, though."

Ted chuckled, then rubbed several days' worth of whisker stubble on his throat. "So who's in there?"

"Ma, of course," Marjie responded, glancing back toward the house. "Benjamin and Jerry and Martha, too."

"Just you and me and Ma—that's the deal," Ted stated coldly. "If we're gonna fight, I'm not gonna do it in front of those guys."

"I said no fight, and I mean no fight," Marjie countered. "But you have to come in. We've got something for you. That's why Benjamin and Jerry are here."

Ted took a deep breath and closed his eyes, then exhaled a big sigh. "What's the game, Marjie?" he mumbled. "This is no time for one of your tricks."

"No tricks. No games," she said. "This was Jerry's idea, not mine. If you want to join us one last time, we'd love to have you. But I'm not going to force you."

Studying Marjie's expression, he asked suspiciously, "So what's Jerry got in mind?"

"It's a goodbye present," responded Marjie, stepping back from the truck. "Wouldn't be right for me to tell you what it is. But it might be something you're going to need."

"Tell me or I'm not coming in," demanded Ted, folding his arms.

"It's a gift for you, Theodore Livingstone," Marjie said as persuasively as she could. "And that's all I'm going to tell you. Now, I'm going into the house, and we all want to see you one last time before you go, and we'd like to give you a present. But if you don't want it, Ma and I will come out here and talk. It's up to you, Teddy."

"Marjie! Come back here!" Ted called but to no avail. Marjie crossed her fingers and kept marching straight into the house.

"What's going on?" Jerry asked as Marjie stepped into the living room, where both he and Sarah were peeking out the window. "Why didn't he come in?"

"I'm not sure that he will," Marjie answered. "I did my best.

Now it's up to him. If he doesn't come in, I told him that Ma and I would come out to the truck and talk. I don't know if he can face you and Benjamin."

Jerry looked back out the window. Marjie noticed that Benjamin's eyes were shut and he seemed to be praying. *Good idea*, she thought and closed her eyes to send up a brief call for help.

"He's getting out!" Jerry exclaimed, then he moved quickly back to his rocking chair. The slamming of the truck door confirmed that it was true.

Ted Livingstone walked reluctantly up the sandy path toward the house, then climbed the wooden steps and pulled the screen door open. He stepped slowly into the living room, and the first thing to catch his attention was the delicious smells wafting from the dining room table. He was shocked to see the table filled with platters and bowls of steaming food and five places set with his mother's best china.

"What in the world?" gasped Ted, turning toward his mother.

"Surprise!" Sarah announced gently, then walked to her son and gave him a rare hug. "Didn't seem right for you to leave without a special meal."

"We made your favorites," Marjie explained, going to Ted and taking his arm. "Ma even made you a plateful of lefse, and you get to eat every lick of it!"

Marjie led Ted into the dining room, and he stood looking over the heavy-laden table, too overwhelmed to speak. "But . . . why?" he finally murmured.

"Ask Jerry," Marjie suggested. "I told you it was his idea."

Ted turned toward Jerry, who had gotten out of his rocker and followed them into the dining room. "Why?" he repeated.

Jerry flushed and shifted from one foot to another. "I guess . . ." he stammered, "because . . . no matter how we feel . . . or how you feel. . . . Well, we just want you to know that . . . that we care for you."

A blank stare was the most that Ted could muster in response, then he colored as well and gave a nervous laugh. Ted awkwardly reached out and shook Jerry's hand, saying "Thanks" under his breath.

Benjamin came up from behind Ted, reached for his hand, and gave it a strong shake. Ted's expression seemed to relax, although he still looked bewildered.

"Let's eat while it's hot," Sarah stated evenly, pointing for everyone to take a chair. "But first, I'd like Benjamin to pray for Teddy and our meal."

"Stop for a minute, will you?" Ted asked, shaking his head. "I didn't expect any of this. You have to give me some time here. I still don't understand."

Ted looked around the room at the faces of those who were there and saw a sadness, discomfort, determination, and loving concern. "I came expecting a fight, not a meal," he sputtered. "Marjie, aren't you mad at me?"

She stared at Ted, and for a moment Marjie entertained the notion of trying to keep the peace by not telling him the truth. But long years of playing with Teddy told her he could always see through her bluffs. She took a deep breath, and one of her eyes squinted a bit as she said, "I've been very angry with you for months, Teddy. I hate what you're doing to yourself, and I hate what you've put Ma through. It's terrible, and you know better. But even if I'm angry with you, that doesn't mean I love you less. You are my brother, and I'm not going to let this awful situation take you from me."

Marjie watched the force of her words strike against the tough emotional veneer that Ted had built up, and for a moment she thought he was going to cry. But Ted simply pulled out the closest chair to the dark oak table and sat down. Closing his eyes, he stunned the others by folding his hands in his lap and sitting motionless. Not knowing what else to do, the others went to their chairs and sat down as well.

Benjamin was about to pray when Ted began to speak quietly with his eyes still shut. "I know I owe everyone here an apology for all the grief I've caused. There's very little I've done in the past months that's been right. But I'm asking you to try to understand that I've got to leave. I don't know why, but I feel like I'm choking to death on this farm and the memories of—I see her everywhere I go.

"Ma," he choked out, eyes still clenched shut. "I'm sorry for the mean things I've said and for leaving you without help. I don't know what's wrong inside me, but I really thought I'd go crazy if I stayed. And the booze and the gambling—I know it was killing you. You really are better off without me, Ma.

"And, Marjie, you've got every right to be angry," Teddy added, finally opening his eyes and turning to her. "But I'm no good, don't you see? I'm no good. The only good thing—"

"Don't say it," Marjie cut him off. "God can help—"

"No! Stop," Ted insisted, holding up his hand. "This God stuff may have worked for you and for Jerry, but it's not for me. And you're not me, Marjie, so please don't push it. Just let me go."

Marjie could read the pain in his eyes and nodded through her tears.

Ted looked back to Sarah and said, "Will you let me go, Ma? No strings?"

Sarah took his hand and looked into her son's eyes with all of her love. "No strings," she whispered. "But that doesn't mean I won't be praying for you. Agreed?"

"Agreed," Ted said softly in return. Then he closed his eyes again.

"Benjamin," Sarah asked, "would you bless this food before it goes cold?"

31

LOVE RETURNS

"Finally," Marjie breathed quietly as she shut the stairway door behind her. "This teething business is a killer. I started to wonder if I'd ever get her down for a nap. Sorry to make you wait so long, Ruthie."

"No problem," Ruth responded with a warm smile. "It's nice just to sit here and gaze out the window. You have such a lovely view; I'm amazed you get so much done around here."

Marjie walked to the dining room window and looked down into the luscious green valley through a break in the pine trees. The Macmillans' herd of Holsteins was grazing on the sloping hill, and several of the black-and-white spotted calves were frolicking in the spring sunshine, enjoying their newfound freedom from the restrictions of the tiny barn pens.

"I never get tired of that scene," Marjie mused contentedly, still studying the landscape. "When Jerry was away, I think I memorized every square foot of grass that's down there."

"And now Teddy's gone," Ruth said.

Marjie nodded and said, "He's on his way. Hard to believe that both he and Paul are in the army. Seems like Paul's been gone forever."

"It doesn't sound like he'll be home for a long time, either," said Ruth. "As far as I can tell, this war isn't showing any signs of being over."

"No," Marjie sighed wistfully. "But now at least we know Paul's alive. Ma finally got a letter a few days ago—from northern Tunisia. He didn't say much, but I gather he's been having a hard time. A lot of his friends got killed in February."

"At Kasserine Pass, I suppose," Ruth stated. "I saw the news reels about that. It was just dreadful; all those inexperienced young men going up against Rommel. No wonder they were defeated!"

"But Paul's all right, thank God," Marjie whispered, shaking her head. "And now the Axis forces have surrendered in North Africa, so maybe all the dying was worth it."

"You wonder at times," Ruth pondered. "And you hope it is. Every time I see Betty Hunter at church, I don't know what to say to her."

"That makes two of us," Marjie agreed, taking in a deep breath. "My man is home safe and sound, and her husband's lying somewhere in a steamy jungle in the South Pacific. I have a hard time even looking her in the eye."

Ruth rubbed her forehead, then rested her head down upon her hand. "So much sadness . . . and worry," she said. "Does your mother worry a lot—about Paul, I mean. And about Teddy enlisting?"

Marjie shrugged her shoulders and raised her eyebrows. "Hard to say," she responded. "She seems all right, but she doesn't talk about it much. Sometimes I think she'd rather bite her tongue off than talk about Paul. I need a good crowbar to pry it out of her."

Ruth laughed, and the gloom that had dimmed the bright spring morning was dispelled with Marjie's smile.

"So why don't you sit down and take a load off your feet," Ruth said, pointing to one of the dining room chairs. "Tell me, how are Sarah and Benjamin faring together?"

Marjie pulled the chair back and sat down. "So far, so good," she replied. "Benjamin just continues to amaze me. He's taken the farm on like it's a mission, and he acts like he's having a ball. All the crops are in, and he's getting at a lot of the work that

Teddy had let slip. I didn't realize how much wasn't getting done."

"What do you think about it?" Ruth asked.

"Whether Benjamin's overdoing it?" Marjie responded.

"No," Ruth replied, fixing her dark eyes on Marjie's brown eyes. "Do you think their arrangement's a good thing?"

Marjie's expression turned to a questioning frown, and she muttered, "Ruth, of course I think it's good. What do you mean by that? Do you have a problem with Benjamin working for my mother?"

Ruth shook her head no and said, "I don't. But there are people who will."

"Who, for heaven's sake?" snapped Marjie, sitting up in her chair and folding her arms. "And why?"

"I'm your friend, Marjie," Ruth assured her. "I'm on your side. But you need to be aware that people around here talk a lot. And they're going to talk about this."

"Why?" Marjie demanded. "What business is it of theirs?"

"It isn't any of their business, but they make it their business to know everything they can about everyone," Ruth said, combing her dark hair back with her fingers. "To some people, a widower and a widow spending every day together is great gossip material."

Marjie stared at her friend in disbelief, but the truth of Ruth's statement slowly began to sink in. "Oh . . . no," she gasped. "You can't mean it. Ruthie, Benjamin's going to be sixty years old this summer."

"That's not so old," Ruth countered, "and your mother's younger. Besides, they were spending time together before this happened. You don't think it went by without people taking notice?"

"I thought of it," Marjie said, rolling her eyes. "This community is so different than where I came from. Most of the people around where Ma lives wouldn't think twice about it."

"Believe me, they do here," Ruth observed. "And you can bet that Benjamin's aware of it, although nobody's going to say anything to his face."

"He never said a peep about it," Marjie said.

"And he won't," Ruth added. "But he must have felt so strongly that it was the right thing to do that he was willing to be talked about."

Marjie's defiant frown changed to a hearty chuckle, and she unfolded her arms. "My mother and Benjamin Macmillan . . . the source of a scandal after all these years. It's too funny to be true!"

Ruth's dark eyes flashed, and she laughed as well. "It is rather funny, but don't be fooled. Rumors are going to fly, and sometimes they get nasty."

"So what can we do about it?" asked Marjie. "Sounds like the damage has already been done."

Nodding, Ruth replied, "There's not much you can do. Perhaps the best defense is just to have yourself prepared not to fight back. You have to trust that the truth of Benjamin's good deed will eventually prevail. To try to fight the rumors will only make it look like you're trying to cover something up."

"That's easy to say, Ruthie," Marjie commented. "But you know I don't do well at keeping my mouth shut. Especially if I hear someone's been lying about someone I love."

"You have to do it—for their sakes," Ruth urged. "Fighting gossip is like throwing gasoline on a fire. You have to let it burn its way out."

"I hate fires," Marjie declared, "and folks who talk about other people. But maybe nothing will come up."

"Let's hope not, but don't bet on it," Ruth warned. "My guess is that people are already talking."

"So be it," Marjie resolved quietly. "If they're that stupid . . . ah, forget it. Did you drive all the way over here to give me this wonderful news?"

Ruth smiled and chuckled. "Not really," she said. "But it was one of the reasons."

"If the next reason is like the first one, I'm not sure I want to hear it. Can you do any better this time?"

"I'm not sure," Ruth said softly, pushing back in her chair and turning her focus out the window.

"Uh-oh, this looks serious." Marjie changed her tone. "What's up? Is everything okay at school?"

"School's fine," Ruth answered, looking back at Marjie. "And we only have a couple more weeks before we close. It's been a wonderful year."

Marjie studied the expression in Ruth's eyes, then nodded in acknowledgment of what she saw. "Shall I tell you why you're here," she asked, "or would you like to tell me yourself?"

Ruth laughed. "Why don't you try and see if you're close," she answered. "Have you been taking lessons in mind reading?"

"That I don't need," Marjie assured her. "I've read this book before. It's about a certain young gentleman named Billy Wilson, I believe. Is that correct?"

Ruth gave her a crooked smile and nodded yes. "What else?" she asked.

"Hmmm," Marjie responded, still observing Ruth's expression. "You're sure you want me to say this?"

"Try it," Ruth urged her. "I want to see how good you are."

"Okay, but don't say I didn't warn you, Ruthie," Marjie deliberated. "You came here today because you want to tell someone that you are falling in love, but you don't know how to handle it. You're afraid of what you're feeling, and you want someone to tell you whether you should go forward or back away."

Ruth chuckled and looked away, but didn't speak for a few moments. "You are very good," she finally acknowledged. "I am scared to death of what I've been feeling. But you're wrong about the falling-in-love business."

Marjie squinted her eyes at Ruth and said, "I know you're not a liar, Ruthie, but 'fess up here. I've seen how you look at Billy, and if that's not love, I don't know what is."

"I didn't say it wasn't love," answered Ruth.

"So, I was right?"

"Close, but no cigar," Ruth replied, then paused. "You can't fall in love with someone you've already loved for years."

"I knew it!" Marjie exclaimed. "I knew it. But Jerry wouldn't tell me the story. He said that if you wanted me to hear it, you'd tell me in your own time. So this explains why you haven't married?"

"I suppose."

"I'll bet that plenty of other guys have been interested in you, right?"

Ruth only nodded.

"How long have you loved him, Ruthie?"

"I can't remember when I didn't," Ruth answered. "I think I've loved him since we were kids. Sometimes I've hated him as well."

"Ouch!" Marjie echoed the feeling in Ruth's words. "Do you want to talk about what happened in the past—or about what's going on now?"

"Both, I guess," Ruth said softly. "May I have a glass of water, though. My throat's not doing so well."

"Sure," Marjie replied as she jumped up and headed for the kitchen. Quickly pouring a couple of glasses of water, she gathered a plate of cookies and headed back into the dining room.

"Thank you," Ruth said after taking a long, cool drink from the glass Marjie had given her. "Your water tastes so good here. Ours tastes like it came out of a tin can."

"Too much iron," Marjie diagnosed. "So what happened in the past between you and Billy?"

"Not much, I suppose, if you couldn't see my heart," Ruth replied with a sigh. "Billy treated me like a sister most of the time—you know, playing ball, going fishing, bickering together. But the summer we turned eighteen, he finally noticed that I'd grown up, and I guess he liked what he saw. After that, we dated every weekend—right up to the day I left for college."

"And before you started dating, you were already crackers over him, right?" Marjie interjected.

"Right," confirmed Ruth. "You can imagine what happened to me once we started going out together. I was absolutely head over heels. He was all I thought about morning to night. I even began to reshape my education plans around the idea of us getting married."

"So what happened when you left for school?"

"He said goodbye."

"That was it?"

"Pretty much," replied Ruth. "He said he'd had a great summer, he'd see me when I came home at Christmas, maybe we could even go out again sometime. And that was it. No letters, no more dates, nothing."

"How could he do that?" snapped Marjie. "Did he know how much you cared?"

"I really don't think so," Ruth responded. "I didn't dare tell him because he just seemed to be in it for a good time. And he'd figured out that he was really as good-looking as the mirror told him, and every girl in the area would melt for a chance to be with him."

"Those latter days I remember," Marjie recounted. "He played the field, that's for certain. But you must have been crushed, I'm sure."

"Devastated," Ruth mumbled and looked longingly out the window. Marjie could see the pain drawn up around her eyes and the pools of tears begin to form around the edges. Taking another sip of water, Ruth continued, "So what I did was lock myself away in my dorm room and become a recluse."

"Not you!" Marjie blurted out.

"Yes, me," Ruth continued and laughed gently. "I became very antisocial for a time, but my grades were outstanding!"

"And Billy?" Marjie asked. "Did you write him any letters?"

"No . . . well, none that I sent him!" exclaimed Ruth. "I must have written him twenty letters that I ended up burning. Then one day, I sort of came to and I decided I had to get on with my life. So the recluse came out of her closet and started talking to people."

"But you never really got over him, did you?" Marjie said soothingly, reaching out and taking Ruth's hand.

"I thought I had," Ruth muttered, then closed her eyes as tears began to press their way out the corners and trickled down her cheeks. Reaching up with her hand, she pushed them away and shook her head slowly back and forth. "I thought it was all over—until Billy came back this time."

"And what now?"

"You tell me," Ruth whispered, squeezing Marjie's hand. "That's why I'm here. Marjie, I'm afraid he's going to walk away again."

"He's changed, Ruthie. That I know is true."

"But how much?"

"I don't know," answered Marjie. "But you've opened your heart to him again, haven't you?"

A slight smile broke across Ruth's face. "I tried to stay my distance, but it didn't work. When he asked me out, I couldn't say no. And now it's too late."

"But it's different this time, isn't it?"

Ruth nodded.

"You've told him your feelings, haven't you?"

"Yes . . ."

"And what did he say?"

Ruth let go of Marjie's hand, and both of her hands reached up to cover her face. Pressing her fingers against her eyes, Ruth began to laugh and cry at the same time, and her shoulders bounced up and down. After a minute or so, she quieted herself, opened her eyes again, and slowly turned her focus back to Marjie.

"He said . . . he loved me!"

32

Never Too Late

"Something really strange is going on, and I don't like it," Marjie murmured as she handed Martha to Jerry. "I've never seen your father act so odd. What do you think is cooking between him and Ma?"

"I have no idea," Jerry assured her. "He got pretty defensive last night. That's not like him."

"Why wouldn't he talk about whether people around here are going to start rumors about him?" asked Marjie. "Ruthie said that—"

"For the tenth time, I don't have a clue," Jerry broke in, holding up his hand. "All he said was that he understood the possibility of rumors, but that it was not going to become a problem. You know just as much as I do."

"Which is nothing," Marjie moaned, grabbing her purse and heading toward the front door. "Guess I'll know pretty soon, though. Why would they want me to come over to talk with my mother while Benjamin comes over here?"

"You tell me, Sherlock," Jerry teased. "Who knows? Maybe it's not working out as well as they hoped? What if your mother feels like she should sell the farm, and she wants to tell you in private?"

Marjie stopped at the door and turned around to face Jerry and Martha. "Could be. . . ." she said reflectively. "But I doubt it. They're both too stubborn to give up this quickly. I better go. Bye!"

Taking Martha's tiny right hand, Jerry waved it and called out in a high-pitched whine, "Bye-bye, Mommy. Please change my dirty diaper before you go. Daddy's no good at it."

Marjie laughed and twirled around. "See you later!" she said, pushing the screen door open. "I'll be back as soon as I can. For sure before choring time."

"Where's the bottle?" Jerry called out as Marjie headed down the sidewalk.

"Right where it always is, goofy," Marjie answered. "If you can't figure it out, ask Benjamin when he gets here. He knows where everything is."

Jerry stepped out of the house, and the screen door slapped closed behind him as he sat down on the front step with Martha in his lap. They watched as Marjie hopped into the car, then waved as she drove down the driveway past them.

Turning out around the corner and onto the gravel road, Marjie was surprised to meet Benjamin's car. She pulled over to the side of the narrow road and stopped. Benjamin slowed and came to a halt beside her.

"You're early!" Marjie called out to him. "You in a hurry or something?"

"Might be," replied Benjamin, smiling and pushing his old cap back on his forehead. "Got some things to take care of here."

"Like what?" asked Marjie suspiciously. "Why all the secrets?"

"You'll find out soon enough," suggested Benjamin. "But my lips are sealed, so you better get on your way. Your mother's waiting for you—with a surprise."

"I want you to . . ." Marjie stopped in midsentence as Benjamin waved and pulled away. "Come back here!" she yelled, but his car kept rolling down the road and disappeared behind the pine trees.

"If he doesn't beat all," Marjie grumped to herself as she let out the clutch and headed toward the highway. "This better be good."

The whole way to her mother's farm, Marjie's mind whirled like a top. But the closer she got, the more she began to expect to see a "For Sale" sign at the end of the Livingstone driveway. As she slowed down and passed the mailbox, Marjie gave a sigh of relief that everything looked the same as usual.

When she was nearly to the end of the driveway, Marjie noticed her mother out under one of the tall elm trees in the side yard. Sarah was sitting on what appeared to be the old wooden yard glider that Marjie's father had built. For years it had gathered dust in a corner of the machine shed. Marjie knew that several of the boards had rotted or broken away, and nearly all of the paint had flaked off. But from the circle of the farmyard, the swing looked brand new.

Sarah waved to Marjie as the glider swayed gently back and forth. Stopping the car in the shade of the elm, Marjie looked over at her mother again and thought for a moment that time had reversed itself. Her hair was tied back loosely, her light-blue dress was blowing gently in the breeze, and Marjie couldn't remember the last time that her mother looked so young and relaxed.

Then Marjie noticed something move in the swing next to her mother, and at first she thought it was one of the cats from the barn. But when it raised its head to see what the noise of the car engine was about, Marjie could see it was a furry brown puppy with long ears.

"Good night!" Marjie muttered as she pushed open her car door and walked around the front of the Ford toward her mother. "Is this what the surprise business was all about?"

"Do you like her?" Sarah asked, holding the puppy up for inspection as Marjie approached the swing. "Isn't she the cutest thing you've ever seen?"

Marjie laughed at the puppy's smiling, foolish face and marveled that her mother would be holding a dog in her lap again after so many years. "She's darling!" Marjie exclaimed. "And she's yours?"

"Sure is," Sarah answered, motioning for Marjie to join her. "Her name is Tinker."

"What?" Marjie asked, taking a seat opposite her mother.

"Tinker," her mother repeated with a chuckle. "That's what my grandmother used to call a wandering beggar. Look at this little beggar's face. Who could resist giving to it?"

"Not me," Marjie admitted, reaching out and taking the dog from Sarah and plopping it into her lap. Marjie laughed as a ropy little tail began to wave back and forth. "What breed is she?"

"She's a cross between a German shepherd and a beagle," Sarah replied. "Look at those long ears and big paws!"

"The ears are definitely the beagle, and the paws belong to a shepherd," Marjie commented, gently stroking the pup's velvety ears. "Where'd you get her?"

"She was a gift," answered her mother.

"A gift?" railed Marjie, glancing up quickly to see if her mother was serious. "Someone gave you a dog as a gift? Who?"

"Benjamin," Sarah said quietly, with only a hint of a smile.

"He didn't."

"He did," her mother assured her. "I happened to tell him how much I used to love having the dogs around the farm, but how I just never had the heart to get another one after Robert died. When Ben heard about the puppies at the Bedford place, I guess he figured it was time I had a dog again."

"And what about the swing?" asked Marjie. "Benjamin fixed it up and gave it a fresh layer of paint? For you?"

"I reckon," Sarah commented with a trace of amusement. "There's nobody else here to do it for."

Marjie's expression was one of baffled wonder, and for a second she closed her eyes and shook her head to clear out the cobwebs. "Okay, now let me figure out what's going on here," Marjie reasoned. "What do the puppy and the swing have to do with why you and Benjamin thought I should come over here today?"

"Nothing . . . at least not much," Sarah replied with a smirk. "You're the one who brought those subjects up."

"I know, but . . ." Marjie paused, then blurted out. "Ma, what's going on? Are you selling the farm?"

"No . . . no . . . no," answered her mother, shaking her head. "Why would you think that?"

"Why else would you call me over here in the middle of the day to—"

"I'll tell you if you can be quiet for a minute," Sarah broke in with a laugh. "But you've got to listen . . . and concentrate on what I say. Can you do that?"

Marjie felt the puppy give a sigh and looked down to see the dog's eyes shutting for a nap. She stopped pushing against the bottom of the swing, and slowly it creaked to a stop. Staring into her mother's eyes, Marjie asked, "All right, so what's the secret?"

Sarah's smile slowly turned to one of serious reflection. She hesitated momentarily, then said, "Here I had it all figured out, and I can't remember a line of what I wanted to say. But I wanted you to be the first to hear this, and to be able to understand."

Holding her tongue, Marjie let her mother gather her thoughts. Sarah paused, looked down at her hands, and rubbed them together before continuing. Soon her clear blue eyes turned upward again and became fixed on Marjie's dark brown eyes.

"Marjie," her mother said in a voice barely over a whisper, "Benjamin asked me to marry him."

The words may have reached Marjie's ears, but the impact was delayed in its arrival. She blinked, then blinked again, and then she tilted her head and squinted her eyes. "What?"

Sarah's eyes were filling with tears, but she didn't look away. Leaning forward, she put her left hand on Marjie's outstretched right hand. Very slowly, as one tear after another began to streak her face, she announced, "Benjamin Macmillan asked me to marry him . . . and I said yes."

"He asked . . . you said yes!" gasped Marjie, clutching her mother's hand tightly. "Just to save the farm?"

Shaking her head no, Sarah did not speak, but softly began to weep.

"Because you love him?" sputtered Marjie as the tears began to fall down her own cheeks. "Do you love him, Ma?"

"Yes!" her mother whispered. With her right hand, Sarah covered her mouth and tried to hold back her crying. "I never thought . . . I could love another man like I loved your father, Marjie. But I've fallen in love again."

Marjie felt the depth of her mother's words, and she was suddenly overwhelmed with a wonderful explosion of joy. Her first reaction began involuntarily in her shoulders, but soon her entire body was bobbing up and down with a wild mixture of laughter and tears. Mother and daughter took hands, and the swing began to shake sideways.

The puppy woke with a start and jumped off Marjie's lap onto the ground. Landing in the long, green grass, the little dog tore around the swing over and over again, yapping up a storm and losing her breath. Finally, as Marjie's and Sarah's emotions quieted, the pup dropped to the ground, panting for air and looking proud to have settled the situation.

The comical sight of the puppy doing doughnuts around the swing had diverted the women's attention, but only for a moment. Mother and daughter dried their tears as best they could, and Marjie wondered what came next.

"And . . . Benjamin loves you as well?" Marjie asked, still holding her mother's hands and searching her eyes.

Sarah nodded yes. "He has for some time," she said with a quiet, raspy voice. "But he didn't dare say anything until he knew that I loved him, too."

"And how did he know?" Marjie asked, reaching back to push away some tears.

"Same way as you always know," her mother assured her. "It's all in the eyes. He doesn't miss a thing."

"You realize he's older than you?"

Sarah Livingstone smiled softly and chuckled to herself. "At our age, what's five or ten years?" Pulling out a loose strand of gray hair, she scrutinized it closely and said, "This isn't about age or looks. Least I hope not!"

Both mother and daughter broke into laughter again, and the puppy jumped up and went back to circling the motionless swing with barking and panting. Sarah reached out to grab her, but the pup flew right on past, then suddenly dropped to the ground exhausted.

Marjie took Sarah's hand again and said, "You're sure about this, Ma?"

"I'm sure, Marjie," her mother responded. "But I was worried how you might react. It would be easy to feel like I was unfaithful—"

"Don't say it, Ma," Marjie broke in. "No one could have been more loving to Pa than you. But he's gone. He would only want what makes you happy."

Sarah closed her eyes tightly and nodded her agreement while another round of tears squeezed through. Taking a deep breath, she opened her eyes and said, "He would be happy then . . . because I am very happy."

"And I am so happy for you, Ma . . . and for Benjamin," Marjie said. "It's just hard to believe!"

"You're telling me!" Sarah exclaimed. "I can't believe it myself. What are people going to say now?"

Marjie shrugged her shoulders. "That all the rumors were true?"

Sarah burst out laughing, then turned toward the road at the sound of a car coming toward the Livingstone driveway. "I believe that will be your husband and my fiancé," she declared with another laugh. "I asked Benjamin to come over as soon as he explained it to Jerry."

Two honks of the horn and the wave of hands confirmed that it was so, and Benjamin's car turned into the driveway and sped toward them with Jerry at the wheel and Benjamin holding Martha. Marjie and Sarah got up out of the swing and headed for the car.

Jerry was out the door almost before they had rolled to a full stop. "Marjie, did she tell you?"

"Yes!" cried Marjie, running to his embrace. "But I can't believe it's true!"

"You better start believing," Benjamin urged her as he pushed open his door and handed Martha to Sarah. "We're too old to have doubters slowing us down."

Benjamin walked over to Marjie, who let go of Jerry and then gave him a very big hug.

"Congratulations, Benjamin," she whispered, choking up again. "You've made my mother so happy. And I'm nearly as happy as she is."

"I love her, Marjie," he sputtered, then the tears took over. "I guess it's never too late for love."

Jerry stepped into the picture and wrapped strong arms around the both of them. Then Sarah and Martha joined the group, and they were all hugging and crying with joy.

"And here all the time I was thinking you two were just good friends," Marjie said as the circle broke up. "Talk about being blind! How could I miss this?"

"Sometimes it's the ones we love the most that escape our notice," replied Sarah with a smile. "Besides, I just figured this out myself. Why should you expect to know before I knew?"

"Because she's Marjie!" Jerry exclaimed, breaking out in laughter. "And she finally missed!"

33

PAYBACK

"Benjamin, what are you working on, anyway?" Marjie walked into the living room balancing a sleepy-eyed Martha on her hip. Benjamin was sitting in his chair busily scribbling on a piece of paper, and Jerry was stretched out on the davenport listening to the radio. "Thought you might like to rock your granddaughter to sleep for the night."

"I'd love to," replied Benjamin, barely looking up, "but I'm sorta busy—and you know full well what I'm working on."

"So why don't you let us help?" Jerry piped up. "Ruthie and Marjie did a knockout job for Chester and Margaret. You don't need to plan your whole wedding by yourself."

"Don't you fret yourself," Benjamin said. "I'll be asking for help soon enough."

"Why not now?" queried Marjie. "You're not going to wait till the last minute and then dump it all on us, are you?"

"What do you think?" Benjamin scolded. "Since when have I ever done that?"

"There's always a first time," teased Marjie, plopping Martha down on Jerry's stomach. "Besides, I've noticed that your mind's been playing tricks on you since you and Ma hit it off!"

"Aw, that's baloney!" Benjamin sputtered. "Where do you come up with this stuff?"

Marjie burst out laughing. "I was born with it," she replied.

"And it comes from my mother's side of the family. Are you sure you know what you're getting into?"

Benjamin laughed and nodded. "I think I do," he assured her. "And I think I'm going to like it!"

"For goodness sake!" Marjie exclaimed. "You're worse than a teenager."

"Takes one to know one," retorted Benjamin.

"You've gone over the edge," Marjie said. "I'm going to call my mother and warn her about you. But not till later," she added. "It's time to get this little girl to bed."

Jerry kissed Martha on the cheek, then Marjie carried her over to Benjamin. He took his granddaughter in his arms and gave her a hug, then a kiss, and then another hug. "I'm gonna miss this," he said with a tired sigh, handing her back up to Marjie. "Good-night, sweetheart."

Marjie carried Martha into the bathroom to change her diaper and was fastening the last pin when she heard Benjamin speak up.

"Jerry, is most of the hayloft cleared out?"

"Yeah. But it looks like we've got enough hay to keep us till the first crop is ready," Jerry answered.

"Is it a mess up there?" Benjamin continued.

"No. I've got it all pushed to the south wall," said Jerry. "Why? You think there's something wrong with the way I'm taking care of it?"

"Not at all," Benjamin quickly assured him. "You can handle it as you please. I'm just checking. What about the Seven Corners piece. You've got hay on that land this year, right?"

"Right," Jerry replied in a bewildered tone. "Same as last year. Why?"

"Just checking," Benjamin replied, then said nothing more.

"Checking what?" Marjie asked suspiciously, stepping back into the living room with Martha. "You've got some cards up your sleeve again, don't you?"

"Me?" Benjamin asked innocently.

"Cough it up, Benjamin," Marjie demanded. "You said there'd be no surprises."

"Pardon me," Benjamin retorted with a beaming smile. "I never said there wouldn't be surprises. I just said that I wouldn't wait till the last minute and dump a lot of work on you."

"All right," Marjie conceded. "Cough it up anyway."

"Not tonight," Benjamin returned. "That would spoil my fun."

"You're too old to be having fun with this!" Marjie joked. "And your fun always seems to be at our expense. When will you tell?"

"Tomorrow, if everything works out," he said. "After Sarah and I talk with the pastor."

"You two have to talk with Pastor Fitchen about marriage?" Jerry asked. "What's he got to do with it?"

"You might be surprised! More than you think, that's for sure," Benjamin replied. "Which reminds me. I need to say good-night myself. It's going to be a busy day tomorrow."

"What time are you seeing the pastor?" Marjie persisted.

"Eleven o'clock."

"So why don't you plan on coming over here for dinner?"

"What're you cooking?" teased Benjamin, getting up out of his chair and stretching.

"Are you suggesting my ma is a better cook?" Marjie muttered.

"She's real good," Benjamin responded. "But we'll be here by noon—anyway."

"Thanks a lot," Marjie said. "I've got some liver to get rid of. You like it fried real dry, right?"

"Don't you dare," Benjamin warned, heading for the stairway. "Anything will do, but keep the liver for another day."

———— ✐ ————

"Your pa's going to drive us crazy if he keeps us guessing about everything he does," Marjie suggested as she turned the meat in the frying pan. "He's wearing me to a frazzle. Was he like this when you were a kid?"

Jerry shook his head. "Not that I can recall. All I remember is him working around the clock. If mother could ever get him to sit down and relax, he was fun to be with. But that didn't happen much. When it did it was mostly in the winter."

"He must have been saving up all his energies to torture us," Marjie said. "I hardly slept last night, trying to figure out this latest mystery."

"Are you kidding? You hit the pillow and started snoring like you'd been taking lessons from my dad. I thought I was in the wrong bed when you let that first blast go!"

"Oh, come on!" cried Marjie, covering the pan with a lid and walking around the counter into the dining room. "I don't—"

"Here they come," Jerry interjected, looking down the driveway and hearing Blue bark from his post on the front steps. "How long do you think Martha's going to nap?"

"I hope she's out at least long enough for the lovebirds to tell us what's going on," said Marjie as Benjamin's car pulled to a stop in the farmyard. "She didn't sleep very well last night, either. Those teeth coming down are making it pretty rough."

"I'm surprised you even heard her above your roar," Jerry teased. "I got up with her twice before you heard her for the first time."

"You didn't!" exclaimed Marjie. "Did you?"

"I most certainly did," replied Jerry with a wink. "I'll tell you about it after lunch. Here they come."

Benjamin and Sarah walked slowly past the large picture window and smiled at Jerry and Marjie as they went by.

"Did you see that look?" whispered Marjie. "This must be—"

The front screen door creaked open, and Jerry met them as they came in. "Don't let the screen bang shut," Jerry urged quietly. "Martha's sleeping."

"Too bad," Sarah complained. "It was my turn to get her first."

"If you can catch her," Marjie said. "She can scoot around here pretty fast now. Just wait till she starts walking."

"Won't be long, I reckon," Benjamin assured. "You better get a hook for that front door. She'll push her way right through it and head for the hills."

Jerry glanced at the door. "You're right," he agreed. "Can't believe I hadn't noticed. But right now we're ready to eat. Come on in and sit down."

"Smells mighty good, Marjie," Benjamin announced. "Where do you want us?"

"You know it doesn't matter where you sit," she answered. "Just take whichever chair you'd like. But I have to warn you . . . no food will be served in this room until I'm satisfied that we have all the details. Understand?"

"Aren't we just a mite testy today?" Benjamin teased as he pulled back his usual chair and sat down. "Not sure I can talk on an empty stomach."

"You'll survive, if you talk fast," Marjie countered. "And I'm not testy. I'm just tired of worrying all night about what you teenagers might pull next."

"I take that as a compliment," Sarah said, sitting down next to Benjamin and taking his hand. "I do feel a bit like a teenager again."

"For the love of . . ." Marjie protested, shaking her head as she plopped down on her chair. "Enough torture. Tell the story!"

"My throat's dry. Will you let me have a sip of my water first?" Benjamin questioned.

"Yes . . . yes . . . yes," sputtered Marjie. "Gulp it down."

Benjamin took a long, slow drink of water, then looked over at Sarah before he began. "Do you want to tell them, or should I?"

"It's all your idea," Sarah replied. "You go ahead."

"I'm not sure where to begin," Benjamin started. "For the past week I've been working on an idea for how we could do our wedding, but we had to talk with the pastor first about whether he'd go along with it."

"I thought you said you wanted to just do something small," Marjie broke in. "A handful of friends at the parsonage, or something. But this is different, I take it."

Benjamin and Sarah glanced at each other and then burst out laughing.

"That means yes," Marjie commented to Jerry. "So the plans

have switched. But what does that have to do with the hayloft and—"

"Now I know!" Jerry hooted. "You must be kidding!"

"What?" Marjie demanded. "Somebody better tell me the plans or I'll start wringing necks one at a time!"

"I thought you might get it," Benjamin told his son. "Let's hear your version, Jerry."

Jerry's face was lit up like a Christmas tree. "Grandpa and Grandma here want to say their wedding vows out on the Seven Corners piece," he explained to Marjie, "and afterward they want to use the hayloft to hold a wedding dance."

Marjorie just looked puzzled while Sarah and Benjamin both nodded yes.

"But why?" Marjie asked. "Have you both lost your minds?"

"Probably," Benjamin said, rubbing his whiskers and beaming a smile to her. "Actually, the story starts with my grandfather, who homesteaded this farm. Shortly before he left to fight in the Civil War, he and my grandmother had their wedding down on that piece of land."

"And they had a wedding dance in their newly built barn," Jerry continued. "Grandma used to talk about how much fun they had at wedding dances."

"In the barn?" Marjie asked with a quizzical frown.

"Where else?" Sarah responded. "The only other place big enough in those days was the church, and some folks didn't think that was proper."

"Still don't," Jerry added. "You realize that some people are going to be scandalized when they hear you're not getting married in the church?"

Benjamin nodded with a grin of deep satisfaction. "That's part of the fun," he said. "Somebody needs to give folks something to talk about."

"You've already done your share," Marjie observed. "But don't you care what they think?"

"Yes, I do, as a matter of fact," Benjamin responded, suddenly serious. "I really don't want to offend anybody. But this is something I really want to do, even if some people don't like it."

"But why?" Marjie asked again. "Why is it so important to you?"

"Simple enough," Benjamin answered. "I've spent sixty years farming these hills, and they've been good to me. It just seems natural for Sarah and me to celebrate our wedding out on God's good earth—where we've spent most of our lives. Anything wrong with that?"

Marjie shook her head no. "And the pastor said he'd do it?" she questioned.

"Took a little persuading," Sarah replied. "Nothing that a little arm bending didn't take care of, though."

Everyone broke out laughing, and Marjie got up out of her chair.

"I'm calling Ruthie," she said as she headed for the phone. "We've got a lot of planning—"

"Not so fast!" Benjamin's voice brought Marjie to a halt. "You promised us lunch once we told our story, and now you've heard it. Besides, Ruthie's probably working at the school till later in the afternoon."

"Let's eat!" Jerry urged her. "I'm starving."

"Me, too," Sarah added. "Can I help?"

"No . . . no," Marjie responded, walking into the kitchen. "I'll take care of it. And how soon before the wedding? Did you set a date?"

"Two weeks from Saturday," Benjamin called out.

"Good night!" Marjie gasped, carrying two serving plates into the dining room. "Couldn't you give us another week to plan?"

"Not at our age," Sarah said. "Every week's a week."

Marjie set the plates on the table, then pulled the lid off the one to reveal three lightly browned pork chops.

"Mmmm . . . mmmm!" Benjamin exclaimed. "Looks good. But there's only three."

"Payback time!" Marjie announced, taking the lid off the second plate. "This one's for you, Benjamin. Beef liver—well done. Just the way you like it!"

34

WHISPERS IN THE VALLEY

"Ma, you look beautiful!" Marjie exclaimed as Sarah Livingstone stepped out of the bedroom in the dark blue dress Benjamin had made such a fuss over. Giving her mother a hug, Marjie whispered in her ear, "Benjamin's a lucky man. Are you nervous?"

"Just a little," Sarah said quietly, holding on to Marjie a moment longer. "But if you want the truth, it's more like a lot."

Marjie pulled her mother even tighter against her. "How can I help you?" she asked.

"Just hold my hand until it's time to start," Sarah replied. "And let's walk instead of driving down there in the car. Maybe I'll relax a bit if I walk."

"You look as cool as a cucumber," Marjie assured her mother, stepping back and smiling. "You'll be fine."

"I hope so," Sarah said wistfully with the shake of her head. Straightening her collar, she looked over at the wall clock. "Time to go. Let's get this show on the road."

Marjie took Sarah's hand and met her mother's blue gaze. "Are you really ready for this, Ma?" she asked.

Without blinking, Sarah nodded slowly, and half a smile curled one corner of her lip upward. "Ready as I'll ever be," she assured Marjie. "But I'm still nervous as a cat. It's been years since I've been with a man, and your father was the only man in my life. But I'll be fine, just like you said. I wish my boys were here, though. What are they going to think of me?"

"They're going to be real surprised," Marjie said and chuckled. "And I'm sure they'll be delighted."

"Let's hope so," said Sarah. "Guess there's not much we can do about it now."

"So let's go," Marjie said. "I'm sure they're ready. Ruthie went down to the field to get everything organized."

"All's well, then," Sarah said, taking a deep breath. "Lead the way."

Mother and daughter stepped from the farmhouse into the bright afternoon sunshine. They were joined by Blue, who appeared to be waiting to escort them down the farm lanes to the hayfield where the wedding would be. A light breeze greeted them as they walked, ruffling the grasses and making the wildflowers nod.

"What a day, what a day!" exclaimed Marjie as they followed the dog down the path toward the fields, crossing into the shade of a stand of willows. "And to think that I was worried about rain. This is the perfect day for a wedding."

Sarah nodded. "The breeze reminds me of something Benjamin and I were talking about a day or two ago. Do you remember when Jesus was talking with Nicodemus and He explained being born of the Spirit by talking about where the wind comes from and goes to?"

"Ruthie made me read that story over and over again," Marjie answered. "I think I've nearly memorized some of those verses."

"Good," Sarah said motioning to the long, tender branches that swayed on either side of the lane. "See those willows moving in the wind, Marjie? Well, I feel like that's what's happened in my life, too. By His Spirit, God is blowing upon me and doing things I never would have expected, and I find them nearly impossible to explain."

"Like bringing you and Benjamin together?" asked Marjie as they neared the end of the tree cover.

"Oh yes," her mother said. "But a lot more than that, too.

Somewhere in the middle of all that's happened since you got married, both you and I discovered the secret that your father found—a real faith in God. Do you remember what you said about that the night before your wedding?"

"How could I forget it?" Marjie whispered, choking up and coming to a halt at the edge of the last tree's shadow. "God has been very good to us, Ma."

"That He has," Sarah said through the first tears of the happy day. Hugging Marjie one last time before leaving the shelter of the trees, she said, "Unbelievably good. I wonder where the wind will blow next?"

Marjie laughed and replied, "Let's go see!"

Stepping into the sunlight, Marjie and Sarah picked up their pace and quickly climbed the ridge that overlooked the Seven Corners hayfield.

"It's just over this hill, Ma," Marjie stated, pointing to the spot.

"I wonder if anyone showed up?" Sarah asked tentatively. "I didn't see a car go by."

"I tried to tell you that the cars were going to go through the other driveway to the fields," Marjie explained as they reached the ridge. "Stop worrying, Ma."

"But what if no one . . ." Sarah's words trailed off as Blue let out a bark and dashed down the hill.

"Look at all the people!" Marjie cried to her mother as they stepped into view of the valley below.

At first glance, the whole valley seemed to be filled with cars. A long line of cars were strung along the farm lane, and a large section of the hayfield that Jerry had harvested in the middle of the week was also covered with vehicles.

"Goodness!" Sarah gasped. "Where'd they all come from?"

"There must be three hundred people!" Marjie burst out. "And they're all waiting for you."

"Oh, my!" her mother sighed. "I can't—"

"Hey, everybody!" Marjie called and waved to the crowd below. "Here comes the bride!"

First a murmur, and then a full-fledged cheer rose up the

gently sloping hillside as Sarah and Marjie made their way down toward the gathered throng. Marjie put an arm around her mother, and joyful tears streamed down their faces and watered the dry earth beneath their steps.

And then, the majestic soprano voice of Margaret Stanfeld rose in solitary perfection to silence the crowd's din. Filling the valley and resonating among the green hills, the familiar notes of "Amazing Grace" stirred the hearts of all who waited for Benjamin Macmillan's bride.

Cupping his hand and speaking directly into Marjie's ear above the music of the band, Jerry said, "Let's sneak away and go for a walk. I've had enough for a while."

"We can't just leave," Marjie responded. "We're the hosts."

"Hosts-smosts," Jerry protested. "Everybody's having so much fun square dancing, they don't need us here. Your mother and my father are doing all the hosting that needs to be done, anyway. Look at them. Chattering away with everyone they ever knew."

"They're having a ball, that's for sure," Marjie agreed, glancing over at Benjamin and Sarah, who were talking with Chester and Margaret. "What about Martha?"

"She and the puppy are in good hands with Ruthie and Billy in the house," Jerry answered. "To speak the truth, I'm a little more worried about those two than I am about Martha and Tinker. I'll bet Ruthie and Billy are smooching on the davenport."

"I certainly hope so," Marjie said and laughed. "Why else do you think I suggested it?"

"Always the matchmaker," Jerry teased. "Busy again, I see."

"Not too," replied Marjie. "Those two are doing fine without me, though a little nudge never hurts. So where do you want to go?"

"Let's just head down toward the creek," Jerry suggested. "We don't need to go far. If I can get a short break, I'll be fine."

They shook hands with several people before they were able to escape the festive confines of the barn. Stepping into the farmyard that was packed with cars, Jerry and Marjie picked their way past several vehicles, ducked quickly behind some tall pines, and headed in the direction of the creek. The day's warm southerly breeze had strengthened to occasional gusts, and a low, full moon easily lighted their path.

"Whew!" exclaimed Jerry as they broke through the trees and stepped out onto the open hillside. Reaching his arm around Marjie, he said, "The quiet feels good, don't it?"

"Sure does," Marjie agreed, wrapping her arm around his waist and snuggling up tight as they made a slow descent toward the creek. "This has been some day. After we get the place put back together tonight, I think I'll go somewhere and sleep for a month."

"Not without me, you won't," Jerry said through a tired sigh. "I can't believe how many people came."

"I didn't realize that our parents knew this many people," Marjie said. "Guess you forget all the lives you touch over the years, especially if you've been good to others. Ruthie did a great job of getting people to help, didn't she?"

"She's amazing," replied Jerry. "It was a great idea to ask people to bring along food for a potluck. I ate like a Trojan."

"More like a threshing machine," Marjie teased, patting his stomach. "It was embarrassing."

"Come on!" Jerry muttered. "I left a few scraps behind."

Jerry and Marjie laughed and headed toward the limestone outcropping that perched above the trickling little stream. Stepping out to the edge of the slab of stone, they stood silently for a few minutes, trying to take in the beauty of the moonlit night.

"Magnificent," Marjie said softly, holding Jerry tightly.

"Yeah," he whispered, taking in a deep draft of air. "So are you."

A sudden gust of wind blew Marjie's hair into Jerry's face, and she reached up to pull it back. "I think I need a kiss," she spoke softly.

"Me, too," Jerry replied. His lips gently met hers, and their arms encircled each other in a strong embrace. The only sound to be heard was the rustling of the wind in the trees.

"That was nice," Marjie said. "Like the first time we walked down here. Do you remember?"

Jerry nodded. "Just keeps getting better, though," he said. "I could use a steady diet of walks with you."

"If you can find a baby-sitter every night, we're in business," Marjie said, still holding Jerry tight.

"Do you hear the whispers in the wind again?" Jerry asked.

"Yeah," Marjie answered quietly, listening hard to see if she could make out what seemed to be muffled words. "When we were walking down to the field today, Ma talked about the wind and the Spirit of God. What if the whispers were the voice of God in the wind?"

Jerry didn't answer at first, and Marjie knew he was listening hard to the hushed tones flowing in the breezes. "I wish it was," he finally responded. "And I wish I could understand what He was saying."

"But maybe it's not as muffled as we think," said Marjie quietly.

Pulling back and gazing down into Marjie's face, Jerry frowned and said, "You're not suggesting you're hearing God in the wind, are you?"

Marjie laughed and shook her head. "No, silly," she said, pulling him back into her arms. "But when you look back over the past year and a half, can't you see God's handwriting sketched all over the place?"

"Plain as day," Jerry said reflectively. "Guess I'd have to be blind to not notice it. But wouldn't it be nice to get a peek ahead at what He's going to do rather than just figure it out when we look back?"

"I'm not so sure," Marjie responded. "I don't think I'd handle it well if I knew what was coming next. Seems like it's better to just know that God is going to be with us, no matter what happens."

Jerry took in her words and chewed them over for a bit. "I suppose you're right," he finally said. "If I had known a few things that were coming, I'm afraid I might have run for the hills."

Marjie laughed, then reached up and pulled his face to hers for another kiss. "I love your honesty," she said. "But if we were able to hear God speaking in the wind, I think I know what He'd be saying about the future."

"Doctor Macmillan knows it all," whispered Jerry. "All right, what would he be saying?"

"I think He'd be telling us that it's time for us really to be on our own," Marjie responded solemnly. "This is your chance to make the farm your own, Jerry. And it's my chance to make the house our home. For us to be our own family."

"And to make our faith our own," Jerry added. "We can't keep depending on Ruthie or my father or Chester to have all the answers."

"Sounds like the voice of God to me," Marjie whispered.

"Sounds a little scary," replied Jerry.

"You won't run for the hills, will you?" Marjie asked.

"Not unless you come with me," Jerry said. "But I think it's wiser to face the music."

"I agree," Marjie said. "And speaking of music, we'd better get back to the barn before someone notices we've been gone."

"One more kiss," Jerry urged. "For the future . . . by the grace of God."

"For the future," Marjie answered him softly.